HEMORRHAGE

A Doctor Cooper Series Novel

HEMORRHAGE

A Doctor Cooper Series Novel

Warren Stucki

SUNSTONE
PRESS

SANTA FE

Sunstone books may be purchased for educational, business, or sales promotional use.
For information please write: Special Markets Department, Sunstone Press,
P.O. Box 2321, Santa Fe, New Mexico 87504-2321.

Book and Cover design › Vicki Ahl
Body typeface › ITC Benguiat Std
Printed on acid-free paper
∞
eBook 978-1-61139-260-9

—————————————————————————————

Library of Congress Cataloging-in-Publication Data
Stucki, Warren J., 1946-
Hemorrhage : a Doctor Cooper Series novel / by Warren Stucki.
    pages cm. -- (Doctor Cooper Series)
ISBN 978-0-86534-985-8 (softcover : alk. paper)
1. Physician and patient--Fiction. 2. Operating rooms--Fiction. 3. Herbs--Therapeutic use--Fiction. I. Title.
PS3619.T84H46 2014
    813'.6--dc23

                    2014002563

—————————————————————————————

WWW.SUNSTONEPRESS.COM
SUNSTONE PRESS / POST OFFICE BOX 2321 / SANTA FE, NM 87504-2321 /USA
(505) 988-4418 / ORDERS ONLY (800) 243-5644 / FAX (505) 988-1025

Acknowledgements

As always, I would like to thank my wife Linda. She was my reader, editor and critic, and though she thinks I never listen to her, I do.

Also, I want express my appreciation to my friend and lunch mate Dana Korn. He also was a reader and editor.

Another friend, Kerry Bradshaw helped immensely with translations.

And my colleague, Dr. Mike Anderson, provided the superb photo for the cover.

Surely, this is a crime, even a heinous crime, like torture, mayhem or murder. The room looks chaotic, resembling a Kansas slaughterhouse, or a grisly crime scene. Blood splatter is everywhere, on the light fixture, the bed and the tracked-through puddles on the white vinyl floor. If caught, the perpetrator will undoubtedly do big time or worse.

But no, not here! Here the perp walks away unshackled, a free man.

Is this carnage somehow different? No, the Utah Criminal Code clearly defines it the same. Why then? A slick lawyer? The right political connections? No, not even by declaring it an act of war. Why then? Nothing more than a common piece of paper, an unconditional pardon, called a professional medical license.

PROLOGUE—MAY 1979

The art of medicine consists of amusing the patient
while nature cures the disease.
—Voltaire (1694–1780)

The paralysis began insidiously enough.

First, it was just a tiny circular spot on the tip of the right big toe of little eight year-old Jonnie, then like river water rising after a fortnight of rain, it started to climb. Within a few days, it ascended to the right calf, then somehow magically bridged open space, jumping to the left leg. After establishing a beachhead there, once again, like a sapling in a rainforest, it resumed its inexorable rise upward. In a week, it conquered both thighs, quickly extinguishing ambulation, like the snuffing out of a candle. Picking up the most distressing hitchhikers, loss of bladder and bowel control, it then moved up to the pelvis and breached his board-thin abdomen, turning those once strong muscles to mush. Now, sitting became impossible. Even more alarming, it nudged his diaphragm and that's when panic set in.

When his diaphragm started to flutter then fail, it made the instinctive act of breathing a conscious labor. Jonnie had to repeatedly remind himself to breathe; otherwise he'd suffocate. Of course, sleeping was downright hazardous, so red-eyed and haggard, Jonnie willed himself to stay awake, scared he might die.

Panic welled in his throat like acute asthma as he realized his worst fear, that of drowning, could actually happen. In a very real way, it was like falling into a pool of cold dark water and sinking to the bottom, like a loose pool tile, with no ability to draw a single breath of fresh air.

When Jonnie saw the stark look of fear plastered on his mother's and little sister Brenda's faces, he knew he was in big trouble.

It all began benignly enough as a virus, a common cold. He'd had the usual cough, sore throat and dripping nose. It was a week or so after his symptoms cleared, he felt the tingling in his right foot, rapidly followed by muscle weakness, progressive paralysis, and the constant raw-nerve pain. At times the pain was excruciating and appeared to originate from somewhere deep within his muscles.

His mother consulted their family doctor, Ron Painter, who quickly referred him to a neurologist. The specialist, however, acted as though he was contagious, and preferred not to touch him even with latex gloves. After just one visit, the neurologist hurriedly shipped him off to Utah's medical Mecca, the University of Utah Medical Center in Salt Lake City, Utah.

At the University Medical Center, important-looking doctors wearing starched white lab coats ruminated, cogitated and stroked their collective gray beards, then called it *French polio,* Guillian-Barre Syndrome. Apparently, this was a fairly new and strange disease, and thought to be autoimmune in nature. Like heat-seeking guided missiles, the boy's own immune system was tricked into sending out nerve-seeking antibodies to ravage his own peripheral nerves.

Unbelievably, they agreed there was no cure, only supportive treatment. Discouraged and depressed, Jonnie and his family headed home. Within days, everything became progressively worse and that's when the breathing problem began. Frantic, almost hysterical, Jonnie's mother was back on the phone to the university graybeards, who advised her to immediately bring him back to the hospital. They planned to insert a plastic tube down his windpipe and connect him to a breathing machine. For how long, his mother asked? No one knew. Maybe forever!

Jonnie was terrified and maybe irrationally, resisted the move. In fact, he threw a hissy fit. Wringing her hands and crying, his mother looked uncertain and enormously frightened. Finally, in desperation, she vowed if the doctors at the university couldn't cure him, she'd find someone who could.

The very next day, a man with wavy, shoulder-length hair and a kindly sensitive face appeared at their door. He was wearing an ivory-colored Russian peasant smock, Roman sandals and faded blue jeans. Jonnie's mother quickly ushered him into the bedroom. Without saying a word, he took Jonnie's hand and stared calmly into his frightened blue eyes. He fished in his pocket and pulled out a small vial of consecrated olive oil. The gentle man sprinkled a few drops on Jonnie's auburn brown hair, then lightly rested his delicate hands on his small head.

Using a clear strong voice, the man asked for the help of God Almighty. Pleading the boy's case out loud, he asked God to raise his mighty hand and smite the evil disease and cure his innocent son, Jonnie. Almost immediately, a serenity descended on Jonnie and somehow, he knew he would be okay. He was absolutely certain he would get better.

Before leaving, the gentle healer gave Jonnie's mother a small bagful of herbs and supplements, all very helpful for severely damaged nervous systems. For the next three weeks, Jonnie's mother religiously gave him daily divided doses of Japanese Sea blue kelp, European lecithin granules, California grape seed extract, St. John's wort and Chinese ginkgo biloba. To these herbs, she added healthy doses of powdered zinc, manganese and vitamins B and C, and then she had him wash them all down with two glasses of pure mountain spring water.

A week later, Jonnie was breathing easier; in a month he was walking with the help of crutches and in two months he was running wild and free. There was no trace left, absolutely none, of that insidious neural assassin.

It was a miracle!

1

Healer of others, full of sores himself
—Euripides (485–406 B.C.)

"Top of the mornin'," the voice sporting a distinct Irish brogue boomed.

"Huh?" Dr. Lawrence Addison Cooper still clung to the last vestiges of a quickly fading, but particularly vivid erotic dream. Kylie had returned, at least in his dream.

"'Tis Joe McCracken service foreman at Saint George Chrysler-Dodge," Joe proclaimed, much too jovial for this early hour.

"Huh," Coop mumbled again, fumbling with the phone.

"Joe McCracken...Saint George Chrysler-Dodge-Jeep," The man snapped, more curtly now.

"Joe McCracken?" Coop parroted, rubbing his swollen red eyes. His stuffy nose conferred a nasal timbre to his voice and he had to breathe through his mouth.

"Blimey, laddie, are you daft?"

"Daft?"

"Tis Joe McCracken, Saint George Dodge...about your lorry."

"Ka-choo!" Coop's sneeze was like a small explosion and he only partially succeeded in covering the receiver with his cupped hand. "Lori? I don't know any Lori."

"No, lorry, laddie. You know, your truck...your Ram twenty-five hundred diesel."

"Oh, yeah, about the transmission."

"I'm sorry, but I have a wee bit-o-bad news." McCracken didn't sound particularly sorry.

Now, fully awake, Coop reached for a box of tissues and glanced at the bedside clock. Damnit—seven o'clock! He was supposed to start cutting in thirty minutes and he certainly didn't have time for a conversation with McClacken. "I...I'm sort of in a hurry," he twanged through swollen membranes. Setting down the phone, he quickly blew his nose. It didn't help. "Can't this wait?"

"Aye, laddie, I suppose it can," McCracken replied, his voice now slow and metered, "but I thought ye might want to know your warranty won't cover the damage."

"What?"

"I hope you saved a good bit-o-quid."

"What the hell you talking about, McClacken?" Coop exploded. "There's not twenty-five thousand miles on that truck!"

"That may be so, but this transmission's been buggered," Mc-Cracken continued, "which automatically nullifies your warranty."

"Ka-choo! What do you mean buggered?" Coop quickly checked his wristwatch. Unbelievably, it really was 7:05 a.m.! He shouldn't have taken the Benadryl last night.

"Do you have any enemies, laddie?" McCracken's voice was suddenly hushed and conspiratorial.

Almost instantly, Coop felt cold, and try as he might, he could not hold back an emerging shiver that snaked up his spine and tingled his scalp. His thoughts, like a trapped coal miner, raced frantically down the blackened corridors of his mind, flinging open dusty and rarely used mental files. "None I can think of," he finally croaked.

"No cheesed-off patients, huh? Maybe some purr chap who couldn't pay your exorbitant bloody fees or someone ye might've butchered."

"Nah...no one I can think of," Coop stammered, his voice twanging like a plucked piano wire.

By now Malachi was stirring on the bed. He stretched and yawned, and wagging his tail furiously, tried to lick Coop's fever-flushed face.

"You saying you always get smashin' good results?"

"Well, yes, most of the time."

"What about purr ole Burt Jensen? A pretty quare thing that was. Now, he has to wear diapers."

How in the hell did he know about that? St. George must be a smaller town than Coop thought. "Not that it's any business of yours, McClacken," Coop barked, "but that is considered an acceptable complication of radical prostatectomy."

"McCracken...the name's McCracken...not McClacken. McClacken sounds like your bleedin' transmission, broke and clackin'. Anyways, I have to report this to Saint George P.D."

"Saint George P.D.?" Coop echoed, wide-eyed.

"Aye, it's the bloody law," McCracken replied. "Don't you get it, buddy? Looks like someone's trying to kill you!"

Coop fell silent, trying to process this most disturbing information. For the moment, he forgot about being tardy for surgery, or how lousy he felt. His pounding sinus headache, stuffy swollen nose, raw inflamed throat and raspy hacking cough, all melted into irrelevance. Now, he was consumed only with the unthinkable, the horrific idea someone out there was actually trying to kill him! But who? And why?

"You still there, laddie?" McCracken finally asked.

"Oh...oh, yeah, sure," Coop mumbled, preoccupied.

"Well then get your butt on down here!" Dr. Stephen Spaulding bellowed, now not a trace of Irish accent. "I'm not going to put this patient to sleep till I see the whites of your baby blues." Dropping all pretense now, he exploded in laughter, "Ha, ha, ha!"

"Steve!" Coop exclaimed. "Steve, that's not at all funny. God will get you for this. No...no, I'm not waiting for God, you better watch your back."

"Ha, ha, ha," Dr Spaulding roared again. "Coops, you're too damn easy."

"Like I said, I owe you one," Coop croaked, "a big one."

Spaulding took another moment to squelch his mirth. "You okay, buddy? You sound like hell."

"Ka-choo!"

"Damn virus...took a couple of Benadryl last night and overslept," Coop confided. "I'll take a quick shower and be there in thirty minutes."

"We can cancel. I'll talk to the family and you can stay in bed."

"No, I'll be alright. See you in a half an hour."

"As usual, Coops, you're operating on surgeon's make-believe time," Spaulding replied. "No way you'll be here in thirty minutes. I'll see you in an hour."

Suppressing a smile, Coop re-cradled the phone. Damn that Spaulding, never a dull minute.

Coop sat on the bed for a moment and stroked his chocolate,

almost a year old Labrador pup. Thinking he needed some company, Steve Spaulding gave Malachi to Coop as a present just after Kylie left; and Malachi was good company, damn good company. Coop had grown to love the dog. As he caressed the soft fur of his ears, Coop's thoughts returned to Spaulding.

Always the practical joker, Dr. Stephen Spaulding also doubled as an anesthesiologist and his best, maybe his only friend, other than of course Jacob. As opposed to Jacob, Spaulding was closer to his age. He and Coop had traded practical jokes for some time now. Lately however, things had escalated into a more treacherous game of one ups-man-ship, each prank more elaborate, more outrageous than the last. This last prank was troubling; Steve had broken serve. It had, in fact, been Coop's turn.

Spaulding and Coop started work at Dixie Medical Center twelve years ago on the same day. The hospital hired another anesthesiologist specifically because of Coop's impending arrival. Both of them present-ed to the O.R. supervisor within a half hour of each other to be assigned a surgery locker. Spaulding arrived only minutes earlier. At the time there was only one empty locker and Spaulding got it. Coop, of course, feigned outrage. The favoring of an anesthesiologist over a surgeon was almost unheard of and obviously contrary to all laws of nature, whether they be Darwin, God or the universe. That small innocuous incident was the beginning of their good-natured rivalry and also their lasting friendship.

Over the years, their relationship evolved into more than just a tennis match of pranks. They frequently worked the same O.R., often socialized together, got divorces within a year of each other, though technically Coop was only separated, and regularly commiserated on the sad state of the sacred institution of matrimony.

Other than occasionally going out with Steve, Coop's hobbies were pretty much solitary activities, like working on the ranch or riding his horses. His more cerebral interests included studying Latin and divining the origin of surnames. For instance, his name Cooper was English, an occupational name for a maker and repairer of wooden vessels such as barrels, tubs, buckets, casks, and vats. And Steve Spaulding's was a variant of Spalding, which literally meant Scottish.

The good news, obviously Steve was working his room today,

which really was a stroke of luck. Steve would not make a big deal of him being late or report him to the Surgical Utilization Committee. With St. George being one of the fastest growing cities in the country, which had attracted literally a covey of new and hungry surgeons, O.R. time was now at a premium. Consequently, the Utilization Committee was far more active and dictatorial. Three late starts resulted in a reprimand, two more probation and another two the offending surgeon was stripped of his O.R. starting time. That was a grand total of seven tardies and Coop was already up to five.

This punishment was more severe than it appeared. Without a 7:30 starting time, the surgeon had no idea how to structure his day. His surgery could start anytime from 7:30 a.m. to after ten in the evening, whenever there happened to be an open room. Regardless of the start time, and often with only minutes of advance notice, he or she was expected to drop what they were doing and start cutting. Trying to schedule time to see patients was a nightmare and more than once, particularly in his early days, Coop had to cancel out the same patient three or four times. This left the surgeon somewhere between the proverbial rock and a hard place, but unfortunately he or she had no option but to take it. If a surgeon didn't cut, he didn't eat.

But Steve was right about one thing; he was an easy mark, mainly because of his lifestyle. Unfortunately, his personal life was disorganized, cluttered and he exhibited an amazing indifference to the mundane details of living, i.e. clothing, household chores and personal appearance. These annoying qualities, plus his exacting schedule as a surgeon, more than anything else, at least in his opinion, contributed to his separation from Kylie. Well, that, and of course Roger Callister.

Glancing at his nightstand, Coop again checked the time, now flashing an alarming 7:10. Damn, he'd better get going. He threw back the covers and jumped out of bed. Almost instantly, everything started spinning. Just before losing consciousness, he collapsed back on the bed, barely missing Malachi, who scooted away just in time.

In college his nickname was Addie Einstein, the Addie from his middle name Addison and Einstein referred to his notable intellect. Most friends figured he would end up sequestered away in some dark and smelly chemistry lab, but to everyone's surprise he chose medicine instead. Even more unlikely, he specialized in surgery and as improbable as it all seemed, he was really quite good at it. Paradoxically, once Coop stepped into the surgical suite his annoying penchant for disarray suddenly disappeared and he ran a very efficient O.R. It was his opinion nurses and techs working in a relaxed atmosphere made fewer mistakes. As a consequence, he ran a very informal operating room, allowing both rock and country music and idle chatter. Though the atmosphere was loose, the crew knew there were limits and almost always respected his boundaries. In the realm of the operating room, Coop's technique was really quite rare; he was both precise and fast. Some said he had the gift of hands.

The second time Coop got out of bed more slowly, but as he stumbled for the shower, he was hit with another paroxysm of sneezing. Almost instantly, his nasal mucous membranes swelled and closed. Now, he could only inhale air through his inflamed raw throat and that was very painful. God, he felt awful!

Normally, Coop was a healthy person. Though he just past forty, he took no prescription medicines, other than Allegra for allergies, and had no sign of heart disease, hypertension or diabetes. In the spring he suffered from pollens, elm, mulberry, sycamore, wild flowers, sagebrush and especially cedar. In the fall, it was the spores, ragweed, pigweed, grasses and mold. In general, though, he was disgustingly healthy, so this cold really caught him by surprise. He hadn't contacted an upper respiratory virus in years.

As Steve suggested, maybe he should cancel the day. Of course that would be a tremendous inconvenience for everyone involved. The patient, Betty Tsongas, had already scheduled time off work and more than likely already taken her bowel prep. Then there was the family to consider. For moral support, a son was flying in from Seattle and a daughter from San Antonio. Both more than likely with non-refundable non-transferable tickets and of course they also had scheduled time off work. Last but not least, there was the psychological distress, which was often considerable. Mentally, the patient spent hours, even days, preparing for this day. It would be devastating, bordering on flippant, to simply say, "let's do this another day. I just don't feel good." No, this was not like a regular job where you could easily call in sick.

Groaning out loud, Coop choked down two more Benadryl, two aspirin and a glass of orange juice. After the O.J., his mouth still tasted like a mixture of mucous and sour battery acid, so he vigorously brushed his teeth, then gargled a half-bottle of mouthwash. He then fed Malachi and climbed into the shower, turning on the warm water. It took a minute for his body to adapt, then he made the shower hotter. It felt so good; he wanted to stay there all day.

The steamy hot water cascaded over his head, onto his shoulders and down his back. Coop could feel his neck muscles relax, his nasal passages open and his superficial capillaries dilate from the soothing liquid heat.

Suddenly, he felt woozy once again as the blood drained away from his head into his now heat-dilated systemic capillaries. Staggering, he backed up and leaned against the tiled wall for support. His head began to spin and he felt his consciousness flee like a zoo animal whose cage was open. He fought to remain standing, then like steamed pasta, his thigh muscles softened and weakened. Without his advice or consent, his knees buckled and he slid down the wet tile to the floor.

Somewhere, in the waning of his consciousness, Coop had a fleeting premonition; he sensed this was going to be a bad day.

2

Surgeons must be very careful
When they take the knife!
Underneath their fine incisions
Stirs the Culprit—Life!
—Emily Dickinson (1830–1886)

After the sinking shower incident, the day somehow righted itself, at least temporarily.

As Spaulding predicted, Coop arrived at the hospital an hour late. He quickly changed into scrubs, then hurried to O.R. #5, his usual operating room. Retrieving an E-Z Scrub brush, he applied some pasty-white Triseptin and mechanically brushed his fingernails.

Idly, he thought, I would like to have ten dollars for every time I've scrubbed at this sink, then it occurred him, he had been paid a heck of a lot more than that. Where had all the money gone? He wasn't an extravagant person, but Kylie was, and unfortunately he was still funding her prodigal lifestyle.

Through the window positioned just above the sink, Coop could see Dr. Stanton Kingsley (from Old English meaning woodland clearing of the king). Stanton, his partner and his assistant surgeon today, was pacing the room, like an expectant father, in his sterile blue gown. Occasionally, he would stop, glance up at the wall clock, perceptibly shake his head, then resumed pacing.

Four years ago, Stan, just out of residency, joined Coop's solo practice. His reason, in his own words, was to learn from the master. Stan, as opposed to Coop, was from a wealthy family and his schooling was all-private, including Harvard Medical School. Coop, on the other hand, was a product of state and public schools.

Lately, Stan seemed restless and Coop suspected some of the honeymoon glow had faded from their relationship. Nowadays, their association had evolved into a mostly *friendly* rivalry, vying with each other for patients and referrals. If he were totally honest, Coop would have to admit Stan was a good, albeit a somewhat impatient surgeon. Stan seemed determined to develop his own technique and acquire an identity separate from Coop. He still had another year on his five-year contract, otherwise Coop suspected he would be gone.

Through the window, Coop noted Dr. Spaulding had finished placing an epidural catheter, a must with these big operations for post-op control of pain. After that, he would insert an arterial line into the left radial artery for continuous blood pressure monitoring, then a second large bore IV in the right arm to deliver fluids, medicines and blood if necessary. Next, he would clip a pulse oximeter on any fingernail without polish to monitor blood oxygen saturation and finally the patient would actually be ready for some anesthesia.

To put the patient to sleep, Spaulding usually gave a bolus of Fentanyl, Propofol and Rocuronium, then a few seconds later, he would insert an endotracheal tube and attach it to the ventilator via a plastic accordion hose. After adjusting the settings on the machine to control both frequency of respiration and tidal volume, and adjusting gas delivery system to achieve just the right mixture of oxygen and Desflurane, the anesthesiologist could then sit back in an easy chair, turn on some good music and read a novel, which is exactly what Dr. Steve Spaulding usually did.

With big cases like the one today, anesthesia preparation time was often thirty to forty-five minutes, depending on the speed and acuity of the anesthesiologist, which varied about as much as the crystalline pattern of snowflakes. What rankled Coop was anesthesia's preparation time was factored into total surgical time, then somehow that was all plugged into a secret formula used to determine how many cases the surgeon would be allowed to schedule on any given day. So, if you had a slow anesthesiologist you might be allowed only three cases instead of the usual four, and it had nothing to do with the speed of the surgeon. Fortunately, Steve, like Coop, was not a dallier.

Thank God, he only had one case today, Betty Tsongas (probably Greek, though the exact origin remained obscure) and fortunately she was in relatively good health. She was born with a pectus carinatum, a pigeon chest, and had a remote history of coronary artery disease treated with an angioplasty and subsequent stents, but none of that should affect today's surgery.

The reason Betty was here, she had a Grade III deeply invasive transitional cell carcinoma of the bladder. A notorious bad actor, this tumor was pretty much both radio and chemo resistant. Unfortunately the only consistently effective treatment was surgical extirpation, the complete removal of the urinary bladder, which in ladies almost always also included a hysterectomy. The absence of a bladder did not, of course, negate the need to somehow eliminate urine from the body with its attendant waste products. The plumbing simply had to be re-routed. Sometimes Coop fashioned a new bladder out of small or large bowel, or both, however with women this procedure was difficult, often resulting in total urinary incontinence. Because of the short urethra in females, if incontinence did occur it was much more difficult to correct.

So with Betty, Coop elected to perform an ileal loop urinary diversion, isolate a small segment of terminal ileum from the continuous twenty-foot ribbon of small bowel, suture one end closed, attach the ureters to the body of the loop, then bring the efferent limb through the abdominal wall as a budded ostomy. Even under the best of circumstances, this was a grueling four to five hour operation.

What made it so tough, the surgeon had to operate deep in the pelvis, directly under the pubic bone. Even in women who tended to have larger and more rounded pelvi, this location made visibility a problem and maneuverability equally difficult. There simply was no room for the surgeon's hands.

Sighing, Coop tossed his scrub brush in the wastebasket, rinsed off the white foamy soap, then while still holding his hands high, backed through the door into the brightly lit operating room.

"Morning all," he greeted the crew with a nasal twang, "sorry I'm late." then sheepishly added, "I overslept."

The surgical team consisted of a scrub tech, Mollie Wilken (German), always happy and eager to please; a circulating nurse, Renae Mackey (Scotland), humorless and a strictly-by-the-book R.N.; a surgical aid, Jared Johnson (English), who also was doubled as a part time pre-med student; and of course Drs. Kingsley and Spaulding.

Inwardly, Coop groaned when he saw Renae. With her in the room, it could be, and often was, a very long and frustrating day.

"You forget something?" Stanton asked abruptly from across the room and Renae rushed him like a linebacker shooting the gap to intercept the tailback.

"Wha-a-t?" Coop asked, but inwardly groaned. It was starting already.

"No!" Renae screamed, planting herself directly in his path. "You can't come in here like that."

"Like what?" Coop looked to his friend Steve Spaulding for help. He just shrugged and grinned, as if to say you're on your own buddy.

"No!" Renae pointed at her own covered face. "No mask. You've got no mask."

Reflexively, Coop almost touched his own face, then caught himself and groaned. Damn, it must be the Benadryl. He'd forgotten to strap on a surgical mask.

"Go back out," Renae ordered, gesturing with her boney forefinger, "put on a mask and re-scrub."

Already, Coop had about had it with Renae. Normally, he could take her domineering, but not today. Battling the virus, he was no mood to also battle Renae. Now was the time to take a stand or suffer the insufferable for hours. "No, damnit, Renae," he thrust out his chin and stood his ground, "we're already an hour late. You tie on my mask and I'll stay sterile." For emphasis, he thrust his hands even higher in the air.

Toe to toe, they glared at each other. No one moved or blinked. After a long tense moment, Renae sighed out loud and lowered her eyes. Without even a cursory attempt to hide her resentment, she grabbed a clean surgical mask, leaned in and with exaggerated movements strapped it on, tying it particularly tight.

"I smell alcohol on your breath," she hissed.

"It's mouthwash," Coop snapped back.

Mollie, who hated discord, nervously gowned and gloved Coop, then went back to the instrument table, fiddling with the surgical tools. Silently, Coop watched as Renae prepped the abdomen.

Unfortunately today, the O.R. was filled with an edgy nervousness, just the kind of atmosphere Coop liked to avoid. Silently, all watched Renae. With her prepping sponge, she took one more angry swipe, covering the indelible ink for the pre-marked ostomy site with brown betadine, then she was done. Finally, a full forty-five minutes after Betty Tsongas entered the room, she was prepped and ready for surgery.

After applying sterile drapes and connecting the electrocautery, Yankar suction and the argon beam coagulator, they were finally ready to cut.

With a # 10 scalpel, Coop made a midline incision, beginning several centimeters above the umbilicus, curving around the vestigial organ, then continuing straight down to the pubic symphysis. Instantly, there was brisk bleeding from subsurface skin vessels. Groaning, Coop glanced up at Stan. He simply sighed and shrugged. They both knew excessive skin bleeding often was kind of a harbinger, the surgeon's equivalent to a mariner's albatross, an unwelcome sign of things to come.

Grabbing the electrocautery, Coop fulgurated the skin bleeders, then charred through two inches of yellow fat down to the midline fascia. A cloud of smoke laced with the nauseating smell of burning flesh permeated the room. After incising the fascia, Coop spread the rectus abdominal muscles with a self-retaining Balfour retractor and used two more self-retaining retractors, Martin's Arms, to retract the abdominal contents superiorly and medially. He was now prepared to take the pelvic lymph nodes. If and when this cancer spread, it almost always did so through the lymph channels.

"What kind of music today, Coops?" Dr. Spaulding asked cheer-fully from the head of the table.

"Classical, maybe something easy on the head, like Mozart." His request was instantly greeted by a collective groan from the rest of the crew. "All right then," he relented, "how about classical rock and roll, not too loud."

"Can do," Spaulding complied by putting on Bob Dylan's, *Mr. Tambourine Man*. "You should have come with us last Saturday," Spaulding continued once the music was blaring.

"The tables good to you this time?" Coop asked as he dissected nodal tissue from around the right external iliac vein. He was one of the few surgeons who could talk and work at the same time. "And could you turn the volume down a notch?"

"Two thousand dollars off the craps tables," Spaulding asserted, then repeated, "you should've come."

"Ah, well, gambling doesn't hold the same fascination for me." Coop handed Mollie a glob of pale pink tissue, allegedly the right pelvic nodes, then after rearranging the retractors, he started on the left ones.

"It gets in your blood," Steve admitted, pulling a novel out of his backpack.

"Yeah, like cocaine," Stan Kingsley growled. He was a devout Christian and did not approve of gambling as well as most other vices. "How much did you lose?"

"None, this time," Spaulding laughed.

"Well, anyway, Steve you might ought to think about toning it down," Coop advised as he grabbed for the Yankar suction. That pesky bleeding was still a problem. "It can get expensive."

"Yeah, well...anyway, Coops, Marty was there." Spaulding grinned behind his mask. "She's dying to meet you."

"I don't know, Steve. I don't think I'm ready yet." Coop's nose was dripping again and his tightly tied mask, like a rain barrel, was filling with sticky mucus. Furthermore, his head was pounding furiously, like the inside of a kettledrum.

"You can't be a monk forever."

"I don't know why not," Coop quipped. "I've been doing a pretty good job so far." He'd just finished with the node dissection, now it was time for the *coup de gräce*, the removal of the urinary bladder. Following that came the tedious portion of the operation, the creation of the ileal loop urinary diversion. "Anyway, I'm still married."

"Ump-h-h," Spaulding snorted, opening up his novel. "That's a pretty liberal use of the word married."

"We got her typed and crossed?" Coop barked without looking up.

"Let me check," Dr. Steve Spaulding quickly leafed through the patient's chart. "Four units—that should be enough. Usually you don't use any."

"I have a feeling this isn't going to be the usual," Coop muttered, as he mopped the blood with a lap sponge. "Any anticoagulants, or aspirin?"

Again, Dr. Spaulding thumbed through the chart. "Was on aspirin, but it was stopped...oh...about ten days ago."

"How about any of the *G-herbs*...garlic, ginseng or ginkgo biloba?"

"Not that I know of...the chart doesn't say," Spaulding was still thumbing through the record. "The pre-op history form really doesn't address herbs."

"Dam-n-n," Coop cussed. Damn and damnit were about the strongest words he ever used. "Stan! Would you suck over here, where I'm working?"

"I can't tell where you're working!" Stan snapped back, but complied anyway.

Coop didn't answer; instead he took down the pubo-vesical ligaments, trying to develop a plane anterior to the bladder and all the way down to the urethra. Though he didn't have as much worry about the dorsal venous complex in women, the urethra was shorter and much harder to dissect.

"You might find it easier if you opened the peritoneum and start below the bladder." Dr. Kingsley pointed out the anatomy with his DeBakey pickups. "You know, develop the posterior plane first."

"I've been doing it this way for years!" Coop growled. "This works the best for me." Almost immediately, he wished he'd kept his mouth shut. That comment made him sound old and rigid, but he was in no mood for Stan's running commentary on his surgical technique. Not today, not with this splitting headache. Once again his nose was swollen shut, except for the continuous dripping, and his throat was dry and raspy from the obligatory mouth breathing.

With difficulty, it was hard to see because the bleeding was getting worse, Coop found the urethra and developed circular plane around it, a difficult maneuver even under ideal conditions due to its short length and adherence to the vaginal wall. Finally, he clamped it with a long Vanderbilt hemostat, then transected it with the #10 scalpel. Now, it was time to do just as Stan had suggested, open the peritoneum, and develop a posterior plane between bladder and rectum, then take down the lateral vascular attachments.

In silence, Coop incised the peritoneum over the dome of the bladder, then with his hand bluntly developed the posterior plane.

Suddenly, it started gushing! Not just the slow steady ooze they'd been dealing with, but more like an uncapped fire hydrant. Within seconds, the entire pelvis filled with blood, then like water in a stoppered bathtub, lapped over the edges of the wound and onto the white vinyl floor. There was absolutely no way to keep up with the massive blood loss, especially using a single Yankar suction, and without a dry field, Coop couldn't see a thing. It was like operating underwater, blindfolded.

"Get me a second suction!" Coop barked at Mollie whose eyes, wide as silver moon hubcaps, reflected her growing panic. "And Steve, you'd better get blood started; this is a bad one. And Steve?"

"Yes, Coops," Spaulding answered, suddenly all business.

"Turn off that damn music!" Bob Dylan's wailing harmonica only compounded the throbbing in his head. He was already beginning to feel light-headed; his surgical mask was three-quarters full of nasal mucous and perspiration was popping out on his forehead, like early morning dew on leaves of alfalfa. So as not to inhale the ponded mucous, Coop carefully sucked in a deep breath through his mouth, then slowly exhaled. He had to take in some oxygen, if he hoped to keep the lurking mental fog at bay.

Without a word, Spaulding snapped off the music and turned to examine his bank of monitors.

"Here," Mollie blurted, shoving another Yankar at Coop, then she yelled at Renae, who just arrived with two units of blood, to hook the tubing to the wall suction.

Even with Coop operating one Yankar, and Stan the other, they still couldn't keep the field dry, nor could they see exactly where or what was bleeding. All Coop knew for sure was it was coming from deep in the pelvis, somewhere in the vicinity of the internal iliac, or possibly the obturator artery or vein. Maybe, even the pudental, though it was a hell-uv-a-lot of blood for a pudental!

The bleeding was getting worse, filling the abdomen and dripping on the floor. There was blood splatter everywhere, on the light fixture, the table and the tracked-through puddles on the white vinyl floor. It looked a massacre. Coop leaned against the operating table to keep from falling.

At first barely perceptible, then rapidly progressing, Coop felt the insidious rise of panic. Soon panic's traveling buddies, light-headedness and beading-perspiration, arrived. The hot water resistant gown coupled with the blazing operating lights and his ongoing viral fever, sent his temperature soaring. He felt like he was wrapped in Saran wrap, then placed outside in the broiling sun. Within minutes, his scrubs and gown were literally soaked. He had to do something fast, damn fast, or Betty Tsongas was going to die.

Struggling for self-control, he barely resisted the urge to start blindly groping and clamping with a long tonsil hemostat. He knew that was futile, nearly always counter-productive and often resulted in worsening the injury, or sometimes creating a new one.

"Pressure's dropping," Steve announced from the head of the table, "seventy over forty."

Coop suspected his pressure wasn't much higher. Now, his light-headedness was definitely worse. He was afraid of passing out and literally tumbling face first into the open wound. Damn, it had to be the antihistamines.

Suddenly, he had an epiphany; the timeless words of his old surgical mentor, Jacob Heinz, came back to him as clear as if he'd somehow bridged fifteen years and was standing right beside him. "Vhen you're up to your ass in alligators, it's hard to remember you vere here to fish. Vell, don't panic, pack the vound as tightly as you can with sponges, take a stool in the corner and think about it."

"Two things, Renae," Coop blurted, "first grab a towel and mop the sweat from my forehead, then open me three more packs of sponges."

Renae stared at Coop in disbelief.

"Now!" he shouted.

At first she didn't move, then reluctantly, dabbed his beaded forehead with a white terrycloth towel. After discarding the towel in the dirty linen bin, and without saying another word, she stomped from the room, returning a few moments later with three more packs of sponges.

As quickly as Mollie handed him the sponges, Coop crammed them into the pelvis, packing them tightly until he could not wedge in another, then he stumbled for the stool in the corner.

To keep from fainting, he quickly lowered his head down onto his lap. Initially, he couldn't concentrate, he couldn't think. Desperately, he fought for consciousness.

He tried to concentrate on the problem, but that was impossible with his mind whirling. Somehow, he must find an anchor, somewhere for his mind to dig in and stop spinning. Finally, strangely, his mind latched onto the idea of premonition. Yes, in the shower earlier this morning, he had a feeling, a hunch, this would be a bad day.

In general, Coop did not believe in premonitions or psychics or even extra-sensory perception. Premonition, he maintained, was an eclectic mixture of pre-conditioned learning, biochemical reactions and enhancing hormones. If one were strictly honest, these inklings, these hunches, were wrong more times than they were right. This morning, as usual, he'd tried to ignore the budding feeling, but this one appeared to have some traction. Today, indeed, had all the right ingredients to produce a bad day.

With head still lowered, Coop's mind did find mooring. Like a spent top, the spinning slowed and finally stopped. His thoughts began to rewind and review what had happened so far. He was searching for a cause, a blunder, something he might correct.

Suddenly, someone was shaking him. That was real aggravating. This was followed by low garbled sounds, but coming from so far away he doubted they were meant for him. There was more shaking. Damn, that was more than irritating and the garbled sound moved closer and was beginning to coalesce into actual words.

"Do you want me to finish the case?"

Now, the sound was right next to him.

"Huh?"

"Doctor Cooper, do you want me to take over?"

"Her pressure's still dropping!" Spaulding shouted from somewhere on the other side of the abyss. "You sure your packs are not occluding the vena cava?"

As though he was looking through a gossamer thin veil of slowly dissipating fog, Coop saw the vague outline of Stanton Kingsley looming over him. Somehow he managed to look both annoyed and incredulous at the same time. Directly to the right of him was an equally scowling Renae Mackey. It was her talons digging into his shoulders as she shook him again.

"Do you want me to finish the case?" Stan repeated.

"No...no," Coop muttered, "give me a minute to think this through."

Coop brushed Renae's hands from his shoulders; she immediately replanted them on her boney hips. "I think Doctor Kingsley should take over," she declared.

"Well, somebody do something," Steve Spaulding pleaded as he plugged another bag of blood into the second large bore I.V. The first

I.V. already had a unit hanging. "This one's number twenty and the last of the matched blood."

"Go unmatched," Stan Kingsley barked.

"You sure she hasn't been on blood thinners?" Coop asked lamely.

"No...no blood thinners," Spaulding snapped as he phoned the blood bank, ordering four more units of unmatched O-negative.

Suddenly, Coop knew what he should do. It was a simple matter of physics. The force causing the blood to leak from the injured vessels (mainly the blood pressure) had to be countered by an equal or greater force, then the bleeding would stop.

"Renae," he ordered, "get me a half-dozen rolls of Kerlix and fast."

Forget about trying to locate, clamp and ligate individual bleeders. Instead, he would do just as he had done earlier with the sponges. He would tie together rolls of Kerlix (a long rolled ribbon of gauze) and jam pack them into the pelvis, thereby creating enough mechanical back pressure to tamponade and stop the bleeding. Once the bleeding ceased, he would simply bring the free end out through a small incision in the abdominal wall. In a couple of days when the lacerated vessels had time to develop mature secure clots, he could carefully advance the Kerlix a foot, or so, each day until the ribbon of gauze was completely removed. It might mean a week or so in the ICU and another week or two on the surgical floor, but it was better than death.

Steeling himself, Coop slid off of the stool, slowly stood up straight, expecting the vertigo to return. It did not. His mind remained clear. Circling around Renae, who watched him like a hawk, he returned to the operating table.

"You're not sterile now!" Renae protested and moved to intercept him, but Coop waved her off. This was no time to worry about the niceties of sterility. He could only hope Betty would live long enough to get an infection.

As he pulled the last of the sponges from the Betty Tsongas's pelvis, the bleeding began again. If possible, it was even more intense and diffuse than before. Like tap water through a colander, now the bleeding was coming from everywhere, skin, subcutaneous tissue, muscle and internal organs, not just the large vessels in the pelvis. It was almost like she had some kind of weird coagulopathy, her blood refused clot.

When the last sponge came out, Coop crammed in the rolls of Kerlix, but at that very same moment he heard Spaulding mutter something unintelligible from the head of the table.

"What?" Coop asked sharply, not looking up.

"I'm losing her!" Spaulding shouted, his voice loud and shrill.

Instantly, Coop dropped the Kerlix and pounded on her chest with a balled fist, then quickly began rhythmic compressions.

"Nothing!" Spaulding called from the other side of the drapes as he groped her left carotid artery. "You're not generating a pulse and no compression waves on EKG either."

Coop pushed harder. Heard a rib crack.

Spaulding shook his head and gave her a bolus of I.V. epinephrine. "Must be the shape of her chest. With that damn pigeon chest, I'm getting nothing up here."

Coop nodded. He knew what he had to do and he had to do it now. Not bothering to ask Molly, he grabbed a scalpel off the Mayo stand, hesitated for only a split-second, then quickly sliced a twelve-inch transverse incision across Betty's chest just under her breasts and roughly between the fifth and six ribs. With large-jawed bandage scissors, he hacked across the bony sternum, inadvertently entering both pleural cavities. Instantly blood poured from these fresh wounds. Using all his strength, he grabbed the cut edges of the sternum and spread them wide. There were more popping sounds as several ribs dislocated or broke. Firmly gasping the heart, still housed in its pericardial sack, Coop began squeezing.

"She's got a pulse," Spaulding confirmed, sounding pleased, "and compression waves on EKG too."

Coop breathed a sigh of relief. Maybe they could save Betty after all. For the next ten minutes, he continued the manual contractions as Spaulding administered more blood, fresh frozen plasma, epinephrine, calcium and sodium bicarbonate. Slowly, the muscles in Coop's hands fatigued and cramped.

"Coop," Spaulding finally said after he'd caught up with her fluids, "let's see if she'll fly."

Holding his breath, Coop stopped squeezing and carefully removed his throbbing hands from her chest.

"Nothing," Spaulding announced. "No pulse, no blood pressure and no electrical activity on the EKG."

Immediately, Coop re-cradled the heart in his hands and resumed manual compressions. Blood continued to pour from the chest wound, filling both pleural cavities, the abdominal cavity, then slopping over to the floor.

"It's no use," Spaulding finally croaked, his voice heavy with both fatigue and resignation. "Her pupils are fixed and dilated, and we're out of blood." He paused then added, "Let's call it."

3

The surgeon is quiet, he does not speak.
He has seen too much death, his hands are full of it.
—*Sylvia Plath (1932–1963)*

"Oh, God, how could this happen?"

Coop rarely prayed, pretty much only in times of disaster, or as a last resort, when there was absolutely nothing else he could do. The last time was just over a year ago when Kylie left him for that itinerant landscape artist, Roger Callister (unfortunately Scottish – short for Mc-Callister). Apparently, they met at the annual St. George Art Festival. It was fast, very fast. Coop hadn't had a clue until she packed her suitcases. Oddly enough, Kylie, as opposed to Coop, was very religious and claimed she had been praying about it for some time, asking for guidance. So, it seems God must have told her to leave him, because she did, and if true what did that say about God's opinion of him?

For the past couple of years, Coop had been on the outs with God anyway and none of this did much to further endear the Almighty to him. Coop concluded God was either being meddlesome or sadistic or Kylie was hearing what she wanted. Bitterly, he suspected it might be all three.

Of course, unlike Kylie, his prayers were not answered. The proof? A year later, Kylie still had not returned. This was only further evidence, at least in Coop's mind, of God's aloofness and/or unbelievable apathy. Was it apathy or absence? He still couldn't decide. And since he wasn't sure he believed in God, these rare and impulsive regressions to prayer were hard to understand, or to justify. Generally, Coop considered them as a sign of weakness. Probably, this baffling recidivism was only further validation of the age-old adage: there are no atheists in foxholes.

But it was simply unbelievable that life so strong, so robust, so vigorous could also be so fragile, so labile and so fleeting. One minute

Betty was evolution's finest, a magnificent human mammal sitting atop the biological food chain, the next minute she was reduced to nothing more than an amorphous lump of common elements and decomposing protein, which would probably sell for less than five bucks from a chemical warehouse. My God, a human life snuffed out and by his own hands! He felt sleazy, and criminal, like a Gestapo storm trooper or a Spanish Inquisitioner. He wanted to cry or hide or both.

Right now, he was sequestered in the tiny windowless cubicle used as a surgical dictation room. For the last twenty minutes, he'd been attempting to dictate an Op/death note of Betty Tsongas, but the words would not come. Without completing a sentence, he re-cradled the Dictaphone and decided to let things marinate for a day or two, then try again. Right now, there was just no way to present this debacle in a favorable, or even an impartial light.

In a few minutes, he would have to face the Tsongas family, but before he did, he'd best get his thoughts collected and his emotions controlled. What to say? How to lessen the blow? How to even start?

He had never before experienced anything like this, a patient bleed so massively, so uncontrollably. Well, maybe once. Years ago he'd performed this same operation on a patient previously treated with five thousand rads of radiation. When the tumor reappeared, the radiation oncologist referred the patient for a salvage, perhaps a more accurate description, a desperation cystectomy. The surgery was nothing short of total mayhem, but he'd known in advance it would be, and had prepared the family. But this was the first time he'd experienced every surgeon's worst nightmare, to actually have a patient die on the operating table. In the worldwide fraternity of surgeons, there was nothing worse.

So why had Betty hemorrhaged? Why does any patient hemorrhage? One possible reason, if the patient was taking anticoagulants, blood thinners like Coumadin, Plavix, Pradaxa or aspirin, he or she would be incapable of properly clotting. Two, if the patient had something genetically wrong with their clotting mechanism, a coagulopathy like familial hemophilia or Von Willerbrand's disease. Three, if the surgeon was blindsided by an anomalous vascular system, the vessels were not where they're supposed to be or there were multiple accessory vessels. Or four, poor and sloppy surgical technique...and that was about it. Coop could think of nothing else. It had to be one of those four things.

As far as he knew, Betty had not been on any anticoagulants, at least in her pre-op physical exam and history she'd denied taking any. Unfortunately, Coop had not checked her clotting factors pre-op simply because she had given him no reason to, in the history form there was no mention of a coagulopathy, inherited or otherwise. Furthermore, at the time of surgery there were no anomalous vessels, at least none he'd seen. So what did that leave? Unfortunately, only sloppy or poor, surgical technique!

Deep down, however, Coop did not feel his technique was bad. Betty had bled from the initial skin incision...from the get go. True, he was battling an upper respiratory virus, felt lousy and was a bit dizzy from the antihistamines. So, being strictly honest, he'd have to admit he had not been at the top of his game, but still that was a long way from sloppy surgery. He simply did not feel the virus had in any way contributed to Betty's demise. But regardless of all that, he had to pull himself together, and quickly. The Tsongas family waited.

The husband, Nickolas Tsongas, was a fiery retired real estate developer of Greek descent. In spite of his seventy-two years, he was lithe, muscular and slender, with a body that belied his years. His dark eyes and graying hair, always-slicked straight back, only seemed to add to his godfather-like image. He had a light olive Mediterranean complexion, pearly white teeth and a couple of expensive gold fillings. Even if you had never met him before, at first glance you'd know he was Greek. He just looked Greek, and his reputation as a hard-nosed businessman was almost as legendary as his reputation as a hothead. It was rumored he'd settled more than one professional dispute with his fists. Over the years, he'd apparently amassed a sizeable fortune, even by St. George standards.

Recently, a lot of new money had moved into the area and St. George was no longer a small struggling agriculture town. For good or bad, depending on your viewpoint, it appeared St. George was heading down the same yellow, or golden brick road as Sedona, Arizona, Palm Springs, California, or Aspen, Colorado. St. George was fast becoming a residential destination for people with money.

"But enough daydreaming," Coop chided himself. Time to get back to the real world, the problem at hand. What to say? And how to say it?

There was simply no way to sweeten or sugarcoat this. Over the years, most surgeons had learned the fine art of how to present their surgical complications in a favorable light, or at least to shift part of the blame to the patient (if you hadn't lifted those fifteen pounds or if you hadn't gotten the incision wet, this wouldn't have happened), or at least they had discovered how to minimize or rationalize them so the complication seemed almost inevitable (I did all I could, but the tumor was just too big, or in all my years, I've never seen anything like this). With unexpected surgical death, however, there simply was no way to do this.

In his mind's eye, Coop could see the faces of the family as he walked into the conference room, bright eager faces with wide expectant eyes, anxious for the good news. Then someone would inevitably ask, "how's mom?" He would have no answer for them other than to simply state the truth, "she's dead!"

At this moment, Coop would gladly trade jobs with almost anybody in America. He could think of no other profession who had to perform this kind of gut-wrenching task, other than perhaps the military or maybe law enforcement, but they were just messengers delivering the terrible news. The death was not their fault.

Coop sighed out loud as he reached for the phone and punched in the number for the reception desk. Might just as well suck it up and get it over.

"Sarah, this is Doctor Cooper," Coop said when the phone was answered. "Is the Tsongas family out there?"

"Yes, Doctor Cooper, they just got back from a late breakfast."

"How many are there?" Coop frowned. Not that it mattered, but he wanted to know how many would be in the firing squad.

"Four, the husband, a son, a daughter and a family friend."

"Could you put them in a private conference room?"

"Sure," Sarah gushed, "anything for you, Doctor Cooper. They'll be in the blue room."

Sighing out loud, Coop thanked Sarah and hung up the phone. After a couple more minutes of silent brooding, he located a box of tissue and blew his nose one last time, then headed for the door.

The family conference room, adjacent to the main surgical waiting room, was a small windowless cubicle conventionally furnished like an upscale formal living room. It featured an over-stuffed couch, two chairs, an oaken coffee table and two end tables with porcelain lamps. The walls were papered and wainscoted, and sported two watercolor paintings depicting well-kept flower gardens. There were no harsh colors, but rather a soothing mixture of gentle pastel colors, mauve, pink and lavender.

Pausing at the door, Coop again hesitated briefly, then slowly swung it open. Nickolas Tsongas was sitting comfortably in one chair; the son occupied the other. He was younger and less gray, but nonetheless a striking likeness of Nick. Seated on the couch were the daughter, actually quite pretty, and a middle-aged man who also appeared to be of Greek descent. All looked up expectantly as Coop entered and shut the door.

"Well, how did it go?" Nickolas smiled. The light gleamed off his two golden teeth as he stood up and strode forward, right hand extended.

"Yeah, how's mom?" the pretty daughter echoed. Her smile was pearly white and simply dazzling. She was wearing the uniform of a flight attendant and her nametag read, Liza Pahl...Southwest Airlines. Obviously she was married.

The other two said nothing but leaned forward, anticipation reflecting off their faces like a fresh coat of Varathane.

"Well," Coop began, then paused as he took Nick's proffered hand. Quickly, he rescanned their collective faces. Damn, there was no good way to do this! "Well," he began again, his cadence slow and deliberate, "I'm sorry, but she...uh...she didn't make it."

Silence quickly permeated the room like thick winter fog rolling up the Virgin River Valley. For a long moment, no one spoke. Very slowly, Nickolas's gilded smile faded and even though light still glinted his golden teeth, his countenance became livid, even rabid.

"What?" he jerked back, disengaging his hand from Coop's.

The daughter sobbed, "oh, my God, oh, my God," while frantically fishing in her purse for a tissue.

Searching his coat pocket, the family friend produced a writing pad and pen, then like a court stenographer, furiously scribbled down every word.

The son stood up and strode forward, joining his father. "What did you say?" he his voice steely, his eyes threatening.

"Again I'm sorry, but she...she's dead. She died on the table," Coop stammered, then quickly tried to fill the deadly silence with the details. "We did everything we could. We gave her over twenty units of blood and I tried every trick I knew, but she wouldn't stop bleeding. Honest to God, I've never seen anything like..."

"...You mean," Nickolas interrupted, "you mean you just friggin' let her bleed to death?" He took another threatening step forward. "It wasn't her heart or her blood pressure or a stroke? You just friggin' let her bleed to death!"

"I promise, we did everything we could," Coop repeated lamely, backing up a step. "Has...has she ever been a bleeder? Or has she been taking any medicines or blood thinners we didn't know about?"

"No!" the son barked. "She damn near cut her finger off in the kitchen last year, cut a tendon and everything, and didn't bleed that much."

"I'm truly sorry, Mister Tsongas," Coop said, voice pinched with emotion. "I don't know what I could have done differently and if I could bring her back, you have to know I would."

More lethal silence.

"So, where is she?" the son finally asked. "I want to see her."

"They have her in an isolation cubicle in recovery," Coop explained. "A nurse will take you back in a minute."

"How do we get her out of here?" Liza, the daughter, sobbed.

"A social worker will meet with you and make the arrangements for whichever funeral home you wish."

Meanwhile the family friend flipped to a new page and continued to write down each word.

"God damn it," Nick roared. "I told her to stay away from surgery—from you!" His face now flushed a scarlet red and his black eyes were glinted like chipped obsidian. "Mary, mother of God," he prayed, "why didn't she just give the Yuccasote a chance?"

"The what?" Coop arched an eyebrow.

"Never mind that," the son snapped.

"I...I want to see my mom," Liza wailed.

Coop searched for something to say. He came up blank. He could think of nothing.

"Mister Cooper," Nick Tsongas hissed, lunging forward, and only being partially restrained by his son. "Mister Cooper," he repeated, gold teeth glinting in the florescent light, then for emphasis he grabbed a fistful of Coop's scrub shirt, "as God is my witness, Mister Cooper, somebody's going to pay for this!"

4

The only weapon with which the unconscious patient
can immediately retaliate upon the incompetent surgeon
is hemorrhage.
—William Stewart Halsted (1852–1922)

Though not yet crested, a hint of morning sun was visible just beneath the shrouded outline of the Colorado Plateau. Its upward bound rays collided with overhead spidery clouds, illuminating a delicate lacy pattern. Initially, a deep burgundy, within minutes it rifled through the reds and oranges before fading into white light.

At ground level, however, the light for now was dull and flat, and the night's cool air lingered, smelling of dew and alfalfa. Unfortunately, this also would be short-lived. As the Helios climbed higher, the morning's gentle air would soon turn heavy, hot and oppressive, all courtesy of a late summer monster-high, which had once again camped over southern Utah.

Coop barely took the time to notice this magnificent light show. With Malachi at his heels, he was in a hurry to finish the morning's tasks. Usually, he took his time; he enjoyed doing ranch chores. That thought made him pause and smile, and would have amazed and amused his father, were he still alive today.

When Coop was a kid, he hated the ranch and everything about it. Undoubtedly, his father was frustrated with him and probably more than a little disappointed. As his only child, Coop suspected his dad had envisioned a hardier boy, one who enjoyed physical labor and perhaps even played a little football. What he'd gotten, however, was a son who loved books, schoolwork and had a lot of allergies, particularly hay fever, and hated all manual labor, including ranch work. Coop could clearly remember the day he'd defiantly told his father if he ever managed to escape the ranch, he would never come back. Yet, here he was.

Furthermore, Coop was convinced if his father had another heir, he would not have left the ranch to him, but he didn't, and he didn't have the time to make other preparations either. Both of his parents died while he was in his last year of residency and both were sudden and unusual deaths. His father rolled a John Deere tractor on a steep ditch bank; the rear tire and roll bar pinned him face down in the ditch. He literally drowned in less than a foot of water. Then not six months later, his mother suddenly died of a blood clot, a pulmonary embolism. What was strange about her death, she had absolutely no risk factors. The doctors speculated it was probably from sitting and brooding for long periods of time, which to Coop seemed a pretty weak explanation. Friends of the family, however, insisted she simply did not have the will to live after her husband passed. Maybe so, though Coop was not convinced one could will death anymore than one could will life.

When Coop first moved back to St. George to begin practice, he planned to sell the ranch, but temporarily he needed a place to live. Flat broke from years of schooling and student loans, he reluctantly moved back to the ranch, but only until he could find another place. That was twelve years ago. He'd expected the old resentments would eventually resurface, but they hadn't. After working all day in the pressure cooker of the O.R., he enjoyed coming home to the ranch and doing something physical. And even more surprising, he found he enjoyed riding horses. It was relaxing and gave him an opportunity to clear his mind. So the horses stayed and so had he.

Coop quickly dumped a half-bucket of alfalfa pellets in each of the five metal feeders, then violently sneezed as a small cloud of alfalfa dust levitated to his nostrils. Damn allergies! The horses, as usual, were edgy, stamping about and jealously guarding their own feeders. They seemed almost as impatient as was Coop.

This morning he had a radical prostatectomy, his first radical surgery since his self-imposed exile following Betty Tsongas's tragic death. Due to his prolonged hiatus, he'd lost his first hour start and was scheduled to follow Dr. Richardson's abdominal-perineal resection of the colon. The O.R. supervisor estimated he should start by late morning. This should give him plenty of time to stop by the office first and get caught up on the never-ending stream of paperwork and callbacks.

Thankfully, this surgery should be pretty straightforward. Gordon

Flowers, the patient, (English from the word flower) had an adenocarcinoma of the prostate. Pathology graded it a Gleason VII, Stage TIIa, a moderately nasty cancer, but in Coop's estimation, they had caught it fairly early.

Dr. Broadbent, an older semi-retired urologist who no longer did radical surgery, had referred Mr. Flowers. According to Broadbent, Gordon had a strong family history; a father and two uncles had died of prostate cancer. Therefore, Dr. Broadbent had followed Mr. Flowers pretty closely with biannual PSA's and digital exams. As soon as Gordon's PSA made a slight blip upward, barely above 4.0, Broadbent performed TRUS, a trans-rectal ultrasound with twelve sectional biopsies, finding the cancer. It was right sided only and in a single core, both favorable signs.

Also, Gordon was an ideal surgical candidate. A recently retired mechanical engineer from Chicago, he was thin, active, athletic and relatively young for prostate cancer, fifty-six. An avid bicycler, he was in excellent health, no obesity, heart disease, hypertension or diabetes and was taking no prescription medicines. In the past, Coop had done this surgery on patients who fit Gordon's profile in about an hour and fifteen minutes, with two hundred cubic centimeters or less of blood loss and two, or at most three days, in the hospital. For radical surgery, it didn't come any easier than this.

After finishing his morning chores, Coop quickly showered, dressed and wolfed down a bagel with black coffee. Before heading out the door, he made sure Malachi had enough food and water for the day, then said goodbye.

Singing along with the radio, Coop guided his maroon Dodge 2500 diesel pickup into his parking space behind the white brick office building. Grabbing an armful of patient charts, along with the notes he'd dictated at home, he walked through the back door. As he strolled down the hall, he hummed a bit of Bob Sieger's, *Old Time Rock and Roll.* For the first time in weeks, he was in a pretty good mood and was even looking forward to going to work.

After greeting the staff and depositing the charts into the arms of his scowling office manager, Christy Dennett (English from the personal name Dennis), she did not approve of him taking medical charts home, he headed straight for his private office.

Still humming, he sat down at his desk and sorted through the small mountain of mail. Most of it was junk: throwaway medical journals, pharmaceutical ads, CME flyers and hospital correspondence, but one letter sporting an officious-looking letterhead caught his eye. It was from Roe, Staples & Bowling, obviously a law firm with a Salt Lake City address. Quickly, Coop ripped open the envelope and extracted the contents and began to read.

> *NOTICE OF INTENT TO COMMENCE ACTION*
> *Nickolas Franco Tsongas, Petitioner*
> *Vs.*
> *Lawrence Addison Cooper, M.D., Respondent*
> *Dixie Medical Center, Respondent*
>
> *Comes now, Benjamin Bowling of ROE, STAPLES & BOWL-ING, counsel for the Petitioner, and serves, pursuant to Utah Code Annotated 78-14-8, a Notice of Intent to Commence Action against the parties listed above...*

Coop did not bother to read the rest. He probably wouldn't understand it anyway. But you didn't have to understand legalese to know what it meant.

Frowning, he stuffed the letter back into the envelope. It's not like he hadn't been expecting it, but enough time had elapsed a tiny seed of hope began to germinate. Somehow, he'd allowed himself the small possibility the Tsongas family had forgiven him. Damn, he should have known better. Always expect the worst, then you're never disappointed. His good mood disappeared, like diamondback rattlesnakes in winter. Sighing deeply, he picked up his desk phone and dialed Christy's extension.

"Christy," his voice now flat and emotionless, "I need two things. First, would you get UMIA, you know my malpractice insurance carrier, on the line, then bring me Betty Tsongas's chart."

While waiting for Christy to get a claim representative from the Utah Medical Insurance Association on the line, Coop leafed through Betty's surprisingly thin chart. Undoubtedly, Nickolas Tsongas's attorney would be requesting her records and he wanted to make sure there was no major blunders like missing dictation, office visits out of sequence, or inappropriate language, and all pertinent lab, x-rays and pathology reports were properly filed.

As he read over the notes again, one detail caught his eye, something he had previously glossed over. It was puzzling to say the least, but he'd actually cystoscoped and biopsied Betty's bladder a year ago last January. Her surgery was performed in June of this year, almost eighteen months later. Why the big delay? The apparent reason, if one were to read between the lines, pointed to Betty. Certainly, he never would have suggested a long postponement like that.

After the initial visit to discuss the biopsy results and proposed treatment (with this kind of aggressive tumor surgery was always the treatment of choice), Betty was scheduled for surgery for the coming week. Then without calling the office, probably just the hospital, she cancelled, giving no explanation and not returning for a full year and a half. Again, why? And furthermore, why was she not already dead? This tumor was infamous for its virulent aggressive behavior, and without treatment the patient usually acquired metastatic disease within six months and was often dead within a year.

Coop shuddered as he remembered that day, Betty's actual death and the uncontrollable hemorrhage. What a nightmare! Forcing his mind back to the present, he thumbed through the lab section. He had not done any pre-op clotting factors, undoubtedly because she had no history of alcoholism or liver disease and had not been on any anticoagulants. Groaning out loud, he closed the chart. Could those missing eighteen months be in someway related to her unexpected surgical hemorrhage? Probably not, but who knows? And why had she finally decided to come back?

Suddenly, his pager squawked, bringing an abrupt end to his musings. Quickly, he checked the message. They were ready for him in the O.R.

No longer in a good mood, he parked the Dodge in the doctor's lot and trudged up the steps to the dressing room. He was still thinking about his impending lawsuit as he donned his blue cotton scrubs, then found his way to the operating room. On his arrival, Steve Spaulding made a great show of looking at his wristwatch.

"Miracles do happen," he grinned, tapping his watch crystal. "You're actually on time."

"Yeah," Coop shrugged. "Sometimes miracles are even bequeathed on the undeserved."

"You mean me," Spaulding laughed, "or you?"

Today, his crew was exactly the same as with Betty Tsongas' ill-fated surgery, Renae Mackey as circulating nurse, Molly Wilken the scrub tech, and Jared Johnson for his aid.

For some time, the hospital had been trying to specialize its operating room crews. The idea was for the same crew and surgeon to work together whenever possible, thereby fostering a better understanding of the surgeon's needs, idiosyncrasies, and the subtle nuances of the surgeries he/she performed. The obvious goal, of course, was to make the operating room more efficient, which hopefully would translate into more surgeries, which should ultimately increase the corporate bottom line. Today, it seems profit, not compassion, was the driving force of American medicine.

To Coop's chagrin, when the new program was launched, somehow he'd inherited the humorless drill-sergeant, Renae Mackey. Privately Coop wondered if there was some ulterior motive when she was assigned to his room. Perhaps, every other surgeon refused to work with her or maybe the hospital planted her as a spy, but then again there was a fair chance it was just plain bad luck. Regardless of intent or the lack thereof, it looked like he was permanently stuck with her. Groaning out loud, he steeled himself for another day with Nurse Chuckles.

As an anonymous and safe way for employees to voice complaints, and to make sure they had a mechanism to be heard, the hospital also recently launched the Incident Report Program. The premise was any employee could file a complaint without having to directly face the person he or she was accusing. As further protection for the whistleblower, the reports were kept strictly confidential, literally taking an act of God or a judicial bench warrant to unseal them. That, however, did not mean the hospital ignored them. Quite the contrary, they were taken very seriously. Often the hospital used them as a club when deciding raises, promotions, surgery block times, etc., and it was rumored Renae was legendary for writing Incident Reports.

Molly was a pleasant contrast. She was always happy and an okay scrub tech, but not yet a great one. To be great, a tech had to master the art of anticipation, knowing instinctively which tool the surgeon needed next and have it ready so the surgeon would not have to stop, ask for the instrument, then wait for the tool to be located and passed. For example if you gave a surgeon a needle holder with suture, you should also be ready to hand him a pick-up (DeBakey for internal organs, rat-tooth for fascia and Addison for skin), followed by scissors to cut the suture he'd just tied. Or, if you gave a urologist a Foley catheter, you should be ready to offer him some lubrication and a syringe to blow up the anchoring balloon. These things always followed in sequence, like the changing of the seasons.

Also, a major part of the art to anticipation was to know where the surgeon was at any moment during the operation. If he/she was deep in the pelvis and asked for a needle holder, obviously it had to be a long one. If he/she were working on the surface, then a shorter one would do. Lastly, this elusive skill included learning the surgeon's preference. For example with delicate dissection around blood vessels some surgeons used a sponge stick and some a Kittner. Coop, however, rarely used either, preferring instead Metzenbaum scissors, employing a spreading and nipping technique.

Although anticipation was a simple concept, almost no one took the time to master it. Hopefully, that was what the hospital had in mind with the new specialization program. On the surface, it sounded good and Coop was willing to give it a chance, even if it meant working with Renae Mackey.

Coop had no complaints about Jared Johnson, the aid. His main responsibility was a gopher, or a go-for, and also to help turnover the room between cases. As a secondary benefit, Jared hoped to secure several coveted letters of recommendation from the surgeons to bolster his medical school application package. Although his job was entry level and thankless, he did it well and without grumbling. Coop had already decided when the time came he would write him a good letter.

And of course, Steve Spaulding was his anesthesiologist. Even before this new specialty program, they worked together a lot, actually almost exclusively. It seemed Steve always requested his room, even demanded it. Now the other anesthesiologists had come to expect and even accept it, and that was okay with Coop. He liked Spaulding. Steve was a good and fast anesthesiologist, and in spite of his ever-escalating practical jokes, his irritating persistence trying to get him hooked up with his friend Marty, and his constant invitations to gambling, he was also a good and true friend.

Finished with draping the patient, Coop was about to make the lower midline abdominal incision, umbilicus to pubis, when Stanton Kingsley walked in, hands held high and still dripping water. As usual, Molly greeted him cheerfully, handed him a sterile towel to dry his hands, then quickly gowned and gloved him.

Inwardly, Coop groaned again. Both Stan and Renae? Now there could be no doubt, if there ever was, he was indeed on God's blacklist. He was perfectly capable of doing this operation without an assistant and he was in no mood for Stan's cryptic running commentary on his surgical technique and how he might do things differently.

Oblivious to the tension, Molly hummed a tune behind her mask as she handed Coop a #10-blade. Accepting the scalpel without comment, Coop made the incision with a single smooth stroke.

Unbelievable! Once again with just the skin incision, there was an impressive show of blood.

"Steve," Coop asked, forehead deeply furrowed, "did I get pre-op coagulation studies on him?"

Quickly Spaulding flipped through the chart. "Nope," he announced, "you want that I should draw some now?"

"Yeah," Coop nodded, "it looks like we could have another bleeder."

With the pelvic lymph node dissection, it only got worse and by the time they were taking down the pubo-prostatic ligaments, the bleeding had achieved the dubious distinction of being classified as uncontrollable hemorrhage. Of course, Coop tried everything to staunch the bleeding, clamp and tie, electrocautery and the argon beam coagulator. Nothing worked. The blood just kept coming. Like a full reservoir during a downpour, the spillway overflowed, likewise blood lapped over the wound edges and dribbled to the floor in streamlets. A large red puddle accumulated on the white vinyl floor and their shuffling feet created disturbing Rorschach patterns.

"Oh sweet Jesus," Coop silently prayed to the God he wasn't sure he believed in, "please, please help me." Then to his chagrin he also offered up a veritable shopping list of promises to sweeten the deal.

Unbelievably, it was happening all over again, like a recurring blip in the continuum of time, or a rerun from the Twilight Zone. For a brief second, the movie GROUND HOG DAY flashed through Coop's mind. What the hell was going on? Once again, he called for a handful of sponges and jam-packed them in the pelvis as tight as he could. Taking a deep breath, he then walked over to the corner stool, sat down and turned his back to the chaos and the stunned faces of his crew.

"BP's now sixty-eight over forty" Steve Spaulding shouted at Coop's back and for once Stanton Kingsley was silent, apparently he had no suggestions.

Coop needed space, a quiet place away from the battlefield to think. What could he possibly do? He'd tried almost everything he knew and nothing worked. But, it was perfectly clear if he didn't do something, and damn soon, he was going to have another surgical death on his hands. He'd already tried all the old techniques, and his old tricks weren't working. So, what did that leave? Prayer? Maybe, this was his foxhole. Maybe, this was his time to reconnect with God. But for God to stop this bleeding would take a miracle and Coop sincerely doubted God would grant him that. He didn't have nearly enough equity in his spiritual bank.

"Well, I never...," he vaguely heard Renae exclaim. "I'm going to get the supervisor." He tuned her out.

Forget the metaphysical, he chided himself, this was not a Greek play, there would be no *machina deus* here. God was not coming to the rescue now, anymore than when Kylie left. Get back to the physical, the real world. If the old wasn't working, then was there anything new? Suddenly, it hit him.

"Renae!" he exclaimed, jumping off the stool. "Do we have any of that new stuff? What's it called? Tissue...uh...Tissuseal. Do we have any of that? The reps were in here detailing it the other day."

"I don't know," Renae growled, stopping just short of the door. "I've never heard of it."

"Well," Coop snapped a definite edge to his voice, "please go check with the O.R. supervisor and if she doesn't know, check with central supply."

Renae did not budge.

"Now!" Coop roared.

Hands on her angular hips and not bothering to hide her disapproval, she glared at Coop for another long moment, then threw her arms up in resignation and marched from the room.

While hanging two more units of blood, Spaulding glanced over at Coop. "Last two units of A-positive, then we go unmatched."

Coop nodded his head.

"You coming to Mesquite with us this weekend?" Spaulding asked as he finished hanging a unit of blood. "Marty will be there."

How bizarre, Coop thought, as he glanced up sharply. What a time to bring that up. "Not now, Steve," Coop muttered.

Spaulding laughed, then more soberly added, "Damn, his pressure's dropped again."

"I don't think we have time for this chitchat," Stanton Kingsley snapped as handed Molly a blood-soaked sponge. "In case you guys didn't realize it, this man is bleeding to death."

At that moment Renae walked back into the room with two small vials. "I've got it," she announced without enthusiasm. "It'll take a bit to prepare it. It has to warm for ten minutes.

"Do it as fast as you can," Coop instructed as he shoved another sponge into the already jam-packed pelvis.

After it warmed, Molly used a pair of identical ten-cc syringes to draw the contents out of the two separate vials; one a gossamer clear liquid, the other mocha brown. Once the syringes were full, Molly attached them to a double-barrel plastic frame, which allowed both plungers to be depressed simultaneously. When the plungers were pushed down, the twin syringes discharged their liquid into an online mixing chamber just before it was extruded through the nozzle.

As Molly finished preparing the Tissuseal, Coop plucked the tamponading sponges from the pelvis, all ten of them. He knew once the last sponge was removed, they would have a very narrow window of opportunity before hemorrhage would begin anew and visibility would vanish.

"Tissuseal!" Coop barked while holding out his right hand.

Smartly, Molly slapped the double-barrel apparatus into Coop's gloved hand.

Orienting the device, Coop inserted it deep into the pelvis and sprayed. Quickly he coated all raw and potentially bleeding surfaces with a thin layer of the clear molasses-like compound. Almost immediately it coagulated, turned opaque, and coated the pelvis in a gelatinous film.

With the double-barrel syringe now empty, Coop stood back and held his breath, waiting for the bleeding to start again. It did not! Almost afraid to look, he waited another thirty seconds, still no bleeding. Slowly he exhaled. Damn, this stuff was actually going to work.

At that moment, Stan Kingsley called for sterile wash water to irrigate the pelvis, the usual routine at the end of a case. Coop immediately placed a restraining hand to stop him, preventing him from pouring the saline.

"No, Stan, if you fill the pelvis with water, you're going to have to suck it out," Coop said sharply, also grabbing the Yankar suction from him. "If you do that, you might dislodge the Tissuseal."

"I don't see how it would hurt," Stan protested. "We always irrigate at the end of a case. Get's rid of any bacteria and loose tissue debris."

"Not this time," Coop insisted firmly, looking Kingsley in the eye.

"You're the surgeon," Stanton said, unable to keep the sarcasm out of his voice.

After one more tentative peek, Coop ordered some #1 PDS to close the fascia. Time to go home.

"You want some closing music?" Spaulding asked. Not waiting for a reply he added, "how about some Jimmy Buffet?"

Kingsley scowled, but held his tongue. Apparently he didn't like Jimmy Buffett.

Quickly, Coop closed the wound, the fascia with a running suture of #1 PDS, the subcutaneous with 3-O chromic gut and the skin with metal clips, then they carefully transferred Mr. Flowers from the operating table to the gurney.

"We'll go to ICU," Spaulding announced as he started the gurney in motion, "if that's okay with you."

Coop nodded his assent. "What was our blood loss?"

"It's hard to say for sure," Spaulding replied, shaking his head, "it was pretty hectic in there for a while. But counting the sponges, the four by four's and guesstimating what dripped on the floor, I'd say somewhere around five to six thousand cc's."

"Wow!" Kingsley exclaimed. "That's sure to get you a call from Peer Review."

"You think you're caught up?" Coop asked, ignoring Kingsley.

"I doubt it," Spaulding replied. "You'll have to check a crit and probably give him more blood later. And it wouldn't hurt to give him a couple more units of fresh frozen plasma."

Once they had Mr. Flowers safely deposited in the ICU and hooked up to all the necessary monitors, Coop sat down at the little wall desk just outside the room to write post-op orders. For a few minutes he wrote nothing, but just sat there reliving the nightmare and wondering if he could have possibly done anything differently.

Sighing, Coop opened the chart, flipped to the order sheet and wrote his usual post-op orders. Suddenly, he remembered Spaulding drew coagulation studies in the operating room. Changing courses, he logged on to the computer, found the hospital applications program and called up Mr. Flowers' coagulation studies. Steve had ordered the whole gamut, including a PT, a PTT, an INR and a Factor IX, not usually included on the routine coagulation panel. Factor IX was one of the ten proteins necessary for the normal cascade of reactions that resulted in clotting and was produced by the liver.

Surprisingly, the only thing abnormal was Mr. Flowers Factor IX. In fact, it was almost zero! Was it possible Mr. Flowers was an undiagnosed hemophiliac? Coop shook his head. No, that was not possible. He sincerely doubted anyone could go through fifty-six years of life with hemophilia and not know it. With hemophiliacs every little bump or a bruise always resulted in a huge hematoma. And a small scratch or abrasion usually produced a major hemorrhage. Even a shaving nick or a dental extraction could be a life-threatening event. No, there was no way Mr. Flowers could have familial hemophilia and not know it. So, if it was not genetic, that only left acquired. And Coop had no idea how one went about acquiring a Factor IX deficiency.

Bewildered, Coop ordered four more units of fresh frozen plasma and ten milligrams of Aquamephyton (Vitamin K) I.M., then stood up and stretched. Might just as well go get it over with, he thought grimly. It was time to talk to the family. He started for the door, then stopped and abruptly sat down again.

Picking up the phone, Coop punched in his office number, then waited. When Christy Dennett finally answered the phone, he instructed her to pull Mr. Flowers' office chart and read him the pertinent information, i.e. the lab slips, pathology reports and office visits.

Frowning, Coop slowly replaced the phone. Unfortunately, it was just as he'd suspected. Dr. Broadbent had performed Mr. Flowers' prostate biopsy almost twenty months earlier (no report of bleeding with the biopsy). After his initial cancer consult with Dr. Broadbent, Mr. Flowers was given an appointment to see Coop about surgery. But after the surgery had been scheduled, Mr. Flowers cancelled out and Coop had not seen him again for a full year and a half! It was Betty Tsongas all over again.

Scratching his head, Coop tried to think it through. Why the missing months? Was this lapsed time in some way related to the massive and uncontrollable surgical hemorrhage? And was it also in some way related to this strange Factor IX deficiency? Coop was beginning to feel more than a little unsettled. One untoward event could be construed as a coincidence, but with two events exactly the same it was beginning to look like a pattern.

Sighing again, Coop stood up again. Time to go face the music. He had Sarah gather the family in a conference room, the very same blue room he had given the Tsongas family the bad news a month earlier.

The Flowers family consisted of Gordon's wife, Jenny; her aging parents, Franco and Lucinda Tucciano (Italian); and a daughter of about thirty, Alexis.

As he introduced himself, Coop noted Alexis was wearing a pink nurses' uniform and her nametag read: *Alexis Flowers—2-West.* She must work here in the hospital on the cardiology floor.

After everyone was seated, Coop gave them an honest, blow-by-blow account of Gordon's surgery. He tried to be impartial, as impartial as he could, considering the circumstances. When he'd finished, he paused and waited for questions. There were none. Instead, a heavy silence hung over the room like a dark shroud over a birdcage.

Finally, Jenny sighed and spoke. "At least he's okay, huh?"

"He's stable and the bleeding's stopped," Coop confirmed, trying not to sound too optimistic, "but we're not out of the woods yet. There's still a long way to go."

"When can we see him?" Lucy Tucciano, the mother-in-law, asked. Her deeply lined face was creased even more with worry.

"In a few minutes, they're getting him settled now," Coop replied. "The ICU is on this same floor about halfway down the main hall. There's a waiting room there. Just pick up the wall phone and ask if you can see him."

Again they lapsed into silence, with the Flowers family apparently trying to digest this unexpected and unsettling news. Coop gave them another minute, then decided he might just as well ask the few questions he had.

"The thing that's got me puzzled," he said, "Dr. Broadbent did the biopsy twenty months ago. Where was Gordon all this time?"

Instantly, Jenny Flowers' countenance changed from worried to upset. She glanced up sharply at her mother, but neither of them said a thing.

"Look," Coop said, continuing to press the point, "it might be important. It could very well save his life."

Squirming uncomfortably in her seat, Alexis looked like an over-inflated balloon about ready to burst. Finally she blurted out, "in spite of my strong professional objections as a nurse, father was seeing a holistic doctor."

"He was very secretive about it," Jenny added, turning red. "He never told us much."

"Who?" Coop asked. "Which doctor?"

"I don't know," Alexis replied. "But I can tell you he was receiving some new kind of combination treatment, including a new herbal medicine."

"What medicine?"

"I don't know," Alexis said again. "But I think it was Yucca...something or other."

"Yucca, huh," Coop said, shaking his head. "Never heard of it." He paused for moment, then continued, "well, can you at least tell me why he came back for surgery now, twenty months later?"

"That part is really quite simple," Alexis replied, "the treatments quit working. His PSA started to climb again."

Coop took a second to mull this over. More than likely this meant the treatments worked for a while; otherwise Gordon would have metastatic disease by now. That in and of itself was quite surprising; usually these herbal remedies did absolutely nothing. The real question was, however, did those treatments in some way cause the bleeding? Probably not, though one could never be certain. Typically, herbal treatments not only lacked any biological activity for a cure, but they also lacked any real potential to do harm. They simply did nothing, except maybe for the placebo effect, and of course they all had a real tendency to drain the pocket book.

Coop decided to give it one more try. "Can you think of anything else? It might just save his life."

They just shook their collective heads.

"So, did you get it all?" Franco Tucciano, the white haired father-in-law, suddenly asked, rising up from the couch.

"All what?" Coop asked, puzzled.

"All the cancer."

As Franco came closer, Coop couldn't help but notice he had an odd, but faintly familiar, odor. It reminded Coop of his leather-riding chaps.

"I guess you didn't hear me earlier," Coop replied patiently. "Because of the massive bleeding, we had to terminate the surgery early. The prostate is still there."

"What!" Franco exploded. "You mean my son-in-law went through all this, damn near died, and the prostate...the cancer is still there?"

"Well...well," Coop stammered, "once he heals up we can irradiate the prostate. His chances are still very good."

"So, why didn't we use radiation in the first place," Jenny asked, "if it's just as good as surgery?"

"Well..."

"...What kind of a...uh...a...," Franco interrupted angrily, pausing to search for the right word. Apparently he couldn't find it. "When I start putting leather on a tree, I damn well finish the job."

"What?" Coop asked. He was not at all following this conversation.

"I said I damn well finish what I promise. That's how we do business in the real world Mister Cooper."

"Pops works with leather," Alexis quickly explained.

"Oh," Coop said, hoping to change the subject, "my grandfather also used to make saddle..."

"*Che tipo di*...uh...what kind of," Franco bellowed, apparently he'd finally found the adjectives he'd been searching for. "What kind of a friggin' chicken shit outfit is this?"

Taken aback, Coop could think of no immediate reply.

With eyes a malignant black, Franco Tucciano glared at Coop, then abruptly turned and stomped from the room.

5

I often say a great doctor kills more people
than a great general.
—Gottfried Leibnitz (1645–1716)

At precisely 7:00 the next morning, Coop parked his Dodge pickup under a solitary Mexican palm tree in the mostly deserted physician's parking lot of Dixie Medical Center. Some of the new crop of physicians, particularly Dr. Sam Kittrel from Huntsville, Alabama, found the hospital's name both amusing and inappropriate.

Of course, St. George, Utah is not located in the true geographical American south, but rather in the southwest desert, and while the true south is hot and humid, St. George is hot and dry. With its striking bluffs, bulwarks and canyons all sculpted from crimson Navajo sandstone, the countryside looks nothing like the verdant pine forests and cypress-lined bayous of the true Dixie. But regardless of those glaring differences, to Coop this was indeed Dixie and these new snickering docs obviously did not know or understand the area's history.

Mormon Pioneers settled the St. George Valley in 1861 under the auspices of the master colonizer, Brigham Young. The reasons for this most southerly colony were manifold. Some say Brother Brigham wanted to further define the southern boundaries of his mountain kingdom, the sprawling Territory of Deseret. Others say Young, a quintessential entrepreneur, wanted to establish a supply station on the southern arm of the old Santa Fe Trail to replenish the California bound caravans right before they entered the forbidding Mojave Desert. But most agree the primary reason for this most southerly settlement, Brigham wanted the battered Mormon people to be self-sufficient, to in no way be dependent on the country that had beaten and forsaken them. Some historians even suggest he wanted Utah to become completely independent, not only economically, but politically as well. The practical reality, however, the Saints needed cotton for clothing. With the recent outbreak of civil war, it had become increasingly difficult to import cotton from the true south. With this in mind, Young called several Salt Lake families (some just arrived from Europe) to be pioneers and move their families to St. George. Once there, they would plant cotton for clothing, grapes for winemaking and mulberry trees to raise silk worms.

The raising of cotton, however, was met with limited success. The fields were small and the fiber was short and of poor quality. Consequently when the Civil War came to a close, St. George's cotton could not compete on the national market and the fledgling industry withered and died. But regardless of the lack of long-term success, this endeavor, plus the mild climate, has forever stamped the St. George and surrounding valleys as Utah's Dixie. Even though farms are now rapidly disappearing in favor of a more lucrative cash crop, golf courses and manicured subdivisions, cotton can still be found growing wild on some of the area's ditch banks or unattended fence lines.

Turning off the ignition, Coop hopped out of the truck, yawned and stretched, then headed straight for the ICU. He had just under an hour to make rounds on Mr. Flowers and do an inpatient consult on 1-West before heading to the office and facing another double-booked day of patients.

In spite of being intubated and on a ventilator, Gordon Flowers looked pretty good, even though he did bear more than passing resemblance to the Pillsbury doughboy. His hands, feet and face were remarkably swollen. Yesterday, in order to maintain his blood pressure, he received a considerable amount of fluid, both blood and saline. That excess fluid made his tissues swell like a tile-setters grouting sponge.

There was no way to communicate with Gordon. He had a breathing tube jammed through his vocal cords and he was heavily sedated, so Coop relied solely on what he could glean from physical examination, the medical chart and various bedside monitors. It was a bit like practicing veterinary medicine.

Surprisingly, Mr. Flowers' vital signs were pretty good. His blood pressure was stable at 112/72, his heart rate steady at 86 and his respirations were 16 (although on a ventilator, he was still breathing on demand). Through the night his urine output was low, but adequate at 400 cc for the last eight hours. But most importantly, there was no blood, absolutely none, oozing from the twin Penrose drains and his hematocrit from this morning's blood draw was a whopping 32. Except for a serum sodium of 132 and a potassium of 3.2, his electrolytes were also mostly normal.

Looking upward, Coop sighed a wordless prayer of thanks to...to whomever. It seemed he couldn't break the irrational habit of prayer. After scribbling a few orders, Coop closed Mr. Flower's chart, replacing it in the metal rack. It was amazing after yesterday's fiasco, on the very brink of death, he could look so good only one day later. Thank God for medical research and thank God, or whomever, for the scientist who developed Tissuseal. Without that recent breakthrough, Gordon Flowers would surely be in the morgue. Now after another day or two in the ICU, Coop should be able to take him off the ventilator, then he should be ready to transfer to 1-West, the post-op surgical floor. Then perhaps after another week or so in the hospital, he would be well enough to go home and a month after that, back on his bicycle. Of course somewhere along they way, he'd have to fit in thirty-five radiation treatments.

Leaving the ICU, Coop checked the waiting room for the Flowers family. It was still too early. Perhaps, he'd catch them on his evening rounds.

The morning was filled with follow-ups, patients who'd previously had cancer surgery. In Coop's specialty, those patients included prostate, bladder, ureteral, renal or testicular cancer. Following surgery, they returned periodically to make sure they were still cancer free and if not to hopefully catch any reoccurrence early. The standard follow-up for most cancers was five years, though that certainly was not carved in stone. Occasionally prostate cancer, and sometimes even bladder, was known to reoccur ten or more years after surgical removal. For bladder, ureter or kidney cancer, Coop often ordered a CT scan to check for lymph node or liver metastasis and a chest x-ray to look at the lungs. Prostate cancer follow-up was much easier, just a digital exam and a serum PSA were adequate. With no prostate, the PSA should remain close to zero for the rest of the patient's life. Testicular cancer also required doing routine CT scans and chest x-rays, but this cancer also had helpful serum markers such as beta human chorionic gonadotrophin and alpha feto-protein.

Coop finished the morning patients forty-five minutes late. Hurriedly he microwaved a frozen dinner in the break room, wolfed it down, then he was ready for the afternoon session. As per his routine, the afternoon patients were usually not follow-ups, but new patients referred for consult and treatment.

The first patient was Arlene Voorhees (Dutch – name of a place in Denthre) referred by Dr. David Devoe, a family physician practicing in Kanab, Utah. Holding a white x-ray folder and a manila envelope, Arlene was nervously pacing the exam room when Coop entered. Her bright flowery cotton summer dress seemed a bit inconsistent with her obviously dour demeanor. She was a thin anxious lady of about sixty. Her sallow face was drawn and deeply lined, and her skin was thickened and weathered, like tanned leather.

As though it was something vile, Arlene quickly shoved the x-ray folder and manila envelope into Coop's hands, then compulsively rubbed her hands together as though ridding herself of any residual residue. After furtively glancing around the room, she eventually focused on the white porcelain sink in the corner. Immediately Coop sensed her need and nodded his okay. She rushed to basin, scrubbed and dried her hands, then without a word sat down and gazed out the window.

"Doctor Devoe wanted me to give you those," she added after a moment, nodding at the folder in Coop's hands, then without making eye contract returned her gaze to the window as though she was expecting someone to join her.

"Hi, I'm Doctor Cooper," Coop said, extending his hand and completing his half of a formal introduction. After a moment, he dropped his unshaken hand and added, "what seems to be the problem?"

"Didn't Doctor Devoe call you?"

"No, but his office did make this appointment."

"Well, you should ask them," Arlene said quickly, remaining aloof, "I don't know."

"Surely, you have some idea," Coop persisted. He was normally a patient man, but Arlene was beginning to test him.

"Well...well they found something," Arlene finally said, gesturing at the folder and envelope like she was shooing a dog from her lawn. "It's in there."

Shrugging, Coop first opened the manila envelope. It contained a couple of pages of photocopied lab results and Dr. Devoe's clinical office notes. The only significant findings were a hematocrit, a bit low at 36, a serum creatinine a bit high at 1.8 and her urine analysis showed significant blood, RBC's—TNC (too numerous to count). And from the barely legible handwritten office notes, the only salient finding was a recent fifteen-pound weight loss. To Coop, it looked like it could be a lot more.

Next, Coop extracted the films, a CT scan, from the folder. Unlike Dixie Medical Center who had gone digital on all x-rays, Kanab's Valley Hospital still processed and printed the films in celluloid. After wedging the films on his now antiquated view box, Coop took a minute to study them. There was an obvious huge ten-centimeter solid mass in the upper pole of the right kidney. It was a little surprising a tumor of this size had not already spread, but fortunately there did not appear to be any renal vein or vena cava tumor thrombus, or any bulky peri-hilar or aortic lymph nodes. And other than a couple of small cysts, the liver was also okay. Likewise, the chest x-ray, other than showing some moderately advanced COPD, was essentially normal.

This was a classical example of what his old mentor, Jacob Heinz, called a "janitor diagnosis." It was so obvious even a janitor passing by could make the diagnosis. Using his pen as a pointer, Coop outlined out the huge mass for Arlene. She took a quick peek, then immediately turned back to the window.

"What is it?" Arlene asked.

"It's a tumor on the kidney."

"Is it malignant?"

"Probably." Coop believed in being honest and up front right at the beginning. This often saved a lot of backpedaling later. "Statistically speaking, ninety percent of all solid tumors of the kidney are cancer. They're called renal cell carcinomas."

"Shouldn't we biopsy it to make sure?"

"That's actually pretty controversial," Coop explained to the left side of Arlene's face as she continued to stare out the window. "Renal cell tumors can seed along the needle tracts, then grow right on out to the body's surface, almost like a mushroom. I've seen that happen."

"So," Arlene said, her affect as flat as the Bonneville Salt Flats, "where do we go from here?"

"These tumors are notorious for being resistant to both radiation and chemotherapy. The only effective treatment is surgical removal."

Her face was as immobile as a wooden mask. Coop looked at her closely to see if she was getting any of this. She did not return his gaze.

After another moment of silence, Coop continued, "with a tumor this size, the sooner the better. They tend to grow very fast." More silence. "Do you want me to go ahead and schedule surgery?"

Finally, Arlene looked away from the window, quickly passed over Coop's face, then focused again on the sink in the corner. "I've heard of another treatment that's quite effective," Arlene said without inflection, "and it's non-invasive."

"What treatment would that be?" Coop asked, frowning.

"I'd rather not say." Arlene's her voice conveyed both stubbornness and finality.

"I feel it is my duty to warn you..."

Suddenly, Coop's pager went off. Retrieving the beeper from the plastic holster on his belt, Coop pushed the button. The LED message flashed: 251-2020. That was ICU's number!

"Arlene, I apologize," Coop said, "but I've got to take this call. Sit tight and we'll talk about this some more in a minute."

Quickly Coop stepped back into his office, picked up the desk phone and punched in the number. The phone rang for thirty seconds before being answered.

"ICU," a female voice barked impatiently.

"This is Doctor Cooper, did someone page?"

"Oh, Doctor Cooper, thank God," the clerk exclaimed. "Let me get the nurse."

It was another thirty seconds before the phone was picked up again.

"Doctor Cooper, this is Nan Franks. I'm the nurse taking care of Mister Flowers." She spoke rapidly, like she was in a hurry.

"What seems to be the problem?"

"Mister Flowers is crashing!" Nurse Franks blurted. "All of a sudden his BP dropped to sixty/forty, his heart rate jumped to a hundred and twenty and bright red blood is pouring from his Penrose drains."

"Is the blood clotting?" Coop asked as he felt the invisible strands of dread knotting in the pit of his stomach.

"No," Nurse Franks reported, "no clots. Blood's thin as water."

"Start a unit of blood and four units fresh frozen plasma," Coop ordered, "run it in as fast as it will go, then just keep the blood going. Start prepping him for surgery. I'll call the O.R."

Hanging up, Coop immediately called the O.R.

"Doctor Cooper," the O.R. supervisor informed, "we do not have a room available right now. The next one to come down will be room eight, an orthopedic case, and that won't be for another hour."

"He'll be dead in an hour," Coop snapped. "Bring in the emergency crew and open the reserve room."

"Are you sure it can't wait?" the supervisor asked. "The emergency crew had a bad night, up all night with a multi-car freeway accident."

"No!" Coop barked. "I need them now."

After taking a couple of seconds to compose himself, Coop hurried back to exam room three and Arlene Voorhees. Even though Arlene also had a potentially life-threatening problem, she would have to wait. He would have to terminate their meeting right now and reschedule. It was a simply a matter of priorities. Mr. Flowers was much more likely to die first.

When Coop opened the door and looked in, Arlene was gone. At the moment, he didn't have time to worry about it. Closing the door, he yelled at his staff to reschedule what patients they could, including Arlene Vorhees, the rest he would see after surgery, then he dashed for the door.

As Coop walked into the O.R., the nurses were already prepping Mr. Flowers' bluish bloated abdomen. Quickly, Coop applied sterile drapes, then using a mosquito hemostat, removed the stainless steel staples holding the skin edges together, allowing them to separate. Using a scalpel, he cut the knot of the #1-PDS suture that roped the abdominal wall fascia together, then grabbing hold of both wound edges he pulled laterally, like trying to pry open jammed elevator doors. The blue PDS suture resisted only briefly, then started to unravel, allowing the abdominal walls to slide apart.

Almost like lancing an abscess, the trapped blood, constrained under pressure, gushed from the abdomen, spilling over the sides, down onto the table, then onto the floor. Coop noted with some concern, there were still very few clots.

For the next two hours, Coop tried every trick he knew to obtain hemostasis. He charred bleeders with the electrocautery, photocoagulated with the argon beam, tissue welded with the harmonic scalpel, suture ligated with chromic catgut and even sprayed the pelvis once again with Tissuseal.

This time nothing worked. It was *de ja vu* all over again. Once again he was stuck on that perpetual treadmill, trapped in that recurring nightmare. It was both real and surreal at the same time.

Suddenly, the awful nightmare slowed and simultaneously the sound track also ratcheted down, became garbled, then went totally silent. Now it was like watching an old black and white movie with the projector running in slow motion and the sound turned off. Jaws moved, but released no sound. Then somehow, Coop managed to extirpate himself from the macabre scene and simply floated above it. No longer an active participant, he became a detached observer, almost a passing tourist. He felt no emotion, other than curiosity.

Below him, Dr's Cooper and Kingsley continued the heroic fight. Frantically, Dr. Spaulding pumped blood as fast as he could, and Molly, Jared and even Renae responded to orders like well-trained soldiers.

But now, it was not his problem. He was nothing more than a casual bystander, a gawking motorist passing freeway gore.

From out of nowhere, a Coleridge albatross flew in, perched on the anesthesia ventilator and began to chant:

> *Blood and hemorrhage everywhere,*
> *Dripping off the bed.*
> *Blood and hemorrhage everywhere,*
> *Soon he will be dead.*

Then, he too fell silent.

Slowly, slowly, in black and white noir, and silent celluloid, Coop watched Mr. Flowers die.

6

As soon as Coop rounded the volcano and headed down the gentle slope to Diamond Valley, the fire was visible, illuminating the night like a coastal lighthouse beacon. It was still too far away to tell for sure, but deep down he knew. In a perverse sort of way, this was a fitting end to a terrible day. It was late, he was physically and emotionally spent, and he certainly didn't need this, but who did? Briefly, Coop thought about turning around and heading somewhere, anywhere, but instead pushed down harder on the accelerator.

After Mr. Flowers died on the operating table, Coop went to face the family. To say they were upset was a gross understatement. They still had not recovered from the bad news of the first surgery, so Coop had not expected they would take this last grim report with any degree of grace. They had not. Who could blame them?

Jenny, the wife, sobbed uncontrollably; Lexy, the daughter, clammed up, bit her lower lip and never uttered another word; Lucy, the mother-in-law, hugged her daughter Jenny while reaching around her to dab her own eyes; Franco, the father-in-law, was visibly angry and paced the room like he was looking for something to hit. Finally, he stopped right in front of Coop, and thrust out his bandy chest and snarled something unintelligible. Coop turned and quickly walked away, afraid it would literally degenerate into fisticuffs.

After that gut wrenching conference, Coop phoned the office. Christy advised him there were still nine patients who could not be rescheduled and were still waiting to be seen. Either they were from out of town, had a pressing problem which could not wait or were too anxious about their newly diagnosed cancer to be put off.

By the time Coop finished with the office, it was almost dark.

Rather than go home to a dark empty house and eat another bland microwave dinner, he stopped at a fast food joint and inhaled a quarter pound hamburger with everything on it, including greasy fries liberally doused with ketchup. For Malachi, he ordered two burgers to go, no onions. Kylie would never let him eat in such a place and wouldn't even allow red meat in the house, but then Kylie wasn't around anymore. It seemed ironic, but Coop now actually missed her constant nagging.

It was well after nine by the time Coop finished eating and started for the ranch, a dozen miles due north of St. George. As he left the city on State Highway 18, the road immediately ascended over the massive bulwark of red sandstone cliffs, then onto the sloping ridge, which angled toward the brooding Pine Valley Mountains. They steadily gained elevation as the highway snaked across several jumbled lava flows, then ran parallel to the rim of Snow Canyon, an elaborate pinnacled and domed chasm carved deeply into that very same red Navajo sandstone formation the road had just scaled. About ten miles from town the highway gently curved right around the base of an extinct volcano. Though it had been approximately seventy thousand years since its last eruption, it still retained a perfect inverted cone shape and was of course the source of previously crossed lava flows. In the dark, Coop could see none of this, but from years of commuting up and down this stretch of road he knew it was there.

Once he circled around the base of the volcano, Coop could see down into Diamond Valley and that's when he'd first caught sight of the fire. Grabbing his cell phone, he punched in 911, then gunned his pickup down the slope and onto the valley floor.

For the past week, a dome of high pressure had camped over southern Utah. That, coupled with no wind, made the smoke layer out over the valley like a dark blanket. As Coop neared the junction to his private road, the air got noticeably hotter and thicker, and smelled like burnt toast. By the time he pulled into his driveway the smoke was so thick visibility was reduced to no more than the length of his pickup. But in spite of poor visibility, the source of the fire was obvious. Flames leaped twenty feet high from his tack and feed shed some fifty yards directly south of the house. Of immediate concern, however, those intervening fifty yards sported a thick carpet of two-foot high cheat grass.

It was tinder dry and if a spark was to land there it would spread to the house in milliseconds, like a gasoline fire.

Of equal concern were the horses. Just south of the tack shed was the horse corral. Coop had five horses, a Tennessee walker, a Missouri fox trotter, a Paso Fino and two quarter horses. Though he couldn't see them through the thick smoke, Coop knew they must be in a panic, racing around the corral looking for a way out. With the gate locked, they were trapped.

Jumping out of the Dodge, Coop ripped off his shirt to use as a smoke filter. Covering his mouth and nose, and running low like a fullback, he dashed for the corrals. Fumbling in the dark and dense smoke, he searched for the gate. His eyes burned and he sneezed and even though he was breathing air through his shirt, he still felt like he was suffocating. There was almost no oxygen in the air, only smoke. After a few moments of groping, Coop managed to locate the gate. Quickly he unlatched it, swung it open, then stepped back. Instantly, seeing their escape route, the horses bolted for freedom, racing two hundred yards across the field to the far fence.

The next priority was to find Malachi. Coop was very attached to that dog. Without Kylie around, Malachi had become his closest companion. As he sprinted toward the dark house, Malachi almost knocked him down in the dark. With his tail wagging furiously, Coop grabbed and hugged him. Thank God, he was okay.

With Malachi and the horses safe, the next order of business was to keep the fire from igniting the tall cheat grass and then the house. Working as fast as he could, Coop lugged a hose out of the garage and located the tap on the south end of the house. Stretching the hose as far as it would reach, he sprayed down the wheat-colored grass. It was none too soon. At that moment, the fire ignited the grass adjacent to the tack shed and flashed toward him. It burned fast and hot, then abruptly stopped at the line he'd just hosed down.

Somewhere out in the night, Coop heard the wail of a siren. Initially faint, it rapidly got louder as it approached the ranch. Thirty seconds later Diamond Valley's sole red and white fire truck roared down his private road and screeched to a stop next to his fire hydrant. Two minutes later, they were connected and spraying a huge arc of water toward the quickly metastasizing fire and the still blazing tack shed.

Though it only took another ten minutes to knock the fire down, the tack shed was a total loss as was the south fence line and two of the horse corrals. Fortunately, however, the house and the horses were okay. Coop breathed a sigh of relief and with his arm around Malachi sat down and watched the firemen work.

After a few minutes of poking through the rubble, the Fire Marshall told Coop he would be back early tomorrow, but from his preliminary investigation he thought it looked suspicious. He added, however, spontaneous combustion fires in stored hay barns were not totally unheard of. Moldy stacked hay, yes, Coop argued, but he fed alfalfa cubes. He'd never heard of a pile of cubes spontaneously combusting.

After the firemen left, Coop found his flashlight and poked around on his own. Everything smelled like a doused campfire. Not only was the tack and feed shed a total loss, but the fire also destroyed two tons of alfalfa pellets, not to mention all of his halters, bridles, saddle blankets and five saddles. Sure, in theory all that stuff was replaceable, but the sentimental value...that was irreplaceable.

One of the saddles, hand-tooled with assorted desert cacti, was a family heirloom, handed down from his grandfather to his father and now to him. His grandfather, an amateur dabbler in leatherwork, actually made the saddle. When Coop was feeling down or troubled, the saddle was a source of solace. He would saddle up one of the horses, usually Stepper, and go for a ride. The saddle was not only the most comfortable, it also was a tangible link to his family, a window to the past, his grounding rod. He was the only one of grandfather Cooper's progeny left. The saddle was somehow proof his problems were indeed transient, they too would pass and life would go on. Most recently Coop used the saddle when Kylie left, then again when Betty Tsongas died.

Sitting down on a charred, still warm, fallen rafter, Coop surveyed the mess. The burnt saddles smelled a bit like his veterinarian's crematory. He had an overpowering urge to give up and move. Maybe start over somewhere else, like Texas. This was too much. After a long moment, he sighed heavily and stood up. No, he would rebuild, for his dad, for his grandfather and for himself.

After completing his inspection of the charred tack shed, Coop headed toward the burned field. With flashlight bobbing and Malachi at heels, he systematically inspected the blackened stubble. He wasn't sure what he was looking for, more than likely he would find nothing, but he had to do something. There was no way he was going to be able to sleep, at least not right now.

Suddenly, Malachi took off, nose close to the ground. Redirecting the flashlight, Coop followed him. After trotting approximately twenty yards to the left, he stopped and sniffed something on the ground. Coop moved in closer. Indeed, there was something lying on the ground. Partially sequestered in a clump of unburned grass, it appeared to be loosely woven fabric. Bending over, Coop patted Malachi for his good work, then picked it up.

What the hell! He refocused the flashlight and for a closer look. He'd seen that fabric before. In fact he was quite familiar with it. What he was holding in his hands was a common surgical sponge complete with a blue finger-loop sewn to its corner. And there was something else; it was greasy. It obviously was doused with some kind of lightly colored oil. Coop held it close to his nose, not much of an odor. He licked a finger. It did not smell or taste like engine oil, but rather like some kind of plant oil.

With fabric like this, so loosely woven, Coop doubted any finger-prints could be lifted, but just in case, he held it by the blue finger-loop and carefully carried it back to the house. In the better light of the kitchen, he examined it more again.

Indeed, it was just as he'd suspected, a common O.R. surgical sponge, and the oily substance appeared to be light in color and tex-ture, more like a vegetable oil than a petroleum product. Rummaging through his cupboards, he found three different kinds of plant-base oil Kylie had in stock, vegetable cooking oil, extra virgin olive oil and a small amount of peanut oil. Coop tasted all three, then tried the sponge again. He repeated the test again, rinsing his mouth with water after each taste. Of course, it was impossible to say for sure, but he strongly suspected the substance on the sponge was olive oil. Fortunately, how-ever, he didn't have to rely on his crude gustatory test. He had another better way to sort it out.

From his college days, Coop had an old friend, actually an old chemistry professor and now the department chairman at Southern Utah University. He could ask to run a qualitative analysis on it.

During his undergraduate years, Coop was a chemistry major and a protégée of Dr. Marcus Westover. Repeatedly, Marcus tried to convince him to make a career out of chemistry and had even talked to the department chairman of Stanford University to secure him a post-graduate position. When Coop chose medicine instead, Marcus was disappointed, but took it all in stride and they had remained good friends. Even though he knew he should hand the sponge over to the fire marshal in the morning, Coop had already decided he would give it to Dr. Westover. In the end, it was not a difficult decision. He figured Marcus would give him faster and more accurate results.

Probably the most important question was not what was used to burn down his tack shed, but who? And why? Was it just kids playing a prank? Albeit, a very dangerous one. Or, was someone actually trying to do him harm? Someone with a vendetta. He could think of no enemies. Everyone pretty much liked him, except...well...now with the exception of the Tsongas and the Flowers family. But surely they wouldn't resort to something like this. They could easily get their pound of flesh through the courts. Was it then just an adolescent prank? Maybe accident? Or, perhaps a random act of arson? It was conceivable he had been a target, but not specifically the target. In the back of his mind, Coop had a sneaky feeling that he might never know for sure.

Feeling a bit unhinged, Coop sat down on a kitchen counter bar-stool to think. After a few minutes of staring at nothing in particular, he noticed the phone answering machine's red light was furiously blinking. Sighing, he got up and punched the play button.

The first message was short and blunt: *Doctor Cooper, this is Doctor Jeremy Faux (French), Chairman of the Surgical Peer Review Committee. We have scheduled an emergency session for tomorrow at 5:30 p.m. and invite, no insist, that you attend. If you have any questions, you can call me at 251-1919.*

Coop had no questions. He knew exactly what that meeting was about, the recent and untimely deaths of Gordon Flowers and Betty Tsongas.

The machine beeped and message number two began: *Doctor Cooper, oh, what the heck, you're still Coop to me. Coop, this is*

Samantha Rose Jardine (English variant of Jardin), remember from college? Anyway, I'm an attorney now with Cannon, Jeffs & Hanks in Salt Lake City. Your insurance carrier, UMIA, has a retainer with our law firm, and I have been assigned by the firm to represent you in the upcoming matter of Betty Tsongas. We need to set up a fact-finding and strategy session. I will be in Saint George tomorrow on other business, is there any way we could meet for lunch, say around 12:15? Let me know if this will work for you. You pick the restaurant. Please confirm by calling 801-565-6666. This number is an answering machine, so you can call anytime. Thanks.

Samantha Rose Jardine! Just the sound of her voice made Coop's heart race and his breath quicken. That was incredible! What were the odds? She was a lawyer. His lawyer!

Just briefly in college during their sophomore year at Southern Utah University, they had dated. They met when she was assigned his lab partner in Invertebrate Zoology. What surprised Coop, not only was she so damn good-looking, but she was also very intelligent and was a great lab partner. Samantha Rose had the whole package. At the time, she had just broken up with her longtime boyfriend, a SUU football player, and Coop was still playing the field...well, playing the field as much as any nerd can.

The fact they got together at all, however briefly, was highly improbable, bordering on the impossible. Samantha was distraught by the breakup with her jock and Coop had a sympathetic ear; he'd always been a good listener. With devastatingly good looks, shiny long auburn hair with just a hint of rust, a perfect hourglass figure, effervescent charm, an infectious smile and a naturally quick mind, Samantha Rose was way out of his league. But nonetheless, probably because he'd caught her on the rebound, they had an intense, wild and thrilling two-week fling. She once confided in him that what attracted her to him was his intelligence and his complete lack of pretension. He was, according to Samantha Rose, the complete and refreshing opposite of her athlete. At least that was something, if only alms for the poor. The boyfriend, however, apparently realizing what he had lost, returned a fortnight later and once again muscled her away.

Somewhat cynically, Coop used scientific theorems to rationalize the irrational and make some cold hard sense of it all. After all, it was clearly spelled out in Gregor Mendel's laws of genetics, or if not it should have been. Or perhaps, it was Isaac Newton's law describing the attraction between two heavenly bodies. But somewhere it was written that beautiful people should mate with beautiful people and have beautiful offspring. So the fact that Samantha returned to the jock should have come as no real surprise. Indeed, it was predicted, even predicated, by immutable laws of the nature and the universe.

Fortunately, the quarter was nearly over, so he did not have to face her again in the zoology lab. Wounded and bitter, even though he'd half-expected it, Coop completely withdrew from all social life. Samantha insisted she wanted to remain friends, but as a mechanism for self-preservation, he purposefully broke off all contact, completely closed her out of his life. Over the years, he had not kept up with her personal or professional life. Until now, he hadn't a clue of what happened to her.

Though he'd completely wiped all traces of her from his life, he'd never really gotten over her and if he were totally honest he'd have to admit he was still in love with her. That's why the sudden increase in heart rate, blood pressure and breathing just at the sound of her recorded voice. If he had any sense at all, he'd request another attorney.

But...but, she was still using her maiden name of Jardine. That must mean she was still single. Whoa, hold on, back up, Coop sharply chided himself, that was not necessarily so. Nowadays married women often retained their maiden name for use in their professional careers.

Damnit, you're doing it again, Coop silently cussed. There was no way he was going to fall again for Samantha Rose Jardine. One broken heart per woman was quite enough. Like any fracture, if you repeatedly broke it in the same place, it eventually would result in a non-union; it would not heal. This, he silently resolved, would be strictly a professional relationship.

With jaw firmly set, Coop picked up the phone, dialed 801-565-6666 and in a flat monotone voice told the recorder he could meet Samantha Rose tomorrow at 12:15 p.m. The Desert Pier restaurant in Ancestor Square would be fine.

Unlike Malachi, who started snoring almost instantly, when Coop finally flopped into bed sleep was a reluctant visitor. Like a detective who continually replays a grainy video from the bank's surveillance camera trying to identify a suspect, Coop kept replaying the events of the bizarre evening. First, there was Gordon Flowers awful death. What the hell was going on? Why were all his patients suddenly bleeding to death? Was it surgical technique or just plain bad luck? Or, was something more sinister going on? He had to find the answer soon and put a stop to it. Psychologically and or financially, he didn't think he could survive another surgical death.

Then there was the fire. He had a nagging bad feeling about it he could not shake. Over and over again, he tried to convince himself it was just another random indiscriminate prank, but the uneasiness remained. The tack shed, of course, could be rebuilt and the tack replaced, but not his grandfather's saddle or the many associated memories. Most of the loss should be covered by insurance, so the financial loss would not be great, but the whole thing left him more than a little unsettled. Was it really possible someone was out to get him? Would he or she strike again?

Lastly there was the message from Samantha Rose Jardine and even it was quite unsettling. What were the odds, considering the number of doctors at any given time being served malpractice claims and the number of lawyers handling malpractice suits, that he would end up with Samantha Rose Jardine as his attorney? Maybe not as unlikely as winning the power-ball lottery, but certainly not very good. The real question, however, would he be able to work with her while keeping his emotions in check? In the past he'd not been very good at that. So why not request another lawyer and be done with it? No...no way! He was not going to give her the satisfaction of knowing he couldn't handle it. Yes, Coop silently resolved, I can and will handle it. Everything will be all right as long as I keep my distance and keep it strictly professional. And what a schmuck he was! What made him think Samantha Rose wanted anything other than a professional relationship anyway?

When he finally dozed off, his dreams were spiked with terrifying visions of orange fire and leaping flames. He groaned and thrashed in his sleep. Though the scenes were vivid, they were often unfinished and disjointed. One minute, he was spraying the fire with a garden hose, the next minute he was listening to the horses' terrified shriek, as they were being burned alive. Then suddenly he was trapped. There was fire everywhere. He could smell burning flesh...his flesh!

Shaking, he forced himself to wake up, then could not get back to sleep. Was that most unsettling dream some kind of metaphor, an allegory or a harbinger of things to come?

7

Medicine is not merely a science but an art.
The character of the physician may act more powerfully
upon the patient than the drugs employed.
—Paracelsus (1692–1741)

The next morning Coop, still shaken by last night's dream, hurried to finish his scheduled patients, then rushed to meet Samantha Rose at Ancestor Square. Glancing at down his watch, he eased off the accelerator. He could easily get there by 12:15 p.m.

The Desert Pier was a trendy outdoor pasta and salad restaurant where young professionals liked to gather for lunch. There they laughed a lot, had a drink or two and plotted how they would and could gladly knife anyone in the back if it were necessary to climb the corporate ladder. Needless to say, this was not Coop's kind of place, but he thought Samantha Rose might like it.

After checking in with the maître d', Coop was shown to a table in the corner, thankfully in the shade, to wait. The usual crowd was there: men in white shirts, ties and slacks, but no coats and ladies wearing anything from jacketless pantsuits to flowery sleeveless summer dresses. Paroxysms of laughter pierced the air and the background chatter was loud and nonstop. Everyone, it seemed had a salient point to make and simply must be heard. To add to the commotion, beepers and cell phones were constantly going off. Sarcastically, Coop wondered if anyone in this crowd had ever had a true emergency. For him a beeper was not a status symbol, but literally was a lifesaving device and figuratively speaking, it was also a proverbial ball and chain. He would gladly give his beeper and cell phone to anyone in this group who would also take them along with their attendant responsibilities.

Frowning, Coop looked away. The loud raucous patrons were

beginning to get on his nerves. He looked up and checked out the over-head shade tree, a honey locust. With long drooping limbs, it looked a bit like a hybrid weeping willow. For a few minutes, he admired the symmetry of the leaves and branches, then checked his watch again, 12:30 p.m. and still no Samantha Rose.

For another fifteen minutes, Coop fidgeted, then got up to leave. Obviously, Samantha must have gotten delayed. When he returned her call last night, he should have left his cell phone number, but he hadn't. Tossing his lime green napkin on the spotless white linen tablecloth, Coop got up and wove back through the crowded tables. As he zig-zagged, he picked up the incongruous odors of Alfredo and alcohol. It was an odd mixture of scents.

At that moment, she arrived, bursting through the door like early morning sunlight. Coop caught his breath. She hadn't changed a bit... well maybe a little. Her face was slightly more mature, but that only added to her beauty, otherwise she looked the same. She was dressed conservatively, wearing black pumps, nylons, a gray plaid business suit and a white satin blouse. The moment she spied Coop she waved and grinned, and Coop's heart melted.

As she jauntily wove her way through the crowd, heads turned, both male and female. He held out his hand, but without hesitating she went right through it, hugged him and kissed him on the cheek. Then, she held him at arm's length, took a long appraising look and nodded her approval. Embarrassed, Coop quickly disengaged and steered her toward her chair. After she was seated, he took a deep breath and sat down opposite her.

"Well how are you, Doctor Lawrence Addison Cooper, M.D.?" She smiled with genuine pride. "My goodness, a doctor!"

Blushing like a schoolboy, Coop was suddenly tongue-tied. This always happened when he was in the company of beautiful women and especially beautiful like Samantha Rose Jardine.

"Uh...uh, well...uh...I'm fine, except for this Tsongas suit," Coop mumbled, trying to stick to business, "and you're a lawyer, huh? I would have never suspected it."

"What did you suspect, Coop?" Samantha asked, her eyes laugh-ing, then quickly added, "I refuse to call you Doctor Cooper anymore."

"I...I don't know," Coop stammered, "probably something...uh...

more visible...like in television or the movies." Then like his tongue had a mind of its own, he blurted out, "Did you get married?"

"Yes, I did get married," Samantha smiled ruefully. "You know him, Chuck Caplin the quarterback."

Involuntarily, Coop winced. He really didn't want to talk about personal stuff. Why the hell did he bring up marriage? And the Chuck Caplin affair was still far too painful to dredge up now or ever. "Oh yeah," he replied as though he had to search the dusty files of his mind to remember. "Any kids?"

"Nope, no kids and for that matter, no Chuck either. We divorced five years ago. Turns out he was about as shallow as a kiddies' wading pool. How about you?"

While waiting for his answer, Samantha stood up, quickly unbuttoned Coop's top two shirt buttons, realigned them, then re-buttoned them correctly. Somehow his top buttonhole was secured with the second button, making the shirt asymmetrical and gap open at the chest.

"Uh...uh, I had a couple of drops of blood splatter on my shirt right before I came over," Coop explained, turning red. "I tried to dissolve them with peroxide, and, uh, I guess put it back on wrong."

"Some things never change. That's what I like about you." Samantha Rose said grinning and shook her head, then continued, "you never answered. What about you? Are you married?"

"Yes...uh...no. Well, I was," Coop stuttered. "I don't know...maybe. Yeah, probably I am, even though I don't have a wife."

"I'm not sure I understood all that." Samantha's faint golden freckles bunched quizzically on her perfect oval face.

"I'm not sure I do either," Coop acknowledged. "She, Kylie, left almost a year ago, but I've never been served divorce papers."

"Why don't you file?"

"Well...well, I don't know." Coop fumbled for something to say. "I guess I just never got around to it."

"I suspect that's another way of saying you hope she will come back." Samantha eyed Coop closely for a reaction.

"Uh...well, why don't I tell you about the Tsongas case," Coop blurted, "bring you up to speed?"

Samantha smiled and nodded. "Yes, we do need to get down to

business. I have an afternoon appointment, then a flight to catch. And I'm sure you have afternoon full of patients."

For the next twenty minutes, Coop went over the whole Betty Tsongas affair from top to bottom. Though he realized it was next to impossible, he tried to explain everything honestly and impartially. In great detail he told her the pre-op rational for surgery and the preparations for the operation. He paused momentarily to see if Samantha was getting all this, then continued on with a thorough description of the uncontrollable hemorrhage and the subsequent events surrounding her death.

As he talked, Samantha fished a yellow legal pad from her bag and began jotting down notes. Periodically, she would interrupt to ask a question, then lapse again into silence and resume writing.

"To paraphrase the incomparable Walter Cronkite," Coop said as he finished. "And that's the way it was."

"Coop," Samantha, Rose was now all business, "and mind you this is just a first impression, but my gut feeling is unless we can come up with some explanation other than surgical technique for the bleeding, this case is going to be a difficult one."

"I know."

"Well then, let's see," she said a little more brightly, "I'll need a copy of your office records and also of Betty Tsongas's hospital chart. Do you think you could overnight them to me in Salt Lake?"

"Sure."

"I'll need a little time to go over the material." Samantha paused for a second for some mental calculations. "The pre-litigation hearing is two weeks from Monday in Salt Lake City. Why don't we..."

"...Two weeks!" Coop exploded.

"Yeah, that kind of surprised me too," Samantha replied. "That's about as fast as I've ever seen a pre-litigation hearing date set after filing the initial Intent to Commence Action. Does Mister Tsongas have connections?"

"If you only knew."

"Anyway, why don't we meet in my office about four p.m. on the Sunday before to go over strategy and organize the material we have?"

"That would be fine by me," Coop stood up and stiffly and extended his hand once more. No goodbye kisses for him; a handshake would do "I'll see you then."

Without giving Samantha Rose a second look, Coop marched out of the Desert Pier. Once outside, he checked his watch, 1:30 p.m., then quickened his pace. He had a full afternoon of procedures, cystoscopies and trans-rectal ultrasound prostate biopsies, scheduled to start promptly at one. He was already thirty minutes late. Oh, well, what else was new?

On his way to the office, Coop reaffirmed his vow of last night; no way was he going to let himself again fall in love with Samantha Rose Jardine. Once burned beware, twice burned a fool. At times, he wasn't very smart, but no way was he a fool.

* * *

Samantha remained seated at the table and with genuine affection watched Coop walk away. How could she not help but like him? He was so different from any other man she'd ever met. So completely unassuming and thoroughly unpretentious, he was both refreshing and amusing. In this twenty-first century where men were every bit as vain as women, Coop was a throw back to the old days. Except that he didn't smoke, in some ways he reminded her of the original Marlboro man. No colognes or fancy perfumes for him, no highlight streaked hair or salon styles, no trendy fashion clothes or male jewelry. What you saw is what you got—and all man.

When she dated Coop back in college, she was attracted to his mind. With his photographic memory, he was the closest thing to a genius she'd ever met and quite unexpectedly she found that sexy. It was true, back then he was a little nerdy. He wore black-rimmed glasses with thick lenses, always carried a calculator, was rail thin, and paid almost no attention to his personal appearance. But my, oh, my, how the years had blessed him. Gone were the thick glasses, he either wore contacts or had LASIK eye surgery. Vanished was the skinny frame, replaced with the lean muscles of a man accustomed to physical labor. Though he was still no fashion statement, his clothes were rugged and western, and looked good on him. Of course, he was every bit as smart as ever and the *coup de grace* he was a surgeon. Samantha would never have guessed that in a million years. She'd always supposed he would end up sequestered away somewhere in a research lab, maybe even win the Nobel Prize for chemistry. But the single most attractive, and at the same time most amusing thing, he still thought of himself as a nerd.

Probably, the biggest mistake she'd ever made was choosing the jock, Chuck Caplin, over Coop. At the time, she knew she hurt him badly and would not blame him if he requested another attorney. Chuck, on the other hand, turned out to be everything Coop wasn't. He was egotistical, vain, lazy, dumb and a philanderer. You could sum up Chuck with one sentence; he figured his good looks and athleticism entitled him to free passage through life.

But she'd best be careful. She was presently involved with another man, Josh Markum. As she had a tendency to do in the past, she needed to be mindful not to string either of them along. Instinctively, she always felt it was better to have a back up, an ace in the hole, and of course that was not only unfair, but often cruel. Certainly, Josh was a step up from Chuck Caplin. He was a lawyer, actually an unnamed partner with her firm, Cannon, Jeffs & Hanks. Also, he was good looking, loved racquetball and scuba diving, but on the flip side of the coin he was quite vain, very materialistic and perhaps even a little superficial. Certainly, he was no Coop, but then again no one else was either. Coop was one of a kind, an American original.

Sighing, Samantha gathered her bag and her writing pad, and got up to leave. She had a whole afternoon scheduled with Dr. Jackson Loebel, an orthopedist. Apparently, he was being sued by a man he'd implanted a Dupey hip prosthesis, another of the growing and seemingly never-ending medical-product class action lawsuits. Following that, she had to catch a late flight back to Salt Lake City.

* * *

As a direct consequence of starting his afternoon patients late, Coop finished late. By the time he saw his last patient, it was 6:00 p.m. and he was already a half-hour late for Dr. Faux's mandatory meeting of the Surgical Peer Review Committee. Jumping in the Dodge, he drove as fast as he could the ten blocks to the hospital. He parked, then sprinted through the front door, dashed down the stairs and arrived at the basement conference room slightly out of breath.

"Glad you could make it," Faux said sarcastically, glancing up as Coop entered. He was standing at the head of a twelve-foot, oval, veneer oak table. Also present were six other docs, each clad in starch white lab coats and sitting around the table at various angles of weariness or boredom. As Coop nodded to those present, he couldn't help but notice Faux's body language did not affirm his initial greeting. He certainly did not look to be happy Coop had made it and for that matter neither did anyone else.

"Sorry, I got hung up at the office," Coop explained, "emergencies." Every doctor used that excuse for everything, to get out of social obligations or church meetings, even with other doctors. It always worked; other physicians realized it was entirely possible.

"Well, you're the only item on the agenda tonight," Faux growled, "so, we've been waiting."

"Sorry, but you didn't give me much warning," Coop said. "No time to rearrange my schedule."

"Let's get on with it then." Dr. Faux pointed to an empty chair at the opposite end of the table. "Take a seat."

Nodding, Coop did as instructed.

After formally stating the mission of meeting for the record, Dr. Faux continued, "now, I'd like to turn the time over to Doctor Raymond Richardson, Chief of Surgery—Doctor Richardson."

Inwardly, Coop groaned. Why did Jeremy Faux always have to be so formal? Everyone here were equals and on a first name basis. Why not drop the formality and the titles? After all, this was not the United Kingdom.

Ray Richardson loudly cleared his throat and looked at the ceiling. "We as a committee have been concerned for a few months now over some very troubling trends on your part, Coop." He paused and cleared his throat again, still avoiding eye contact. "Within the last three months, you've had two surgical deaths, both associated with massive blood loss, over six thousand cc per case. This is most unusual, even for radical cancer surgery, and...uh...we would like to hear your side of the story."

Frowning, Coop stood up. "Honest to God, Ray, I have no idea. Frankly, both cases were bizarre. Both patients were relatively healthy, no liver problems and not on anticoagulants. I've spent literally hours and hours racking my brain and have come up with nothing, no plausible explanation."

"That only leaves you, doesn't it," Faux interjected, "surgical error, incompetence or impairment. Perhaps, all three."

"You guys know my history," Coop argued. I've been on the staff here for twelve years and in the past my surgical judgment and competence have never been questioned. I'm just having a run of bad luck."

"What about the issue of impairment?" Dr. Harvey suddenly asked. He was sitting next to Coop, directly on his left.

Coop frowned again and shook his head. "Impairment? What are you talking about, Harv?"

"We have in our possession an Incident Report from a nurse who claims you were operating on," Dr. Richardson paused briefly to check his notes, "on Betty Tsongas impaired, possibly drunk."

Damn that Renae, Coop thought bitterly. He should have known. "That's preposterous," Coop tried to control his rising anger. "I had a cold, a virus, and took a couple of Benadryl...uh...and some mouthwash. It was very stressful in there, but I was not drunk and I was not impaired."

"Well, right now we have no way to prove it one way or another," Dr. Faux admitted, still eyeing Coop, "but I can tell you without any equivocating, it just doesn't look good. Your performance not only reflects badly on the surgery department, but on the entire medical staff and on this institution as a whole."

Coop could think of nothing to say, so he simply glared back at Faux.

After a moment of tense silence, Dr. Harvey stepped in again. "Coop, are you having personal problems? We hear rumors."

"Well, yes." Coop decided he might as well be honest. "As you probably know, my wife left me a while back, but I swear it had nothing to do with this."

"This is so unlike you," Dr. Balantine, a heart surgeon, remarked. "It's almost like we should look for other factors."

"Well," Dr. Faux took charge again, "well, I don't think there is anything further to gain by batting this around all night like a cricket match. I'll entertain motions right as to how the committee wishes to deal with this problem. Your options include suspension of surgical privileges, probation, a written reprimand or no action."

"I don't think we have enough evidence of impairment, just her word against his," Dr. Balantine argued, "so, I vote against suspension. However, the situation does bear close monitoring. I'll make a motion for a year's probation."

"The chair has a motion for probation," Faux echoed. "Do I hear a second?"

"I'll second," Margaret Toolsen, an emergency room doctor sitting next to Harvey, called out.

"Are there any other motions?" Faux asked, then after a moment of silence he continued, "then the chair would like to forward a motion for suspension. We are unduly exposing the department to possible legal action if we do nothing. Will anyone second this motion?"

No one spoke.

"Uh...well then," Faux muttered, his face mirroring both surprise and betrayal, "let's vote on the first motion. All in favor say aye."

A chorus of ayes resounded loudly.

"Those against say nay," Faux then instructed.

There were none.

"It appears the voting is unanimous," Faux bitterly conceded, "but I need to warn you, Doctor Cooper, this really is a probation in every sense of the word. One more offense and your operating privileges will be summarily suspended."

8

As to disease make a habit of two things:
to help, or at least, do no harm.
—Hippocrates (460–377 B.C.)

Years ago while still in high school Coop was registered for an early afternoon chemistry lab. That particular winter afternoon was cold and overcast consequently the windows were closed. Their assignment was to construct a hydrogen generator using Pyrex flasks, glass tubing and rubber stoppers. Once they had the generator operational, they were to collect the hydrogen gas (a byproduct of the reaction) in an inverted test tube. Hydrogen is lighter than air so it rises and therefore would theoretically get trapped in the down-turned tube. To confirm, they had indeed created and collected the volatile gas, the manual instructed them to ignite the inverted test tube and listen for the characteristic pop, much like the sound of a wine bottle being uncorked.

Even now, decades later, Coop could still recall the chemical formula, $2Al\,(s) + 2NaOH(aq) + 6\,H2O > 2Na+(aq) + 2(Al(OH)4)- +3H2(g)$, but of course he could remember most esoteric facts. What he had trouble with were the mundane details of daily living. In big bold letters, the lab manual warned: **DO NOT LIGHT THE GENERATOR ITSELF**, and the teacher also went to great lengths to reemphasize that point. Naturally, anything forbidden only made Coop more curious. When everyone else was busy making popping sounds, he took his Bunson burner and held it up to the tip of the glass capillary tubing exiting from the generator itself.

KA-BOOM!

The generator exploded with the force of a stick of dynamite. As the flask blew apart, tiny glass shards were launched into the air, like flying razor blades. As they sliced across the room, they cut through or pegged into anything and everything in their path: wallboard, supporting columns, blackboards, hanging lab coats and wooden cabinets. The concussion from the blast also cracked two windows as well as most of the lab glassware in the neighboring bays. Miraculously, no one was seriously hurt, though several students were impaled by little missile shards, some had to be plucked out with tweezers and a magnifying glass. Needless to say, Coop ended up in the principal's office.

After fifteen minutes of harangue, the principal ended his lecture by stating, "Lawrence, I'm really disappointed in you. This is so out of character for you." And it was. Normally, he was not a rebel, but could not resist the temptation to find out what would happen if indeed a hydrogen generator was lit. It was more an act of curiosity than of defiance or delinquency.

Even to this day, he could never forget the feeling of humiliation as he shuffled head down and red faced from the principal's office. Everyone stared at him or at least he imagined they did. Today leaving Jeremy Faux's conference room, he felt very much the same way.

In less than an hour, the superbly confident and much heralded cancer surgeon was reduced to an ordinary man filled with misgivings, self-doubt and very little self-esteem. In the slanted evening light, Coop's haggard face reflected the strain. For the moment, he appeared confused, looking around as though he were lost. Finally, he sighed out loud and seemed to have come to a decision. From his shirt pocket, he fished out his cell phone and punched in the number of Dr. Jacob Heinz.

Jacob was a pre-WWII Nazi refugee from Schlamending, Austria. His emigrant parents brought him to America as a pre-teen. And though he spoke perfect English, except he still had a little trouble with his 'W's', he enjoyed pretending he understood very little English and claimed one could learn a lot by playing the dumb foreigner.

Coop and Jacob went back a long way. When Coop was in training at the University of Utah, Jacob was not only his mentor, but also his friend. At the time, Heinz was approaching retirement age and took Coop under his wing as kind of a personal project or perhaps his final bequest to mankind. Much like an aging artist wanting to leave at least one masterpiece as a legacy. Jacob taught Coop everything he knew about the healing arts and surgical medicine. In fact, it was Jacob who insisted he use Metzenbaum scissors for dissection rather than Kitners or sponge sticks, even around major blood vessels or small nerves. Coop could still hear Jacob's admonition, "any surgeon vorth his salt should learn the fine art of delicate dissection." Though he was impatient with sloppy work, he was a kind and understanding friend, and always had a ready ear.

After his retirement from the U. of U., Dr. Heinz, like many northern Utahns, moved to Utah's Dixie to get away from brutal cold winters, the backbreaking chore of shoveling snow and to work on his golf swing. Over the years they stayed in contact, with Coop visiting Heinz on the average of three or four times a year. This year, however, Coop was delinquent with no visits at all, but then again this had not been a very good year.

"*Guten Tag,*" Jacob answered the phone, sporting a thick German accent.

"Jacob, this is Coop and you're speaking German."

"*Ja, Ja,* I know," Heinz laughed. "Never know vhen it's going to be a politician or a telemarketer."

"How are you, Jacob?" Coop asked. "I'm sorry I haven't been by lately."

"*Mir geht's gut,* and you?"

"Fine," Coop replied, then hesitated, "actually, not so good. I've been having some trouble with surgery."

"*Wie das?*" Jacob asked, then switched to English. "How so?"

For the next five minutes Coop explained to Jacob in detail the last two surgical catastrophes, then concluded by telling him about the just completed meeting of the Surgical Peer Review Committee. Jacob offered no immediate comment. Then just as a slumping professional golfer might ask a colleague to analyze his swing, Coop asked Heinz to scrub with him on his next surgery, specifically to critique his technique and offer any other criticisms or suggestions.

"I don't know," Heinz wavered, "you really think that's necessary? You're one of the most gifted surgeons I know. I doubt I vould be of much help."

"It would help me a lot just to know you still think my technique is still okay. These last few months have been hell on my confidence. You still have courtesy privileges don't you?"

"*Ja, Ja*, of course," Jacob replied, then paused to think. "Okay, you let me know vhen is your next case and I'll vill scrub."

"*Danke*, Jacob," Coop said. "You don't know how much that means to me."

Folding up the cell phone, Coop replaced it in his pocket, then glanced down at his watch. It was almost seven-thirty. If he hurried he could still make it to the St. George Convention Center in time to hear the wildly famous Dr. Jonathan Clifton Ford speak.

It seems lately Dr. Ford (English - a topographic name for someone who lived near a ford) was all the rage. A chiropractor by trade, he had greatly expanded his original practice from simple spinal adjustments to organize a very successful health institute and in the process it seems he had become an expert, though probably self-proclaimed, of holistic medicine and the natural healing arts. Reportedly a dynamic speaker, the charismatic Ford had recently taken his health message on the road to large and enthusiastic audiences.

The chairman of the Ethical Practices Committee, an ad hoc appendage of the UMA (Utah Medical Association), asked Coop as past president of the Washington County Medical Association and current delegate to the Utah Medical Association, to quietly investigate the enigmatic Dr. Jonathan Clifton Ford. So far, Coop hadn't come up with much, just anecdotal evidence and personal testimonials, actually most of them quite flattering if not glowing.

Though he was rumored to have a brick and mortar clinic somewhere in the desert, Dr. Ford recently made personal appearances in several towns scattered throughout the tri-state area, (southern Utah, southern Nevada and northern Arizona) and even addressed much larger crowds in Las Vegas. This, however, was his first sojourn into St. George. Curiosity, plus the mandate from the Ethical Practices Committee, was enough incentive for Coop to attend, though after the day he'd had he would have preferred go home to Malachi and a quiet evening of brooding. Oh well, he would reward Malachi with a bacon cheeseburger and a dose of Jonathan Clifton Ford might just take his mind off his own problems.

The St. George Convention Center was a newly-constructed, multi-level, terracotta brick building located at the far south end of the valley right on the banks of the perpetually muddy Virgin River. It was pretty much surrounded on the other three sides by hotels and restaurants, but unlike convention centers in other states there were absolutely no bars or gentlemen's clubs. This, after all, was Utah. In lieu of nightlife (though it was not always easy to convince conventioneers there was a substitute for nightlife), a paved riparian walkway along the Virgin River had been constructed for those attendees who fancied a quiet evening stroll. One of the largest and most visible buildings in town, it was close enough to I-15 to provide easy freeway access for out-of-towners.

Tonight, the convention center was hot, noisy and packed. Certainly it looked as though Dr. Ford had no trouble in attracting an audience. With head bowed low, so as not to attract too much attention, particularly from old patients, Coop entered through the twelve-foot high glass door, then quickly weaved through the dense milieu of bodies crowded in the foyer. In a very real way, the baying and milling crowd reminded Coop of penned cows at the Southern Utah Cattle Auction. He squeezed through and around them, eventually finding an entryway down the slanted walkway into the auditorium.

Even though the room was large, a capacity over two thousand, it was already packed and reeked of perspiration, stale deodorant and cheap perfume. Patiently, Coop worked down the aisle, searching for a seat. There were none. About two thirds the way down, he realized he would not find a chair and subsequently gave up. Instead, he leaned back against wainscoted wall, mauve paper and walnut paneling, patiently waiting for the show to begin.

Not only was it hot, it was also very loud. On the stage, a brass band belted out *Give Me That Old Time Religion.* That, plus the ongoing crowd noise, was beginning to give Coop a headache. He closed his eyes and tried to tune it out, then he felt a tugging at his elbow. Grudgingly he opened his eyes instantly recognized the face of a patient. A second later his photographic memory produced a name, Eldon Hunsaker. So much for trying to remain *incognito.*

"Doctor Cooper!" the elderly man exclaimed, almost jubilantly. "I didn't know you approved of this sort of thing."

"What sort of thing, Eldon?" Coop forced a smile.

"This sort of thing." Mr. Hunsaker gestured at the audience with a wide sweeping arc. "This kind of medicine. The old time traveling medicine show."

"I can't say for sure," Coop tried to remain cordial, "if I do or not. I'm not sure what kind of medicine this is."

"Well, it does work," Eldon insisted, then sheepishly added, "I'm sorry I haven't been in for a while, but I've been doing fine."

"I'm glad you're doing well," Coop shouted. The band started up again, making further conversation almost impossible

Silently, Coop recalled Eldon's medical history. Yeah, he remembered the details, like he remembered everything else. Eldon Hunsaker had prostate cancer, a Gleason grade VIII, stage TIIB. He had a biopsy, but no treatment, at least not from Coop, yet he still looked fine. The puzzling thing, that was over two years ago.

Abruptly, the band stopped playing. The overhead lights went out and the spotlight highlighted only the drummer as he executed a loud cascading drumroll. Eldon disappeared back to his seat. The spotlight then swung to the center of the stage as a smiling waving Dr. Jonathan Ford parted the curtains and marched onto the stage. The resultant applause was immediate and thunderous.

Ford appeared to be about Coop's age, in his early forties. His naturally wavy hair was shoulder length and almond brown in color, as were his eyes. He was wearing a white Russian peasant smock garnished with fancy red embroidery. His pants were faded blue jeans and his sockless feet were covered with leather Roman sandals. He sported a short well-trimmed beard, had a kind gentle face, doe eyes and a smile that was almost angelic. Waving, he bowed low to the crowd, his long hair falling forward, covering his face. It was an opening fanfare, Coop thought, befitting a rock star.

After another full minute of almost deafening ovation, Dr. Ford bowed one last time, then patted the air down repeatedly, asking for silence. After loudly clearing his throat a couple of times, he finally began his speech. His voice had a musical quality and he spoke with the natural cadence of a poet. All in all, it was really quite captivating.

"Every man is either a fool or a physician after the age of thirty," Ford boldly proclaimed, then paused for dramatic effect. "What did John Ray mean by this most provocative proverb? What he meant, of course, is we are ultimately responsible for our own health, not the government, not your insurance company, or even your family doctor.

And, I suspect this is the reason you are here this evening. Tonight, I not only intend to inspire you to become captains of your own ship, but also to become masters of your own fate, ministers to your own souls and physicians of your own bodies. You can do this. Indeed, health and happiness are as inseparable as shipmates, bunkmates joined at the hip, married for life."

For the next hour, Coop listened to Dr. Ford. Not once did he yawn or did his mind wander. Without question, Dr. Ford was a fascinating and hypnotic speaker. His impassioned speech had all the superficial trappings of a science lecture, but felt more like old time gospel preached in a revival tent, or perhaps even a fiery political rally in a small town square.

As Dr. Ford wound down his remarks, Coop tried to analyze what he actually said. Basically all he gleaned from the last hour, Dr. Ford subscribed to and preached one basic tenet, treat the whole patient, mentally, physically and spiritually. Unfortunately, he skipped over the boring details and offered absolutely no specifics on how to accomplish this. It was more like a pep rally before a big football game, than a team meeting to map out a game plan. His speech, Coop decided, was about as controversial as motherhood and apple pie.

Ford concluded by offering his personal testimony. Where had he learned this revolutionary, this all-encompassing approach to health and disease? Through study, prayer and through the school of hard knocks. He too once was a patient, a patient on his deathbed and was healed.

After another rousing ovation, Dr. Ford, like Moses descending from Mount Sinai, raised his hands high and started down the ramp, leaving the safety of the stage to mingle with the crowd.

Positioned on the far side of the great hall, Coop immediately worked toward the doctor. Doggedly, he fought and wedged through the milling swarm, steadily pushing his way toward Ford. After five minutes of dodging, bobbing and weaving, he finally stood directly in Dr. Ford's projected path.

"Doctor Ford," Coop extended a hand as Ford looked up, "I'm Doctor Lawrence Cooper."

Smiling broadly, Dr. Ford firmly grasped Coop's hand in both of his. "You can call me Cliff, Doctor Cooper."

"That was quite a speech, Cliff," Coop continued. "You certainly managed to hold their attention."

"I assume your approach to medicine is a bit more conventional," Dr. Ford said, still smiling warmly, his eyes soft and gentle.

"Yes," Coop nodded, "I'm of the old school. I still cut out disease."

"Ah, a surgeon," Dr. Ford exclaimed, "the intrepid health warrior armed with an eagle's eye, a lion's heart and the hand of a lady."

"Yeah, well, I guess," Coop shrugged. "That may be a bit too flowery for what I do, but I'm still not clear on your approach."

"It's really quite simple, prevention, prevention, prevention, but when treatment is required, treat the whole person, not just a single organ."

"But I guess that's where I'm confused," Coop persisted. "Treat them how?"

"We have a very effective combination therapy," Ford smiled and groped for Coop's hand once more. "It was very nice to meet you, Doctor Cooper. I'm sure we will meet again."

Then he was gone. Ever the consummate diplomat, he continued to work the huge crowd.

Coop watched him go, then slowly wormed his way out of the convention hall. Dr. Ford was not at all what he'd expected. He was affable, charming and appeared, at least superficially, to be honest, sincere and totally dedicated to his work. There was, however, one disconcerting thing that bothered Coop, and it wasn't just his rather generic speech. There was something elusive, something intangible about Ford. It was hard to put a finger on. Maybe, he was just too slick or too confident or too polished or smiled just a bit too much. He was everything Coop was not. Maybe that was it. Perhaps what Coop was feeling was nothing more than a healthy, all-American dose of professional jealousy.

Maybe, but then there were his eyes. Sure they were gentle and without question they were sincere, but there was also something else. Ford's eyes, depending on your take, shone with the radiant light of truth and righteousness or glinted with the flinty zeal of fanaticism. But regardless of his vague suspicions and general sense of uneasiness, there really wasn't much to report to the UMA.

* * *

The next week Coop scheduled Mr. Hector Perdenales Gonzalez (Spanish or Mexican from the personal name Gonzalo) for surgery. Mr. Gonzalez presented with gross hematuria, blood in the urine, but no pain on urination. Cystoscopy confirmed the bladder was clean, but a CT scan of the abdomen revealed an obstructed left kidney with marked hydronephrosis (back up of urine). The exact point or cause of the obstruction was not clearly defined, though it appeared to be somewhere in the distal third of the ureter. To further delineate, Coop took Mr. Gonzalez to the surgical suite and under anesthesia performed ureteroscopy (scoping the ureter). That study solved the mystery. Coop saw a fleshy sessile mass in the ureter about four centimeters above the bladder. A biopsy revealed a high-grade transitional cell carcinoma and subsequently Hector Perdenales Gonzalez was scheduled for surgery.

This would be a fairly technical surgery. First, Coop would have to resect the entire distal third of the left ureter, the part containing the cancer. Of course, this would shorten the ureter considerably making it impossible to plug the remaining stump back into the bladder, even the dome. To compensate, a long bladder flap would be outlined, incised, then swung upward toward the transected end of the ureteral stump. Step two, the ureteral stump would be implanted in the upturned bladder flap. Step three, the flap would be rolled into a tube, thereby creating a neo-ureter, replacing the previously resected six centimeters of tumorous ureter. Lastly, the defect would be closed to make the bladder watertight again.

As usual, today Coop was in a hurry. After taking care of Malachi and the horses, he rushed from the house fifteen minutes late, but rather than feeling harried, he felt relaxed. Just knowing Jacob Heinz would be assisting rather than the always-critical always-cynical Stanton Kingsley made all the difference in the world.

Even though he was fifteen minutes late, when he arrived at the operating room there still was no patient, only a scowling and pacing Renae Mackey. Curtly, she informed him of a newly instituted hospital policy: *when operating on paired organs, the surgeon must mark the correct side with a permanent felt marker before the patient leaves the pre-op suit.*

Sarcastically, Renae continued, "as far as I know the ureter is still a paired organ," then after glancing down at her wristwatch she added, "they've been waiting on you for twenty minutes."

As Coop sprinted to the pre-op area, he was fuming. Not only was he upset with Renae, she was her usual caustic and irritating self, but also with the hospital. Obviously, this was another blatant attempt by them to absolve themselves of any responsibility and place all liability squarely on the shoulders of the surgeon.

After accepting the expected ribbing for being late, Coop quickly marked Mr. Gonzalez's left side, initialed it, then walked to the doctor's lounge for a cup of coffee and a slice of toast. It would be another twenty minutes before Dr. Spaulding would have the patient asleep.

Coop choked down a half-cup of stale coffee and burnt toast, then headed for the O.R. He couldn't help but smile when he saw the familiar profile of Dr. Jacob Heinz through the window. He was sitting on a stool and thumbing through the patient's chart.

A short energetic man in his early-seventies, Dr. Heinz had thick grayish red hair, so coarse it looked like it would have to be cut with a hedge-trimmer. Also, as one might expect, he had equally thick and bushy eyebrows, which seemed to perfectly match his unruly hair. At first glance, Jacob looked like he could pass for Vincent Van Gogh as he appeared in his self-portrait, except of course Jacob had two ears. Meeting him for the first time, one would never suspect he'd been one of the finest surgeons to ever set foot in the state of Utah. He just didn't look the part and maybe that's why he and Coop got on so well. Coop didn't look the part either.

"Hi, Jacob," Coop greeted him warmly as he entered the room, "glad you could make it."

"*Ja, Ja,* it does the old bones good to get out and do something vorthwhile every now and then," Heinz laughed. "But, let's not make this too long...the old knees."

"Fine by me," Coop agreed, "a quick in and out. No complications."

"Everything looks *sehr gut,*" Heinz acknowledged, pointing to the patient's chart. "Normal clotting factors. It ought to go vell."

"I hope so," Coop offered Heinz a hand, helping him up from the stool. "Let me introduce you to everyone."

Starting with Spaulding, Coop introduced Jacob to the team.

"*Guten Morgen, Herr Doktor*," Jacob said as he shook Spaulding's hand, then he acknowledged the rest of the team.

With introductions completed, they then went back out in the hall to scrub.

Five minutes later, when they re-entered the O.R., Steve Spaulding completed his tasks and was just turning on his ever-ubiquitous music.

"Do you have any requests, Doctor Heinz?" Spaulding pointed to his Bose Sound System.

"*Jawhol,* how about some Bach or Beethoven?"

Spaulding searched for a moment. "No can do, Professor. The closest thing I have to classical is the Beatles."

"The Beatles are fine," Jacob conceded, "just not too loud."

As Coop and Jacob gowned and gloved, Spaulding continued his idle chatter. "How about it, Coops?" he asked. "This Saturday night at the Oasis Casino. They're having a quarter-slots tournament."

"I don't know, Steve. I've got a lot to do."

"Like what?"

"Like...uh...like the horse stalls need to be cleaned and..."

"...What horse stalls?" Spaulding interrupted. "I thought they burned down. Anyway, I've already told Marty you were coming."

"I don't know, let me think about it."

"No...I'm not taking no for an answer this time. I'll pick you up at eight." Spaulding insisted, then he turned to argue his case with Jacob. "He hasn't been out in over a year, ever since Kylie left."

"It vouldn't hurt you to go out and have a little fun," Heinz agreed. "A man needs a vay to release a little pressure or he vill *explodieren.*"

"Huh?" Spaulding asked.

"Explode," Coop translated.

"Yeah, so how about it, Coops?" Spaulding was nothing, if not persistent.

"Okay, okay," Coop finally relented, "but I'll meet you there. I'll take the Dodge in case I need to escape."

"Ha, ha, ha," Spaulding roared. "I can guarantee you'll not be wanting to escape from Marty."

From the opening incision, Coop sensed they were in trouble again. As before there was a brisk ooze just from the superficial skin bleeders. By the time they entered the pelvis it was too late to turn back. And even with the sage advice and experienced hands of Dr. Jacob Heinz, things rapidly degenerated into bloody chaos.

"*Gott im Himmel!*" Jacob exclaimed, as he stuffed more sponges into the pelvis. "Vhat the hell is this?"

Mentally, Coop again started to withdraw, though physically he still went through the motions. Distantly, someplace in the periphery of his mind, he heard Spaulding bellow for more blood, Jacob demand another Yankar suction, Mollie shriek for more sponges and Renae and Jared frenetically dashing about, trying to locate those items.

Ever so briefly amid all this confusion, Coop had a flashback. He was about twelve, and back on the family ranch. Sternly, his dad pointed at twenty white Leghorn chickens, showed him a large mulberry stump, handed him a spruce-handled axe, then walked away. By the time Coop finished, it looked more like a Civil War battlefield than a family henhouse. Blood, bodies and heads were scattered everywhere. And to Coop it felt much more like carnage than Sunday dinner. Everywhere was the stench of fresh blood, and death and vomit. His vomit!

9

It was late Sunday morning and Coop was in the Dodge, heading to Salt Lake City. Out of his window, he could see Cedar City, a quaint college town and home of his undergraduate alma mater, Southern Utah University. It was also this campus where his good friend, Dr. Marcus Westover, taught and ran his research chemistry lab and lastly it was home to the much-heralded Tony-award-winning Shakespearean Festival.

Coop exited at the middle exit, then worked his way through a middle-class subdivision to the Westover home. After a few minutes of catch-up conversation, Coop gave him the baggie containing the oily sponge, declined an early lunch and thirty minutes later was again back on the freeway.

In approximately five hours, at 4:00 p.m., he was supposed to meet Samantha Rose at her office in Salt Lake City's Triad Center. A week ago Samantha called his office and confirmed the date with his office manager, Christy Dennett. Christy informed Coop Samantha wanted a quick strategy session to prepare for the upcoming Tsongas pre-litigation hearing, which was scheduled for the next morning at nine a.m. Obviously Samantha understood how professional offices worked. It was much better to schedule these things with Christy and let her add it to his calendar. If she'd called him directly, more than likely he would have gotten it wrong or would have forgotten. Well, maybe not, since it was a meeting with the beautiful Samantha Rose Jardine!

After arranging for the neighbor boy to watch Malachi and take care of the horses, Coop headed out of Diamond Valley just as every-one was getting ready to go to church. Sunday mornings were often associated with recurring pangs of guilt, especially when he saw the neighborhood families, scrubbed and clean and in their Sunday best, crowding in their vans or Suburbans and heading for the chapel. This was the way he was raised and this is what he used to do on Sunday mornings. Nowadays, however, a couple of things prevented him from participating in the family/church routine. One, he didn't have a wife much less a family and two, intellectually he didn't really know about God or at least the traditional Judeo/Christian version. But if he were completely honest, deep down he missed it.

But it was not only seeing families on their way to church that had him in a funk. This whole past week, it seemed, was composed of nothing more than rotating periods of guilt and shame or both.

To start the week there was the unbelievable Hector Perdenales Gonzales fiasco and death. It alone was enough to stock him with a whole year's worth of guilt. To once again go through the gut-wrenching experience of having a patient expire on the operating table, then immediately after having to explain the unexplainable to the family was almost more than he could bear. Needless to say, it was incredibly hard.

Coop could, and did, predict the family's reaction. He was becoming something of an expert on this. Their initial reaction was incomprehension, a collective blank face. Next came shock, then disbelief, followed by denial. There's just no way something like this could happen, not in the twenty-first century. After denial came anger. In this day of modern medical miracles, this should never happen. Nobody is supposed to die nowadays, at least not in a hospital surrounded by all this marvelous technology, and if a patient does die it means somebody must have really screwed up. Lastly came revenge. By damn, somebody's going to pay for this and pay dearly. In the U.S., this usually meant attorneys and money.

And Coop did feel a profound sense of guilt even though Jacob assured him he'd done nothing wrong. Nevertheless, he was the captain of the ship and someone died on his watch. Ultimately, he was responsible, just as was the captain of the tanker *Valdez*, even though he wasn't actually on the bridge when the ship ran aground and spilled millions of gallons of oil on Alaska's pristine coast. Every lawyer understood this principle and Coop knew soon the vultures would be circling.

He also felt guilty as well as some shame for what happened

last night. As promised, though he'd tried to think of every excuse he could to get out of it, he reluctantly steered the Dodge south on I-15 to Mesquite, Nevada. It was only thirty-five miles, but it seemed like over a hundred. First of all he didn't care much for gambling; it never held much fascination for him. Second, he still felt nervous partying and drinking around his patients. A lot of the St. George retirees headed for the gaming tables in Mesquite on weekends and it was likely he would bump into some of his patients. Sure, he knew doctors did it all the time, but somehow he felt physicians should tread a slightly higher ground, like pastors or presidents. This attitude, Spaulding lectured him, was not only archaic, it was also completely unwarranted. Even though most surgeons thought they were gods, he said, in reality they were not. And as mortal men, they were allowed to have some fun and even harbor a couple of vices.

Coop, as usual, arrived late, then it took another fifteen minutes for him to find Spaulding. From the looks of it, Steve was already having a good night. On his own admission, he'd already imbibed a fair amount of alcohol, participated in the slots tournament and won a couple hundred dollars or so he said. But then again, Spaulding always claimed he won. His companion, Shannon, was young, built, blonde and brainless, just the way Steve liked them.

Though a little older, Marty was also built, though probably from silicone. She differed from Shannon in that she was a brunette, maybe not quite as dumb, but very clingy. Constantly clinging to Coop's arm, she chatted incessantly, never letting him out of her sight. Idly, Coop wondered what would happen when he went to the bathroom.

While Spaulding and the blonde played the tables, Coop and Marty went to get something to eat at one of the casino's four restaurants. For most of an entire hour, Coop never uttered more than five sentences. He didn't have to. At first he tried to be an active participant in the conversation, then eventually gave up. Occasionally, he would smile or nod, but other than that he tuned her out. To pass the time, he imagined he was in a huge vacuum tube, a vacuum meant no air and no molecules to conduct vibrations, hence there would be no sound. After inserting himself into the imaginary vacuum, when he looked out he saw her lips move at a torrid pace, but there was absolutely no sound. It was pretty cool. Then suddenly, for no explainable reason, her face mutated to that of Kylie, but that was okay, Kylie also liked to talk. He looked away for a moment and when he looked back somehow Kylie's face transfigured to that of Samantha Rose Jardine. Immediately, Coop decided it was time to get out of the vacuum tube and once again Marty's moving lips projected sound. A lot of sound.

When it came time to go home, Marty clung to him as if he was her purse. Coop repeatedly refused her invitation to go home with her, claiming he had to get up very early to go to Salt Lake City, which was mostly true except for the early part, then she switched and wanted to accompany him to his place.

Feeling more than a little guilty, she seemed so lonely and desperate, Coop managed to extricate himself and go home alone. Once in bed, however, he tossed and turned for two hours before giving up, getting up and taking a shower. Taking his time, he fed the horses, had breakfast with Malachi, then hopped in the truck and headed north to Salt Lake City.

Coop sighed out loud at the memories, then checked his watch. Though he was still over two hundred miles away, there was no need to hurry. He had plenty of time.

Right at four o'clock, he pulled into the Triad Center's underground parking, quickly found a spot, then located the elevator. The Law firm of Cannon, Jeffs & Hanks occupied the entire fifth floor of the ten-story building. As soon as Coop exited the elevator, he was there, directly in front of suite # 501. A note, taped to the inch thick tempered glass door, fluttered like an autumn leaf in the current from the air conditioner. It was from Samantha Rose Jardine.

> *Be back in a minute. Door's open. My office is all the way to the end of the hall on the left.*
> *Make yourself comfortable,*
> Samantha

By following her instructions, Coop ended up in a spacious office featuring a large bank of windows overlooking downtown Salt Lake City and Temple Square. Furnished in the ultra-modern style, the room was dominated by a large cedar wood desk. Looking a bit like a huge red amoeba, it was cut from an irregular slab cedar, then finished and highly buffed. Though it seemed to float on air, an angled pedestal forged from copper actually supported it. On opposing sides of the desk were two black leather chairs and a matching leather divan positioned over by the bank of windows. Several paintings and prints adorned the walls, mostly of the modern genre or cubism. On the wall behind the desk were three of framed diplomas and a summa cum laude certificate. Houseplants were abundant and included macho and mother ferns, a xanada philodendrum, an oasis plant, a lady palias and a money tree. Coop chuckled at that. A money tree seemed more than appropriate for this lavish office.

With a jaundice eye, Coop continued to survey the room. It amazed him the differences in this office and his. His was a bare skeleton with no meat, no muscle and no fluff. Simple and cluttered, he sported a cheap laminated desk with an equally cheap set of vinyl-covered chairs and that was about it. No plants, no pictures, no personal mementos, though he still kept a picture of Kylie sequestered away in the top drawer of his desk. The only other furniture was a precut, self-assembled, Home Depot bookcase, which housed his assorted medical texts, most of them sadly out of date.

All though he felt a twinge of guilt for snooping, Coop couldn't help himself. After furtively glancing over his shoulder, he took a closer look at Samantha's desk, particularly her personal knickknacks. On the mostly immaculate desk were four seemingly random objects: a bronzed courtroom gavel, the ubiquitous justice-is-blind balance scales, a fractured piece of chalky-white elkhorn coral and a solitary six-inch photograph.

Framed within the picture was of a strikingly handsome man in his late thirties, maybe early forties. Wearing a knee-length wetsuit, his black curly hair was still dry as though he was planning to, but had not yet gone scuba diving. At first glance, Coop knew it was not her ex, Chuck Caplin, or her father, and as far as he knew she had no brothers. He picked up the photograph for a closer look. It was signed: *love, Josh.*

"Hi! I see you made it."

Flinching and nearly dropping the picture, Coop froze like he suddenly had a gun pressed hard into his back. Fortunately, the voice came from directly behind him. Taking a full second to compose himself and using his body as a shield, he carefully replaced the picture, then attempted to erase guilty look from his face as he turned to face Samantha Rose Jardine.

"Yeah, I just got here," he answered, trying for, but failing, a poker face. A raspberry blush seeped into and fought to replace the natural tan color of his face.

"Sorry about the note. I just ran over to the convenience store for something cold. Is ice tea okay?" Samantha Rose handed him a sixteen-ounce cup.

"Yeah, great," Coop replied, accepting the tea.

Quickly Samantha Rose leaned over and pecked him on the cheek. "You drive or fly?"

"I drove," Coop answered, still wondering how much Samantha had seen. "I never know how to get around when I fly."

"I would have picked you up at the airport." She circled around the floating desk and sat down. Today, she was wearing faded blue jeans, a white sleeveless cotton blouse and matching white sandals. Sitting in the streaming light in from the bank of windows, her hair appeared to glow. The direct sunlight seemed to inflame and infuse more red into her auburn hair.

"Well, I kind of like having my own wheels," Coop replied a little more gruffly than he intended. Today he needed to be very careful, keep his distance from Samantha Rose Jardine.

She looked at him intently. "Well then," she was suddenly all business, "have a seat. But before we get to the Tsongas case, there are a couple of new developments we need to discuss."

"What developments?" Coop sat down stiffly opposite Samantha. The strange amoebae desk floated between them.

Samantha Rose hesitated, bit her lip, then jumped in. "I just received official notification on Friday from the attorney for the Flowers family. They also intend to Commence Action."

"I...I kind of expected that," Coop mumbled, but inside he was churning. Damn it! Rather than a operating room, it looked like he was going to spend the next couple of years in the courtroom.

"Also, I suspect it's only a matter of time till the Gonzalez family will follow," Samantha added.

"Yeah, I suppose," Coop agreed listlessly. Fulfilling his agreement of full disclosure, he'd called Samantha right after the Gonzalez surgery. Coop was silent for a moment, then tried to change the subject. "This is a first for me. How do you want to handle the hearing tomorrow?"

Samantha didn't answer, but continued to eye Coop closely. "I guess I might just as well tell you the other thing right now."

"What other thing?"

"It's kind of a long story."

"I've got all afternoon."

"On Fridays," she began, "the University Law School has a weekly series called Judicial Grand Rounds. They serve lunch and some of the more complex and/or thorny legal cases presently working through our courts are discussed."

"I'm following you. We have the same thing, medical or surgical grand rounds depending on your specialty."

"Well, anyway," Samantha continued, drawing in a deep breath, "not only is it a good place to learn, it's also a good place to pick up on gossip, legal and otherwise."

Coop nodded.

"At the last grand rounds, an attorney from Saint George, an old classmate of mine, was there and she told me..." She paused again.

What?" Coop blurted. He could do without all the dramatics.

"Well, she told me she'd heard some rumblings down in Saint George that the Tsongas family was working with Saint George P.D. and the Washington County Attorney about the possibility of charging you with negligent homicide."

"What?" Coop frowned. "What does that mean?"

"It's death caused by gross negligence, like vehicular homicide, but in this case we trade the automobile for a scalpel."

"But...but I'm licensed to carry a scalpel."

"Most people charged with vehicular homicide are licensed to drive a car," Samantha explained, "the difference being they're usually driving impaired or drunk or both."

"Well, that certainly doesn't apply to me or my scalpel," Coop replied tersely. He could already feel his blood pressure rising.

"Hold on for a minute," Samantha held up her outstretched hand like a traffic cop, "we're both on the same side. However, it appears they have a nurse who is willing to testify you were operating impaired, perhaps drunk, the day you worked on Betty Tsongas."

"Renae Mackey!"

"Who?"

"Renae Mackey, she was the nurse. She's never liked me."

"Well, anyway, if they do charge you, that would be a criminal case and would be moved to a criminal court, not a civil court."

"You're joking."

"No, I'm afraid not. Coop, this is serious business."

"Wha...what's the penalty," he asked, though he was not sure he wanted to hear the answer, "for negligent homicide?"

"As with a similar malpractice verdict, it can include a large fine, but the big difference it also allows for substantial jail time."

"How much jail time?"

"One to five."

"Years?"

"Yes, years."

"Does my malpractice insurance cover that, the legal fees and court fines?"

"Unfortunately, no. Malpractice insurance only covers civil cases. With criminal cases, you're strictly on your own."

"So, you'll represent me if they do file?" Coop's tone more subdued now. This latest curveball had really shaken him.

"No, regrettably, I can't." Samantha's brown eyes reflected the frustration in her voice. "Our firm's contract with your insurance carrier won't allow it."

Coop was stunned.

"Well, hopefully it will never come to that," Samantha Rose added quickly. "Now let's turn to more pressing matters—tomorrow's hearing."

Immersed deeply in thought, Coop didn't answer.

"Coop," Samantha said, her voice now slightly louder. "Shall we go over our game plan for tomorrow?"

"Oh...well...yes." Coop forced his mind back to the present.

"Okay, first let's talk about Nurse Mackey and her rumored allegations of impairment. Are there any documents she might have filed which the other side could have gotten hold of?"

"Nah, there's nothing on the patient's chart. She may have filled out an Incident Report, but those are strictly confidential and tightly sealed. It would take an act of congress to get hold of them."

"So, you're pretty sure we'll not be blindsided by any of this impairment stuff?"

"No...and there was no impairment. And as far as I know there's nothing on the record and certainly there was no blood alcohol or a breathalyzer tests."

"Okay, then let me tell you about some of the procedural rules for tomorrow's hearing," Samantha continued, though she still looked worried. "Each side will be given about thirty minutes to present their case with the plaintiff always going first. There can be absolutely no interruptions while the presentations are being made. After the initial presentations, each side will be given a ten-minute rebuttal period. Witnesses are not allowed and we cannot directly question the other side, nor them us, though the panel may ask questions of anyone at anytime. Unfortunately, for a pre-lit hearing the plaintiff is not required to back up his claims with documentation no matter how outrageous, but it surely helps if he does. Written testimony and/or any physical evidence such as x-rays or hospital charts are permissible. Any questions?"

"So, we can't question them about their story, even if it's grossly inaccurate?" Coop asked.

"No, not directly. In our presentation, however, we can address and refute any claims listed in their Intent to Commence Action brief. Then of course, we'll have our own ten-minute rebuttal if something surfaces not listed in the original complaint. The rational is they don't want the hearing to degenerate into a finger-pointing and name-calling shouting match."

"Okay," Coop nodded, "so how do you want to proceed?"

"When our turn comes, I will introduce you to the panel, then ask you about your qualifications, you know where you went to medical school, your board certification and so on."

Coop nodded again.

"Then I'll simply have you tell the panel in your own words what happened. Try to be as honest and forthright as you can. The panel can pick up on dishonesty in a heartbeat. Finally we'll conclude by addressing the specific charges on the filed complaint, which basically is your negligence caused Betty Tsongas's death..."

By the time Samantha Rose finished, Coop was pale, clammy and perspiring. He sat back in the chair and exhaled slowly. No question about it, tomorrow was going to be an ordeal.

"You look like you could use a real drink," Samantha suggested, also sitting back in her chair. "You name it, we've probably got it."

Coop hesitated for a moment. When Kylie first left and before Malachi, he started drinking. Ostensibly, he rationalized, to cope with the loneliness. Not that he became an alcoholic, but his drinking became a bit a little more than just social drinking. After a few months, when it looked like it could develop into a problem, he'd simply stopped. And of course by then Steve had given him Malachi, which helped considerably with the loneliness.

"How about scotch on the rocks?" Samantha Rose asked when he did not answer.

Coop nodded. What could it hurt? Might calm his nerves.

When Samantha returned, she juggled two crystal glasses, a bucket of ice and a bottle of Glen Levitt. She sat them all down on her floating desk.

Still shaken from their previous conversation, Coop watched as she made two stiff drinks, then handed one to him. He downed it in two gulps, then handed the glass back to her. He didn't speak again till he was working on his third scotch.

"It's amazing," he wrinkled his brow. "I've been trying to figure the odds."

"What odds?" Samantha asked with a quizzical grin.

"The odds you'd end up as my attorney. I mean considering all the malpractice cases in the state of Utah and all the malpractice attorneys, it's got to be one in a thousand. Maybe more."

Samantha grinned slyly. "I have a confession; I helped the odds just a little. To get this case, I not only had to bully my colleagues, but I had to call in all my outstanding markers and threaten to quit."

"You...you mean you actually wanted this case," Coop stammered. "Why?"

"You're a smart guy. I'll let you figure it out." Samantha winked as she sat down on the leather divan. "Come over here." She patted the soft black leather. "You'll be more comfortable."

Somewhere in the back of his mind, he knew it was a bad idea. It was the very thing he'd been trying to guard against, but somehow his feet didn't obey his mind. They appeared to have a will and purpose all their own. In spite of all his good resolve, his personal oath, Coop somehow ended up on the couch sitting next to the beautiful Samantha Rose Jardine.

From there, things rapidly went downhill. Not that Samantha was always the aggressor. He probably was most of the time. It must have been the scotch or maybe the subsurface need for some kind of emotional catharsis or maybe it was just the accumulated loneliness from Kylie leaving or maybe it was yet just another flagrant manifestation of his weak character or perhaps all three, but regardless of the exact etiology Coop gave up, gave in…completely. For the next hour he totally immersed himself in the incredible body of Samantha Rose Jardine.

It was everything he'd remembered, but over the years had not dared dream. Even before they were finished, he knew what he feared most, had somehow just happened. Once again, like a laboratory white rat, he was trapped. For better, but probably for worse, he was once again completely irrevocably in love with Samantha Rose Jardine.

At some point, he remembered asking, "Who's Josh?"

"Don't you worry about Josh," she replied vaguely between kisses.

* * *

Back in her condo in the trendy City Creek Center in downtown Salt Lake City, Samantha Rose was dismayed, mostly with herself. She had a pounding headache and an upset stomach, probably from mixing Scotch with a full jigger of guilt, three tablespoons of uncertainty and a dash of ecstasy. What had she just done? Was she back to her old tricks again? The ones she'd thought she'd outgrown a long time ago. Was she again trying for a whole string of boyfriends?

When she and Coop parted company two hours ago, at first she basked in the glow of Coop, God how she'd missed him, then gradually the qualms of what she'd done set in. She had no right to toy with his feelings if she was not serious about him. She knew damn well he was not a one-night-stand sort of guy. Had she really thought this through? They certainly were not college kids anymore and it surely was not fair to Coop for her to approach this as a casual fling. And, of course, there were other considerations too.

First and foremost was Josh. While it was true they were not officially engaged and neither had asked for exclusivity, they were, nevertheless, seeing a lot of each other. Six months ago, Josh made partner with Cannon, Hanks & Jeffs and promised he would do everything in his power to see she would soon follow. Even though he'd never predicated his support on her continuing affection, Samantha couldn't help but feel his endorsement would be somewhat less enthusiastic if they were to break up.

But the real question, did she prefer Josh to Coop? It really was not a fair question and truthfully she barely knew Coop. Yes, they dated some twenty years ago, but that was only briefly and a lot could have changed in two decades. However, if you just considered this most recent event and asked her if Josh excited her as much as Coop, the answer would have to be an unequivocal no. They were so different. It was like trying to compare a pampered thoroughbred to a wild mustang. Samantha smiled at her analogy. Yes, the nerd in his own way was now a wild mustang.

Also, what about Coop? Was he even available? Technically, he was still married to Kylie and more than likely was still in love with her. Samantha could think of no other reason for a guy to stay married to a woman who'd up and left him a year ago. Obviously, he was holding out hope for her return. So, was she being presumptuous to assume she could have Coop if she wanted? That all she had to do was to simply make her decision. There were at least three very big reasons he might reject her. One, he was still married and loved his wife. Two, she'd dumped him once before and he may not have forgiven her. And three, he was certainly no fool. More than likely he'd be wary about jumping into another relationship with her.

Then there was the somewhat murky ethics of it all. Lawyers fraternizing their clients did not have quite the same severe negative connotation as doctors or psychiatrists consorting their patients, but it was nevertheless frowned on. And even though it was not something for which one could be disbarred, it was still considered to be very much ill advised. Considering, however, they already had a past history, they were once lovers, that somehow seemed to make the act less egregious, at least in her mind. It was like married couples getting back together after a trial separation because they were lonely or just to give it one more chance. But if she were truthful, it wasn't nearly that clear-cut. Her head ached from thinking and worrying. It was all very confusing.

Tonight, Samantha planned on going over the material for tomorrow's pre-litigation hearing one last time, but she couldn't concentrate. Instead, she fixed herself a cup of hot herbal tea and went to bed, but sleep would not be her guest tonight. Eventually, she got up again and pulled out Coop's already thick file. Listlessly, she looked at the papers, shuffled through them several times, but never really read them.

When her alarm sounded at six-thirty, it did not wake her, nor did the red crescent rim of sun as it broke through her window. She was awake and already showering.

10

Diseases and sin—these are the same as motion and heat. One passes into the other.
—*Leo Tolstoy (1828–1910)*

The pre-litigation panel consisted of four members: the chairman, Ms. Suzanne Erickson, a private banker from Ogden; a urologic oncologist, Dr. Reed Black from Salt Lake City; a medical malpractice attorney, Mr. Roy Leonard, also from Salt Lake City; and a non-affiliated lay person, Mrs. Laura Frank, an overworked mother of five from Provo. By their relaxed attitude, the exact opposite of Coop's, he could tell they had done this before.

Five minutes late Chairman Erickson called the meeting to order. Coop took a deep breath and braced himself for the worst.

Following established protocol, the plaintiff went first. Since the injured party could not present her case in person, Betty Tsongas was dead, the plaintiff's attorney, Mr. Benjamin Bowling (English - a variant of Bolling), did most of the talking.

Attorney Bowling was a massive man both in height and weight. Easily six-foot-six in height and weighing well over three hundred pounds, Ben Bowling was a commanding figure and a natural leader. When he talked, he expected people to listen and usually they did.

Displaying an impressive command of the English language, he painted a disturbingly vivid picture of the horrors of that day. It appeared his account was compiled from subpoenaed witnesses, from medical records and from the obviously biased account of the Tsongas family. To Coop's way of thinking, it was an incomplete composite of the day's events, containing some truth, some half-truths and some absolute fable. The apparent gist of Bowling's twenty-five minute oration, Dr. Cooper's sloppy and woefully deficient surgical technique had directly contributed to and caused the death of Betty Tsongas.

After finishing his most impeaching anthology, he used his last five minutes to elicit testimony from the husband, Nickolas Tsongas. Uncharacteristically subdued, Nick nevertheless looked quite striking in his dark pinstripe suit. With his gray/black hair slicked straight back, he also wore a mauve shirt with a dark purple tie and expensive Italian shoes.

Using gentle, but leading questions Bowling had Nick tell the panel how Dr. Cooper never explained the potential risks of the operation and certainly never mentioned the possibility of massive hemorrhage resulting in death. Blinking away the tears, Tsongas confided how much he missed his wife, how his children were forever deprived of a mother and his grandchildren a grandmother. He finished up by stating how Dr. Cooper's gross incompetence has created a huge void in his life, which can never be filled. He took another poignant moment to wipe away more tears, then sat down.

Suddenly, it was their turn.

Also striking in her gray business suit, but weighing in at a mere one hundred and thirty pounds, Samantha Rose stood, introduced herself to the panel, then presented Dr. Lawrence A. Cooper.

Today she was all business. All morning, she had made absolutely no reference to what happened in her office yesterday. Coop should have been relieved, but he wasn't. To him her ongoing silence was more than a little disconcerting. Now, he had no idea what their relationship was or even if they had a relationship. Was she just trying to maintain a firm division between personal and professional life and now it was time to be professional? Was yesterday a one-night stand and today he once again had been demoted to just another client? Or was yesterday just a lie, a sordid tryst? Had she in fact been cheating on Josh and now had an attack of the guilts? One thing for sure, her cold shoulder made it hard for him to concentrate on the hearing.

After the formal introductions, Samantha immediately began asking questions.

"Doctor Cooper, could you tell the panel from which medical school you graduated and the year?"

"Stanford University, nineteen ninety."

"Any honors?"

"Summa cum laude with additional honors in surgery," Coop replied, while privately thinking that Samantha Rose was not the only one capable of graduating with such distinction.

"Where did you serve your internship and residency?"

"Duke University, North Carolina—for both."

"Are you board certified?"

"Yes, twelve years ago."

"Any further training?"

"Yes, Ma'am, (he could be professional too), a two-year fellowship in uro-oncology right back here at the University of Utah Affiliated Hospitals in Salt Lake City under the auspices of Doctor Jacob Heinz."

"What operation did you perform on Betty Tsongas and why?"

"A radical cystectomy with ileal loop urinary diversion. That's taking out the urinary bladder and using a piece of small bowel to divert the urine through the abdominal wall into a bag. The reason for the surgery was high grade invasive cancer of the urinary bladder."

"Is this a surgery you do frequently?" Samantha asked crisply, not even a hint of a smile.

"Yes, in my field it is a common surgery."

"How many of those operations would you guess you have you done over your career?"

"Well over a hundred, I'd say."

"Have you ever had one bleed this badly before?"

"No, not like this. Once I did have one bleed, but it was a patient who'd had previous pelvic radiation, a so-called salvage cystectomy."

"So this outcome is totally aberrant to your previous experience."

"I've never before had a patient bleed to death with this surgery or any surgery," Coop declared and technically that was not a lie. The Flowers and Gonzalez cases both came later.

"Why do you think this patient bled so much?"

"I really don't know." Coop slowly shook his head. "It was almost like she was on blood thinners, but as far as I know she wasn't. Her blood simply would not clot and when blood won't clot it pours out of blood vessels like water through a colander. We simply could not stop the bleeding, though not from the lack of trying."

"Doctor Cooper, why don't you take a minute and describe for the panel what happened that day as seen through your eyes."

For the next ten minutes, Coop gave a detailed, blow-by-blow, account of what happened, purposefully neglecting to mention he was also battling a virus. It had not affected the surgical outcome, so there was no point in adding on extra baggage, which was not needed and might easily be misconstrued. He tried to be sincere and forthright and as best he could tell the panel seemed sympathetic. When he finished, the urologist, Dr. Black, asked a couple of technical questions, then Samantha Rose continued her line of questioning.

"So, Doctor Cooper, in your heart do you feel Betty Tsongas's death had anything to do with your surgical technique as claimed by the plaintiff?"

"No, I honestly do not," Coop answered, looking straight at the panel. "I think the bleeding was due to some kind of intrinsic failure of her blood to clot. And I personally don't believe there's a surgeon in the country who could have saved her. In retrospect, I can't think of a thing I would do differently."

"Thank you, Doctor Cooper," Samantha said formally, then turned and addressed the panel. "By its very nature surgery is a risky business. Our hearts go out to the Tsongas family, but this appears to be one of those rare idiosyncratic events beyond the control of medical science and Doctor Cooper. He feels terrible about the outcome, but there was nothing else he could do. It was simply out of his control." Samantha paused to look each panel member in the eye, then continued, "this concludes our presentation. I know you all are busy people and I thank you for your time."

Nodding, Chairman Erickson then turned to Attorney Bowling and Nick Tsongas. "Rebuttal, Mister Bowling?"

While Ben Bowling collected his papers, Samantha leaned over to Coop and whispered, "very good! I think we'll be okay."

Standing, Benjamin Bowling loudly cleared his throat and eyed the panel. "Just a couple of things. First I see no objective, i.e. laboratory evidence, that Mrs. Tsongas was a bleeder as the defense claims. So, I suspect this diagnosis of inability to clot is an afterthought, thrown up as a smokescreen." Bowling paused for a moment, looked Coop in the eye, then sighed out loud. "I was hoping I wouldn't have to do this; trusting it wouldn't be necessary. Deep down, I thought Doctor Cooper would do the right thing, come clean on his own accord, but it doesn't look like that is going to happen."

He reached a huge paw into his briefcase and retrieved a manila folder bound with an elastic band. Taking off the band, he continued in a loud clear voice. "I have a sworn affidavit here authored by a nurse, Renae Mackey. She was the circulating nurse attending Betty Tsongas's surgery." He paused again, then passed out two stapled sheets to each member of the panel and another to Coop and Samantha Rose. "Here, as you can see, Nurse Mackey claims, and without equivocating, Doctor Cooper was operating impaired, probably from alcohol, on the day in question. She was so alarmed by the event, she reported it to Dixie Medical Center using their standard Incident Report form."

A painful silence settled over the room as all heads tilted down to read the affidavit. Stunned and more than a little angry, Samantha glanced over at Coop. He had no trouble reading her face. Her eyes asked, "where the hell did this come from?"

"This is not a copy of the Incident Report," Samantha quickly objected.

"I never said it was," Ben Bowling answered calmly. "It's Nurse Mackey's affidavit attesting to what she wrote in the Incident Report."

"I would like to see the actual report," Samantha barked.

"So would I," Bowling replied, "but that's like getting a top secret file from the C.I.A. The hospital claims it is sealed and refuses to give it up. It looks like I will have to obtain a warrant to get it, but Nurse Mackey remembers perfectly well what she wrote and this is her notarized affidavit."

Nobody said a word. After a long moment, Bowling continued, "I think I need say no more, this says it all." Ben Bowling held the papers up high above his head, then sat down again, trying hard to squeeze his huge frame back into the under-sized chair.

Slowing rising to her feet, Samantha Rose was obviously searching for some kind of a rebuttal, some way to mitigate the damage. "Other than Nurse Mackey's personal opinion, I see no actual documentation of this outrageous claim. I see no blood alcohol levels or a serum toxicology report. This statement could easily qualify for this week's talk-is-cheap award. There has been bad blood between Doctor Cooper and Nurse Mackey for some time now. Obviously, this is simply a case of spite or vengeance or both. Without any actual documentation it boils down to her word against Doctor Cooper's and I prefer to believe Doctor Cooper."

As Samantha sat down, Chairman Suzanne Erickson cleared her throat and rose from her chair. "Is there anything else?" She paused for a moment, then continued, "I want to thank you all for coming and for your presentations. The panel will meet after lunch and discuss this case and render an opinion. In a few weeks an official transcript of these proceedings as well as the panel's formal opinion will be mailed to both attorneys, but if the counselors wish to call my office later this afternoon I will give them a verbal report."

Still dazed by this unexpected twist, Coop staggered from the room, blindly following Samantha Rose. As they waited at the bank of elevators, Nickolas Tsongas along with his attorney Ben Bowling walked up. No longer appearing subdued, Nick glowered at Coop, then suddenly lunged forward, grabbing a fistful of lapel, shirt and tie. He pulled Coop in close, uncomfortably close, nose to his Greco/Roman nose. Coop could see the fluorescent light gleam off his gold teeth and he could smell the stale odor of cigars on his breath.

"So, how did you like that, Mister Cooper?" He pulled Coop even closer. "And this is just beginning."

Quickly, Ben Bowling wedged his huge body between them, then hustled Tsongas toward the stairwell. A little unnerved Coop tried to compose himself before turning back to face Samantha Rose. At that moment, the elevator arrived and the doors slid open. Without comment, they stepped in and Samantha pushed the button for the ground floor.

Out in the parking lot, things seemed even more strained. All Coop wanted to do was get away, away from Salt Lake City and away from Samantha Rose Jardine. Samantha didn't seem to particularly want to tarry either. They quickly said their goodbyes, this time without any overt display of affection. Samantha promised to call as soon as she heard anything from the panel, then abruptly turned, fumbling in her purse for the keys to her Lexus. Coop watched as she skillfully wove in and out of the late morning Salt Lake City traffic. If nothing else, she was a good driver.

Thoroughly confused and fighting depression, Coop climbed in the Dodge, headed down 6th South and straight for the freeway. If he hurried, though there was really no good reason to, he could be back in St. George by 4:00 p.m.

Unfortunately, the four and one half hour trip home gave him plenty of time to think. He couldn't decide which was more unsettling the way the hearing had gone or the way Samantha Rose treated him.

With the obvious benefits of hindsight, he realized it was a huge mistake not to mention the fact he had a cold the day of surgery. Now it looked like a cover up and they would surely crucify him for it.

He had no idea, though maybe he should have, they would get hold of Renae Mackey. Until today he wasn't even sure the Incident Report existed, though he suspected it. And before Bowling presented Renae's affidavit, it appeared the panel was leaning his way. Now it would take a miracle for them to find this lawsuit non-meritorious.

And just as disconcerting or maybe inexplicable was Samantha Rose's behavior. Today they'd behaved like two awkward teenagers after their first time, not knowing how to deal with it the next day. He was not a mind reader and had no way of knowing what she was thinking, but there was several possibilities. Was last night just a fling? Or one last tryst to make sure she'd made the right decision in dumping him years ago? Or had she entertained thoughts of renewing a relationship with him, but last night he'd failed the test, come up short, so to speak? Was she cheating on the Josh in the picture and this morning had an attack of conscience? Was she feeling guilty about the questionable ethics of having sex with a client and hence her formal cold demeanor? No smiles, no hand touches and certainly no greeting or goodbye kisses. Without her volunteering any information, all he could do was speculate and one possible explanation did not seem much better than the next. One thing was for damn certain, however, he should have stuck to his original plan and kept his distance from Samantha Rose Jardine. She was bad news, real bad news, but he already knew that. If he had any sense at all he would call Cannon, Jeffs & Hanks and request a new attorney...well, maybe that was a bit rash, but never again would he fall for Samantha Rose Jardine! Softly cursing himself under his breath, Coop once again renewed his vow to keep their relationship strictly hands off, strictly professional.

About ten miles north of St. George, his cell phone rang, jolting him out of his gloomy reverie. Signaling left, he pulled onto the freeway shoulder and fumbled for his cell phone.

"Yeah," he growled.

"Coop, it's Samantha Rose."

"Yeah?" He resolutely kept his answers brief and gruff.

"I just heard from the panel."

"Yeah?"

"I'm sorry, Coop," Samantha had a catch in her voice, "they voted unanimously for meritorious."

Coop was silent for a few seconds. "So what happens now?"

"They are free to proceed with their suit and undoubtedly they will."

"So that means there will be a trial?"

"Yes, unless you want us to try to settle first?"

"No!" Coop snapped. "I did nothing wrong."

"Well, as your lawyer," Samantha said, using her professional voice, "I must warn you unless we can come up with some reason for her bleeding other than your alleged impairment or incompetence we have no case. The prudent thing might be to settle."

"How much would that cost?"

"With negligence resulting in death, it could easily run into the millions of dollars."

"No," Coop said tersely, "at least not now. So realistically, how long before we'd go to trial?"

"It varies, but usually somewhere between three to six months," Samantha replied. "However, considering how fast they got the prelim scheduled it could be anytime."

"Give me a little time to come up with something."

"Okay," Samantha agreed. "I'll keep you informed of any new developments on my end."

Before any meaningless goodbyes could be proffered, Coop simply hung up. Two could play the cold shoulder game. Even though Samantha's news was really no surprise, it nevertheless was most depressing.

Samantha's quick assessment of the cost to make this case go away also was not totally surprising, but nevertheless it was bad news for a couple of reasons. One, to settle out of court always gave the appearance of a *de facto* admission of guilt and would undoubtedly serve as bait for the other circling sharks to join the feeding frenzy. Without question that would be enough to convince the Flowers and Gonzalez families to go ahead and file a claim and more than likely enough to persuade Nick Tsongas to go ahead and pursue criminal charges. The second problem, his malpractice insurance limits were one million dollars per single case and three million per aggregate. With this suit and potentially two others, and if Tsongas did convince the police to charge him criminally, it could possibly leave him with a debt of maybe ten million or more dollars. Hell, he could easily use up the entire three million dollar aggregate on this first case. Then from the other cases, that would leave him millions to pay from his own pocket, which of course he did not have.

Coop rehashed the whole scenario several more times as he drove the last few miles to St. George. With each mile, and no matter how he massaged it, or from what angle he viewed it, it got no better.

Twenty minutes after talking to Samantha, he was back in Diamond Valley. Coop breathed a loud sigh of relief when he noted everything appeared to be okay. Nothing looked amiss. There were no more fires.

First, he headed straight to the Snow house to get Malachi. Unlike Samantha Rose, Malachi had no reservations the day after. Coop was instantly lathered with a plethora of Malachi's kisses. Next, he checked on the horses. They also looked fine and the stables were clean. Todd Snow did a good job; he'd have to remember to give him a good tip. Before entering the house he collected a bundle of mail from the mailbox along with his accumulated newspapers. Standing at the kitchen counter, he sorted through the stack of mail. Out of the corner of his eye, he noted the message light was blinking on the phone answering machine. Mechanically, he punched the play button as continued to separate the mail into piles.

It was the haughty voice of Dr. Jeremy Faux. *Doctor Cooper, this phone call is to inform you of the action taken by the Surgical Peer Review Committee at an emergency session today. As it appears your hemorrhage problem is ongoing, most recently Mister Hector Gonzalez. The committee has decided it has no choice but to suspend your surgical privileges, effective immediately. Any surgery you may have already scheduled will have to be transferred to the care of another surgeon, perhaps Doctor Kingsley. If you have questions or wish to appeal you may forward either to the Committee in writing.*

Click...that was it. No expression of sorrow or regret. With a single chorus of ayes, the committee summarily removed Coop's only source of income. Bitterly, he wondered how one acquires that kind of power? Fifteen long years of intense technical training and now all for naught. Wiped clean, like erasing white chalk markings from a blackboard. In mere seconds, everything changed. Now, he had no way to pay bills, buy food, or feed the horses and no way to give Kylie the seven thousand dollars a month he'd promised in lieu of her filing divorce papers. Of course, he had a little savings, but with the looming colossal malpractice settlements, filing bankruptcy may be his only option. At least for now, well at least for a couple of months, he could survive on his savings.

Still reeling from Faux's message, Coop pulled up a barstool, sat down at the counter and once again began going through the mail. It appeared to be the usual assortment of bills, credit card solicitations and advertising flyers. At first he was hopeful, but as usual there was no letter from Kylie. She had only written two letters all year. There was, however, a letter sporting an official logo, which instantly caught his eye. He plucked the letter from the pile to take a closer look. It was from the UTAH STATE BOARD OF LICENSURE. Quickly, he ripped open the envelope and fished out the single page.

Dear Dr. Cooper,

Recently we have received several complaints concerning your surgical conduct and have been notified of three recent surgical deaths. Subsequently, we are scheduling a hearing, October 21 at 2:00 p.m., to discuss these grave concerns and to address the status of your Utah State license to practice medicine.

Please plan to attend or send representation.

Harry Jacklinson, M.D., Board Chairman

In anger, Coop hurled the letter to the floor. He hadn't seen that one coming, but he should have. Son-of-a-bitch, things kept getting better and better.

But realistically, what difference did it make? After the action taken by Faux's Surgical Peer Review Committee, he really couldn't effectively practice medicine anyway, at least not surgical medicine and that was all he knew. If the Utah State Board of Licensure revoked his medical license, so what? That was kind of like shooting a man after he was already hanged. Undoubtedly, the bullet wouldn't hurt or accomplish very much. Bending over, he retrieved the letter. Not that it would make much difference, but he better fax it to his lawyer, Ms. Samantha Rose Jardine.

Trying to calm himself, he picked up the newspaper, *The Daily Spectrum*, then wandered into the living room. Exhausted both emotionally and physically, he sank down into his maroon leather LazyBoy and picked up the first page. With all the wars, suicide bombings and school massacres, the world was such a mess his troubles looked almost insignificant. Sighing, he finished with the most unsettling first page, set it aside, then opened the second page, Utah and Local News. In large caps, a bold black headline immediately caught his eye: *DR. JEKYLL, MR. HYDE OR DR. COOPER?*

With growing apprehension, Coop rapidly scanned the body of the story. It was written by the Spectrum's own investigative reporter, Sally Morgan. Through sources who wished to remain anonymous, Sally had uncovered a major and growing crisis at Dixie Medical Center, a potentially dangerous problem that could affect the whole community. A hospital staff surgeon, Dr. Lawrence Addison Cooper, had recently experienced a series of, three to be exact, surgical deaths. Also, these same unnamed sources maintained Dr. Cooper had, at least on one occasion and possibly more, presented to the operating room impaired, on drugs or alcohol or both. In the source's opinion, operating in this impaired condition without question had contributed to these untimely surgical deaths. A hospital spokesman, Mr. Reed Blackum, however, assured this reporter steps had already been taken to ensure the public's safety and preserve the hospital's national reputation. Ms. Morgan ended the piece by provocatively asking, "as with the recent airline pilot inebriation scandal, the same question needs to be asked here. Do surgeons have the same problem? Is Dr. Cooper just the tip of the iceberg?"

Coop slumped low in the LazyBoy. There just was no anger left, just a hollow empty space in his chest and another one in his head. Without a doubt, this had been the mother of all days. First, there was the cold shoulder from Samantha Rose, next the pre-litigation hearing and the subsequent adverse verdict, after that Dr. Faux's curt message stripping him of his right to work, then the ominous letter from the Utah State Board of Licensure and finally this withering expose' in the Daily Spectrum. Add to this his ongoing personal problems, an estranged wife he was still supporting and an ex-girlfriend who enjoyed toying with him, and he'd about had it. Was this what life was all about? Is this all there was? If it was, he'd about had enough.

Both physically and emotionally drained, and spiritually tapped out, Coop had no fight left. They had completely and thoroughly beaten him. He seriously doubted there was any way to rebound from all this. He was in much too deep of a pit and he had no will or way to climb out. He had no will even to live another day.

Struggling out of his chair, he shuffled into the bedroom. On the top shelf of the clothes closet, he searched and located his well-stocked first aid kit. From it he pulled out an empty sixty cc syringe, an eighteen-gauge needle and a rubber tourniquet. Lying down on his bed, he tried to calculate how much air he needed to inject into his vein to cause death. Would sixty cc do? Or would he need more? From medical school, he tried to remember the mechanism of how an air embolus caused death. The bubbles would travel through the vein and eventually collect in the right atrium. There they would displace the blood and prevent future filling. The lower chamber, the right ventricle, would subsequently have no filling and no blood to pump to the lungs. No blood to the lungs meant no oxygen to any organ including the heart and brain. With no brain function, the switchboard would go black and within seconds completely shut down. Five minutes later, it would become permanent...the blessed black void of nothingness.

Grim faced, he strapped the tourniquet to his upper arm.

11

Cap off
and then what? The brains as
helpless as oysters in a pint container,
the nerves like phone wires.
God, take care, take infinite care
with the tumor lest it spreads like grease.
—Ann Sexton (1928–1974)

For almost an hour, Coop remained motionless on the bed, overwhelmed by the crushing weight from the twin grim reavers, futility and depression. His chest hurt, his pulse was erratic and his breathing was shallow and labored. Perhaps he would die here in bed without lifting a finger or using the tourniquet and the air syringe. That would be best. Suicide was a messy and cowardly thing to do. If he could possibly have a spontaneous heart arrhythmia, a run of V-tach resulting in flatline, it would be much better.

After another thirty minutes, he realized he would not be that lucky. His heart rate and breathing slowly returned to normal. His chest pain, probably psychogenic, faded. Now he really had only two options, take his own life using the air syringe or quit whining, exit the pity party, get his butt off the bed and take charge of the situation.

From seemingly out of nowhere, Malachi suddenly jumped on the bed and licked his face. A tear collected in the corner of his eye. He would surely miss that dog. Slowly the tear disappeared and was replaced by resolve. His jaw muscles tightened and his eyes focused. He drew in a deep breath and held it in for a moment.

Damnit, he would fight! He'd done nothing wrong. If there was any justice in the universe, there had to be a path through this maze, a way to set things straight, a way to clear his name. Jaw still set, he gave Malachi a hug, got up off the bed, picked up the phone and punched in the number of Dr. Jacob Heinz. What he really needed now was not to wallow knee-deep in self-pity. What he needed right now was a good friend and some sage advice.

Though it was late, Jacob instantly invited him over. Apparently, or so he said, he couldn't sleep either and would enjoy some company. Coop loaded up Malachi, fired up the Dodge and headed down the hill to St. George.

At 10:30 p.m., Coop pulled up to Jacob's Spanish/Mediterranean style house situated right on the seventh fairway of the Entrada Golf Course. Entrada was unique even for St. George golf courses. Even though it too had spectacular views of the looming bank of Navajo sandstone cliffs and canyons, it also had the distinction of being built right on top of a lava flow. Most fairways were not flanked by tall fescue grass, but rather jumbled heaps of black lava rocks.

Heinz greeted Coop and Malachi warmly, then grabbed a pot of coffee and headed straight through white French doors to the backyard patio. Coop and Malachi followed.

Coop took a moment to admire the night. Above him and constructed of redwood slats, a lattice covered the patio and was almost totally overgrown by flowering trumpet creepers. The night was warm and a mild desert breeze rustled through the red creepers. High in the southern sky a three-quarters silver moon provided a splash of ghostly light, barely illuminating the adjacent fairway. Off to the right, Coop thought he could smell the musty odor of a pond and imagined it was ringed with cattails. His suspicions were confirmed when he heard a frog croak. Though he couldn't see it, undoubtedly a water hazard must be close.

Jacob placed the hot coffee pot on a coaster right in the middle of the circular wrought iron table, then pulled up a chair and motioned for Coop to do the same. After pouring two cups of steaming coffee, Heinz settled back on the padded cushion and took a careful sip. Contented, Malachi curled up at Coop's feet.

"*Ach, ich liebe Kaffee,*" he sighed, "*auch im Sommerziet.*"

"Me too," Coop agreed, then added, "Jacob, English please."

"So how have you been, *mein Freund*?" Heinz took another sip, then eyed Coop closely.

"Fine," Coop hesitated, then blurted, "actually not so good."

"Vell, do you vant to talk about it?"

Coop nodded, then shifted his gaze from Heinz to the patio floor. The moonlight filtered through the lattice and produced a nearly perfect-checkered pattern.

For the next fifteen minutes, Coop told Jacob everything, everything except the part about Samantha Rose. He doubted Jacob, a dedicated bachelor, would be of much help with troubles of the heart. "And so in summary," he concluded, "I've got no surgical privileges. I've got two, most likely three, malpractice lawsuits pending which more than likely I will lose. A negligent homicide criminal case will probably soon be filed. Undoubtedly, my Utah state license to practice medicine will be revoked and my name's been smeared in the local newspaper so even if I could practice medicine, I doubt anyone would come."

"And that's it?" Jacob feigned astonishment. "That is all! Come on, Coop, tell me vhat's really bothering you."

"No, seriously, Jacob, that article really upset me."

"Ha, ha, ha, Doctor Jekyll," Jacob laughed. "I saw the paper. That vas really quite clever."

"Maybe from where you sit," Coop said sourly. "I thought it was a great example of tabloid journalism."

"*Ja, ja*, a classical example of S*chadenfreude*."

"What?"

"Delight in downfall of others," Jacob explained, then after a moment asked, "vhat else?"

"What else, what?"

"That's all little stuff, now tell me the big stuff. Vhat's really bothering you?"

"That's it," Coop sighed, "except for the obvious. I have absolutely no way of making a living now."

"And that's vhat's got you down?" Heinz arched a bushy eyebrow. "Did I ever tell you about the days before ve left Austria?"

"Yes, Jacob, several times."

"*Ach wirklich*," Heinz shrugged, "this isn't so bad."

"I'm sure you're right," Coop acknowledged. "But where do I go from here?"

"Vell," Heinz stroked his chin. "Like a rogue stem cell that's gone vild, all your problems have grown from a single cell, a single incident,

120

and that cell is surgical hemorrhage. So rather than several problems, you've really only have one. Solve that and the others vill fall into place."

"But I...I'm not sure where to start."

"I scrubbed with you, remember?" Jacob continued. "There is absolutely nothing vrong vith your surgical technique. If anything, you are a better surgeon now than years ago in your residency and I must say you vere gifted then."

"So?"

"So, if the problem is not vith you and is not vith your equipment or help, then it has to be vith the patients. Something vas not right vith those patients. They could not and vould not clot. Nobody could have saved them. You need to dig deep into those patients and their lives. Find out vhere they vere and vhat they were doing in the days and veeks before surgery." Jacob leaned over and patted Coop's arm. "And I'd villing to bet my tiny U. of U. pension you'll find something."

They sipped the coffee in silence for a few minutes, then Coop sighed loudly and set down his empty cup. "Thanks, Jacob, you have no idea how much this has helped."

"*Ja, ja*, next time don't be so long in coming and next time," he paused and looked slyly at Coop.

"Yes?"

"And next time bring by some of them Viagra samples with you."

Coop looked sharply at Heinz, then grinned. "Jacob, I had no idea!"

"*Ja*, they're very expensive," Jacob said. "That's vhat you could give me for my birthday—or any day for that matter."

"At your age, Jacob!" Coop feigned surprise.

"You ever use them?"

"Nah, they don't do any good if you don't have opportunity."

"Vell, there is a certain *Fraulein*...," Heinz said sheepishly, then quickly diverted the conversation. "You need to get on with your life too. Time to forget that Kylie."

"Yeah, I suppose you're right, but I...I still love her."

"Love and dependency are not the same thing, Coop," Jacob insisted. "Time for a new start, time for a divorce."

"I...I don't know. I'll have to think about it. Anyway, I can't afford a divorce right now."

"Are you still sending her seven thousand dollars a month?"

"Well...yes," Coop replied, getting flustered. He'd forgotten he told Jacob about Kylie's money. But what he hadn't told Jacob was the seven thousand dollars a month was more than just subsistence money for Kylie, it was also guilt money. His guilt. If only he'd been more attentive, a better husband, then Kylie would still be with him today. No, he wasn't unfaithful, but nevertheless he cheated on her... with his time. With mandatory hospital call, emergencies and just trying to build a practice, he essentially placed her in the second or even in third position in his life. No vacations, no long weekends together or even just leisurely evenings reading novels or watching T. V. And there was very little quality bedroom time as well. He was always bone-tired when he got home or his damn beeper went off, more than once right in the middle of lovemaking. And some days he never left the hospital. Twenty-four hour workdays were fairly common. Now those all those career choices seemed less important and his behavior seemed more and more inexcusable. Yes, if he'd just taken the time, Kylie would still be here today. He would gladly trade all his professional success just to get her back. Ha, ha, that was a laugh. Now it appeared there was nothing left to trade.

"Take my vord for it, a divorce would be cheaper," Heinz continued. "Particularly, since she's the one who shredded the marriage vows."

"Well, I'm no hurry," Coop shrugged. "It's not like there is a long line of women out there waiting to get at me."

"You keep this up and there never vill be, at least not the good ones." Heinz was silent for a moment. "Coop, I may be vay out on a limb here and I probably ought to keep my mouth shut, but...,"

"Spit it out. I can take it."

"Vell, ever since I've known you, you've had this huge inferiority complex. Not with science, surgery or medicine, but with personal things. You think you are clumsy and not very athletic. And you think you are not very good-looking and you think there is no vay you can compete for the good women. Am I right?"

"Well, I...I guess so," Coop stammered. This conversation was getting damn uncomfortable.

"Vell, let me break the news to you," Jacob said firmly. "You're wrong. Dead wrong on all three counts."

They sipped coffee in silence for a minute.

"Well, anyway, I've got to go." Coop finished his cup and set it back on its saucer. "But I do appreciate your advice, both professional and personal." He stood and motioned to Malachi.

"*Ja, Ja,* keep me informed," Jacob also stood, "and don't stay away so long next time."

Though he promised he wouldn't, when Coop got home he couldn't help it; once again checked the messages on answering machine. There was nothing from either Kylie or Samantha Rose.

In spite of the lack of phone messages, Coop slept well for the first time in weeks. If he dreamed, he didn't remember. The next morning he awoke feeling renewed and determined. It was time for him to change professions from surgeon to sleuth, from physician to gumshoe. He couldn't perform surgery anyway and he was getting damn tired of being batted around like a tumbleweed on a windy day. Today he would become pro-active; today he would seize the initiative.

After a quick breakfast of coffee and a toasted bagel, he phoned his office manager, Christy Dennett, right at eight o'clock.

"Christy, I need three small favors from you."

"I hope they won't take too long," she whined. "Doctor Kingsley is seeing patients today and you know how hectic that can be."

"Yes, I know Stan is in today," Coop replied testily, and wanted to add, but I pay your salary. Instead, he said, "but this won't take long."

"Well, okay, what is it?" Christy said unhappily.

"First, I need you to run a computer search of all of my patients. Specifically, I need the names of all patients who had a positive cancer biopsy in the last four or five years."

"That shouldn't be too hard," Christy admitted.

"Second, and I don't know if the computer can do this, but I would like the names of the group of patients who did not come back after the initial cancer talk or delayed the return appointment for three months or more."

There was a moment of silence as Christy thought about this. "Okay, I think I know how to do that."

"Lastly, I need all charts pulled for that no-show or tardy group."

"Now, that could take some time," Christy whined. "The computer can't do that."

"Take all the time you need," Coop said firmly, "as long as it's done within the hour."

Again Christy was quiet for a moment. "Uh...uh, Doctor Cooper?"

"Yes."

"Uh...what am I supposed to do with your patients?"

"What do you mean?"

"Well...uh, I've heard rumors and Doctor Kingsley said..."

"...Said what?"

"Well...uh, he said you might not be practicing medicine any more."

News travels fast, Coop thought, gritting his teeth. "For now, I will continue to see my post-op and cancer follow-up patients, but all new patients should probably go to Doctor Kingsley."

"Okay," Christy replied. "What about the surgery you've already got scheduled?"

"Make appointments for them to come in and talk to me. They'll either have to go to Doctor Kingsley or I'll have to find them another surgeon."

"That's a lot of extra work," she complained.

"Can't be more than three or four patients," Coop snapped and hung up.

Coop stared at the re-cradled phone and shook his head. At forty-five, Christy was a bitter mousey blonde unhappily suspended between marriages. She was fairly intelligent and it was obvious she considered office work beneath her skills and deserved station in life. At times Coop wondered why she was still at Urology Associates. Clearly, she was not happy, constantly complained about her salary and frequently badgered him for a raise. He sighed and shrugged his shoulders. Oh well, he'd worry about Christy another day, right now he had bigger and more pressing problems.

When Coop walked into the office an hour later, Christy looked harried as she slammed a stack of charts on his desk. It was apparent by her body language she wanted him to know what a major pain he was. Politely, he thanked her, shooed her out of his office, then closed the door. He wanted no interruptions for the next few hours.

Three hours later Coop was beginning to get a better understanding of things, see the bigger picture. Indeed, there seemed to be something of a pattern emerging. In the last four years, he saw a total of one hundred and four patients with positive cancer biopsies or masses highly suspicious for cancer. They ran the whole urological gamut: kidney, ureter, bladder, prostate and testicular tumors. Of that one hundred and four patients, unbelievably twenty-five, almost one-fourth, never returned or substantially delayed their return after the initial cancer talk. This was incredible considering they all had life-threatening diseases. When first informed they had cancer, most patients were chomping at the bit to get something done, but not so with those twenty-five. All of them were scheduled for surgery, then canceled at the last minute. Why? He could think of no good reason. It was almost like someone got to them and convinced them to go elsewhere. Coop forced a nervous laugh. He was beginning to feel a bit unnerved and more than a little paranoid.

After thinking about it for a few more minutes, Coop picked up the phone and called Dr. Kenneth Keys, a friendly competitor. After the usual pleasantries, Coop got right down to business.

"Ken, I've noticed a strange pattern with some of my cancer patients. Either they're canceling their surgery or delaying it for months. Have you seen anything like that?"

Dr. Keys paused for a moment to think. "Not off the top of my head. I may have lost one or two, usually to you," Ken laughed. "But nothing that I would consider a pattern. If you like, I could have my girls run a computer check to make sure."

"If you don't mind, Ken, and let me know. Oh, and Ken, have you had any problems with surgical hemorrhage lately?"

"No, just my usual excess of a thousand cc's or more per case." Keys chuckled again.

Coop didn't laugh. With his last three surgeries, he lost much more than that--an average of six to seven thousand cc's and that was no laughing matter.

"Any of my patients come your way?"

"Not that I can think of."

After hanging up the phone, Coop factored in what Ken just told him into what he already knew. When stirred, like flour gravy, the plot thickened. As far as he knew, and since they worked in the same office undoubtedly he would, Stan Kingsley did not have a problem either. So it appeared to be just him. Again why? Was he specifically being targeted? If so, by whom? And how? A cold shiver ran down his spine as he stared out the window at the half full parking lot. He had to shake it off. He was beginning to act like one of those conspiracy nuts.

After mulling things over for several more minutes, Coop picked up the phone again and punched in the number for the records department of Dixie Medical Center. When they answered, he requested they pull the hospital charts on those same twenty-five no-show patients. Possibly, the reason they never came back was they simply switched to another doctor. From their hospital charts, he could tell if they'd received treatment from another physician, at least if it were one on the staff of Dixie Medical Center.

Still preoccupied, Coop somehow managed to navigate the ten blocks to the hospital without an accident or traffic ticket. Making a beeline for the records department, he accepted a stack of charts from the head of the department. It was probably his imagination, but she seemed hostile and a little reluctant to turn over the charts. Perhaps, Jeremy Faux had sent all hospital departments a memo about his suspension and she wasn't sure if he still had privileges to go through hospital records. But more than likely, he was seeing ghosts where there were none. As with Christy, the records department was undoubtedly overworked and didn't have the time or manpower to pull his charts.

For the next two hours, Coop pored over the stack of manila charts. If possible, these charts were even more baffling than his office charts. Of the twenty-five patients in question, none of them switched doctors! Or if they had, it was a doctor out of town. But that was not the most perplexing thing. A second pattern seemed to be emerging. Of the twenty-five patients, fifteen (eighty percent), at varying times over the last three years had presented to the emergency room with life-threatening hemorrhages including G.I bleeds, severe nose bleeds, intracranial hemorrhage, gross hematuria, retroperitoneal hemorrhage or spontaneous subcutaneous hematomas. Even more ominous, an unbelievable fourteen of the fifteen died from those very same catastrophic events. That was over a ninety percent mortality rate! Not very many diseases boasted that kind of lethality.

Since all of those fifteen patients presented to the E.R. with severe bleeding, all had coagulation studies performed. In all fifteen, the pro-thrombin times, partial prothrombin times, INR's and platelet counts were normal. In spite of the lab tests most were empirically transfused several units of fresh frozen plasma (a concentrated serum containing an abundance of all clotting factors, platelets and proteins needed for coagulation.) It was, however, almost always to no avail, as fourteen of the fifteen bled to death anyway.

Of the fifteen who hemorrhaged, unfortunately only three were checked for Factor IX deficiency, not usually included in the routine coagulation panel, and just like Mr. Gordon Flowers all three were ex-tremely deficient.

His interest now piqued, Coop zeroed in on those three charts. He thumbed to their history and physical examination page. None of them had a prior history of congenital hemophilia. What was left if not congeni-tal? Only acquired hemophilia. The only problem with that theory, as far as Coop knew, there was no reported syndrome of acquired hemophilia. Scratching his head, he tried to come up with a working hypothesis. The only thing that made any sense was somehow these patients must have come in contact with some substance that depleted the body of the liver-produced clotting protein, Factor IX, much like the AIDS virus depletes the body of the proteins necessary to produce antibodies.

So to summarize, three of them, perhaps all fifteen, there was no way to know for sure, had acquired a Factor IX deficiency. That was all very interesting, but where did he go from here? What was his next step? At least now, he had a working theory, certainly a good first step, but what he needed now was tangible evidence. Slowly, a plan was beginning to germinate in his brain. Quickly, he gathered up the charts, returned them to the director of records and headed back to his office.

When once again in his office, Coop skimmed through his com-puter printout sheets. What he was looking for was the very last cancer patient who was a no-show. It took a few minutes, but finally he found a name, Nathan Reed. Nate was a twenty-three year old stuttering college student from Milford, Utah. He moved to St. George two years ago to go to Dixie State University and was majoring in, of all things, abnormal psychology. Coop didn't know this for sure, but suspected Nate hoped psychology might cure his stuttering.

Almost three months ago, Coop performed a right radial orchi-ectomy, removing the testicle and cord, on him. Pathology confirmed it was an embryonal cell testicular cancer. His serum markers, alpha feto-protein and beta human chorionic gonadotrophin, were both fairly high. A CT scan of the abdomen confirmed probable peri-aortic lymphadenopathy, multiple enlarged lymph nodes, and a chest x-ray revealed golf ball size masses in both lungs. Without question, he had metastatic disease. Fortunately, however, even with advanced disease young men usually did not die from this cancer, not if they got proper treatment. After the orchiectomy, what Nathan Reed needed was the works: chemotherapy with adjuvant radiotherapy and possibly more surgery to remove any persistent enlarged retroperitoneal nodes, ones that did not melt away with the previous treatments. If he did not get these treatments, there was a very good chance he would die. And as far as Coop could tell, he had not received any of these treatments.

After a few more seconds of perusing the lab section of his chart, Coop flipped to the patient information page. Nathan lived in off-campus housing fairly close to the University. Quickly, Coop scribbled down the address, 366 South, 600 East, Apt. # 4. It was less than ten minutes from his office.

Leaning back in his chair, Coop stretched muscles and groaned out loud. His eyes burned from all the reading and his head ached from the hours of intense concentration. For now, however, he'd done enough research. It was time for some traditional detective work, time to pound the pavement, time for some conventional gumshoeing. It was time for a good old-fashioned stakeout.

12

He is in great danger, who being sick,
thinks himself well.
—Thomas Fuller (1654–1734)

Three o'clock found Coop parked across the street from Nathan Reed's apartment, just two blocks from Dixie State University. It was a 1930's sienna brick prairie-box house, which was partitioned into four smaller student flats, all with separate entrances. There were two rentals on the main floor, one upstairs and a new one in the recently remodeled basement. Nathan lived there.

Once a neat middle-class neighborhood with quiet streets lined by stately sycamore and pecan trees, it had pretty much morphed into low rent student housing. The front yards looked seedy and unkempt, the paint on the trim and eves was scaling and pealing, the window and door screens were torn or missing and the sidewalks were chipped, cracked and buckled. Landlords, of course, no longer resided in the neighborhood and ever profit-conscious they were reluctant to make costly repairs, scrimping on even routine lawn and yard maintenance. The subdued background noise of neighbors quietly chatting over back-yard fences, the chugging of gas lawnmowers or the laughing of children playing street games was now replaced by blaring rock music, loud cars and all night keg parties.

Coop had already cased Nathan's apartment, at least as best he could from the outside. It appeared no one was home even though there was an old battered 1990 white Toyota pickup parked in the driveway. Inside, it was quiet with no lights or noise. Satisfied Nathan probably walked to school and more than likely was still there, Coop returned to the Dodge, slumped down in the seat and prepared to wait.

It was late-September and the fall semester classes had been in session for almost a month now. To confirm it really was fall, Coop glanced up at the sycamore trees. They were no help. They still sported the seaweed green leaves of late summer. And even though the air was a bit cooler, everything still smelled stale and dry, probably because there had been no appreciable rain for at least two months. Though invisible to the naked eye, Coop knew the fusty autumn air was saturated with billions of spores, blissfully released by maturing perennial plants and weeds. And needless to say, Coop's seasonal allergies flared once again, this time with a vengeance.

Lowering the truck window, he tried to catch a breeze. He immediately sneezed, even though there was no appreciable breeze. The air was dead and nothing stirred except for the occasional comings and goings of the scruffy looking students. They were a shabby lot, dressed in the standard Dixie State University uniform: knee-high shorts, flip-flops and ragged t-shirts. Even this early in the semester their clothes looked old, faded and frayed. Apparently, the annual ritual of buying new clothes to begin the school year was long dead.

For a man usually on the run, this unexpected inactivity combined with the relative tranquility and the warm afternoon conspired to make him sleepy. His eyes burned and itched from allergies and his lids felt weighted, like the leaded cars of the Cub Scout derby, and began to droop. He closed his eyes for only a moment, that did feel better, then his mind slowly emptied, like water swirling down a drain. Then he slept.

For a while, his mind floated aimlessly, searching for a place to land. Finally, it made one last random loop, then once again settled on fire, lots of fire. As he raced out of his house, forty-foot flames soared high into the ebony night sky. Once a safe distance from the house, he stopped, turned and faced the blazing inferno. The house was totally engulfed, being swallowed whole by a huge orange mouth of fire. Suddenly, he remembered Kylie was still in there! Racing back to the house, he dove into the firestorm, screaming her name. Dropping to his hands and knees, face only inches from the floor, he tried to find the bedroom. Frantically, he searched for what seemed like an eternity through the pugnacious black cloud, then finally he found her in the bedroom. It was also choked with smoke, making his lungs ache and his eyes burn, but there she was lying unconscious on the bed. Overhead the burning roof cracked loudly and spit sparks and chunks of glowing coals. Frantically, he noted a fiery rafter was about to give way and crash down the bed, right on top of Kylie. He lunged for her.

KA-BOOM!

Involuntarily, Coop flinched and his eyelids jerked open. It took him a couple of seconds to erase the image of fire and re-establish his bearings. Somewhere close by he heard the hum of a gasoline engine. The explosion must have come from a combustion engine backfiring. Peeking out his window, he saw the old white Toyota pickup slowly backing out of the driveway. As it rolled out onto the street, it momentarily stopped adjacent to the Dodge. Still slinked down in his seat, Coop nevertheless got a good look as the driver tried to shift gears. Even though his hair was a little longer and he now sported a scraggily unkempt beard, there was no mistaking, it was his former patient Nathan Reed (English - a variant of Read). After finally completing the gear shift, Nathan pressed down on the gas feed and the old mini-truck started forward.

Coop just wanted to talk to Nathan, but now it was too late. Quickly, he hit the ignition, made a U-turn in the middle of the block, then followed the Toyota at a safe distance. Nathan turned right onto Seventh South, then proceeded east twelve blocks to Bluff Street. At Bluff Street, he turned south and headed straight for the I-15 on-ramp. Touching the brake, Coop slowed down and tried to stay far enough behind so he wouldn't be too obvious, but not so far back as to lose him. This technique, Coop decided, was not as easy as it appeared in the movies. Gunning the Dodge, he ran the next red light so as not to lose Nate completely.

Cruising five miles an hour under the speed limit at seventy, Nathan headed southwest on the freeway. Thirty-two miles later, after crossing the state line into Arizona, he took the Littlefield exit and drove straight through the small town. Without signaling, he turned left at the first intersection onto a washboard rutted gravel road. It appeared to be well traveled and headed straight out into the vast Mojave Desert.

Coop pulled the Dodge to side of the road, but left the engine running for the air conditioning. There was no worry now; he could easily follow Nate's progress by the telltale billowing cloud of road dust. Conversely, his dust plume would be just as visible to Nate through his rearview mirror. Coop was not worried. He suspected in this remote section of the Mojave Desert there was only one road in and if he followed it he would eventually find Nathan Reed.

While he was parked waiting for Nathan's dust cloud to disappear, Coop used his cell phone to call the neighbor boy, Todd Snow. He asked him to feed the horses this evening and look after Malachi. With that worry resolved, he settled back to wait.

Always the amateur scientist, Coop passed the time by trying to identify the roadside plants. They were typical Mojave Desert flora. Off to his, right he noted several clumps of stunted salt brush and some stands of rabbit brush. Further away the dull gray flats were peppered with oily creosote bushes, sporting their signature spindly limbs and small crinkled green leaves. To his left, he spotted a variety of cacti. Close to the truck there was a cylindrical barrel cactus, then further out was a cluster of blue/green-spiked yucca. In front of the truck, he spied a multi-lobed prickly pear cactus, a wickedly branched cholla and on the horizon a venerable stand of stately Joshua trees. At this distance, they looked a bit like saguaro cacti, but Coop knew they weren't. Native saguaros were not found this far north.

Out of the corner of his eye, Coop saw a blue lizard scurrying from one patch of shade to another. Though unseen, he suspected other common desert fauna skulked nearby. The Mojave and sidewinder rattlesnakes, Gila monsters, scorpions, kangaroo rats, jackrabbits and of course the ubiquitous coyote were permanent residents.

At last, Nathan's swirling vortex of dust disappeared from the horizon. Coop shoved the Dodge in gear and once again started down the corrugated gravel road.

For the next five miles, Coop gradually climbed a sloping plain, apparently formed by erosion of the distant craggy peaks. About halfway up the piedmont, he noted a battered road sign, peppered with bullet holes, welcoming the desert traveler to the State of Utah. As odd as it seemed, the road must have looped back around and he once again was in the state of Utah.

As he got closer to the looming peaks, the piedmont got progressively narrower and just before it funneled into the gapping mouth of a high rocky gorge the road abruptly veered to the right, dropped off the plain and into an adjacent canyon. Employing multiple switchbacks, the road gradually snaked down the steep canyon to a dry wash some five hundred feet below. In its descent, it looped around several house-size boulders and splendid old cedar trees, before eventually arriving on the narrow valley floor. From here, it maintained a more gradual descent, roughly following the same course as the canyon's dry wash.

Once on the valley floor, Coop picked up speed, steering the Dodge down a rare stretch of fairly straight road. Suddenly, he slammed on the brakes. Up ahead was a large bulwark of sandstone, seemingly blocking the road. As he eased forward, Coop could see the road actually circled the rocky rampart, then disappeared on the other side.

Slowing to a crawl, Coop entered the turn, hugging to his side of the road in the event of oncoming traffic. Abruptly, he hit the brakes again. Directly ahead was a ten-foot high white stucco wall capped with terra cotta tile and strands of coiled barbwire. The gravel road terminated right in front of a eight-foot high iron portcullis, glowing brightly in the slanted light of the westward setting sun. To Coop, the wall and portcullis looked about as impenetrable as the ancient city of Troy must have looked to the invading Greeks.

Quickly, he shifted the Dodge into reverse, backed up around the huge stone formation, then looked for a place to park. To the left of the road, he spied a thick copse of mesquite trees, fifty yards up a feeder arroyo. He headed for it and somehow managed to wedge the Dodge into the dense grove. As he sat in the thicket contemplating his next move, he watched the sun slip behind the west canyon wall. It would be dark in less than an hour. If he were going to scout out the place, he'd better to do it while he could still see. But thinking ahead, he nevertheless grabbed a flashlight from the center console, climbed out of the truck, then trudged down the sandy bottom of the feeder arroyo back toward the main road. Pausing briefly, he glanced back at the truck. Unless you knew it was there, the pickup was pretty much invisible.

Keeping off the main road and using strewn sandstone boulders and creosote bushes for cover, Coop worked his way back to the huge portcullis. On the wall just to the right of the huge metal gate he spotted a mesh-covered speaker imbedded in the stucco wall and just below that a red button. Directly above the portcullis, and anchored on each side to the stucco fence, was a large arch. Suspended from the arch was an ornate eight-foot wooden sign. On the left margin, a good likeness of a creosote bush was carved and the right margin featured a

Spanish bayonet yucca. Both plants were painted with the appropriate colors. Embossed in large golden letters and centered between the two desert plants was the eye-catching inscription: **MOJAVE INSTUTE OF THERAPEUTICS AND HEALTH**.

Squatting behind a large spiny hopsage, Coop considered his next move. Should he push the red button and simply ask to be let in? Surely if they went to this much trouble for security, they would not open the doors for just anyone. More than likely, they would want to know his business, then what would he say? Oh, I was just curious. Or, I was just passing by and wondered if you offered tours. Or, should he tell the truth and simply say, I saw one of my patients go in and I was wondering what in the hell he was doing there.

From far behind him, Coop thought he heard the faint hum of a combustion engine. Turning around, he saw a red car approach the crest of rimrock, then begin its descent down the switchbacks. It was hard to say for sure, but it looked like a late model foreign car, possibly a Nissan or Honda. It was too far away to tell for sure.

Coop sprinted back to the safety of the feeder arroyo and hid behind a sandy cutbank. A few minutes later, he heard the steady purr of the engine and the crunch of the tires as it picked up speed down the canyon road. The car slowed as it approached the sharp curve and as it did Coop strained to get a look at the driver.

Abruptly, his jaw dropped! Quickly, he took a quick second look. What the...? There was no doubt about it; the driver of the red car was none other than his office manager, Christy Dennett! What the heck was she doing here? Coop was stunned. This made no sense at all. For a minute, he couldn't think, then slowly his mental gears began to turn, grinding out a half-dozen possible scenarios, none of them very reassuring.

As the car passed, Coop clamored over the bank and followed it around the stone pillar. Once in front of the portcullis, Christy stopped, rolled down her window, punched the red button and spoke something unintelligible into the speaker. She then sat back and waited. A few moments later the huge metal gate groaned and slowly slid open.

Suddenly, he realized there it was, right in front of him, his opportunity to get inside. Briefly, he wondered once in, how would he get back out? When faced with difficult problems, Coop's usual pattern was to step back and carefully analyze all possibilities, all ramifications, but there was no time. Christy's car was already moving forward. He may not get another chance. He had to make up his mind and right now.

Crouching low, like a marine storming Omaha Beach, Coop sprinted through the open portcullis right behind the Nissan. A few seconds later, he heard the mammoth gates clang shut behind him. For better or worse, he was now inside The Mojave Institute of Therapeutics and Heath.

Almost immediately, Coop veered to the left, leaving the road and hiding behind the slender trunk of a tall desert palm. Christy, on the other hand, continued on toward a large central parking lot. From the safety of the tree, Coop surveyed the grounds and structures within the compound. It was literally a desert oasis. Lavishly landscaped, it featured an abundance of mother ferns, desert palms, stately saguaros, pencil thin ocotillos, robust Mormon tea bushes and tall sleepy mesquite trees. Periodically, these arid gardens were spiced with a desert oasis or lush lagoon, also landscaped with the appropriate flora. The grounds looked like they were somehow shipped directly from a posh Arizona resort, from the Camelback Mountain, to the Mojave Desert of southern Utah.

The ten-foot stucco wall appeared to go all the way around the compound, but there was only one gate, the one through which he had just entered. Within the compound itself, there was no gravel. The road and parking areas were paved and well maintained. It was a beautiful place. The only inconsistency, the only glaring incongruity was the coiled strands of barbed wire capping the stucco fence.

Centered in this five-acre compound was a striking single-story hacienda. It was constructed with a large central pod and four equally spaced wings, angling off in roughly the four directions of the compass. To Coop, it looked a bit like a huge white crab lying on its back with legs extended. It sported the classical Santa Fe Pueblo architecture with a flat roof, an enclosing parapet and protruding poles or *vigas*. The walls were plastered white and troweled to the classical mission finish and the windows were framed with rough-hewn planks, stained a dark chocolate brown. The doors were constructed with those same thick planks and the fixtures, knobs and hinges were all hand-forged rustic iron. To add accent, terra cotta tile was set on most windowsills and around most door jams.

From the safety of the corrugated palm tree, Coop watched as Christy parked in the main lot, then walked briskly toward the central pod and the primary entrance. A quick survey of the parking lot also revealed Nathan Reed's white Toyota pickup parked in the last row. That was really no surprise as there was only one road in and it ended here.

After checking his wristwatch, Coop glanced up at the rapidly changing evening sky. It had deepened to a navy blue, but off to the far west a few feathery clouds still glowed a bright crimson red, inflamed from below by the upward angled rays from the now invisible sun. The compound itself was now suffused in a gray flat light, typical of sunset. There was no breeze and hot air lingered, trapped by the circling stucco wall.

Coop decided to wait for dark before making his move. But if he was going to stall for time, he'd better find another place to hide. The slight trunk of this palm tree didn't offer much cover. Off to his left, he noted a thicket of date palms, feathery mesquite trees and numerous giant macho ferns. Keeping low, he dashed to the grove, then quickly sequestered himself amongst the ferns. Almost immediately, his nose started to itch. By firmly pinching his nostrils, he managed to stave off an impending sneeze. With nose still itching and eyes watering, he quickly found another hiding place, this time on dry sand. He rested his back against a date palm, then he waited. By scooting a couple of feet to his left, he had a window through the foliage, giving him a narrow view of the parking lot and main entrance.

To help pass the time, Coop thought of Kylie. He couldn't help but wonder where she was, what she was doing, and wishing she would come back. What did Roger Callister have he didn't? He didn't even want to think about that. Finally his thoughts turned to Samantha Rose, which was no better. He wondered once again why he ever got involved with her. Was he brain dead? What was he thinking? Obviously, he wasn't.

After another half an hour, the lights around the compound, apparently connected to an automatic timer, flashed on. First was the outside lighting of the grounds and garden, next the tall metal pole lights of the parking lot and lastly the security floodlights, strategically spaced about every ten yards atop the stucco fence.

As if somehow cued by the lights, the cars immediately left the parking lot, including both Christy and Nathan's, and headed for the main gate. Fifteen minutes after that, the whole lot was empty and though still bathed in artificial white light, the entire compound looked deserted. Apparently, the workday was over. Probably, somewhere there were security guards, but for the moment none were visible. Coop suspected they were huddled in a small room behind a bank of video monitors, munching doughnuts, telling war stories and drinking coffee.

While the darkness slowly deepened to night, Coop forced himself to wait another thirty minutes, then he got up and stretched out the kinks. Sticking strictly to the shadows, he carefully made his way toward the hacienda, then cautiously worked around the entire structure, including all four wings, checking for unlocked windows or doors. There were none. Briefly, he saw a security guard patrolling the periphery over by the fence. He simply crouched back in the shadows till the guard passed.

At the southwest wing, opposite from the main entrance to the central pod, Coop found a large mesquite tree growing adjacent to the building. It was tall enough to reach the roof and looked stout enough to hold his weight. Clenching his jaw with resolve, he grabbed a branch and began climbing. It had been thirty years since he'd climbed a tree and even as a kid he never liked it. As he climbed higher, the branches got progressively smaller, groaning and trembling under his weight.

C-R-A-C-K!

Suddenly, a limb snapped! Coop plunged downward a foot or so before grabbing hold of a stouter limb and holding on. The limb swayed and bowed, but held. With heart pounding, Coop took a deep breath and considered a change in strategy. Unfortunately, he could think of no other way, so he took a deep breath and started climbing again, this time with more care. Eventually he worked high enough to reach the top of the parapet. Using maximum effort, he grabbed hold and hoisted his body up and over it, tumbling onto the flat roof. With chest heaving from the exertion, he lay spread-eagle on the roof, gulping air. God, he was out of shape.

After his heart rate and breathing returned to normal, Coop struggled to his feet and looked around. The roof was gently slanted for drainage and externally the parapet was dotted with canaliculi, jutting out like water spouts. On the roof, however, there was nothing, nothing other than a few breather pipes, some shuttered heater vents and scattered skylights. No apparent way to get inside the building, unless...

One by one, Coop checked the large plastic caps over the skylights. Directly over the central pod, one was a little loose. Apparently during construction, the carpenter set the skycap, but forgot to sink the screws. By rocking it back and forth, Coop worked the cap from its wooden frame and set it aside. Now he could look straight down into the main foyer of the central pod. A large reception desk was directly below him, apparently placed there to take advantage of the light.

Coop firmly grasped both sides of the framework, then slowly lowered himself down through the aperture. Supporting his full weight with one hand, he used the other to work the plastic cap back in place.

This accomplished, he fully extended both arms, but still couldn't reach the desk even though he was sure it was right beneath him. It couldn't be more than a foot or so. His arm and shoulder muscles stared to fatigue. Taking in a deep breath, he let go, crashing down on the reception desk, shattering a plastic desktop file and scattering papers, staplers, printers, pens and telephones everywhere. Obviously, it was a little further than he thought.

With his shins still stinging from the impact, Coop slowly rolled off the desk, scattering even more papers and pens. Once on solid ground, he paused to take inventory of his injuries. Other than a strawberry abrasion on his right elbow and a slightly twisted left ankle he was okay. Not bothering to gather up the scatter, except for the loudly beeping phone, Coop pulled the flashlight from his back pocket, turned it on and surveyed the room. As he suspected, he was in the spacious central pod. From where he stood, he could see four hallways, the entrances to the angled wings.

Straight ahead were the massive main doors and between them and the desk a lofted atrium arched over a huge oval planter. The odd thing about the planter, it contained only two plants, both of them quite large and robust. On one end was a coppice of waxy creosote bushes and the other a huge colony of Spanish bayonet yucca.

Redirecting his flashlight, Coop checked out the four wings. He debated briefly, then started his search down the wing labeled: *Research & Development*.

As Coop walked down the hallway, his flashlight ballooned any and all shadows, creating eerie ghostly shapes dancing on the white plastered walls. After roughly a hundred feet, the hall made a right-angle turn, then abruptly ended at another solid plank door. Coop checked the door fixture. Surprisingly, it was unlocked. Cautiously, he pulled it open, then instantly sneezed. The odor effluxing from the room was both acidic and corrosive. Not only did it burn his nasal membranes, but also blistered the lining of his lungs. It smelled like...like what? The best he could come up with was an unlikely mixture of hot roofing tar and cheap Mexican tequila.

Stepping inside he closed the door, then systematically swept his light around the room. It was a large windowless space and even if he didn't have a chemistry background, he still would have known it was some kind of laboratory. There were four rows of wooden cabinets topped with black Formica counters and sporting an array of laboratory equipment, both large and small. Coop immediately recognized Bunson burners, glass flasks, round beakers, coiled glass tubing, metal crucibles, water baths, furnace ovens and storage bins. But what really caught his eye was a huge eight-by-eight wooden vat at the far end of the room. Looking a bit like a square wine cask, but larger, it was constructed entirely of oaken slats. To the immediate right of the vat were a half a dozen long aisles. Ten-foot high metal racks flanked each aisle and sported eight shelves per rack. All shelves appeared to be well stocked.

Coop carefully wove through and around the laboratory bays, then made his way toward the vat. Grabbing hold of the corner of the heavy lid, he cracked it open an inch. Instantly, he gagged, dropping the lid and staggering backward. There was no question about it; this was the source of the room's vile odor. Holding his breath, he raised the lid high enough to poke his head in, then refocused the flashlight. The vat was about half full, containing a lumpy mash, semisolid in consistency and looking a bit like a bowl of oatmeal, but darker. Coop quickly lowered the lid again, then inhaled deeply. Unfortunately, the air was still tainted and triggered another round of coughing, followed by a jag of sneezing. Whatever that stuff was, it was potent.

Still sniffling and with eyes watering, Coop wandered over to the long aisles of metal racks, redirecting his flashlight as he went. His light beam sparkled off countless pieces of glassware. The glass crystal occasionally split the light into a rainbow prism of color. On closer inspection, the shelves contained hundreds of containers of every size. There were three, six and twelve ounce bottles, as well as pint and quart jars. All containers were filled with a thick amaretto brown liquid.

Picking up a six-ounce vial, Coop focused the light directly on the label. It simply read, *YUCCASOTE*. The plastic screw cap was slightly crusted with golden brown crystals. Using all his strength, Coop managed to twist off the cap. Once again, he sneezed. The opened vial smelled exactly like, though not quite as strong, as the soupy mash in the adjacent oaken vat.

Suddenly, on the other side of the plank door, Coop heard a noise, like boots scuffing on a concrete floor. Quickly, he snapped off his flashlight, pocketed the six-ounce vial of Yuccasote, then crouched low behind a tall metal rack.

Creaking on its cast iron hinges, the plank door slowly swung open. Two powerful light beams entered, erratically bobbing as they silently, almost eerily, surveyed the darkened room. After a moment, the echo of footfall followed the beams into the room. Finally, the shadowy forms of two uniformed security guards emerged from the darkness, one quite short and rotund, the other tall and skinny. Once inside, they paused again, sweeping the room with their powerful lights.

"Who's in here?" the taller one said loudly.

"Satch, there's no one," the short one whispered, still arcing his light.

"No," Satch argued, "there's some one in here alright."

Briefly they huddled, mumbled something unintelligible, then separated, the short one heading left, the tall one angling to the right.

Coop was trapped! The only way out was straight down the middle, right through the cluttered maze of laboratory bays and stacked research equipment. Dropping down to all fours, and without the aid of the flashlight, he crawled in the general direction of the front door.

Down low the heavy fumes were even more concentrated. Coop's nose itched, then watered, then twitched.

Suddenly, he sneezed! Immediately, the two beams swung in his direction. Clamoring to get away from the light, Coop collided with a metal storage rack. Top heavy, it rocked back and forth on its short steel legs, sending dozens of Yuccasote vials sliding from the shelves and crashing to the concrete floor.

"Over there!" the tall guard shouted. Instantly both flashlights readjusted and arced in his general direction.

Staying low and on all fours, Coop scrambled forward, but the scattered glass shards lacerated his hands and abraded his knees. Further compounded by the spilled Yuccasote, the caustic fumes were even stronger and Coop started sneezing violently.

Now, there was no point in trying to maintain cover. They knew exactly where he was. Standing up, Coop sprinted for the door. In his haste, he collided with a laboratory counter, sending flasks, beakers and Bunson burners smashing on the floor. Reeling to the left, he crashed into another metal rack, this time completely upending it. Glassware flew off the shelves and shattered on the hard concrete floor. Coop lunged forward, hurling debris out of his way as sprinted for the west wall. A quick right turn at the wall and he would be back at the entrance!

He'd gone no more than a half-dozen steps before he spied the rotund guard directly in his path, frantically grappling to release the snap on his holstered revolver. Lowering his shoulder, Coop charged, hitting him squarely in the chest. The impact carried them both into another laboratory bay. As the guard's gun flew from his hand, Coop once again heard the unmistakable sound of breaking glass.

Like a cat, he was on his feet again, ready to break for the door. In midstride, he suddenly stopped, stood still, then slowly stiffened, like advancing rigor mortis.

"Enough of this shit," Satch hissed, the cold barrel of his .357 Magnum pressed hard against Coop's left temple.

13

A physician can sometimes parry the scythe of death,
but has no power over sand in the hourglass.
—Hester Lynch Piozzi (1741–1821)

Coop was in purgatory—both literally and figuratively.

The Washington County Correction Facility was located about halfway between the cities of St. George and Hurricane on a lonely stretch of badlands known as Purgatory Flats. Consequently, the prison complex was also affectionately known as Purgatory.

Purgatory Flats was an exceptionally desolate tract of land dotted with countless weathered hills carved from ancient bands of blue, gray and crimson clay. With its genesis dating back to the Jurassic Period, this strange geologic formation was created over millions of years in several distinct stages. First, sediment from an ancient inland lake was deposited, creating a soft mud bed, which eventually solidified into Chinle shale. Over many millennia the lake water slowly evaporated, then multiple volcanoes erupted adding several more layers of thick ash, completely covering the Chinle shale. This volcanic ash eventually compacted into today's colorful strata of banded clay. Through the eons, rainwater and fierce winds condensed and eroded these layers, sculpting them into hillocks and creating a classic badlands formation.

The oxidation of imbedded heavy metals produced the rich colors: manganese for blue and purple, iron for red and crimson. Depending on the culture, this unique formation was known by a couple of different descriptive names. The early Utah pioneers christened it the Painted Desert, but the Native American name was even more descriptive... Land of the Sleeping Rainbows. Today, however, it is simply known as Purgatory Flats.

Though Coop was quite conversant with the area's history and geology, this was not what presently occupied his thoughts. In lieu of sleep, he was reliving last night's fiasco, blow by blow.

After the security guards captured him, they were not sure of what to do. First, they frisked him, discovered and confiscated the 6 oz. bottle of Yuccasote, then fished his wallet from his back pocket and checked his I.D. Without returning his wallet, they then forced him to the ground, face down, and handcuffed him. Once he was secure, the guards engaged in heated debate as to their next move.

Finally, Satch pulled his cell phone from its hip holster and called headquarters for instructions. He listened intently for a few moments, then hung up and immediately punched out another number. Catching only brief snatches of the conversation, Coop gathered he was talking to the Washington County Sheriff's Department. From the sound of it, he also concluded they were having a jurisdiction squabble. After a brief and occasionally heated argument, Satch finally convinced the deputy they really were in Utah, more specifically Washington County. After more haggling, Coop heard them arrange to meet halfway.

Satch hung up, then grabbed Coop by the hair, roughly jerking him to his feet and shoving him in the back seat of a late model SUV. Coop's head throbbed from the rough treatment and he wondered if he was missing a divot of hair, wrenched from the scalp and hanging by the roots. With his hands cuffed behind his back, there was no way to confirm.

The exchange took place in the dark just outside Littlefield, Arizona. Still cuffed, Coop was unceremoniously yanked from the SUV and deposited in the back seat of the black and white Washington County Sheriff cruiser. Briefly, he considered escape, like in the movies, but quickly decided against it. Movies were scripted; real life was not. He could get shot or perhaps even worse he might actually make it and escape into the great Mojave Desert with no water and hands still cuffed. Once inside the cruiser, however, it became a mute point. There were no handles on the doors, the windows would not roll down and the thick Plexiglas partition separating the back seat from the front was as solid as tempered steel. Now, there was no way to escape. He sat back and closed his eyes.

From Littlefield, they took him directly to the Washington County Corrections Facility at Purgatory Flats and booked him. As luck would have it, the booking officer was the son of one of his prostate cancer patients. Oddly enough, he seemed embarrassed for Coop. Without looking him directly in the eye, the desk officer advised him of what to expect. Tomorrow, he would be formally charged with breaking and entering, attempted burglary and the wanton destruction of private property. Also, he explained, by tomorrow they would receive a more accurate appraisal of damage, but from the preliminary report, the value of the property destroyed would probably bump the charge up to a felony.

After booking, Coop was sent to photography, then on to finger-printing. Next on his to do list was wardrobe, a euphemism for a standard orange jumpsuit commonly worn by Washington County prisoners. Lastly he would be assigned a cell. Neither happened. Apparently, the house was full and since he was likely to make bail within a few hours, they didn't bother. Instead, a deputy deposited him in a large holding cell, still in his street clothes, to wait out the night. Tomorrow he would appear before Judge Judith Pleasants and be formally charged and bail set. In lesser cases, this took place right from the jail via video hook up, though the officer hesitated to say for sure it would happen in his case. Coop wasn't certain, which he preferred, but a video hearing might be less humiliating than facing the judge in person. After the preliminary hearing, all he had to do was come up with money for bail and he could go free, at least until the trial, whenever that might be.

Coop was informed he could make a phone call, but by then it was well after midnight and he didn't know Samantha's home phone number. Sighing in resignation, he decided he would wait until 9:00 tomorrow morning, then call her at the office.

Sitting down on a scarred, unpadded bench between two inmates, Coop surveyed his surroundings. He was somewhat disappointed when he realized the cell did not feature the classical vertical steel bars. Rather, it was constructed, at least on three sides, of thick two-inch reinforced safety glass. It was a bit unnerving, like being a prisoner in an ant colony. The fourth wall, the back wall, was solid rebar reinforced concrete. Standing up, Coop wandered over and touched the glass wall. Though it didn't look it, the glass felt solid enough. Undoubtedly, you couldn't break it with a sledgehammer. Oddly, Coop still wished he had bars to grab.

Wandering back to the bench, he sat down and surreptitiously studied his fellow cellmates. On his right was a kid, eighteen years old or so. He had long shaggy unkempt hair and equally scruffy facial stubble. Dressed in a torn faded t-shirt and dirty Levi shorts, he reeked of alcohol and cigarette smoke. Coop had no way of knowing for sure, and he certainly didn't want to ask, but if he were a betting man he'd put his money on a DUI.

The other man was middle-aged with a hardened pocked-scarred face. He wore a colorful Hawaiian short sleeve shirt, unbuttoned half to his belly, exposing a tanned and hairy chest. His eyes were cold, gray and vacant, and his jet-black hair was slicked straight back. Coop guessed he was some kind of a flimflam man or maybe a pimp. From the looks of it, he wasn't planning on staying long either. Again he had no way of knowing what his offense was, but he was willing to bet he'd been here before. He just looked like a repeat offender.

Fortunately, neither man seemed very talkative. The kid's silence was probably alcohol induced; he looked like he was nursing a hangover. As for the other guy, this was probably old hat. He felt no need for nervous chatter.

Suddenly, Coop had an overpowering sense of humiliation, of embarrassment. What was he doing here? He'd not felt this kind of shame since being sent home from church for playing chess in sacrament meeting or the high school chemistry lab fiasco. This was no place for a man of his stature, with his education and his professional skills. More than likely, he was the only surgeon ever jailed here. Undoubtedly, and if you believed in a hereafter, his deceased mother was turning over in her grave and his father was shaking his head and saying, "Mary, I told you so." Coop sighed out loud. Other than those possible celestial spirits, he assumed, with a sense of relief, no one else knew. Then he remembered the booking officer recognized him and furthermore *The Daily Spectrum* always published a daily compendium of the county's arrests. In their *Public Record* column they included names, addresses, reasons for apprehension as well as the dollar amount for bail. You couldn't buy that kind of publicity, Coop thought dryly. It should go a long way in helping his already faltering medical practice.

At the thought of his name in the newspaper, Coop groaned out loud. Both of his companions turned and stared, and he instantly wished he could disappear into the concrete wall. Instead, he got up and wandered back to the thick glass wall and focused his attention on the digital clock fixed on an outside wall. It flashed a disappointing 3:05 a.m. He still had six long hours before he could call Samantha Rose Jardine. Closing his raw and sore eyes, he let his mind wander. Like a migratory goose looking for a pond, someplace to light down and rest, his thoughts circled and circled, then finally landed back on the disturbing events of yesterday at the MITH compound.

Trying to figure out why Nathan Reed was at MITH was not all that difficult. It was not a terribly big leap of logic to assume he was there for cancer treatments, probably with Yuccasote. But the puzzling thing, however, the treatments must be doing some good. Nathan looked too good for them for them to be doing nothing. Three months ago his disease was so far advanced without treatment Coop expected he would be in far worse shape, possibly even dead. Obviously, this wasn't the case. Coop sighed again. Too bad the guards confiscated the Yuccasote he'd purloined. He would love to have Marcus Westover at Southern Utah University analyze it.

Christy Dennett, on the other hand, was not quite so easy to figure. At first glance, one would have to consider the possibility she was passing information about cancer patients to MITH, maybe even recruiting or at least encouraging them to leave Coop. When he was combing through the hospital charts of his tardy and absent surgery patients, it had occurred to him someone was getting to them before surgery and diverting them in another direction. As further proof, Dr. Keys stated he was not having a similar problem and neither was Stan Kingsley. If Christy was referring patients to MITH, what was her reason? The motive was obvious—money, plain and simple. She constantly bellyached about the lack of money and her desperate need for a raise, even within days after just getting one. Maybe, she'd stumbled on a way to supplement her income. Try as he might, Coop could think of no other reason for Christy Dennett to be at MITH.

Time passed slowly. Coop hashed and rehashed everything again and again. His head ached from too much thinking and the acute lack of sleep, and his fall allergies continued to make his eyes itch and burn. The air in the cell was heavy and stale, reeking of alcohol and the body odor of his two companions. Changing positions, he sat on the floor and leaned against a wall corner, then closed his eyes, trying to shield out the glare of the florescent lights. He frankly doubted he could sleep in this fishbowl, but somehow he must have dozed. The next thing he knew someone was shaking his shoulder. Warily, he cracked an eye open. It was the longhaired kid. Over the kid's shoulder, Coop noted the outside wall clock now flashed a welcome 8:00 a.m.

"Hey, dude," the kid was saying. "You wanna go to breakfast?"

"Huh?" Coop rubbed his eyes again.

"Yeah, man, they got some real good grub here."

Somehow Coop doubted that, but got up anyway and followed the kid. He certainly looked better this morning; his hangover must be better. A guard escorted them to a large windowless dining room with two dozen, or so, long fiberglass tables and accompanying benches. Service was cafeteria style.

For prison grub, Coop had to admit it wasn't half bad. He was served hard scrambled eggs, crispy bacon, black coffee and whole wheat buttered toast. Since Kylie left, he almost never ate this well at home. If he ate at all, his usual breakfast consisted of a toasted bagel and black coffee, both on the run.

Once he'd finished breakfast, he again checked the time. It was now after nine and time to call Samantha Rose. After repeatedly signaling by banging on the glass wall, Coop finally got the attention of a guard. The guard, obviously irritated by the interruption, escorted him to a wall phone over by booking, then leaned against the wall well within earshot and impatiently waited.

First, Coop called the neighbor boy, Todd Snow, and asked him to continue to feed the horses and care for Malachi. He hung up and glanced over at the guard. He was presently engaged in heated conversation with another deputy. Coop quickly punched in the number for Cannon, Jeffs & Hanks.

The phone rang an agonizing ten times. With each ring, Coop's spirits sank a little lower. Was no one going to answer the damn phone? Maybe Samantha was in court today or sick or even worse on vacation, probably scuba diving with Josh. Finally on the eleventh ring, the receptionist, already sounding harried for this early hour, picked up the phone.

"Cannon, Jeffs and Hanks!" she snapped.

"Uh...this...this is Doctor Lawrence Cooper," Coop stammered. He rarely used his title for muscle, but he'd never been in this situation before. "I...I'm a client of Samantha Rose Jardine and I really need to talk to her. It's urgent."

"Miss Jardine is in a staff meeting this morning and can't be disturbed," the receptionist said brusquely.

"This is a matter of life and death!" Coop blurted. Yes, he knew he was being overly dramatic, but to him it felt that way. "Can you at least go ask her if she will take the call?"

There was a moment of silence as the receptionist considered his request.

"Please," Coop pleaded, "tell her it's Doctor Cooper."

"Well, okay, wait on the line, Doctor," she sighed and punched the hold button. Quickly, the phone static was replaced by elevator music.

After a full five minutes of Barry Manilow, Coop heard the button click again.

"Hi, Coop." Samantha greeted him, "I'm glad you called. I was going to call you anyway after the meeting. I have three important bits of news."

"Oh." Coop decided to hold his news until he heard what she had to say.

"First," Samantha continued, speaking as though she was in a hurry. "The firm has given me permission to represent you at your hearing with the Utah State Board of Licensure next week." She paused for Coop to comment. When he didn't, she continued, "their rationale, meaning Cannon, Jeffs and Hanks, is the result of any action taken by the state licensure board might directly impact your upcoming malpractice trial."

"Okay," Coop replied without enthusiasm.

"Second, the Betty Tsongas malpractice trial has been scheduled to begin two weeks from Wednesday...and without any new evidence we are still in trouble. Have you given any more thought to settling out of court?"

"No."

"No, you haven't thought about it," Samantha seemed unperturbed by Coop's curt answers, "or no to any kind of settlement?"

"No settlement."

"It would probably be cheaper in the long run and certainly a lot less headache for you."

"No."

"Okay," Samantha sighed, "now for my third bit of news. Just this morning, through my friend from Saint George, I received a tip the Washington County Attorney has decided to go ahead and charge you with at least one count of negligent homicide. Apparently, he's still trying to decide about Misters Flowers and Perdenales."

"So what does that mean?"

"That means sometime in the next few days you'll probably be arrested, formally charged, then released on bail pending the outcome of that trial. Or possibly, hopefully, some kind of plea bargain in lieu of a trial." Samantha quickly added, "Coop, I am so sorry."

"Yeah, well, I guess it was expected."

"Yeah, I guess," Samantha agreed, then paused. "Oh...Coop, I apologize. I've done all the talking. Why did you call?"

"Well, I've got some news too. I'm already in jail."

There was a moment of complete silence, filled only with background static of the telephone. "You're not kidding, are you?"

"No."

"Do you want to tell me about it?"

"What do you want to know?"

"First of all, what are the charges?"

"As best I can tell, I think there will be four," Coop shifted the phone to his other hand, "criminal trespass, breaking and entering, attempted burglary and wanton destruction of private property."

"How much private property?"

"Why?"

"It's like theft. Depending on the value of the items stolen, it can be anything from petty theft, a misdemeanor, to grand larceny, a felony," Samantha explained. "So how much private property do you think you destroyed?"

"A lot."

"More than five thousand dollars?"

"Probably."

"When's the hearing?"

"Sometime later this morning," Coop answered, then asked. "Is that when I plead guilty?"

"No, at this hearing you will be formally charged, the judge will make sure you understand the county's charges against you, then set bail." Samantha Rose quickly added, "but when the time comes, I don't think it's a good idea to plead guilty."

"Why? I am."

"Yes, but if you plead guilty you loose all muscle with the county attorney, all possible leverage to make a deal. By their very nature, county attorneys are both lazy and overworked. Even if they have sure thing, a slam dunk, they will often make a deal just to avoid the time, effort and expense of a trial. If you plead guilty, you are waiving your right to a trial and the county attorney has what he wants without having to give you a thing. After that there will be no deals and you basically trust yourself to the mercy of the court. Unfortunately, the court's mercy can be about as fickle as Utah's weather."

"Or Samantha Rose Jardine," Coop mumbled, mostly to himself.

"What?"

"Oh, nothing."

Samantha said nothing and neither did Coop. Finally, and as if it took great effort, he broke the silence. "Samantha, it appears I'm in big trouble. I'm really going to need your help."

Once again there was a long pause.

"Coop," Samantha carefully measured her words, "I wish I could, I really do, but we've already gone over this. Cannon, Jeffs and Hanks won't allow it and neither will your malpractice insurance carrier. Our contract with UMIA specifically states we will not get involved in criminal cases. And UMIA won't touch it either."

"But this is my life we're talking about." Coop voice raised a decibel. "Not only my freedom, but also my very ability to make a living."

"I know, Coop," Samantha Rose replied softly, "but..."

"...But I kind of thought I was a little more than the average client."

"You are, Coop."

"You must have studied criminal law in school," Coop persisted, "just like we study general medicine in medical school."

"Yes, Coop, I did, but I've never practiced criminal law."

"I've never practiced orthopedics, but I know how to set a broken bone."

"It's not the same thing."

"I fail to see the difference."

More silence.

"I'm asking you as a friend," he despised how desperate he sounded, "but right now I need a big favor."

"I can't, Coop," Samantha whispered, her voice choked with emotion.

Coop said nothing more. Samantha Rose had said it all.

"Coop...Coop let me try to explain," Samantha blurted. "I'm up to make partner this year. If I were to directly violate policy then..."

"...Remember we're talking about my life here!"

"We're talking about my life too," Samantha snapped back. "You're not the only one with big things at stake."

More uncomfortable silence followed, then Coop, feeling there was nothing left to say, hung up.

* * *

Samantha Rose Jardine was sitting at her desk when she heard the line go dead. Rather than also hanging up, she stared at the phone, idly rotating it in her hands. What had just happened? Had she just broken up with Coop?

Of course, he was being unreasonable. All he could see was the deep hole he'd dug for himself was starting to crumble and cave in. Maybe, it was just panic talking, because it sure didn't sound like Coop.

On the other hand, who could blame him? It was a pretty nasty mess. And he was right about one thing, if you stacked his potential losses against her possible losses, it would be like comparing the Great Wall of China to a white picket fence. But regardless of the relative gains or losses, what it had done was force her to make a decision. If she continued her fence sitting, the decision would be made for her. It would be over with Coop. He needed her help. He was desperate for her help and if she didn't lift a finger, there would be no reconciliation... ever.

Yes, she did have a lot to lose too, but how much did those things really matter? How much did she really want to make partner? If she lost this job, she could surely get another. And what about Josh, it was time to make a decision there too. God, how she hated being forced into a corner and making a decision under pressure. She much preferred taking her time or even better continuing with the status quo.

Suddenly, the phone started its electronic bleating. Sighing deeply, she hung it up, but still did not get up. Idly, she ran her hand over her amoeba redwood table and stared out her bank of windows at nothing.

"Miss Jardine," her secretary poked her head through the half open office door.

Samantha flinched at the sound of her voice. "Yes, what is it?"

"Your nine-thirty is here."

14

You are a physician, doctor.
You would promise life to a corpse
if he could swallow your pills.
—Napoleon (1789–1821)

Over late morning coffee at the Quail Run restaurant, Coop sat across from Dr. Jacob Heinz. They sipped in silence.

Coop was still trying to come to terms with Samantha Rose's refusal to help. Frowning deeply, he set down his cup. Perhaps, she was not the girl he'd thought she was or maybe she was. She had abandoned him before, so why was he surprised now? Sure, she had her reasons, making partner, but to Coop that just didn't wash. In his line of work one of the first things you learned was how to prioritize, then triage. In medical school, you were taught to take care of the most life-threatening problems first, then the lesser ones later when you had time. In his mind, if you were to stack his present and very real problems next to Samantha's potential ones, there was no question whose should take precedence, whose were more life-threatening. Coop realized he was being petty and self-centered, but after all he'd been through he was entitled to a little selfishness.

Shortly after he'd hung up on Samantha, another deputy grabbed him for his preliminary hearing. The preliminary hearing was indeed conducted by video camera and television link up. It was cold and impersonal, but that was okay. It's not like he was auditioning for a part in a play or interviewing for a job. He hoped it provided a layer of anonymity not possible with a face-to-face appearance, but in reality that benefit was probably more perceived than real. Judge Judith Pleasants informed him he would be charged with two separate felonies, burglary and wanton destruction of private property. Apparently, the county attorney dropped the criminal trespass charge and merged breaking and entering with attempted burglary, thereby creating one offense, plain old burglary. Both offenses, however, were felonies and carried a possible penalty of a substantial fine and up to five years in jail, or both.

After the judge was sure Coop understood the charges, she counseled him to find a lawyer, then she set bail at ten thousand dollars. Coop protested, but Judge Pleasants quickly dismissed his complaint and the screen abruptly turned to static and falling snow. That's when he called Jacob Heinz. Good old reliable Jacob had, without even asking why, readily agreed to come and bail him out.

Not realizing the court would refuse a personal check, they accepted only cash or a cashier's check, Jacob was initially turned away. He then went directly to his bank, withdrew $10,000 from his retirement fund and purchased a cashier's check. Returning to Purgatory, he then posted bail.

On leaving the jail, Coop also visited his bank, withdrew some spending money and made sure he had enough in his checking account to repay Heinz. Jacob, as opposed to Purgatory, would accept personal checks, then they met for coffee.

Setting down his coffee cup, Coop took a blank check out of his wallet, wrote it for the ten thousand, signed it, then handed it over, along with his gratitude, to Heinz.

"Ha, ha, ha, looks like that Kylie vill have to go vithout her check this month," Jacob laughed merrily.

"I've got this month covered," Coop replied, "but this could be it."

"You're not serious!

"I...I've already sent it," Coop stammered, turning red.

Heinz shook his head, then changed the subject. "So, did you get away with any of that Yuccasote?"

"No, the security guards confiscated it before they turned me over to Washington County."

"*Das ist schade*, that's too bad," Jacob took a sip from his mocha flavored cappuccino. "*Mein Gott*, this is good coffee," he exclaimed, setting down his cup. "I have a feeling that Yuccasote is the key. It could be our Rosetta stone. Nobody could make sense of ancient Egyptian until Jean-Francois Champollion found it.

"Yeah," Coop agreed glumly, "Yuccasote has to be the key."

"The vay I see it," Heinz continued thoughtfully, "you'll eventually need some of your patients to come forward and testify they were taking Yuccasote. But there's no sense in doing that until you can prove Yuccasote is a blood thinner and in order to do that you've got to have some."

"Getting patients to testify won't be easy." Coop remembered how hard it was to get the Flowers and Tsongas families to open up. "And as I just recently found out, getting Yuccasote isn't all that easy either. Unfortunately, they don't sell it at Walgreens."

"*Nein, nein*. No one said it vould be easy," Jacob agreed, "but you'll find a way."

"You have more faith than I do."

"Also, you need to talk to your office manager, Christy Dennett," Heinz drained his cup, then grabbed a paper napkin to wipe the foam from his face, "see vhat that *klieine Dame* is really up to."

"Yeah, I agree." Coop also finished his coffee, then he pulled out his wallet.

Reaching over, Heinz stopped him. "*Nein*, this one's on me. You save your *Geld*, you'll be needing it," He paid the bill, then set two quarters down on the table for a tip. He then looked up at Coop and grinned. "But I am still vaiting for them Viagras."

Coop nodded and smiled. "I'm sorry, Jacob, with all that's going on I forgot. The next time I'm in the office, I'll raid the sample closet and get you a stock bottle."

"How many in a stock bottle?"

"Three, I think."

"Three! Is that all?

"That ought to last you for at least three years," Coop joked, "maybe more."

"Ha, ha, very funny," Jacob growled, but smiled anyway. "You should talk."

As Jacob walked away, Coop surreptitiously added another couple of dollars to Jacob's coins. From past experience, he knew Jacob was a notorious under-tipper.

After saying goodbye to Jacob, Coop headed straight for Urology Associates. Fortunately, Stanton Kingsley was in surgery today so he could talk to Christy and not feel like he was interrupting her busy day.

With as much of a poker face as he could muster, he asked Christy to step into his private office, then he closed the door.

"Uh...uh, Christy," Coop stammered, suddenly losing his poker face. He hadn't yet decided how he was going to broach the subject. Quickly, he settled on the direct approach. "Uh...Christy, what were you doing at Mojave Institute of Therapeutics and Health yesterday?"

"Huh?"

"I think you heard me."

"How...how did you know?" she mumbled, turning red.

"I saw you."

"You were there!

"Well," Coop stuttered, "well...uh..."

"You followed me!" Christy exclaimed, her voice ripe with indignation

"No, I was already there," Coop quickly explained, which was technically true. He'd followed Nathan Reed.

"What were you doing there?" Christy asked, clearly surprised.

"That's not important," Coop snapped. "Let's stick to the original question. What were you doing there? And I do want an answer."

"Well..."

"Well, what?" Coop was convinced her answer would go a long way to solving his problem.

"Well, if you must know," Christy finally blurted, "I went there to apply for a job and...and if they offer me one, I...I might just give my notice."

Coop was speechless. Certainly, this was not the answer he'd expected. Was she telling the truth? She seemed quite nervous, but maybe that was because she felt disloyal. He studied Christy's face. So, was that all there was to it, a job interview? No grandiose convoluted plot to proselytize and convert his patients to MITH. Was his little conspiracy theory blown to bits? Suddenly, he felt very foolish. Maybe he had jumped the gun. In general, he loathed alarmists, conspiracists... those people who saw sinister plots and ulterior motives in everything. Now it appeared he was doing just that.

"May I ask why?" Coop asked, though he thought he already knew the answer.

"They start out at two bucks an hour more than you're paying me right now."

"Well," he added lamely, "if you do decide to leave, give me as much notice as you can."

After excusing Christy, Coop sat down and lowered his head on his desk. Not only did he feel foolish, but also very discouraged. He was banking too much on Christy being the key, the Rosetta Stone. Now once again he was back to square one, still treading water and getting nowhere fast. Where should he go from here? As Jacob said, he needed some Yuccasote. Stating the obvious was the easy part; the difficult part was getting some. As far as he knew, there was only one source of Yuccasote, the MITH compound, and that would require another covert operation...

...But maybe there was another way. In his mind, Coop slowly worked out another plan. It was not very complicated, but try as he might he could think of nothing else. This time he decided on the direct approach, a frontal assault. What did he have to lose? Certainly, last night's covert operation netted him nothing—nothing except an indictment on two separate felony charges.

Thirty minutes later Coop was speeding down I-15 toward Little-field, Arizona. If he hurried, he might make it to MITH before closing time. After exiting at Littlefield, he flew through the town, fortunately there were no cops, then he took the first left into the forbidding Mojave Desert. For fall, it was uncharacteristically hot and in the distance he could see heat waves scintillating up from the hot desert floor.

By the time Coop steered the Dodge around the gray sandstone pillar, he still hadn't made up his mind on how he was going to do this. The only thing he'd decided for certain, he wasn't going to break in again.

Easing the Dodge up to the huge iron portcullis, Coop came to a stop next to the speaker box. He hesitated for a couple of seconds, then punched the red button.

An officious male voice crackled through the speaker. "Please state your business."

"I...I want to talk to the person in charge."

"And whom should I say is calling?"

"Cooper...Doctor Lawrence Cooper."

"And what shall I say is your business?"

"Uh...uh...it's medical." Coop tried to keep his voice firm.

There was a moment of speaker static. Apparently, the guard was checking with a higher authority. After a moment the male voice was back. "Okay, proceed to the large parking area, go into the central building and present yourself at the reception. Absolutely no detours. Understood?"

"Yes, sir," Coop said smartly, then shifted the Dodge into drive. That was much easier than he'd expected.

Simultaneously, as the speaker went dead, the heavy iron gates groaned, then slowly slid open. Following instructions, Coop parked in the central parking lot, the same place Christy and Nathan had parked, then headed straight for the main entrance. A huge portico, constructed of massive Douglas fir logs, arched over the entrance, protecting the two heavy plank doors.

Inside, it was magnificent. Even though Coop had been there before, it was in the dark and he really hadn't appreciated the true splendor of the place.

Continuing with the southwest theme, the lobby was tastefully decorated with an assortment of chest-high clay pots, Navajo blankets, kiva ladders and woven reed baskets. Colossal log pillars supported a twelve-foot high ceiling and carved into each pillar were at least two *nichos*, containing rare Hopi kachinas. The walls were adorned with large hand-woven Navajo tapestries and priceless tile and sand paintings. Coop took a moment to appreciate the room, then headed straight for the reception desk; the very same desk he crash-landed on the two nights earlier. Obviously, the mess he made was cleaned up.

"Hi, I'm Doctor Cooper," he said. "I would like to see..."

"...Oh, yes, Doctor Cooper," the receptionist flashed a grin. "Assistant Director Rob Belton will see you now. Richard will show you the way."

Dressed in the standard navy blue security guard uniform, which Coop was now quite familiar, Richard escorted Coop back to Dr. Belton's office. Thankfully, as far as Coop could tell, this guard was not one he'd wrestled with the other night. He was a bit older, roughly six feet tall, a hundred-and-eighty pounds and was definitely more polished, more used to dealing with the public, than those from the other night. Those guards were probably assigned to the nightshift.

With Richard leading, they crossed the central pod and proceeded down the wing just opposite to the one he chose the other night, the one to the Yuccasote laboratory. The sign over this wing simply read: *Business and Administration.* At the first door on the left, Richard stopped and knocked. When he heard an answering grunt, he opened the heavy plank door and let Coop enter first.

The room's decorations were also southwest and were also impressive. Native American handicrafts were scattered around the room. Several big clay pots were used as planters and contained an assortment of cacti: a tall Peruvian, an organ pipe and an Argentine toothpick. The walls were adorned with original paintings, mostly southwest landscapes by prominent artists. Coop couldn't help but wonder if one of Roger Callister's, Kylie's boyfriend, might be hanging there. In the center of the room and facing a large window overlooking a verdant lagoon was a black walnut, hand-carved Spanish desk.

With a single glance, Coop took all this in, then his eyes finally found the man. Appearing somewhat insignificant amongst all this this opulence, he was seated at the ornate Spanish desk.

At once he stood up and quickly walked toward Coop. Smiling he thrust forward a well-manicured hand.

"Hi, I'm Rob Belton, Assistant Director. I'm sorry but the Director is out of town." Belton's smile broadened to expose perfect white teeth. "I guess you'll have to be satisfied with the second string."

As Coop shook his hand, he quickly sized up Belton (English - a habitational name from any of various places called Belton). He was a small, but energetic, man in his early fifties. Everything about him was spotless and manicured. Adorned a pearl white lab coat, his short sandy hair was parted on the left side, recently trimmed, lightly oiled and neatly combed. As opposed to Jacob, his goatee was well groomed, as was his mustache. Under his starched white lab coat, he wore an equally starched and white shirt, a conservative navy blue tie, matching slacks and glossy black loafers. Surprisingly, there were no wrinkles in his pants, no spots or blemishes on his shirt and the underarms of his lab coat arms revealed no hint of yellow stains. Superficially, at least, he seemed friendly and forthright.

"Doctor Lawrence Cooper," Coop completed his half of the introduction. "Second string is fine by me."

"Come on in," Belton enthusiastically took Coop's arm and led him across the room. "Let's sit down where we can be more comfortable."

Belton chose two fur-upholstered, probably fox, willow chairs positioned directly in front of the picture window. Coop took the closest chair and Belton circled around to the other. Surprisingly the chairs were more comfortable than they looked, but Coop couldn't help but think PETA would have a stroke if they ever saw them.

"Can I get you something to drink? Ice tea or lemonade?"

"No, no thanks." Coop shook his head, even though lemonade did sound good.

"Well then, what can I do for you today, Doctor Cooper?" Belton leaned forward as though he really was interested.

"Well...well," Coop hesitated. As was becoming a pattern, he hadn't really thought this through. "Well, I've had several patients tell me what a marvelous place this is, so I thought I would come and see for myself."

"You've never been here?"

"No, first time," Coop lied. "It's a beautiful place."

Belton glanced sharply at Coop. "Why Doctor Cooper, you were here just last night."

So, that's the way he was going to play it, no fencing, no dancing and no pretense. That was fine by Coop. "Well...well, I want some information on one...no two things," Coop stammered, red-faced.

Belton nodded.

Coop plunged on. "First, I want to know what is going on here. What you're all about. Two, I want to know if my office manager, Christy Dennett, is really applying for a job here."

"Yes," Belton immediately acknowledged. "Miss Dennett is applying for a job, but if that is going to present a hardship to you, I will simply remove her application from consideration."

"Well," Coop hesitated. He hadn't expected that.

"No, I insist, I'll remove her from our candidate list."

"No, that won't be necessary," Coop replied, while silently thinking, perhaps I could pay you to take her. "She's not been happy with us anyway."

"We want nothing more than to maintain a good relationship with all the local medical community and particularly with you Doctor Cooper." Belton's smile was magnanimous.

"Why particularly me?"

"Well, let's just say you're the only one with whom our relationship looks a bit strained, like it has the real potential to go sour," Belton replied smoothly. "So as a gesture of good faith we are willing to drop all of the charges from last night."

"Can you do that?" Coop raised an eyebrow. "I thought it was out of your hands and now in the hands of the county attorney."

"Well, technically it is," Belton agreed, "but since we are the victims, I'm sure the county attorney would listen to us."

"What about the damages?"

"We have insurance."

To say Coop was amazed was an understatement. Dr. Belton seemed sincere, honest and gracious. "Thank you," Coop mumbled, "I do appreciate it. Right now I have plenty of other problems to deal with."

"I'll bet you do," Dr. Belton nodded.

"So you never answered my second question," Coop persisted, though now more subdued. "What is going on here?"

"We are a health and therapeutics clinic," Belton explained. "It's as simple as that."

"Yeah, I read the sign."

"We strive for a holistic approach to medicine," Belton continued, a bit condescending, "We treat mind, body and soul."

"Can't argue with that," Coop said. "That's kind of the holy trinity of medicine, like baseball, apple pie and motherhood."

"Huh...yeah...well, I suppose."

"So, what is Yuccasote?"

"What?" Belton answered a little too quickly.

The first little crack in the plaster façade, Coop though, suppressing a sly grin. "Yuccasote. You know the stuff I tried to steal last night."

"Oh, you mean Yuccasote," Belton laughed and recovered quickly. "I'm afraid I didn't hear you. It's a brand new chemotherapeutic drug we have developed and is now producing marvelous results."

"So, you are conducting human trials?"

"We don't have to. It's a natural product."

"But you are keeping statistics on your results and side effects?"

"Of course."

"Could I see that data?"

"It's not compiled yet," Belton said quickly.

"How about just telling me," Coop persisted. "Any problems with hemorrhage?"

"None."

"Are you sure?"

"I'm not at liberty to divulge that information."

"Yeah, I'll bet." Coop shifted his weight in the fur chair, generating small prickly bolts of static electricity.

"Well, if there's nothing else." Dr. Belton stood up.

Might just as well swing for the fences, Coop decided, also standing. "May I purchase some Yuccasote?"

"You know, Doctor Cooper, I would love to," Belton smiled, "however, there are patents pending. You know how that is."

"No, I don't guess I do," Coop couldn't keep the sarcasm out of his voice, "but I take it you are saying no."

"I'd really love to, but you know how it is."

"So, you treat cancer patients and develop new drugs. Is that your stated corporate mission? Anything else?" Coop was still bait fishing.

"Since you've asked," Belton sat down again. His perpetual smile now seemed more relaxed, more genuine. "There is more. We are doing a great and vital work here. You might even say God's work."

"God's work?"

"If healing the sick is God's work, and certainly Jesus thought it was, then that's what we are doing...God's work."

"Hippocrates said first do no harm," Coop quipped.

"Know the truth and the truth shall set you free," Belton quickly answered. "Jesus to his disciples."

"Who dares to say that he alone has found the truth?" Coop countered sharply. "Henry Wadsworth Longfellow."

"For this I was born, and for this I have come into the world, to bear witness to the truth...Jesus."

"Nothing's more dangerous than a pious man armed with a grain of truth...Lawrence A. Cooper."

"Like a stone cut out of a mountain without hands," Belton proclaimed, eyes shining fiercely, "nothing can stop the work of God...the Book of Daniel."

On the way back to St. George, Coop mulled over his visit with Dr. Rob Belton. Doctor of what? Coop still was not sure. It was a strange visit to say the least. He wasn't quite sure what to make of it. On one hand, Belton seemed friendly enough, sincere and compassionate. On the other hand, he appeared to possess a missionary's zeal, a crusader's determination and the classic tunnel vision of a fanatic. Even though Coop appreciated his offer to drop the burglary and destruction charges, fanatical anything made him uncomfortable.

The visit was friendly enough, but on closer analysis what had he learned? Very little, except Christy Dennett was indeed applying for a job at MITH and they offered their patients some kind of holistic treatment. Unfortunately, he still had no idea what that meant. Furthermore, he had no idea what Yuccasote was, other than a brown smelly liquid, and even more distressing he still did not have a sample. As Jacob Heinz aptly pointed out, Yuccasote was the Rosetta Stone and it if his investigation was to move forward it was imperative he obtained some. But the real question was how? Certainly, Coop did not want to launch another covert operation and he'd just tried the direct approach, which had netted him nothing.

Frustrated, he glanced out the window at the passing Mojave Desert. His eyes were heavy from spending last night in in the Washington County Correction Facility and the associated lack of sleep. He willed them to stay open and tried to concentrate on the passing desert.

In the golden glow of the setting sun, the pygmy desert plants looked less threatening, almost cartoon-like with exaggerated shadows ballooning way out of proportion to their size. The shadow from a six-foot Joshua projected some thirty-feet or more. Mesmerized by the desert and the play of sun and shadow, Coop momentarily forgot his troubles. Without really noticing, he turned onto the piedmont plain.

In the spring, fall and winter, the desert was indeed a beautiful and fascinating place. It had evolved its own unique ecosystem not found anywhere else in the world. Plants, like cacti, gave up their broad leaves in favor of needles and waxy skin. Likewise the fauna was just as well adapted. Reptiles, snakes, lizards, and tortoises survived by evolving a protective scaly skin. Unlike humans, the lacked sweat glands and stubbornly clung to the older, but more efficient energy system of cold-blooded metabolism.

I wonder, Coop idly thought, if cold-blooded creatures get cancer like his patients...

...Cancer! His patients! That was it. It suddenly dawned on him where he could get some Yuccasote. Stomping down on the accelerator, his trailing parachute dust cloud immediately ballooned higher. If he hurried he could make it back to St. George by dark.

It was so simple he was embarrassed he had not thought of it earlier. The solution was right in front of him all the time and with his own special brand of tunnel vision, he'd failed to see it. College students were almost always broke!

15

Doctors will get off their pedestals
when patients get off their knees.
—Anonymous

Back in St. George, Coop watched the streetlights wink on as he drove through the rapidly gathering dusk. Turning off Bluff Street, he headed straight for Dixie State University. A block before the campus he turned left and onto Nathan Reed's street. As he parked the Dodge squarely in front of Nate's basement apartment, he was relieved to see a light on and the white Toyota in the driveway. Nathan must be home. Coop climbed out of the Dodge and stretched out his cramped muscles, then headed straight for Nathan's door.

Standing in front of the door, Coop raised his hand to knock. He hesitated, taking a moment to collect his thoughts, then pounded on the door.

As Nathan opened the door, his eyes slowly widened with both surprise and disbelief. Then he flushed a crimson red, like he'd just been caught with his hand in the Salvation Army's Christmas pot.

"D...D...Doctor Cooper!" he finally stammered.

"Hi, Nathan," Coop greeted him.

"W...w...what'cha doing here?"

"Why don't we go inside and talk?" Coop suggested, then pushed past him.

"O...o...okay, Doctor Cooper," Nathan stuttered, stepping aside, allowing Coop to lead the way.

Nathan's apartment was just what Coop expected for a bachelor student apartment. There was clutter everywhere. Books and computer paper, some full sheets some wadded, littered the threadbare over-stuffed couch, as well as the blonde coffee table and the dirty green-shag carpet. Occupying the far half of the room was what Coop presumed was the kitchen, only because he could see dirty silverware, dishes and plastic cups heaped on the counters. On closer inspection, some cups still contained an unidentifiable liquid with floating furry islands on a layer of film. Some of the dishes were stippled with unknown food particles, a few growing a gray green fungus.

Separate from the main room, but still visible through the open door was the bedroom. Even from his vantage point, Coop could see dirty clothes strewn everywhere, covering the unmade bed, nightstands and heaped on a small student desk, which looked like it hadn't been used in a very long time. He suspected the bedroom floor was hardwood, though it was difficult to tell for sure. It also was carpeted with a thick layer of clothing.

Abruptly Coop sneezed. The apartment had a stale moldy stench, like mixing the odor from of a gym locker with that of a root cellar. Still sniffling and wishing he had a brought a Benadryl, Coop pinched his nose and looked for a place to sit down. Undoubtedly, it had been a very long time since this apartment was cleaned or even aired out.

Sweeping some discarded computer paper aside, Coop quickly inspected the now visible fabric, decided nothing was moving, then gingerly sat down on the green couch. Nathan grabbed one of two metal folding chairs from the kitchen, positioned it on the far side of the cluttered coffee table, then sat down facing Coop.

"W...w...wha'cha you doing here, Doctor Cooper?" he croaked.

"How are you feeling, Nathan?" Coop ignored Nathan's question. But Coop's question was not a merely rhetorical, as Nathan's former doctor he really was interested in his health.

"I...I'm sorry about the mess," Nathan blurted, glancing around the room. "I...I never seem to have the time..."

"That's okay, Nate. You didn't know I was coming." Coop then softly added, "I was once a college student."

"And I'm sorry, Doctor Cooper, that I never came back."

"That's okay too," Coop replied, "I'm not here to chastise you, but I really am curious how you're feeling."

"O...o...okay, most of the time. At first real good, now some good days and some bad."

"Any nosebleeds or prolonged bleeding, say if you cut yourself shaving?"

"I...I don't shave much, Doctor Cooper." Nate stroked the scraggily hair on his face.

"Well, you look pretty good," Coop observed. "I really thought without treatment you'd be in much worse shape."

Nathan blushed and looked down at his feet. "A...a...actually, I am getting some treatment."

"Oh!" Coop tried to look surprised. "From a doctor I know?"

"Nah...no, I don't think so," Nathan stuttered. "It's not traditional medicine."

"So what kind of treatment are we talking about?" Coop tried to sound casual. He sensed Nathan was about to clam up. "You can tell me Nathan. I'm probably the least judgmental person you know."

For a minute, Nathan was silent. He sighed deeply, then continued, like he was happy to finally have someone to share his burden. "It's a holistic approach, treating the whole patient, mind, body and soul."

Coop frowned. Just a few hours ago he heard the very same thing from Rob Belton at MITH. Trying to hide his annoyance, Coop shrugged and instead said, "sounds intriguing."

"M...m...my parents are dead against it."

"They're only concerned for what's best for you."

"I...I...I know." Nathan seemed close to tears. "We had a big fight and don't talk anymore."

"You should give them a call, Nathan, and try to make up. Some day you might need their support."

"I...I...I know, but they just don't understand."

"Nevertheless, you should try. You might be surprised."

"M...m...maybe I will." Nathan wiped away a tear.

After a moment of silence, Coop continued, "so where are these treatments administered?"

"Sometimes at the center and sometimes right here in my apartment."

"Where's the center?"

"I...I...I can't tell you, Doctor Cooper."

"That's okay," Coop said quickly. He knew anyway. "I understand the need to treat the whole patient, but they must be using a drug too. You look too good for only receiving counseling and spiritual therapy."

Again Nathan hesitated, then forged ahead. "Yeah, it's a new drug, really a wonder drug. They call it Yuccasote."

"Never heard of it," Coop fibbed, "but I must say it looks like it is working."

"Yeah, it is...mostly" Nathan agreed. "I was much better at first, but maybe not feeling quite so good now."

"Do you have some here?"

Nathan nodded. "In the bathroom."

"Can I see it?"

After another moment of hesitation, Nathan nodded again, got up from the chair and disappeared into the bedroom. A minute later he returned and handed Coop a brown glass bottle.

Coop was very familiar with the bottle. It was exactly the same as the ones he'd found stocked in the laboratory at MITH. The same ones he'd knocked over and tried to steal. Nathan's was the larger size, a pint bottle with a cork stopper. It was about two thirds empty, the bottom third contained the same syrupy amaretto liquid. The pint bottle sported a plain white label. Though a bit stained and smudged, it simply read: **YUCCASOTE**. No directions on how to take it, no list of ingredients, no directory of possible side effects and no instructions on how to handle an overdose.

"You got any more of this?" Coop idly rotated the bottle in his hands.

"Yeah, I've got another whole week's supply."

"How long will this last?"

"That's about two days worth," Nathan calculated. "It tastes like shit...uh...sorry Doctor Cooper. It tastes like crap."

"Don't worry about it," Coop grinned. "I've heard that word before. Maybe even used it myself once or twice."

"Yeah, well, I suppose." Nathan smiled for the first time. "I just don't want to teach you any bad words, D...D...Doctor Cooper."

"Nathan," Coop leaned forward, suddenly all business. "Nathan, I would like to buy this bottle from you."

"I...I don't know, Doctor Cooper," Nathan replied, shaking his head. "I'm not supposed to do that. They keep pretty close track of it."

"Tell them you knocked it over and spilled some, or you got mixed up on the dosage and had been taking a little too much."

"Well, I have been taking a little extra," Nathan admitted.

"So you'll run out early anyway."

"But I'm supposed to return the empty bottles."

"Tell them you accidentally knocked it off the sink and broke it."

"W...w...why would I do that?"

"Look, Nathan," Coop reached for his wallet, "I'll pay for it. Here's a hundred dollars."

"I...I...I don't know, Doctor Cooper," Nathan shook his head again. "I could get into big trouble."

"How so?" Coop still waved the bill in front of him. "Nobody will ever know. How about two hundred dollars?" Coop pulled another hundred-dollar bill from his wallet, dangling it like a carrot in front of Nathan.

Nathan hesitated, then gulped, but did not take his eyes off the money.

"Unless things have changed drastically since I was in college, you must be strapped for cash." Coop further tempted him by holding up two Ben Franklins to the light.

Nathan waffled for a couple more seconds, then grabbed the bills like they were birds about to fly. He then shoved the bottle of Yuccasote into Coop's hands.

"Do you want to make some more money?" Might just as well go for it now while the iron was hot.

"How?" Nathan asked guardedly, his eyes narrowed.

"You say sometimes they do your holistic treatments right here?"

"Yeah."

"I'll give you another two hundred dollars if you'll let me watch."

"T...t...they'll never allow that," Nathan stammered.

"Hide me somewhere in here." Coop gestured by sweeping his hand around the jumbled room. "They'll never even know." Then silently he added, "in all this clutter."

Nathan stared at the money in his hand and thought about it a moment longer. "H...h...how much you willing to pay?"

"Another two hundred dollars."

"M...m...make it three."

"Okay, three it is," Coop agreed. "So tell me when the treatment will be."

"I don't yet know myself."

"Well then as soon as you can, let me know."

"Where's my m...m...money?" Nathan asked suspiciously as he watched Coop replace his wallet.

"You'll get the money after you let me watch."

"O...o...okay, I'll call you, but I'll need your number."

Coop scratched down both his cell and home phone numbers on his business card and gave them to Nathan.

"Give me as much lead time as you can." Coop stood up and began to leave. Halfway out the door he turned back. "And Nate, I really do think you should to come to my office and let me check you out. Get some blood tests, a CT scan and maybe a chest x-ray."

"I...I...I can't afford it."

"We'll work something," Coop assured. "I won't charge you a doctor's fee and there're government programs available for the rest."

"I...I...I'll think about it, Doctor Cooper," Nathan stuttered as Coop closed the door.

Crossing the street, Coop climbed back in the Dodge. He couldn't help but smile as he held up the pint bottle of Yuccasote. Though it was now pitch dark, the light from the overhead streetlight glinted off the opaque brown glass, giving it an almost golden or caramel sheen.

Coop nodded his head with satisfaction and placed the bottle in the glove compartment. At long last, he was making some progress. For the first time in a very long time, he was in a good mood. Things were finally going his way. Tomorrow he would take this bottle of Yuccasote to the Cedar City campus of Southern Utah University and have his old friend, Professor Marcus Westover, analyze the contents. Marcus was in his own right a fairly renowned scientist. His specialty was the chemical toxicology of desert plants, so having him investigate Yuccasote should be right down his alley.

Also, it would give Coop a chance to follow up on the oily cloth sponge he'd previously dropped off after the tack shed fire. He still strongly suspected it was olive oil, but it would be nice to know for sure.

In the dark, Coop smiled again and shook his head again. With all that had happened lately, he'd almost forgot about the surgical sponge. Even though it was only a little more than a week since the fire, it seemed like it was a lifetime...probably because his present life bore no resemblance whatsoever to his previous life, the one of just a month ago. Lately, his life resembled a rollercoaster ride or perhaps a better analogy, an EKG strip showing frequent runs of ominous life threatening V-tach.

Suddenly, Coop realized how exhausted he was. Firing up the Dodge, he headed for home. He ached deep in his bones and his muscles felt like boiled pasta. It was no wonder he was tired; he really hadn't slept much for forty-eight hours. Now he longed for nothing more than to be recumbent, for a good night in his own bed with his good buddy Malachi.

As he turned into Diamond Valley, he once again became anxious. Ever since the fire, he fought a wave of foreboding every time he entered the valley. Quickly, he scanned the black void ahead. Thank God, there were no leaping orange flames, but nevertheless as he drove down his gravel road he couldn't shake the feeling something was wrong.

Parking in the driveway he got out and immediately checked the house. Malachi rushed up, his tail wagging, and Coop breathed a long sigh of relief. At least Malachi was okay. And from the outside, the house appeared to be okay as well. The doors were locked; none were forced open. Inside, everything looked okay too. No evidence of unwanted guests, nothing broken and nothing out of place. Grinning sheepishly at his paranoia, Coop decided he might have overreacted.

Nevertheless, he grabbed a flashlight and headed for the horse corral. Pausing briefly at what was once the tack and feed shed, he flashed the light on the charred skeleton. "Damn, what a shame," he mumbled to himself. With everything happening so fast, he'd not found time to clean up the mess, let alone rebuild. At this rate, maybe he never would. Sighing loudly, he continued on to the horse corrals.

The pipe gate was gapping wide open! Why? Feeling a renewed sense of dread, Coop entered the darkened corral, quickly arcing his flashlight back and forth. At the far edge of the corral, he thought he saw a dark indistinct mound. He stopped and refocused his light on it. It didn't move. Probably, it was nothing. Maybe a large pile of horse dung. He turned away, but Malachi bolted for the object and began sniffing. Coop moved in closer. The mound took shape. It was a large animal.

Oh my God, he had a horse down!

Sprinting the remaining ten yards, he dropped down on a knee to examine the horse. It was one of his two duns. Then he recognized the white star on the forehead and the three white-stocked feet. It was Stepper! His Tennessee walker, his favorite riding horse. Stepper was lying on his left side, his head resting on the ground. Though his eyes were wide open, they looked vacant. His mouth also gapped wide, allowed his purple tongue to flop out over his alabaster teeth.

Coop groped the neck for a carotid pulse. There was none. As he withdrew his hand, it felt wet and sticky. Redirecting the light, he immediately shuddered. His hand was smeared with bright crimson blood!

Fighting to control his emotions, he forced himself to investigate further. There was a large puddle of partly congealed blood, forming a halo around Stepper's head. Coop inspected his open mouth. It was clean, no blood on the tongue, teeth or pooled in the oral cavity. He then inspected the anus. No blood there either. Obviously, the horse bled to death, but not from the G.I tract. Next he flashed the light on the penis. Again there was no blood. That most likely ruled out a urinary tract hemorrhage.

Calling Malachi, Coop backed off, sat down and tried to think. He was damn fond of that horse and struggled to control his emotions. He forced himself to concentrate. Using his medical training, he took it step by step, starting with what he already knew. There was no question about it, the horse bled to death, of that he was certain. Unfortunately, he was becoming something of an expert on hemorrhagic death. Anyway, it didn't take a doctor or a sophisticated lab to make that diagnosis. The proof was right there in front of him, right on the ground, at least a couple of gallons or more. But, if the blood didn't exit from a natural orifice that left only one other possibility, it had to come from an unnatural orifice, more specifically a wound. Furthermore, the location of the puddle, where the blood was most concentrated, would suggest a head or neck wound.

Getting up once again, Coop steeled himself, then leaned over the gelding. Parting the hair with one hand and directing the light with the other, he systematically inspected the neck and head. The first time over he found absolutely nothing and neither did he the second. He tried to roll the horse over so he could examine the downside, but couldn't budge him. The horse weighed well over a thousand pounds, couple that with the rigidity of his muscles from rigor mortis and there was no way he was going to roll Stepper.

Still fighting with his emotions, Coop headed back to the garage. After some searching, he found a twelve-foot link chain, fired up his Kubota tractor and headed back to the horse. Carefully, he looped the chain around both the front and hind feet, then secured it to the cross-bar of the Kubota. Climbing back on the tractor, he slowly worked the gas feed forward and rolled the horse to his right side. Now he could inspect what had been the downside of the head and neck.

About mid-neck, he noted a small clot clinging to the horse's hair. Holding the flashlight with his teeth, Coop gently parted the hair. At first he saw nothing. Moving in closer, he meticulously went over the area again, this time scrapping off the small clot. What the hell was this? He looked again to be sure. No question about it, there was a tiny puncture wound, no bigger in diameter than an ice pick. Coop saw the wound missed both the jugular vein and carotid artery, but by no more than an inch. He was convinced, however, those major vessels had been spared. But regardless of that, it appeared this small wound was the source of the disproportionate and massive bleeding.

For the next fifteen minutes, Coop once again covered every square inch of the head and neck, then went over it again. There was absolutely nothing else. There were no other wounds, scratches or abrasions, no matter how small.

Sitting down again, Coop tried to think this through. It was puzzling to say the least. There was just no way a horse should bleed to death from a wound this small unless it penetrated a major vessel. And this one definitely had not. Normally, a small wound would clot and seal within five minutes with maybe ten to fifteen cc of blood loss at most. There was no way a horse, or a human for that matter, should bleed to death from such a trivial injury unless there was some kind of a concomitant coagulopathy, something wrong with their clotting mechanism. In fact, it would have to be a scenario very similar to what happened Betty Tsongas, Gordon Flowers and Hector Gonzalez.

Another puzzling thing, it was a puncture wound and looked like it surely could have come from an ice pick. The problem was, however, nobody used ice picks anymore. Coop couldn't remember the last time he'd seen one. Of course, the injury didn't necessarily have to be an ice pick; it could be from anything small and round, for instance 12-penny nail. But it would be next to impossible to hand drive a nail into a horse's neck and have him hold still long enough to do it. No, it had be a weapon, one with a shaft like an ice pick, and also a handle. Something for the perpetrator to grip in order to generate enough force to penetrate skin and something which could be swung with enough speed the horse wouldn't have time to react.

Even though it was a warm night, Coop shivered at the thought. Suddenly he felt cold, very cold. Was it possible? Could there be a link between Stepper's death and his surgical deaths? They all bled to death under the similar and very strange circumstances. Was Stepper killed by the same thing his three patients? He knew it sounded farfetched, but was Yuccasote somehow also involved in all this?

Certainly, a horse could not take Yuccasote on his own volition. A horse had to be deliberately fed or injected the compound, whatever it was. Assuming all this was true, then this was first-degree murder, the premeditated taking of a life! Then it followed there must be an equine murderer out there. The next question begging to be answered was who? Who would do such a cowardly thing? Obviously, it had to be someone with access to Yuccasote. If he had enemies at MITH, he surely didn't know it. Yes, he broke into their compound and smashed up their lab a bit, but Rob Belton already indicated they were ready to forgive him. Was Belton serious or just toying with him? Had he offered to drop the charges just so he could exact his revenge another way? No way to know for sure, but that seemed a little farfetched. So, if not MITH, then who? Questions swirled in Coop's mind like driftwood in a whirlpool, but answers were not immediately forthcoming.

Of course, if there were no answers, the best he could do was to continue his investigation. First, he needed to stop all this wild speculating and figure out for sure who and what killed Stepper. To do that, he needed proof, physical evidence. Perhaps, he could also have his friend, Dr. Marcus Westover, analyze Stepper's blood, checking for any trace of Yuccasote. To do that, however, he would need Stepper's serum, but by now his blood had all clotted or was spilled on the ground. He could have Marcus analyze the clotted blood, but that probably would do no good. He sincerely doubted there would be any Yuccasote or any other drug for that matter, contained in the clot. Drugs were only found in the serum.

After thinking about it a little more, he finally gave up and walked away, Malachi following at his heels. There was simply no good way to do it.

After a few halting steps, he stopped and scratched his head. As with the placenta, most drugs passed through the eye-blood barrier into the vitreous humor, the fluid filled compartment directly behind the lens. The difference being, unlike blood the vitreous humor did not clot.

Just the thought made Coop recoil. He didn't know if he could do it. After all this was his baby, he'd raised him from a colt. Unfortunately, he had no choice. There was simply no other way.

Struggling to compose himself, he slowly shuffled back to the horse. Then gritting his teeth, and with tears streaming down his face, Coop reached down and with considerable effort plucked out Stepper's right eye.

16

Coop woke up late the next morning with Malachi snoring gently beside him. With all that was going on, including the death of Stepper, he didn't think he would sleep, but he must have. The lack of sleep and the seemingly endless stress must have finally caught up with him.

Nursing a bit of a sleep hangover, he felt listless and sluggish and struggled with a vague headache somewhere behind his eyes. Slowly, he crawled out of bed, then shuffled toward the kitchen. Tail wagging, Malachi jumped up, stretched and followed. Mechanically, Coop ground coffee beans, placed the grounds in the drip chamber and added water, then put a sliced bagel in the toaster.

Still half asleep, he fed Malachi, then slouched down on a kitchen chair, closed his eyes once again and waited for the bagel to pop up. Cracking open an eye to check on the toaster, he caught sight of Stepper's eyeball, magnified by the thick glass of the Mason jar. It was a grotesque sight. Shuddering, he removed the jar from the table, placed it onto the counter, then covered it with a checkered red and white kitchen towel—one of Kylie's. When he went to bed last night, he worried he would spend the entire night with grisly nightmares about Stepper, but if he had he didn't remember. Maybe exhaustion does rob us of our dreams.

Sitting back down at the table, he mentally went over his plans for the day. First, after finishing breakfast and showering, he needed to make arrangements for somebody to come bury Stepper. The problem was not enough room on the ranch for the grave, obviously there was.

No, the problem was digging the grave. If he were to dig a grave that size by hand, it would take several days. By then, Stepper would be bloated and decomposing. What he needed was a backhoe.

Next, he needed to take his two specimens, Nathan's bottle of Yuccasote and Stepper's eye, fifty miles north to Cedar City and personally deliver them to Dr. Marcus Westover. While there, he hoped to get a report on the surgical sponge. After last night's murder, he was pretty certain someone was out to get him. It was hard to pass off two acts of violence committed within a single week as random. No, these acts appeared to be directed and the target was him!

Suddenly, the bagels popped up accompanied by a thick plume of black smoke. The carbonaceous odor of burnt toast rapidly filled the kitchen. Before the smoke alarm went off, Coop threw open a window along with the kitchen door, hoping to create a cross draft, then he grudgingly scraped the charred layer into the sink. Once he was down to brown, he slathered on some margarine and poured himself a cup of steaming black coffee. Sighing, he took a bite of crispy bagel and watched the cloud of smoke funnel out of the open door. At least the coffee should be good. Raising the mug to his lips, he took a long draught. The hot liquid running down the back of his throat felt good and...and gritty. He gagged! Hurrying to the sink, he spat out a mouthful of coffee grounds. Damnit, he'd made shepherd's coffee. Somehow, he'd forgotten to place the paper filter into the plastic basket.

God, how he missed Kylie! He really wasn't much of a bachelor.

Throwing the coffee down the sink, Coop munched on the burnt bagel. It wasn't bad if you liked the taste of charcoal. He longed for the lazy mornings, in reality they were very few, when he and Kylie would sit here, sipping coffee, real filtered coffee, and read the two-inch thick Sunday newspaper. He would grab the world news, she the southwest living section. That seemed like a long time ago. Where was she now? Probably still in Phoenix. At least that's where he sent her checks, not to a residential address, but to a post office box. Sucker checks, as Spaulding called them. He hadn't heard from her in over three months, but he almost never did unless the money was late. Jacob was right; this was insane. Why not go ahead and get a divorce?

At first he'd thought she would sow a few wild oats, then come back. But that was beginning to look less and less likely. And why should she come back? He was basically paying her to stay away. What a chump he was. Already, it was almost time to get another check off in the mail. There was no way he was going to continue doing that. Not only was it insane, like Jacob said, but now as an unemployed man with massive looming bills, he simply couldn't afford it.

He brooded in silence, then his thoughts drifted to Samantha Rose Jardine. Right now she was probably wrapped in a satin robe drinking cappuccino with Josh on a quaint Spanish patio overlooking the flawless turquoise water of the Caribbean. They would have a leisurely breakfast, certainly not burnt bagels and shepherd's coffee, then go scuba diving at Palancar or Santa Rosa Reef. Oh well, there was nothing to gain in worrying about that. She was now, and always had been, way out of his league anyway. Later today, right after he got back from Cedar City, he would call his insurance carrier, UMIA, and request another attorney. He still had an upcoming malpractice trial to prepare for and probably two more to follow. No, there certainly was no point in torturing himself with the likes of Samantha Rose Jardine.

Checking his watch, Coop choked down the rest of his burnt bagel with a glass of water. Time to get going. He reached for the phone and called a neighbor from across the valley who had a backhoe and arranged for him to come and bury Stepper. Just as he hung up the phone, the doorbell rang. Groaning out loud, he got up from the kitchen counter and with Malachi at his heels headed to the front door. The one thing he didn't feel like today was early morning visitors.

The moment he opened the door, Coop knew this was going to be another bad day. For standing there under his arched Spanish portico were two officers, both wearing the uniform of the Washington County Sheriff's Department. They looked fairly young, clean-shaven, well muscled and serious.

The shorter one, built like a refrigerator on steroids, all torso and no neck, did most of the talking.

"You Lawrence A. Cooper?" he demanded, not bothering with pleasantries.

"Good morning to you, too," Coop said sarcastically. He'd about had it with men in uniform. "And who might you be?"

Somewhat taken aback, the square one hesitated, then apparently decided it was a legitimate question. "I'm Sergeant Kim Gaye," he nodded at his partner, "and this is Deputy June Posey."

In spite of the situation, Coop couldn't help but smile. Talk about oxymorons, names that didn't fit. The incredible hulk certainly didn't look like a Gaye and the other deputy did not resemble a June Posy. "What can I do for you, Sergeant Gaye?" Coop asked, suppressing a grin.

"Somethin' funny?" Gaye demanded.

"Nah, I just got off the phone," Coop nodded back toward the house as though that was the answer. "Is there something I can do for you?"

"We are here to arrest you," the linebacker declared flatly, his confidence now fully restored.

"On what charge?" By now Coop knew he was entitled to that much.

"Negligent homicide." Sergeant Gaye quickly stepped forward with cuffs in hand and grabbed Coop's shoulder, attempting to turn him. For a big man, he was surprisingly light on his feet.

Seeing that as a threat, Malachi snarled, bared his fangs and wedged himself between Coop and the Sergeant. In his haste to retreat, Gaye stumbled backwards, dropping the handcuffs and stumbling off the porch.

Coop was both amazed and proud of Malachi. Like most labs, Malachi was social and affectionate by nature. Coop had never seen this side of him.

"Hold on a minute." Coop took advantage of Malachi's protection. "Can I at least shower and put on some clothes."

Visibly shaken, Gaye considered his request. "You can put on some clothes, but no shower. And take care of that dog before I shoot him."

"I wouldn't even joke about that," Coop's voice turned deadly, "if I were you."

They glared at each other for a couple more seconds, then Coop called Malachi over and settled him down. Then with Malachi in tow and Sergeant Gaye following at a safe distance, Coop headed for the bedroom. Gaye instructed Deputy Posey to maintain his post at the front door. Briefly, Coop toyed with the idea of attempting an escape, but there was no way he could out run or out muscle young Sergeant Gaye.

With a frantic Malachi watching, Gaye and Posey stuffed Coop into the backseat of their cruiser, then handcuffed him. Forty-five minutes later, he was back at the Purgatory Flats Correctional Facility.

Unfortunately, the same booking officer was on duty. Of course, Coop remembered his name, but pretended he didn't. He wanted to avoid any lengthy conversations which familiarity often breeds. Fortunately, the officer still seemed embarrassed and wanted to keep things strictly professional.

Without looking him in the eye, he told Coop he would definitely be in jail for the rest of the day. More than likely his preliminary hearing would not be scheduled until tomorrow. The hearing, the Sergeant went on to explain, probably would not be via video linkup as was the last one. With homicide charges, the accused usually faced the judge in person. At that time, the charges would be officially filed and bail would be set. "And," the Sergeant added, "this is maybe overstepping my bounds, but for a case like this I would strongly recommend you have a lawyer present."

"Can't I represent myself?" Coop asked. He certainly was not going to call Samantha Rose again. "That's what I did the last time."

"Yeah, you can, but this is much more serious, a Class A felony," the Sergeant advised. "Trust me, you're going to want an attorney for this one."

"I don't know any attorneys."

"Use the Yellow Pages, they're full of 'em."

Coop did make a phone call, but not to a lawyer. Once again he called the neighbor boy, Todd Snow, to care for Malachi and the horses. Though Todd readily agreed, Coop suspected both he and Malachi were getting a little tired of this. Coop sweetened the deal by offering to pay him double, a gesture he really couldn't afford.

This time he was issued the standard apparel for Washington County prisoners, a bright hunter orange jumpsuit and he did get his own cell, the last on the right in A-block. Finally, he thought with wry grin, they're taking me seriously. But in a way, he was happy for the privacy. At least, he did not have to talk to anyone and the only time he had to mingle with other prisoners was for meals and periods of exercise, which he mostly declined. Other than that, the solitude gave him plenty of time to think and plan.

Coop considered randomly selecting an attorney from the yellow pages as was suggested; there were eleven pages of them, most with color photographs. But he didn't know any of them and furthermore tomorrow was not the trial, only a hearing. Surely, he could handle that by himself. Tomorrow, the important thing was for him to get out on bail and get those samples, the Yuccasote and Stepper's eye, up to Dr. Westover.

Once again, Coop did not sleep very well, but certainly better than his first night in jail. At least he had a cot. Maybe he was getting used to prison life after all.

Following breakfast, Coop was informed his hearing was scheduled for 1:00 p.m. in the 5th Circuit Court of Judge Judith Pleasants. His spirits sagged a little when he heard the news. Judge Pleasants was the same judge he'd appeared before yesterday via teleo/videoconference. Hopefully, Coop thought, she does this so much she won't remember me, but deep down he knew this was probably wishful thinking.

At 12:30 Coop was plucked from the lunchroom by two deputies and escorted via patrol car to Judge Pleasants' court. Flanked by the officers, he was seated in the gallery, first row.

Coop surveyed the courtroom with the interest of a tourist. In his forty-one years, this was his first time here or in any courtroom for that matter. It was a large rectangular room with a raised dais on one end on which featured the judge's massive desk or in legal jargon, the bar. On the wall above the desk, or bar, were two picture portraits, one of the present governor of the great state of Utah and the other of the president of the United States of America. Slightly lower than the bar off to the right was the witness stand, then a bit further to the right, the jury box. Directly in front of, but below the judicial bench, were two rectangular oaken tables, apparently one for the plaintiff and his or her counsel and the other for the defense. Separating this working area from the gallery and running the entire breadth of the room was a restraining rail fence, also constructed of oak. Jutting out over the gallery was a small balcony, presently cordoned off and closed. Apparently they were not expecting a large crowd today. There were no windows and all light was artificial, giving the place the ambiance of an over-illuminated cave.

Promptly at 1:00 with black robe tails fluttering behind her, Judge Pleasants (a name for someone from Piacenza, Italy-formerly called Placentia) marched briskly into the court.

"All rise," the bailiff barked, "the Fifth Judicial Court in and for the county of Washington in the state of Utah is now in session. The honorable Judge Judith Pleasants presiding. Please come to order."

Without offering a single glance at her court, Judge Pleasants brusquely took her seat, then still without raising her head, waved for everyone to sit down. With gray head bowed, she silently consulted her docket.

"The Fifth District Court of the State of Utah will now proceed with the preliminary hearing of the State of Utah verses Lawrence Addison Cooper," she announced, head still bent. Finally she looked up and peered down over her reading glasses at the court. "Who will represent the state of Utah?"

"I will, Your Honor," Assistant County Attorney, Bryan Bledsoe (English from Gloucestershire), replied, standing. The whites of his blue eyes were bloodshot and his sandy hair was mussed, as was his three-piece suit. In a word, Bledsoe looked overworked.

"Come, come now, Mister Bledsoe," Pleasants chided, "by now you know the routine. State your name for the record."

"Bryan F. Bledsoe, County Attorney," Bledsoe responded, unable to fully conceal his irritation.

"Now then, who will represent Mister Cooper?" the judge asked.

"I will, Ma'am," Coop stood, parroting Mr. Bledsoe.

Judge Pleasants' scowl deepened even further. "You may address me as Your Honor," she snapped. "And who might you be?"

"Lawrence Addison Cooper, but my friends call me Coop. I...I guess I'm the defendant."

"Ah, yes, Mister Cooper or should I address you as Doctor Cooper?" Judge Pleasants said, a trace of sarcasm imbued in her gravelly voice. "I remember you from yesterday. You're becoming quite a regular."

Coop's heart sank. The anonymity he hoped for just vanished. "Yeah...yes, Ma'am...uh...Your Honor, I will represent myself."

"Surely, doctor," Judge Pleasants growled, "you remember the old proverb, he who serves as his own physician has a fool for a patient?"

Coop nodded.

"Doctor Cooper, please answer verbally," Pleasants admonished. "The court stenographer cannot record a nod."

"Uh...yes, I've heard it."

"Well, that same proverb holds true for the practice of law. Please retain a lawyer, Doctor Cooper."

"I...I will, Your Honor," Coop stammered. "I thought I had one, but it didn't work out."

"Humph!" Pleasants snorted, then turned to the county attorney. "Mister Bledsoe, what charges do you bring against the good doctor this time?"

"The county wishes to charge Doctor Lawrence Addison Cooper with negligent homicide, a Class A felony, Your Honor."

"Just to make sure this is not some kind of vendetta or legal harassment of the good doctor," Pleasants said, "why don't you briefly tell me what you have?"

"Well first of all we have a dead patient, bled to death in the operating room, then we have an affidavit from the O.R. nurse stating Doctor Cooper was operating impaired, under the influence of drugs or alcohol or both. Finally we have a warrant copy of an Incident Report from the operating room filed that same day, which also claims Doctor Cooper was impaired."

"May I see them?" the judge asked.

Bledsoe handed over the documents without further comment.

"I see," Pleasants frowned. "No toxicology screen?"

"No, Your Honor."

"No blood alcohol level?"

"No, Your Honor."

Judge Pleasants' frown deepened as she mulled this over. "Okay, I guess this is enough. I will bind Doctor Cooper over for trial on the charge of negligent homicide," Judge Pleasants turned to Coop. "Do you understand this charge brought against you, Doctor?"

"Yeah, I guess, and I...I plead, not guilty," Coop blurted. In the heat of the battle, he'd forgotten Samantha's earlier advice.

"This is an arraignment," Judge Pleasants snapped, "we do not plead here. Would you like me to explain the charges or not?"

"Well...uh...yes, I guess, Ma'...uh...Your Honor,"

Pleasants fired Coop a warning glance, then began, "Negligent homicide is the willful taking of a human life by one's own carelessness or neglect. Usually, this is a life, which was in someway entrusted to his or her care. It is a Class A felony punishable with a substantial fine, up to ten thousand dollars, and jail time up to fifteen years or both. Any questions?"

"Uh...what is the difference between this and the negligence of malpractice?"

"I suppose it's a matter of degree" Judge Pleasants replied. "Gross or wanton negligence is a crime, simple ineptness is malpractice. Any other questions?"

"No...uh...Your Honor."

"Now, then," Judge Pleasants said, "let's talk bail. Your thoughts, Mister Bledsoe?"

"As you know, Doctor Cooper is a repeat offender and I think he is definitely a flight risk. He has the money and means to go anywhere he..."

"...Hold on a minute, Ma'am...uh...Madam!" Coop blurted out. "I'm flat brok..."

"...Doctor Cooper!" Judge Judith Pleasants roared. "You do not have the floor and I am not your mother and I do not run a brothel. I am certainly not a Ma'am or a Madam and if you call me that one more time I will add contempt to your growing list of offenses. And please do not interrupt again, this is a courtroom not a local bar," she paused for a moment and glared down at Coop. "Better still, let's postpone this bail hearing until you have found adequate representation."

"But, Ma'am...uh...uh...Your Honor!" Coop was on his feet. "I really need bail set now."

"You still do not have the floor," Judge Pleasants thundered, then shook her head. "Okay, I'll bite, why is that, Doctor Cooper? Why do you need bail now?"

"I...I can't stand to spend another night in here and I have things I simply must take care of that can't wait."

"Such as?" Pleasants arched a gray eyebrow. "Previously scheduled surgery?"

"Well...uh...no," Coop sputtered, then decided he might as well tell the truth. "I have to prepare for an upcoming malpractice trial."

"My, my, Doctor Cooper," Judge Pleasants chided, "you really are

184

a regular consumer of our legal wares. Negligent homicide, however, easily takes precedence over a common malpractice suit," she paused and frowned, "and I think it would do you some good to spend another night with us." Judith Pleasants raised her gavel high. "So, until you obtain proper counsel, this hearing is adjor..."

"...**Your Honor!**" A loud voice interrupted from the back of the gallery near the doors. "Your Honor, he does have counsel."

Coop turned just in time to see Samantha Rose Jardine, stunning as usual, striding confidently toward the bench.

Gritting her teeth, Judge Judith Pleasants' scowl, if possible, deepened even more. "And who might you be?"

"Samantha Rose Jardine from the firm of Cannon, Jeffs and Hanks of Salt Lake City, Utah." She flashed her all-American girl smile. "I was admitted to the Utah bar in nineteen ninety-eight."

"Well, now, Ms Jardine," Judge Pleasants slowly meted out her words. "If you ever again make a grandstand entrance like that in my court again or if you ever show up late again I will automatically hold you in contempt. Do I make myself clear?"

"Yes, Your Honor," Samantha replied meekly, but as she turned and walked back to the desk she winked at Coop.

"So, Doctor Cooper," Judge Pleasants asked, "for the record, is this your attorney?"

"Uh...uh," Coop hesitated. Did he really want to get involved with Samantha Rose again? Briefly, he again recalled the old saying, burned twice a fool, but what did the proverb say about three times. Surely, that was way beyond foolish. On the other hand, what choice did he have? He really didn't want to spend another night in jail and he didn't know any other lawyers. Even taking all that into consideration, it was not an easy decision. One he wished he had more time to think about it.

"Well, Doctor Cooper, we are waiting. Do you accept Miss Jardine as your attorney?" Pleasants asked again, more impatiently this time. "This is not a trick question, but I do need a verbal answer, a yes or a no."

"Uh...uh...I guess, Your Honor."

"What did I just say?" Judge Pleasants growled. "A yes or a no. I guess is not an option."

"Y...y...yes," Coop stammered.

"Okay." Pleasants was all business again. "Now that's settled, let's proceed with the bail hearing. Regardless of what you all might think, this is not my only case today. Ms Jardine, what say you?"

"If there is a flight risk in this court, it is certainly not Doctor Cooper. He was born and raised here and his roots go back generations. He has a busy surgical practice and a home and a ranch in the area. No way is he going to up and leave all this on the flimsy case presented by the prosecution. Your Honor, Doctor Cooper will be here the night they turn the lights out in Saint George, Utah."

"Very eloquent, Ms Jardine" Judge Pleasants said sarcastically. "Mister Bledsoe, what do recommend for bail?"

"One million dollars!"

"You've got to be kidding?" Samantha laughed. "That might be the appropriate for capital murder, but..."

"...It has to be high enough," Bledsoe argued, "to deter..."

"...Five hundred thousand dollars," Judge Pleasants slammed her gavel down. "Next," she barked, once again lowering her head to study her docket.

"Your Honor, may I confer with my client for a minute?" Samantha asked as the courtroom rapidly cleared, preparing for the next case.

"Yes," Judge Pleasants looked up over her glasses, "you certainly may, but back in the conference room at Purgatory. I need my court-room. Next."

Coop arrived at Purgatory before Samantha, but he didn't have to wait long. Within fifteen minutes, a deputy opened his cell and escorted him to a conference room.

The room was small and cheerless with no windows and no accessories. The walls were painted a faded cream soda and the only furniture was a scarred pine table with two equally worn chairs.

Samantha Rose was already seated when Coop was ushered in. Again vowing to maintain a safe distance at all times, Coop sat down opposite Samantha, taking care not to touch or get too close to her. Certainly, no kissing on the cheek, not even a handshake.

"I'm surprised you're here," he said curtly.

"My friend, the one here in Saint George, heard you'd been arrested and called me. She knew you were my client. So, I hopped on the first available flight and as you saw barely made it."

"That's not what I meant."

"Oh, you mean Cannon, Jeffs and Hanks," Samantha forced a laugh. "They don't know yet."

"So what happens when they do?"

"Well, what will happen, will happen," Samantha shrugged. "I can't control everything."

Coop was silent for a moment. "Uh...I...uh...do want you to know I appreciate this," he finally mumbled.

"Not a problem," Samantha flashed her most disarming smile. "What we need to worry about now is making bail. How do you want to do it? Pay the five hundred thousand refundable security deposit or go through a bail bondsman?"

"How much will a bail bondsman cost?"

"Ten percent, that's fifty thousand dollars, but that's not refundable. You're simply giving away the fifty thousand dollars."

Coop took a moment to consider this. "Neither sounds very good."

"Well, I personally hate giving a bail bondsman money for doing nothing. You are not a flight risk, there's no question you'll show up for trial, so they make fifty thousand dollars for essentially doing zilch."

"I guess, that's like the line from the Dire Straits song," Coop said with a crooked grin.

"Huh?"

"You know...money for nothing."

"Ah, and your chicks for free," Samantha completed the stanza. "I remember. Why do guys always like that song?"

"I have no idea," Coop grinned, then quickly caught himself. He was going to have to watch himself around Samantha Rose Jardine.

"Can you come up with five hundred thousand?"

"I could probably almost make it," Coop replied after taking a couple of minutes to do the mental calculations, "if I cleaned out my savings, liquidated my retirement fund and took out a second mortgage on my house."

"It's a tough decision, I know," Samantha said. "It's up to you. Either way, I'll help as much as I can."

"Well, I kind of agree with you," Coop said after another moment. "I too hate to throw fifty thousand dollars away when I suspect I'm going to need the money sometime in the very near future."

Samantha Rose nodded

"So, I'll get the five hundred thousand back as soon as I show up for the trial?"

"That's correct."

"Okay, let's go ahead and see if we can get it together," Coop reluctantly agreed, "but unfortunately it leaves you doing most of the leg work."

"That's okay," Samantha smiled, as she scooted back her chair and stood up, "but you realize, it may take a few days."

"I know," Coop said with a tight smile. "This place sort of grows on you."

17

Mrs. Mease told me when dying
that among other things she had to repent of,
one was too much confidence in my remedies.
—Benjamin Rush (1745–1813)

Coop languished in jail for over a week. In the meantime Samantha Rose was very busy. After calling her office in Salt Lake City and arranging for a week off, she spent her days ferrying papers back and forth from the bank and Merrill Lynch to the jail. As if was watching all his assets disappear with each stroke of the pen, Coop groaned, but signed every paper.

Early in the week, she also managed to run up to Salt Lake City and represent Coop at his State Licensure Board hearing, though she doubted it did much good. On her way, she hand delivered the bottle of Yuccasote and Stepper's eyeball to Professor Marcus Westover. Coop had warned her about the eyeball, so she mostly kept the Mason jar wrapped in the kitchen towel. Curiosity, however, did briefly get the best of her and she took a quick peek. Once was enough, though it didn't bother her as much as she'd thought. Maybe, she proudly told Coop, I could have been a doctor after all.

Even though Samantha Rose volunteered to get a hotel, Coop insisted she stay at the ranch. Not only would it save money, but he needed someone to take care of Malachi, feed the horses and watch the house. By now, he'd pretty much exhausted Todd Snow as a resource.

As Coop predicted, he did have to drain his savings, the entire seventy-five thousand dollars. Plus, he cashed in his retirement fund valued at two hundred and fifty thousand dollars, a second mortgage on his house and ranch netted another one hundred and fifty thousand and that was it, he was completely tapped out. That still left him a full twenty-five thousand dollars short and try as he might he could not figure out a way to get it short of selling the ranch. "You can't wring water out of a stone," he despondently told Samantha Rose over the phone. "And regardless of the Dire Straits lyrics, there was no free money,

Just as he made up his mind the next time she visited he would tell her to forget the five hundred thousand dollar security deposit and call a bail bondsman, a deputy jailor appeared and without explanation unlocked his cell. Not waiting to see if it was a mistake, Coop quickly stepped out and followed him. As they walked down the hall, curiosity got the best of him and he asked the deputy jailor what was going on. The deputy just shrugged and said bail was posted and he was instructed to let him out, and that was all he knew. The possibility of freedom was just too tempting, so without further interrogation or hesitation Coop collected his personal items and headed for the door.

As he walked out of the secured area, once again a free man in street clothes, Samantha Rose was waiting for him in the lobby. The instant she saw him, she dropped a magazine and rushed over, planting a kiss on his cheek.

Caught off guard, Coop didn't have time to turn away.

"I'll bet you're glad to be out of there," she exclaimed. From her smile, she was happy too.

"Once you swallow your pride and learn not to fight the sexual predators, it's not all that bad," Coop deadpanned.

"Really!"

"No, just kidding," Coop laughed. "Just like in the real world, no one made any advances at me."

"That's not funny," Samantha feigned annoyance, "nor is it true. If you remember correctly, I recently made a pass at you."

"I thought it was the other way around."

"No, I'm pretty sure I was the aggressor."

"Well," Coop changed the subject, "I'm still a little puzzled how I made bail?"

"It's really quite simple. We posted the money and now you're out. That's how the system works."

"I know how the system works, but I was twenty-five thousand short."

"I found some assets you didn't know you had." Samantha shrugged, avoiding Coop's gaze. "It just took a little more digging."

"No you didn't."

"Well, the court gave us a little leeway."

"Oh, kinda like a game of horseshoes, you get points for coming close. Come on, Samantha Rose, even I don't believe that."

"Well...well, I don't know," she stammered. "They let you out, so let's not worry about it."

"But I am worrying about it."

"If...if you must know, I chipped in a little."

Coop was silent for a moment then continued, a catch in his voice. "You didn't have to do that."

"What are you talking about?" Samantha joked with mock indignation. "How do you think it looks, me being a lawyer and all, to have my man in jail? It's kind of like having a patient you've operated on end up in the morgue. It's just not good publicity."

Coop didn't know what to say. He was not very good at expressing gratitude. He seldom had to. "Well...," he fumbled for the right words. "Well, I do appreciate all you've done. I hope you know that."

"My pleasure," Samantha smiled, then turned to go.

"And for taking care of Malachi and watching the house."

"I like your house and I love Malachi." Samantha grinned. "But I've never slept with a dog before." She paused for a moment. "Come to think of it, maybe I have, once or twice."

Coop grinned in spite of himself. "I hope that crack wasn't aimed at me."

"No, long before you."

"And I hope the reason you helped wasn't because I made you feel guilty when I called you after being arrested."

"No, not at all," Samantha Rose replied. "It was more like I needed time to get my priorities straight."

"Well, I owe you a big one," Coop insisted, "with all that driving back and forth to the bank and to Cedar City...,"

"...Oh, speaking of Cedar City," Samantha interrupted, "Doctor Westover phoned me yesterday. He said the oil on the surgical sponge was definitely olive oil and imported from Italy."

"Italy?" Coop echoed, not able to conceal his surprise. "How'd he know it was from Italy?"

"Apparently the oil had minute traces of selenium."

"So?"

"According to Doctor Westover, neither California, Spanish or Greek olives have selenium, or anywhere else in the world for that matter, only Italian olives."

"I suppose we import a lot of Italian olive oil?"

"I think that would be safe to say."

"So that narrows things down considerably, huh?"

"Yeah," Samantha Rose agreed. "I doubt there's more than fifty million or so Americans that buy Italian olive oil each year."

Coop mulled that information for a moment, then shook his head. "How about giving me a ride home?"

Samantha's rental was a silver gray Lexus, much like her own, with very comfortable leather seats. It wasn't his Dodge pickup, but Coop decided he could get used to a car like this and being chauffeured wasn't half bad either.

Like a man returning to his hometown after a forty-year absence, Coop hungrily took in the familiar sights on the way home. All he knew for certain, there was no way he was ever going back to jail.

He did not speak again until they were almost halfway up the hill to Diamond Valley. "Samantha, do you know much about prescription and drug laws?"

"I'm not sure what you mean."

"You know the laws that regulate the FDA, Food and Drug Administration, and the entire health food industry."

"Yeah, a little. A couple of years ago I had to research the subject for a trial."

"Can the doctors at MITH legally sell Yuccasote without the seal of approval from the FDA?"

"Yes, unfortunately, they probably can."

"How's that?

"As long as they claim it is a food supplement or has all natural ingredients, they don't need approval from the FDA."

"Any laboratory testing?"

"No, none."

"So, they don't even have to know if there are any active ingredients?" Coop asked, as the passed the little town of Winchester Hills. "And if so, what they are and what they do?"

"Unfortunately, most of the health food manufacturers have no idea what chemicals are in their products."

"And they don't have to do animal and human trials?"

"Not with food supplements," Samantha insisted "no more than General Mills has to run human trials on its cereal. And, they don't have to back up their advertising claims either. They can claim anything: good for the liver, fights arthritis, kills viruses, strengthens the immune system and battles cancer. I know of some supplements that claim all of those."

"Miracle drugs, huh," Coop said tongue-in-cheek. "So, the consumer has no way of knowing if the stuff really works or if it has side effects?"

"None, no way at all," Samantha agreed, "but they are supposed to put a list of ingredients on the label."

"Well then, that's certainly a violation," Coop declared as he watched the cinder-peppered slopes of the dormant volcano go flying by.

"What's a violation?

"The label on the Yuccasote has nothing listed."

"I suspect that may be the least of their transgressions." Samantha turned off the highway to Diamond Valley.

"Well, that's quite a racket."

"Nationwide, a multi-billion dollar per year racket," Samantha Rose agreed, turning on Coop's private road and passing under the pole entryway sign.

Coop fell silent as he took a moment to scan the ranch and house. Thankfully, everything seemed okay.

"So what happened to Josh?" he abruptly asked.

"Who?" Samantha looked surprised.

"You know, Josh the scuba diver. The one in the picture."

"Oh, that Josh," Samantha laughed. "He was never as big a deal as you thought. Don't worry; I've taken care of him. But now I have a question for you."

"Uh...uh...okay," Coop stammered, instantly realizing he should have kept his mouth shut. Now he'd left himself wide open for Samantha to ask the same question about Kylie. Was he ready to give Kylie up? Could he honestly say, don't worry I've taken care of that.

"So, what do you want for your birthday?"

"Huh?"

"Your birthday, it's coming up this Friday, the day after Thanksgiving," Samantha repeated, then confessed. "I know from looking at the information your insurance carrier sent over."

"Uh...uh...I don't know. How about let's forget my birthday this year? It's hard to think about going for a swim in the ocean when you see the dorsal fins circling."

"Well, we'll see," Samantha Rose said vaguely.

Malachi was beside himself when Coop and Samantha drove up. Privately, Coop was a little miffed when Malachi seemed just as happy to see Samantha Rose as he was to see him.

Even though she had been staying at the ranch for the last nine days, Samantha still wanted Coop to give her an official tour of the place. For roughly a half-hour, he guided her around the ranch. His tour not only included the land, the horses and charcoal heap that was once a tack and feed shed, but was also spiced with anecdotes and vignettes of family history. Samantha seemed particularly dismayed by the loss of the tack, especially when Coop explained he presently did not presently have a single riding saddle. If he had, he would gladly take her out for a horse ride.

After the tour, Samantha, putting on one of Kylie's aprons, declared she was going to prepare Coop a home-cooked meal to compensate for his nine days of prison food. At first he was a bit dismayed to see her in Kylie's apron and almost told her to take it off, but she did look good and anyway he was hungry.

While Samantha cooked, Coop gathered up his stack of unopened mail and newspapers and sat down in his LazyBoy. Deciding to save the mail till last, he picked up *The Daily Spectrum* and began reading. After finishing with the first page, national and world news, he opened the second page, Utah and Local News. Immediately, his hands began to tremble and the paper began to rattle. To calm himself, he took a deep breath, then slowly reread the first paragraph to make sure his eyes weren't playing tricks. Unfortunately, it still read the same. There in bold one inch-high print blazoned the headline: ***DISTINGUISHED PROFESSOR DIES IN LAB FIRE.***

The newspaper slipped through Coop's numb fingers, falling to the floor.

After he stopped shaking, he forced himself to reach down and retrieve the newspaper. Like passing a bad accident on the freeway, Coop had to force his eyes away from the headlines to read the rest of the story.

According to Jill Thorpe, the Spectrum's Cedar City reporter and whose name was attached to the dateline: *Dr. Marcus Westover, winner of the prestigious J.D. Bryant Award in Research Chemistry, died last night at approximately 1:15 a.m. in a tragic, work-related fire. Apparently he was alone and not even his colleagues had any idea what he was working on, only that he'd been very secretive. When interviewed, his distraught wife, Edith, also stated she had no idea what her husband was working on, only that for the last week or so he seemed preoccupied and had been in the lab late almost every night.*

Even though the Cedar City Fire Department's response time was less than ten minutes, the fourth floor laboratory was a total loss and there was also major smoke and some structural damage to the two upper floors of SUU's Physical Science Building. Fire Marshal Bud Daniels confirmed his initial impression was the deadly blaze was accidental. "Sadly," he stated, "it's a hazard of the trade when working with highly combustible chemicals. I'm surprised we don't see more of these kind of fires."

Coop felt cold and empty, and totally responsible. Deep down he knew this was no accident. Damn, he hated to think a thing like this could happen to a nice old guy like Marcus Westover—and all because he was doing him a favor. Not by intent, of course, but nevertheless Coop felt he was responsible for his friend's death. It was a terrible feeling to know you caused a death, and twice as bad when it was a close friend.

Numb with shock, at first Coop couldn't think, but eventually he tried to make some sense of it. The more he thought about it, the more he knew this was arson and murder. After years of studying both the physical and biological laws of nature, Coop was not a great believer in coincidence and the timing of this fire was too suspicious. Furthermore, Marcus knew his chemicals and from personal experience Coop also knew Marcus was ultra-cautious and always emphasized safety. Questions begged to be asked and demanded to be answered. Who would do such a thing? And why? And where would it all end?

Choking back the tears, Coop called to Samantha Rose and showed her the article. Overwhelmed, she slumped down into his lap. Just last week, she'd met with Professor Westover and only yesterday she spoke with him on the phone, now he was dead. It was so unreal, it bordered on surreal. Putting her arms around Coop, she pulled him in close.

They sat in silence for a few minutes, then a timer went off in the kitchen. Sighing deeply, Samantha got up to go check. With the back of his hand, Coop wiped a tear from his eyes, but more followed. He needed a tissue.

As he stood up, the pile of mail setting on his lap fluttered to the floor. Scattered among the mail were two official-looking letters. One was quite thick and bore the official logo, a bristlecone pine, of Southern Utah University. The other sported the familiar beehive stamp of the great state of Utah.

Bending down, Coop retrieved those two letters, leaving the others untouched. First, he ripped open the thick Southern Utah University envelope and quickly rifled through the pages. Unbelievable! It was Westover's analysis of both Yuccasote and the vitreous humor of Stepper's eye. Marcus must have mailed them right before the fire. Locating, a box of tissue, Coop settled back into the chair and thumbed to page one.

According to Dr. Westover, Yuccasote was derived from both the yucca cactus plant (*yucca shidigera*), also known as Spanish bayonet and Spanish dagger, and the creosote bush (*creosote larrea tridentate*), also commonly known as chaparral or greasewood. In the past, both plants were used for medicinal purposes by the desert dwelling Chuilla Indians as well as many of the early southwest desert pioneers.

On page two, Westover detailed his chemical analysis of both plants. It was technical data, but with his years of chemistry training Coop could follow most of it. With the Yucca plant, traditionally only the root was harvested. Once gathered, it was split and boiled. The root extract did contain phytosterols, naturally occurring steroids. Also, often a fungus, *Streptomyces caespitosus*, was known to colonize its roots. As a point of comparison, Mitomycin, a well-known chemotherapeutic agent, was also derived from the broth of a similar fungus. Westover then went on to explain, "without further testing it would be impossible to say for certain, but it was entirely possible Yuccasote, like Mitomycin, may indeed have some anti-tumor activity."

As far as creosote was concerned, it also had a number of chemically active compounds. The Indians prepared it by harvesting the tiny crinkled leaves and yellow blossom flowers, grinding them to a pulp. Following this, they dried the mulch in the hot sun, then mixed the residue with water and brought it to a boil. After letting it cool, they simply drank the supernatant. The active ingredients: eighteen distinct flavone and flavonol aglycones, a single dihydroflavonol, larretic acid, two guaiuretic acids including the very important nordihydroguairetic acid (NDGA) and several quercetin bioflavonoids. Also, creosote contained large quantities of 3-(acetonylbenzyl)-4-hydroxycoumarin, a compound very similar to warfarin and may indeed have potent anticoagulant properties by inhibiting the liver from synthesizing the essential clotting protein Factor IX.

Lastly, pure grain alcohol, ten percent by weight, was added to the mixture.

On page three, Westover speculated possibly how the compound Yuccasote was prepared by MITH. Compared to the Indian or traditional way, there were some minor differences when preparing the two herbs as a mixture. The Yucca root and the creosote leaves and flowers more than likely were ground together, then water added to make a soupy mash. Next, over low heat, the pulpy mixture was simmered, not boiled, for several days and the thick supernatant collected and filtered. Finally grain alcohol would be added in a one-to-ten proportion, then the liquid was bottled and corked or capped.

The last page, number four, was quite brief. It contained the analysis of Stepper's vitreous humor. Very simply, it contained high concentrations of 3-(acetonylbenzyl)-4-hydroxycoumarin from the fungus *Streptomyces caespitosus.* In other words, Yuccasote.

"Oh sweet Jesus," Coop softly murmured, "that is a lot to digest." Setting Westover's report aside, Coop tried to comprehend all he'd read. In a nutshell, no a bombshell, Marcus Westover had confirmed

Yuccasote contained both anti-cancer and anticoagulant properties! This would explain the bleeding.

Of course when he had time, he would reread it more carefully, but now he wanted to check out the other letter, the one from the State of Utah. Actually it was from the office of the Utah State Board of Licensure.

> Dear Dr. Cooper,
>
> After convening a formal hearing on the matter, receiving input from your attorney and giving it considerable thought, we feel it is in the best interests of everyone, the State of Utah, you, and your patients, to temporarily suspend your license to practice medicine in this state pending the outcome of your negligent homicide and malpractice trials.
>
> We hope you understand. Any request for an appeal must be made in writing.
>
> Sincerely,
>
> Harry Jacklinson, M.D., Board Chairman

Unfortunately, this letter, unlike Westover's, came as no great surprise. The only thing mildly surprising was the speed at which it arrived. After all, it had been only nine days since he was arrested and charged. I suppose, Coop thought bitterly, they'd thought they had to move fast to remove this dangerous public menace off the streets or in this case out of the operating room.

Professor Westover's letter, however, was nothing short of explosive. It was literally a smoking gun. It was the break they were looking for.

Over dinner Coop and Samantha discussed the letter. Apparently, Yuccasote coupled with the neck puncture wound had killed Stepper. And it was not too big a leap of faith to assume Yuccasote coupled with surgery killed Betty Tsongas, Gordon Flowers and Hector Gonzalez. Then reality set in. Unfortunately, to qualify as indisputable evidence in court, Samantha added in between bites, they were still lacking a critical piece of evidence. Yes, now they could prove Yuccasote was an anticoagulant, and they could prove it killed Stepper, and they could prove Nathan Reed was taking it, but what they couldn't prove was Betty

Tsongas, Gordon Flowers and Hector Gonzalez were taking the deadly herb.

"Coop," Samantha added as he finished her chicken cacciatore and she cleared the table. "I strongly feel, and I know you do too, that Professor Westover's death is somehow related to the Yuccasote and MITH. So, we're talking murder here! I think you should go to the police."

"It won't do any good," Coop declared, rinsing and drying the dishes as Samantha washed. "They won't believe me. Right now I have zero credibility with them."

"You need to at least try. You owe it to your friend."

There was no way Coop could argue with that logic. He could never repay Westover. How do you repay someone for giving their life? Glancing down at his watch, he noted the time. It was just a little past seven. Nodding, he finished the dishes and got ready to go.

"Great cacciatore," Coop said as he winked at Malachi. "Not quite as good as Purgatory's creamed chicken on a shingle, but with a little practice...,"

He never finished. Like a bullwhip, Samantha loudly snapped the dishtowel, popping him hard on the behind.

"Where did you learn to do that?" Coop whined.

"I've had a lot of practice," Samantha quipped, "on people who complain about my cooking."

"I'll be back in an hour," Coop laughed as he leaned over and kissed her.

"No need to hurry," Samantha Rose hugged Malachi. "I have some-one here who appreciates my food."

Pretending he was upset, but smiling inside, Coop grabbed the Westover letter and left.

Things went pretty much like he'd expected. The officer who in-terviewed him immediately recognized him, even before he opened his mouth. Politely, the deputy jotted down everything, but Coop couldn't help but feel he wasn't taking him seriously. When he'd finished, the officer assured him they would look into it, but somehow Coop doubted it would be a high priority. More than likely his report would be filed in the nuisance bin and soon be forgotten.

Coop left police headquarters discouraged and depressed. Climb-ing back into his pickup, he did what he usually did when he was down;

he headed straight to Jacob Heinz's place. Somehow talking to Jacob always made things look better. He had a knack of taking major problems and shrinking them down to their proper size.

When he arrived unannounced, Coop was surprised to find Jacob was already entertaining a visitor, a lady. It appeared they had been out on the back veranda enjoying the evening with a late cup of coffee. Coop immediately apologized for intruding and excused himself, but Jacob would have none of it. Grabbing him by the elbow, he steered him through the French doors to the patio and the wrought iron table. The aroma of the gourmet coffee filled the night air and Coop couldn't help but marvel how good Jacob's coffee always smelled. It tasted pretty good too.

"Sophie, this is Doctor Lawrence Cooper," Jacob introduced him with pride. "He vas my very best student."

Coop firmly shook Sophie's small hand. Wearing a flowery yellow summer dress, she was tiny, petite, seventy, and quite a looker. "Nice to meet you, Sophie, and please call me Coop. If you call me Lawrence, I probably won't answer," Coop laughed. "Sometimes I even forget that's my name."

Slowly, Sophie looked from Jacob to Coop, then back again. "I have a feeling you two have things you need to discuss. How about I go inside and watch a little MTV?"

Quickly, Coop glanced over to see if she was serious. Sophie just laughed, grabbed her cup of coffee and made her way back through the French doors.

"*Sie ist schön?*" Jacob asked, grinning like a schoolboy.

"Yes, Jacob, she's very lovely," Coop nodded his approval. "How did you meet her?"

"At the supermarket. Vhere else?"

"I thought maybe at one of the local bars," Coop suggested with a wry grin.

"In Saint George," Jacob hooted. "Vhat bars?"

"You've got a point there, my friend."

"So, *wie gehts*?"

"Not so good," Coop answered, then quickly added, "and Jacob, we've about reached the limits of my German."

"*Ja, Ja,*" Jacob found a clean cup and poured Coop some coffee, "so bring me up to date."

For the next twenty minutes, Coop explained in detail his second trip to MITH, his attempt to buy a bottle of Yuccasote and how he'd finally gotten a sample from Nathan Reed. He also informed Jacob of his second visit to Purgatory, his incarceration and how Samantha Rose came to the rescue. Then with a mixture of bitterness and sadness, he told Jacob of the deaths of Stepper and his friend Professor Marcus Westover. Struggling to control his emotions, he then simply handed over Westover's letter for Heinz to read, then sat back nursing his coffee.

"Vell," Heinz said after finishing the letter, "it appears the reason your patients were able to delay their surgeries for one or two years is that Yuccasote does indeed have cytotoxic and anti-tumor properties."

"Yes," Coop nodded, "it does appear that way."

"And," Heinz continued, "just like conventional chemotherapy, after a vhile the tumor cells become resistant to the drug and starts to grow again."

"It looks that way."

"Or, I suppose," Heinz added, still looking at the letter, "it is possible that rather than tumor resistance, the more recent batches of Yuccasote did not contain the root fungus, *Streptomyces caespitosus*. Or at least not in large enough quantities."

"Yes, I guess that too possible," Coop replied thoughtfully. "And I doubt the people at MITH ever knew what made their drug work."

"But regardless of vhy it quit working, it still had enough time to damage the liver so it quit making Factor IX." Heinz folded the letter a stuffed in back in the envelope.

"Yeah, that's the way I see it."

"So with the tumor growing again, they returned, you took them to surgery and they bled to death."

"It appears so."

"This is not unlike the experiments the German doctors did in the concentration camps," Jacob declared, "totally unsupervised with a free hand to do vhat they vanted and vith no regard to the consequences."

"That might be a bit of a stretch."

"Vell, hell," Jacob's voice rose with anger, "these people are dangerous! Patients are dying. They need to be stopped!"

"Yes, you're right, Jacob."

"You know vhat you need to do, don't you?"

"Yeah, Jacob, I think I so."

In silence, they finished their coffee. Sighing out loud, Coop put down his empty cup and stood up to go. "Jacob, my friend, I've taken enough of your time," then nodding toward Sophie, he added. "I'll let you get back to more important things."

"How about you?" Jacob also stood. "You still vaiting for that Kylie?"

"Nah," Coop shook his head, "not anymore. I've got Samantha Rose staying with me out at the ranch."

"Ah, I vould love to meet her sometime," Heinz opened the French doors. "But if you like her, I know I vould too."

"You will meet her," Coop assured him, "and I do like Sophie."

"*Ja, Ja*, but I still need the little *blaue pille*." Jacob grinned slyly.

"Oh!" Coop looked at Sophie watching T.V. "Oh, Jacob, I'm so sorry. With all that's going on..."

"I tried it once," Jacob lowered his voice, "vhen it first came out. Doctor Mueller from the university gave me some. It vorked good, but then he moved to the Mayo Clinic."

"I promise," Coop picked up his empty cup and saucer, "I'll get you some. We always get office samples—almost weekly."

"You should try it. Now you've got that Samantha."

"I did once," Coop blushed, then quickly added, "uh...uh...not with Samantha Rose, but it gave me a headache."

"You need some more of them headaches."

18

A wise doctor does not mutter incantations
over a sore that needs the knife.
—Sophocles (496–406 B. C.)

The day of the Tsongas malpractice trial arrived with Samantha Rose still representing Coop. Apparently Cannon, Jeffs & Hanks were not yet aware of her recent foray into criminal law or they decided to turn a blind eye. For the duration of the trial, Samantha decided to move to St. George. Initially, she reserved a room at the Courtyard by Marriott, but Coop thought that was silly and insisted she stay at the ranch. Halfheartedly, she argued against it, then gave up and moved in. That way, she rationalized, it would be easier for them to quickly conference or just bat around ideas.

It was a perfect late November day. The cobalt sky was faultless and autumn's golden sun was shining brightly, but not with the same intensity as summer. The sycamore leaves had turned a dull pottery brown, the maple leaves blazed a brilliant picante red and the quaken aspen added a lemon yellow. Overhead, as a cool breeze rustled through the brightly festooned leaves, it picked up a couple of hitchhikers, the musty odor of autumn as well as pitchy smoke from the valley's many wood burning stoves. It was a light sweater day, but also a day that begged to be outdoors, taking in the sights and smells of the season.

Coop, however, was not outdoors and was not enjoying this perfect day. Rather, he was stuck indoors and was quite uncomfortable. Inside the courtroom, it was stuffy and hot. There was no breeze and it smelled like furniture polish and floor wax.

Even with a wholly composed Samantha Rose Jardine seated at the oaken table next to him, he was still nervous—nervous as an intern making his first surgical incision. He blushed with embarrassment as that memory flashed across his mind. His attending surgeon had dryly commented. "What's the matter, boy? Your hands are shaking like a dog shitting peach pits."

Today, however, he had good reason to be nervous. His whole life was at stake. He had everything to lose or conversely he had everything to gain. It was all on the table. If he lost the Tsongas case, it would tip the other already teetering dominos, triggering a sequential free-fall. The upcoming Flowers and Gonzalez trials were essentially clones of this one and if he couldn't win this one it was most unlikely he would prevail with the others.

The accumulative jury awards could run into the tens of millions of dollars and unfortunately his aggregate malpractice policy would only cover a grand total of three million dollars. Plus now, there were no more assets he could liquidate. He'd depleted them all to make bail on the negligent homicide charge. Also, by the time it was all over, his legal costs, those from the criminal case not covered by his malpractice carrier, could be astronomical.

As with the other two malpractice cases, the negligent homicide trial was also pending. The verdict of this trial more than likely would also be a barometer for that trial. Even though they would be tried in different courts, criminal rather than civil, undoubtedly the same evidence would be used and the same expert and character witnesses would be called. With the criminal trial, however, not only was there the potential of a substantial fine, but also the real and scary possibility of considerable prison time. If he lost today, undoubtedly it would change his life for a very long time, maybe forever.

Today was day three of the trial and so far it was not going well. Day one was spent entirely with jury selection and Samantha Rose seemed satisfied with the jurors that were selected. She wanted women because she thought they would be sexually attracted to Coop, an argument Coop sincerely doubted. She also favored people with a college education, professional people who could empathize with Coop and understand technical aspects of the case. Blue-collar jurors, she was afraid, would have no sympathy and might bring with them the prejudicial baggage of class resentment, *the rich doctor got what he deserved.* What she got, however, were six women out of the ten jurors and five of them held college degrees. All in all, not too bad, she informed Coop.

Day two was wholly consumed with procedural instructions from Judge Pleasants, the disposing of pretrial motions and opening statements by Benjamin Bowling, the plaintiff's attorney, and Samantha Rose. It proved to be a gut-wrenching day and by the end of it Ben Bowling had almost convinced Coop he was an incompetent surgeon and a terrible human being. On the other hand, Samantha did a credible job presenting their point of view: basically, Betty Tsongas bled to death, not from surgical misadventure, but from an intrinsic and acquired defect in her clotting mechanism caused by a new combination herbal drug. Of course, the jury had no way of knowing Samantha Rose had absolutely no evidence to back up her contrasting claims, but they soon would.

Day three, today, was the beginning of the evidentiary portion of the trial and as per protocol the plaintiff would go first. Their job, of course, was to present their case to the jury, using all available evidence and witnesses to substantiate their claims.

After the usual call to order by the bailiff, Judge Judith Pleasants seated herself, fussed with her gown and scowled at her notes, then turned to Bowling. "Looks like you're up, Counselor."

Without bothering to rise from his chair, Bowling loudly announced, "As our first witness, we call Doctor Stephen Spaulding."

Almost too eagerly, Spaulding jumped up from his seat near the back of the gallery and rapidly made his way forward down the aisle. As he passed Coop, he paused and grinned.

"Haven't seen you around lately, Coops," he whispered. "Marty still wonders what happened."

"As you can see," Coop replied with a thin smile, "I've been a little busy."

"Your Honor," Bowling immediately barked, "I object! The witness should not be allowed to converse with the accused, especially right before being deposed."

"It's your witness," Judge Pleasants said dryly, "you control him."

"Doctor Spaulding!" Bowling bellowed. "Please take the stand—now."

"Give me a call sometime," Spaulding said over his shoulder as he continued toward the witness box.

"Do we have to worry about him?" Samantha whispered, leaning in close.

"Nah," Coop shook his head. "Steve's okay. He may be their witness, but he's in our camp."

"I hope so."

Bowling struggled to haul his huge frame out of the chair, but briefly it stuck, wedged by his ample buttocks. Grudgingly, it finally relented to gravity, banging loudly back to the floor. As Bowling trudged toward the witness box, each ponderous step made his massive thighs jiggle and the hardwood floor creak. After establishing Spaulding's credentials as a doctor and a board certified anesthesiologist, Bowling got right down to business.

"So, Doctor Spaulding," he asked in most commanding voice. "Were you the anesthesiologist attending Betty Tsongas on the day in question?"

"I was." Clean-shaven and hair trimmed, Spaulding looked dapper in his white starched lab coat and fuchsia purple tie. In spite of himself, Coop couldn't help but smile. He'd never seen Steve look quite so... uh...so clean.

"Was there anything unusual about that surgery?"

Spaulding rolled his eyes. "A better question, was there anything usual?"

"Doctor Spaulding! Please don't try to put words in my mouth and do not answer my question with a question."

"Oh!" Steve feigned embarrassment and a forced laugh, "I didn't realize I had."

"Could you give us some specifics?" Bowling continued undeterred. "What made that day so unusual?"

"Well, I'd say hemorrhage and death are a little unusual," Spaulding quipped, "at least they are in my practice."

Ignoring Spaulding's flippant tone, Bowling pressed on. "How often do you have patients die in surgery?"

"Almost never."

"Could you be more specific? Give me a number."

"Well, up until then none, but since I've...," Spaulding appeared catch himself and immediately clammed up.

"What did you mean by *since*?" Bowling quickly asked, emphasizing *since*.

"Well, since then we've had several..."

"...Objection! Your Honor." Samantha was instantly on her feet. "Mister Bowling is treading on inadmissible ground. You already specifically ruled on that in the pre-trial motions."

"Side bar," Judge Pleasants ordered, then turned off her microphone. "Miss Jardine, I don't know if the witness's testimony is inadmissible until I've heard it."

"Obviously, he was going to mention the Flowers and Gonzales cases," Samantha insisted.

"Are you also a mind reader?" Bowling argued.

"Well, ask him now, during side bar," Samantha suggested, "then rule. If it is admissible he can repeat it to the jury."

Judge Pleasants considered this for a minute, then turned to Spaulding. "Whisper to me what you were going to say."

"Well," Spaulding murmured, just slightly louder than a whisper and the jury strained to hear. "I was going to say, since the Tsongas death we've had two more cases of pretty much the same thing, two more bled to death."

Coop caught just enough words to get the gist of what Spaulding was saying and undoubtedly the jury did too.

"Your Honor," Samantha objected again, "that was hardly a whisper and as you know those two cases both have trials pending." She lowered her voice and added, "And you've already ruled that testimony is inadmissible."

Nodding, Judge Pleasants dismissed the side bar, then loudly announced, "objection sustained. Counselor, ask another question."

"Yes, Your Honor," Ben Bowling replied coolly. He'd made his point anyway. Bowling studied his notes for a few seconds, then continued. "How much blood would you say Betty Tsongas lost?"

"I don't know...roughly ten thousand cc's, give or take," Spaulding shrugged. "It was hard to keep an accurate count."

"Why is that?"

"Well, there was blood everywhere, on sponges, drapes and the floor. Just too much to keep track of and...and I had other pressing duties."

"Such as?"

"Such as trying to keep the patient alive," Spaulding snapped.

Bowling paused again to consult his notes. "Ten thousand cc's, how much would that be in fluid ounces?"

Pausing, Spaulding thought about it, then did the mental arithmetic out loud. "Uh...let me see, there's thirty cc's per ounce; that's thirty-three and a third ounces in a thousand cc's; times that by ten and that comes to three hundred and thirty-three ounces for ten thousand cc's of blood loss. There are one hundred and twenty-eight ounces per gallon. Divide that into three hundred and thirty-three. Uh...I guess that's a little less than three gallons, if my figures are correct."

Immediately, an audible collective gasp issued up from the gallery. Coop glanced over at the jury. Spaulding's math made a big impression on them as well.

"Three gallons!" Bowling boomed, then paused to let those startling figures marinate in the courtroom's stagnant air. After a moment, he continued, "with a surgery like Betty's, a radical cystectomy, what would you say is the average blood loss?"

"I don't know, probably four, maybe five hundred cc's," Dr. Spaulding paused again to do the math, "that's roughly thirteen to sixteen ounces."

"So, Betty Tsongas lost...um...lost over twenty times the normal amount?" Bowling declared. He looked like a big jungle cat ready to pounce.

"Yeah, something like that."

"Did anyone check her clotting factors prior to surgery?"

"Uh...no."

"Why was that?"

"I suppose Doctor Cooper didn't feel it was necessary."

"Not necessary! Why is that, Doctor?"

"She was not on blood thinners and no history of bleeding, alcoholism or liver disease."

"So there was nothing, nothing at all," Bowling pressed the point, "to indicate she'd had a prior bleeding tendency?"

"Well, not that I know of."

Bowling paused a moment to let that point sink in, then suddenly changed directions. "Did surgery start on time that day?"

"No, as I recall we started about an hour late."

"Why the late start?"

"You can start an operation," Spaulding laughed derisively, "without a surgeon."

"So, are you saying Doctor Cooper was late?"

"Yeah," Spaulding shrugged, "I suppose."

"Did he say why?"

"Overslept. Said he wasn't feeling well."

Samantha fired a helpless look at Coop. Spaulding was killing them.

"Did he seem okay during the surgery?"

"I suppose, as good as you can with a virus."

"Could you be a little more specific?"

"Well, he seemed sort of out of it. Not his usual self. He was real quiet, then got dizzy." Spaulding squirmed uncomfortably in his chair.

"Anything else?"

"Uh...he had to sit down on a stool for a bit."

"And all the while Betty Tsongas was bleeding to death!" Bowling blurted, raising an incredulous eyebrow.

"Objection!" Samantha was on her feet again. "That's not a question, but a statement, and an inflammatory one at that. And...and it's pure conjecture."

"I certainly think," Bowling shot back, "Doctor Spaulding has the qualifications to know if someone's bleeding to death."

Judge Judith Pleasants glowered at the attorneys. Through the grapevine, Coop heard she hated objections. She liked fast and streamlined trials with no stalling, no bickering and no interruptions. "Sustained," she growled. "Strike that from the record. Mister Bowling, you know the rules. Stick to them."

"I have no further questions of this witness," Bowling said abruptly, then lumbered back toward his chair. "Your witness, Counselor," he added, looking smugly at Samantha Rose.

Coop realized there was very little Samantha could do with her cross-examination. Everything Spaulding said was true enough, though he might have been a little more vague and used a less vivid and inflammatory language.

"Doctor Spaulding," Samantha Rose began, her rust hair gleaming in the bright fluorescent light, "how many of these operations, these radical cystectomies, have you provided the anesthesia?"

"I don't know, maybe a hundred."

"So you've seen a lot of them. What do think went wrong?"

"Objection!" Bowling shouted from his chair. "This calls for speculation on the part of the witness."

"Not at all," Samantha countered evenly. "You've already established his credentials as an expert and he's done over a hundred of these cases. I'm asking his professional opinion."

Judge Pleasants looked unhappy. Scowling, she considered both arguments. "Objection overruled," she finally barked, then added, "Can we get on with it, you two?" She glared down from the bench for a moment at both lawyers, then turned to Spaulding. "You may answer the question, Doctor."

"I can't remember the question." Spaulding smiled apologetically.

"What do you think was the main problem with Betty Tsongas's surgery?" Samantha asked again.

"Well," Spaulding replied thoughtfully, "I've never seen anything quite like it. I really don't know."

"Do you think Doctor Cooper's surgical technique or his illness had anything to do with it?" Samantha asked bluntly.

Coop knew Samantha knew she was taking a big risk with this question, but it wasn't as risky as it seemed. He knew Spaulding would back him up.

"Well," Spaulding hesitated and looked down at his feet. "Coop is my friend. I'd rather not say."

Samantha looked alarmed and at the same time a little unsure, but now she had no choice. She started this line of questions; she had to push on. "Please, just answer the question, Doctor."

"Well, I don't know," Spaulding hedged. "I was too damn busy trying to keep her alive to spend a lot of time observing technique. Anyway, I'm not a surgeon."

Frustrated, Samantha quickly thanked Spaulding and excused him.

Wide-eyed, Coop watched his friend walk by. That was either a very clumsy attempt to help or a very well concealed stab in the back.

Sitting back down next to Coop, Samantha leaned in and whispered angrily. "What the hell was that?"

"I have no idea," Coop mumbled.

"Well, I do," Samantha hissed under her breath. "In the words of Alexander Pope, that's called damning with faint praise."

Next, Bowling called Dr. Stanton Kingsley to the witness stand. Even Stan's stride cried out with arrogance. His demeanor was haughty and his appearance striking. Wearing expensive Gucci shoes Dr. Kingsley also sported dark Armani slacks, a spotless white shirt, a striped red tie and a starched knee-length white lab coat. As opposed to Coop, he had the look of a successful doctor. Quickly, Stanton was sworn in and his impressive credentials established.

"Doctor Kingsley, what part did you play in Betty Tsongas's surgery?" Bowling asked.

"I was the assistant surgeon." Kingsley's delivery and enunciation were perfect.

"Did Doctor Cooper arrive late for surgery that day?" Bowling's voice carried around the room like a trained stage actor.

"Yes, well over an hour."

"What kind of shape was he in when he did finally show up?"

"He seemed distracted, out of sorts."

"Was he sick?" Bowling pressed.

"I couldn't say."

"Did he do anything unusual or peculiar during the surgery?"

"Well," Stan Kingsley hesitated and looked Coop straight in the eye. "Right in the heat of the battle, he sat down on a stool and appeared to pass out."

"Did he fall off the stool?"

"No, but he did slump over, put his head down in his lap and didn't seem to hear me when I asked if he wanted me to finish the surgery."

"What would you say about Doctor Cooper's surgical technique that day? Was it was okay?"

"Objection!" Samantha yelled. "Calls for conjecture."

"Expert witness," Bowling replied smugly, then toughed two fingers to his forehead as kind of a salute. "*Touché*, Counselor."

"Overruled," Judge Pleasants ruled with hesitation. "You may answer the question, Doctor."

"I'd rather not say." Kingsley stubbornly thrust his chin forward. "Doctor Cooper is my partner and I still have to work with him."

"Your Honor," Bowling appealed to the bench. "I need some help here."

Judge Pleasants looked sternly down from the bench. "Doctor, this is not dealer's choice. Answer the question or I will hold you in contempt."

"Well, then, I will say this much," Kingsley carefully measured his words. "Uh...let's just say he didn't do things the way I would have."

"I see. Have you ever seen blood loss like this before?"

"No, but I have since," Kingsley divulged.

"Would you care to elaborate...,"

"...Objection!" Samantha shouted, instantly on her feet. "Again this line of questioning is not allowable. We've already gone over this."

"No further questions," Bowling said brusquely, sporting a poorly concealed smile.

Once again Samantha made a few minor points with cross-examination, mainly showing Stan Kingsley and Coop really didn't get along, but other than that she did very little to discredit his testimony or impugn his integrity. Apparently, he was a man of few vices and no hidden skeletons. As Dr. Kingsley stepped down from the stand, he looked satisfied, maybe even a little self-righteous. Facing straight ahead, he never looked at Coop as he walked stiffly back up the aisle.

Judge Pleasants frowned at the opposing counsels, sighed, then consulted her watch. Silently, she debated for a couple of seconds, then ordered a two hour recess for lunch. She loudly banged down her gavel, then rose, and with her black robe tails flaring, marched from the courtroom.

Somewhat shell-shocked, Coop watched Samantha calmly gather up her papers and carefully place them back in her briefcase. Her face was unreadable as they headed for the exit. As Coop opened the door for her, their path was suddenly blocked. Totally suffused in the brilliant sunlight, Coop initially didn't recognize him. His smile was thin, strained and malicious, and his silver black hair was slicked straight back, but it wasn't until the midday sun glinted off his gold teeth that Coop identified him. It was none other than Nickolas Tsongas!

"How do you like it so far, Mister Cooper?" he sneered, getting up close in Coop's face. Almost immediately big Ben Bowling grabbed him and shoved him through the door. Nick broke free long enough to hiss, "don't think for a moment this is over. It's just the beginning!"

19

I read once of a man who was cured of a dangerous illness
by eating his doctor's prescription which he understood
was the medicine itself.
—Samuel Butler (1835–1902)

Coop and Samantha had a quiet lunch at Jose Garcia's, a quaint little Mexican restaurant located downtown and only two blocks from the courthouse. Samantha ordered a taco salad, Coop a bowl of chili verde. Silently, they toyed with their food. There wasn't much to say. They both knew the trial was going badly and neither had the slightest idea of how to change it. Finally, Samantha gave her salad one last stir with her fork, looked at her watch. "We'd better get back," she said. "Judge Pleasants has already warned me once about being late."

Coop nodded and scooted his plate aside. "Yeah, I remember," he stood up and tossed his towel on the table. "At my preliminary hearing, she threatened you with contempt."

Once the court was back in session, Benjamin Bowling continued with his parade of witnesses, by calling Renae Mackey to the stand. Rigid as advanced *rigor mortis*, she stiffly placed her right hand on the Bible as she was sworn in.

"What is your title, Ms Mackey?" Bowling asked, "and your hospital position?"

"I am a registered nurse," Renae's her voice was flat and her face about as animated as a fifteenth-century Dutch still life painting, "and I work in surgery."

"Where did you go to school?"

"I got my degree right here at Dixie State University."

"What was your job during Betty Tsongas's surgery?" Bowling struggled out of his chair, but this time with his right hand he made sure he left the chair behind.

"I was the circulating nurse."

"What does a circulating nurse do?"

"I oversee the operating room and make sure the surgeon has everything he needs."

"Kind of like a movie producer?"

"Yeah, I guess."

"Do you agree that Doctor Cooper was late the day in question?"

Renae nodded her head with conviction.

"You need to answer verbally, Nurse Mackey," Mr. Bowling reminded her, "it's for the record."

"Yes...yes, he was quite late."

"Now then, Nurse Mackey, will you describe Doctor Cooper's bizarre behavior on that day."

"Objection, Your Honor!" Samantha was instantly on her feet again. "He's leading the witness. Nobody's established there was any bizarre behavior."

"Side bar," Judge Pleasants growled from her desk.

When the two counselors gathered under the bench, she covered the microphone and hissed. "I'm getting damn tired of this. You two are experienced lawyers, you know the rules, now play by them." She then uncovered her mike and barked, "Objection sustained. Mister Bowling, please rephrase your question."

"What kind of a state was Doctor Cooper in when he arrived for surgery?" Bowling asked smoothly. He did not appear to be in the least embarrassed by the judge's reprimand.

"He seemed out of it," Renae answered, "you know, confused."

"Why do you say that?"

"First of all, he forgot to put on a surgical mask, then when the bleeding started he didn't seem to know what to do."

"Did you also witness the stool-sitting episode?"

"Yes, sir."

"Do you think Doctor Cooper fainted?"

"Yes...but it was more like he passed out."

"What's the difference?"

"Fainting is usually a medical condition. Passing out is related to medication or drugs of some kind."

"So, how do you know he passed out?"

"Objection!" Samantha howled, "this calls for a personal opinion."

"Expert witness," Bowling snapped back.

"Objection overruled," Pleasants growled, looking like she might explode.

"Could you elaborate, Nurse Mackey?" Bowling continued.

"I think he was intoxicated or on drugs," Renae declared, her thin jaw stubbornly thrust forward, "or both."

"Why do you say that?"

"I smelled alcohol on his breath, he was dizzy," Renae said, "and I've seen this sort of thing before. I know what an impaired person looks like."

"Thank you, Nurse Mackey." Bowling squeezed his huge frame back into his undersized chair. "Your witness, Counselor."

Samantha didn't immediately rise from the table, but instead took a few moments to fiddle with her laptop computer.

"Ms Jardine," Judge Pleasants finally barked, "do you have questions for this witness?"

"Uh...yes, Your Honor."

Slowly, Samantha Rose got out of her chair and approached the witness box. Once again, all heads turned. They always did when Samantha walked by. "Nurse Mackey, are you experienced in all fields of medicine or are you strictly a surgical nurse?"

"No, I've worked most areas of medicine except O.B," Renae replied.

"Psychiatry and drug and alcohol rehab?"

"Well, no."

"But you do know a little about flu and upper respiratory viruses?"

"Yes, I worked pediatrics for five years."

"Could you tell us the symptoms of the flu or a bad cold?"

"You can run a fever, have a lot of nasal congestion and drainage, and have a headache," Renae answered confidently.

"How about dizziness?"

"Yes, and that too."

"It seems to me you just described Doctor Cooper's symptoms of that day."

"Objection!" Bowling bellowed. "There was no question here. It seems as though the Counselor is offering her own opinion."

"Sustained," Pleasants barked, then not bothering to cover her mike, she added, "I'm warning you two for the last time."

"Have you ever gone to work with a cold, Nurse Mackey?" Samantha continued unfazed.

"Well...," Renae hesitated.

"Remember, you're under oath."

"Well, yes, a time or two," Renae admitted, frowning. "Sometimes in this business you've got no choice."

"I see..." Samantha paused, and looked pointedly at the jury, then back at Renae. "Now let's change direction a little. You say Doctor Cooper was impaired that day, did you obtain a blood alcohol level?"

"No."

"How about a drug and toxicology screen?"

"No."

"So, how do you know Doctor Cooper was drunk or impaired?"

"I know drunks when I see them," Renae declared stubbornly.

"Your professional opinion?"

"Yes, ma'am."

"Oh," Samantha said facetiously, "so you did work in alcohol rehab?"

"I must object," Bowling shouted, trying to struggle to his feet, then giving up. "Really, Your Honor, Counsel is badgering this witness."

"Ms Jardine," Judge Judith Pleasants hissed. "I now find you in contempt of this court. We'll discuss your penalty later."

"May I ask on what grounds?" Samantha asked, seemingly not in the least dismayed.

"I'm warning you," Judith Pleasants' voice was lethal, "don't try me."

"I have no further questions of this witness." Samantha abruptly sat down beside an astonished Coop.

To say Coop was amazed was a gross understatement; he was in awe. Not only was Samantha Rose a great lawyer, she was also a master magician. She had just made something out of nothing.

Judge Pleasants scowled down from her bench, then turned to Nurse Mackey. "You are dis...,"

"...Re-cross!" Bowling shouted, abruptly standing up. Again his uprooted chair clung briefly to his bulging behind.

"Is this going to accomplish anything?" Pleasants asked bluntly. "This is not a tennis match you know. You don't always have to hit the ball back."

"Yes, Your Honor, I'm pretty sure it will," Bowling replied as his trapped chair suddenly released and clattered back to the floor.

Pleasants nodded her consent.

"Nurse Mackey," Bowling began after a moment's contemplation, "you may not have worked on an alcohol rehabilitation unit, but you do have some experience with alcoholics. Would you care to tell the court how?"

"I...I would rather not," she stammered, turning red.

"Please, Ms Mackey," Bowling coaxed. "It's important."

Renae hesitated and bit her lower lip. "Well, if you must know, I lived with an alcoholic for twenty years. My...my late husband Elliot died from cirrhosis of the liver."

Silence descended on the courtroom like a fresh blanket of snow. After a long theatrical pause, Bowling continued. "Thank you for sharing that, Nurse Mackey. I know that was hard."

After dismissing Renae Mackey, Judge Judith Pleasants looked like she'd about had enough and made a great show of consulting her wristwatch. Scowling down at the courtroom, she appeared to make up her mind. "This court is recessed for the day. And since tomorrow is Thanksgiving," she added, thinking out loud, "and since I'm going out of town, Friday will also be a court holiday. Therefore, this court will not reconvene until Monday morning at 9:00 a.m. sharp." She banged down her gavel, bunched up her robe up around her waist and quickly walked from the room.

During the ride home, Samantha explained to Coop what to expect on Monday. The plaintiff had one more witness to call, Nickolas Tsongas. Obviously, he would give a biased, heart-wrenching account of how Coop ruined his life. On cross-examination, Samantha would try to badger him into admitting Betty was taking Yuccasote, but she suspected he would simply deny it.

After Tsongas, it would be their turn to call witnesses and present evidence. She had already arranged to call Dr. Jacob Heinz as a character witness and she would try to submit Dr. Marcus Westover's letter as evidence. However, if they couldn't prove Betty Tsongas was taking Yuccasote, then Westover's letter was pretty much irrelevant and for that same reason it might be ruled inadmissible. Two weeks ago Samantha had subpoenaed Betty Tsongas's patient records from MITH, but was informed by mail they had never heard of her and they had no record of such a patient.

As a final act of desperation, Samantha informed Coop she planned to call him to the stand, a potentially tricky and chancy maneuver. As a witness she suspected he would do a credible job of telling his side of the story. After all, he did have an honest look about him and certainly did not appear to be incompetent, but calling him to the stand would also open the door for the prosecution. Undoubtedly, in cross-examination Bowling would verbally assault him and unmercifully bash his character. Then, that would be it, caput, they were done, finished. This could be one of the shortest and flimsiest defenses in the history of malpractice jurisprudence. If she deliberately stalled, their defense could take a half-day at most. By mid-afternoon, it would be time for each side to present their summations and the whole thing could possibly go to the jury as early as Monday afternoon or Tuesday morning at the latest. "And I doubt," Samantha concluded, "the jury will have to deliberate very long with this one. It is entirely conceivable we could have verdict as early as midday Tuesday."

Then she fell silent and Coop didn't have to ask what she thought the verdict might be.

At first, he felt the insidious creep of vulnerability and helplessness. In short order, that was followed by a tidal wave of raw panic. His throat tightened. Were they really that close? So by Tuesday the last domino would topple and the chain reaction he most feared would begin. Literally, the floodgates would open, destroying everything in its path. He had no choice. He simply had to go back to MITH and find some kind of documentation. Something to verify Betty Tsongas was a patient there, was indeed taking Yuccasote and that's what killed her. He shuddered at the idea, but he what other option did he have? Anything less would not help.

Reluctantly, Samantha Rose agreed. She could think of no other way either, but stubbornly insisted this time she would also go.

Coop steadfastly refused for several of reasons. One, if caught in a criminal act she would surely be disbarred. Two, he needed her to stay here on the outside, to alert authorities if he didn't come back. And lastly, he needed her to keep an eye on the ranch, horses and Malachi. With an unknown assailant, murderer and arsonist still at large, he didn't dare trust those things to the Snow boy. Grudgingly, Samantha agreed, but she made sure he knew she didn't like it.

It was after five o'clock when they arrived back at the ranch and as usual, Malachi was beside himself to see them.

With Malachi following and begging for attention, Coop and Samantha headed straight for the house. The first thing that caught Coop's eye when he walked into the kitchen was the red light flashing on the answering machine, almost never good news. Taking in a deep breath, he punched the play button.

D...D...Doctor Cooper, uh...this...uh...this is Nathan Reed. I'm having a treatment at my a...a...apartment at eight o'clock tonight. I...i...if you still want to come, be here by seven-thirty. And...uh... bring the money.

Samantha sighed and made coffee.

Coop arrived at Nathan's apartment right on time. Somewhat grudgingly he paid the three hundred dollars, actually Samantha Rose's money, then looked around. Not that it was spotless, but Nate had cleaned the place up a bit, particularly the living room and kitchen, and he'd blocked the view of the bedroom by simply closing the door. The scattered textbooks were collected and shelved and the autumn-leaf carpet of discarded computer papers had been raked and bagged. The kitchen's dirty dishes were washed, or at least removed from sight, but unfortunately the stale locker room smell remained. Silently, Coop suspected things were not quite as clean as they appeared.

Nate was nervous, almost jittery as he escorted Coop to the bathroom, which had not been cleaned, and showed him a one-inch hole he'd bored through the common wall to the living room. From the living room, the hole was pretty much invisible as Nate had placed a motel-quality desert landscape painting over the hole, then right through a saguaro cactus he drilled a matching hole. After instructing Coop to not screw this up, Nate left, closing and deliberately locking the door behind him. With his right eye pressed to the peephole, Coop could see him anxiously pacing in the living room.

Coop didn't have to wait long. Within ten minutes, he heard a loud knock on the door. With hands visibly shaking, Nate opened the door to Dr. Rob Belton. The doctor was wearing a powder blue sweatshirt, faded jeans, white sneakers under a white lab coat. Even when he tried to look causal, he looked formal. Coop suspected as a kid, he never knew the joys of mud and water. Without so much as flinching, and much to Coop's surprise, Belton walked over and sat down on Nathan's grimy, possibly infested, green-felt couch. Grabbing a metal folding chair from the kitchen, Nathan turned it backwards, then sat down facing Belton. Once again Coop was struck by Belton's apparent sincerity.

"So, how are you feeling?" he asked, leaning forward.

Coop strained to hear.

"G...g...good days and some b...b...bad ones. Probably not as good as a month ago," Nathan replied, resting his elbows on the back of the chair.

"Are you taking your medicine?"

"Y...y...yes sir, I never miss."

"If you don't start feeling better by next visit, I can give it I.V," Belton advised. "We've just finished formulating and new a new intravenous preparation. It works much faster and is more potent."

"I...I...I hate needles."

"Well, we'll see," Belton said softly. "Are you making it to your classes?"

"Yeah, getting mostly straight A's."

"How about that girlfriend?" Belton winked. "What was her name?"

"J...J...Jenny. She still comes around sometimes. Maybe even later tonight."

"Well, then," Belton loudly slapped his knees, "I guess we'd better give you your treatment now so you can get on with your life."

"Y...y...yeah," Nathan agreed, "t...t...this is a busy night for me."

"May I use the bathroom to wash up before we get started?" Belton held his hands up high, as he got up and headed for the bathroom. "It was a long drive."

"Uh...uh...no!" Nate shouted and scrambled to block his path. "I...i...it's out of order."

"Well, okay," Belton shrugged, dropping his hands. "Are you okay, Nathan?"

"Yeah, I'm fine, D...D...Doctor Belton." Nathan followed Belton back to the living room. "I...i...it's just the toilet overflowed and I haven't had a chance to clean it up yet."

"Well, if you can stand my dirty hands, then I guess I can," Belton smiled. "Let's get on with it."

Somehow, Coop suspected his hands were spotless.

Nathan grabbed the metal chair and placed it in the exact center of the room, then slumped down on it. Fishing in his jeans, Belton produced a small vial of what appeared to be oil, sprinkled a few drops on Nathan's already greasy black hair, then placed his hands lightly on his head. He closed his eyes, tilted his face upward, then using a clear strong voice, he began droning what sounded like a prayer.

"Oh, God, in the name of Jesus Christ and by the authority of the holy Melchizedek priesthood, I invoke thy divine power. Today I pray for you to heal thy son, Nathan Reed, to make him whole again. As you know, Nate is engaged in a life and death struggle with the devil. The Dark One has placed an evil spell, yeah even the scourge of cancer on Nathan, but we know with your help we can deliver him from all evil, just as Jesus drove the unclean spirits from the man called Legion. But as we do this, we acknowledge your great wisdom and humbly submit to your will. For blessings already received, we thank you and vow to remain faithful servants and rededicate our lives to your kingdom and glory. For thine is the power and the Glory, Amen."

Belton let his hands linger on Nathan's head for a few seconds, then slowly removed them, helping him up from the chair. After warmly embracing him, Belton looked Nate in the eye and reminded him of his covenant with God and MITH. Lastly he extracted a twelve-ounce brown bottle of Yuccasote from his lab coat pocket and handed it to him.

Coop groaned inwardly, almost out loud, when he saw Nathan fish in his Levi pocket and pull out the very same money Coop just gave him, offering it to Belton. Smiling like a benevolent grandfather, Belton took the money, hugged him again and asked for his empty bottle.

"Uh...uh I broke it," Nate stammered. "W...w...when the toilet overflowed I was scrambling around, trying to shut it off and I...uh... knocked in onto the toilet bowl and broke it."

"You sure?" Belton asked, giving Nathan a sharp glance. Nate nodded and after one more critical look, Belton wished him well and was gone.

Coop was dumbfounded. So this is what was meant by combination therapy, the much-ballyhooed treatment of the whole person, the physical, the mental and the spiritual. The entire treatment consisted of cursory conversation about school and girlfriends, the laying on of hands, the chanting of incantations and the delivery of a bottle of Yuccasote. Oh, and of course, the exchange of money.

Unlocking the bathroom door, Coop returned to the living room. With no hug or smile, he also looked Nathan straight in the eye.

"Nathan, this is madness! Tomorrow, I want you to come by my office and get those blood tests and x-rays."

"I...I...I'll think about it, Doctor Cooper," Nathan stammered, his eyes wide with surprise. As Coop walked toward the front door, Nathan added, "m...m...maybe after the holidays.'

"I'll see you in no later than next week," Coop said sternly.

Thirty minutes later, Coop was back home. Sitting at the kitchen table and over a cup of decaffeinated coffee, he narrated the entire episode for Samantha Rose.

"I can't believe what I just saw," he concluded.

"It does seem pretty bizarre," Samantha agreed.

"Almost like I'd somehow time-traveled back a century or two," Coop shook his head, "back before the dawn of science and modern medicine."

"Sounds a bit like an old time traveling medicine show," Samantha added, "complete with it's own patent medicine."

"Yeah, it was quite a show, all right," Coop's his forehead was creased with concern, "but I am worried about Nathan."

"Maybe, he will come to the office to be checked."

"I sure hope so...,"

Suddenly, there was a loud knock on the kitchen door!

Startled, Coop and Samantha looked at each other, then at the door. Coop frowned and shook his head. He hated late night visitors. It was almost never brought good news.

Another knock. Even louder this time.

"Okay, okay, I coming," Coop grumbled as got up and headed for the door.

Shrugging, Samantha took another sip of coffee, almost cold now, as she silently stared out the window into the black night.

Flipping on the porch light, Coop swung the door wide open, then immediately caught his breath!

Quickly, he glanced back over his shoulder at Samantha Rose, then tripped over the threshold as stepped onto the landing and closed the door. Regaining his balance, he tried to speak, but no sound came.

At first he thought it was an apparition, conjured up in his muddled mind from extreme loneliness and months of endless yearning, but it was not.

It moved! Its feet made little scraping sounds on the concrete! It had a definite scent, that of cheap French perfume! It spoke! And when it spoke, he knew for sure it was no ghost. Its voice was high-pitched, almost whinny, and very familiar.

"Hi, there, Coops."

He remained rooted and speechless! For there standing on the porch, bathed in soft incandescent light and as beautiful as ever was his long-estranged wife, Kylie Evans Cooper!

20

It is a mathematical fact
that fifty percent of all doctors
graduate in the bottom half of their class.
—*Author Unknown*

Coop didn't know what to say. He didn't have to. Kylie began talking the second he opened the door.

"Coops, long time no see," she gushed as she rushed forward to kiss him. "I'm sorry I didn't call first, but, you know, I just couldn't find the nerve." She continued to jabber as she opened the door and pushed past him into the kitchen. "Sometimes it's just easier to do things in person, you know. Phones can be so hard. If you would just learn how to text."

From past experience, Coop knew when Kylie did this, talked fast, literally nonstop, she was nervous. Obviously, she was nervous now.

"Things just didn't work out so well with Roger, you know, not that he wasn't a good man. But as it turned out, he was not a world famous painter, pretty much a nobody. You know, what they call a regional artist, whatever that means."

Over the years, Coop had also learned to read between the lines. As Kylie prattled on, he silently interpreted. *An unknown painter meant no life of glamour, no spotlight in the society section of the newspaper, no highbrow socials or parties.*

"In fact, you know, he was pretty much a bum most of the time," she continued. "He could only paint when the inspiration hit him. But, you know, inspiration is a pretty bad shot. It didn't hit him very often."

No money, no life of luxury.

"After a while things got unbearable, you know. And as God knows, I tried."

224

They ran out of money. And he hadn't sent her a check this last month.

"Anyway, I didn't know what to do. So I prayed about it for days and days. And fasted too."

Couldn't figure out how to come back and still save face. But if God commanded it, who could argue? Kylie pretty much used prayer to validate what she was planning to do anyway.

"Then, it just came to me, probably an answer from God, you know, but what I had here was pretty close to perfect and I'll bet Coop still loves me and...," Kylie stopped in mid-sentence as she caught sight of Samantha Rose sitting quietly at the table. As Samantha lowered her cup onto its saucer, Kylie's mouth dropped.

Coop quickly stepped in. "Samantha Rose, this is Kylie Cooper. Kylie, this is...uh...uh...my lawyer, Samantha Rose Jardine."

As she stood up, Samantha Rose frowned and looked sharply at Coop. Slowly, she replaced her frown with a thin smile and extended her hand to Kylie.

Coop instantly realized his error. He'd made a huge colossal mistake by introducing Samantha as his lawyer and not his girlfriend or at the very least his friend. Unfortunately, there was no way to retract it now.

"Nice to meet you, Misses Cooper." Samantha's face was now a mask.

"A lawyer?" Kylie shamelessly appraised Samantha Rose from head to foot. "Coops, why ever do you need a lawyer? You never said a word to me."

"It's a long story," Coop replied vaguely, but silently thought, "I didn't tell you because you weren't here."

Kylie paused and looked puzzled.

"Well," Samantha Rose said following a long awkward pause, "you two have a lot to talk about. I'll just get my stuff and leave."

"Can I talk to you for a moment in private?" Coop asked, then not waiting for an answer grabbed Samantha by the elbow and steered her into the bedroom.

"Samantha...uh," Coop stammered, "uh...you've got to believe me, I had no idea she was coming."

"I believe you."

"You...you don't have to go."

"So you'd like a *ménage a trois*?"

"No!"

"Then that must mean you're going to ask Kylie to leave?"

"Well...uh...,"

"Your hesitation tells me everything," Samantha said brusquely. "Let me get my stuff, I'll leave you two alone."

"Where?"

"Where, what?" Samantha snapped

"Where will you go?"

"I don't know. Maybe back to Salt Lake."

"What about Monday?" Despair seeped into Coop's voice. "What about the trial?"

"Don't worry," Samantha pulled clothes from the closet, "I am a professional. I'll be there. Just make sure you are." She turned her back on Coop and threw clothes into her suitcase.

A few minutes later Samantha and Kylie, both dragging suitcases, passed in the hallway. Kylie headed straight for the master bedroom and Samantha Rose for the door. Coop followed her out to her rental car.

"Good bye, Coop," Samantha's jaw was firmly set. "I'll see you Monday."

"Can...can we at least have Thanksgiving dinner together tomorrow?" Coop pleaded. "We could go out to a restaurant."

"No, you spend tomorrow with your wife. You need some time to decide what you want." Samantha shut the car door firmly, then drove off into the black night.

With equal parts of confusion and despair, Coop watched her taillights disappear around the first turn. For months, he dreamed of this moment, now it didn't feel exactly like he thought it would.

Back in the house, Kylie wanted to talk. She always wanted to talk. As though she was talking to a girlfriend rather than a husband she'd abandoned over a year ago, Kylie babbled on about Arizona, the southwest circuit of art shows and the towns she visited with Roger Callister. She just loved Sedona, Arizona. It was a lot like St. George, but classier. Unfortunately, Roger said they couldn't afford to live there, etc., etc., etc.

Just like old times, Coop began to tune her out. So this was it?

This was what he had dreamed of. This was what he'd yearned for and even prayed for. This was why he'd never filed divorce papers and this was why he'd faithfully sent seven thousand dollars a month for well over a year. So, if this was it, why wasn't he happy? Even overjoyed? He'd finally gotten what he wanted. For a man who had trouble finding even one girlfriend to suddenly have two was almost a cruel twist of fate. Perhaps there was a God after all, if so he was laughing. He or she had a sick sense of humor. Coop figured his God had to be one of those ancient Greek Gods. The sadistic ones who delighted in toying with their mortal's lives, enjoyed placing them in impossible awkward positions and watching them squirm.

"Actually, Flagstaff wasn't bad either and not as expensive as Sedona, but no red rocks, you know. I could've lived there in the ponderosa pines and all, but the altitude really flared up Roger's emphysema, you know, the cigarettes, and he really didn't want to settle down anyway or give up the cigarettes. He said he wanted to paint every sunrise and sunset in the west, but then mostly he sat on the couch...,"

In the end, it wasn't really much of a decision. Coop really didn't need time to think, to thoroughly analyze it from every angle, as was his usual routine when tackling difficult problems. Quite simply, he wanted Samantha Rose Jardine. Why hadn't he been honest with Kylie right from the beginning? It would have been so simple, "Kylie, I'm so sorry, but things have changed. This is my girlfriend, Samantha Rose. No, I don't want you back, Samantha makes me happy." That's what he should have done. It was the shock of it all and the fact she'd actually come back. Momentarily, that unhinged him, confused him. Unfortunately, the memory of Kylie was more desirable, more attractive than her actual presence. Already, she was starting to drive him crazy. He almost wished his beeper would go off calling him to the E.R. Unfortunately, being suspended, that wasn't likely to happen.

"So, you know what I did? I got down on my knees and prayed, really prayed, and God showed me the way. He told me in no uncertain terms, this is where I belong. This is my place, my home and Coop is my husband," Kylie gushed with conviction, then actually paused for Coop to comment.

He didn't. After another moment of silence, she said something totally out of character.

"So how about you, Coops? What have you been up to?"

Suddenly, it dawned on him; here was a way out. He cleared his throat, sat down, then in vivid and depressing detail explained all that had happened to him in the last few months. He told her about his present lawsuit, how it was going badly and he had at least two more pending. To an increasingly somber Kylie, he also revealed he was charged with negligent homicide and that trial would begin sometime in the near future. With absolutely no attempt at sugarcoating, he disclosed his gloomy financial status, how he was already broke with the real potential of soon being millions of dollars in debt. With no job, a debt like that may take a lifetime to settle. He felt a little guilty about what he said next, and though it was a little heavy-handed, technically it was true. In the eyes of the law, the spouse, meaning Kylie, was also responsible for any debts accrued during marriage. As she attempted to digest that, Coop explained there was also a very real possibility he might even go to prison.

For the first time all night, maybe the first time ever, Kylie was speechless. He hated being so rough on her, but in truth he was just telling it like it was. Coop could almost see the gears of her mind turning, but she remained quiet. Obviously, down there in Arizona, she'd heard nothing of his problems. Coop smiled to himself. Perhaps, he wasn't as big a desperado as he'd thought. It looked like he and Roger had something in common after all. Roger was a regional painter and he was just a regional thug.

Looking down at her hands, Kylie fussed with Samantha's table centerpiece, an autumn bouquet featuring a long stem cattails, red chrysanthemums and colorful fall leaves, then smoothed out the checkered linen tablecloth. Sighing deeply, she stood up, declared she was tired and going to bed. As she walked away, Coop told her he would sleep in the guest bedroom. She simply nodded, but still offered no verbal response.

During the night, Coop heard Kylie get up and wander about the house several times. He didn't sleep much either. Though his decision was made, he continued to mull things over. His was the classic story of long distant relationships. Perhaps separation really does make the heart grow fonder, but the mechanism seems to be memory inflation.

When something or someone is taken from you against your will, its memory becomes exponentially more dear, more treasured with the passage of time. For example in death people almost always attain a stature way out of proportion to their true standing in life. It seems the deceased are invariably canonized. Nobody gets up at a funeral and says, "he was a no good lazy son-of-a-bitch."

By morning Coop had pretty much planned and prioritized what he must do. First he must deal with Kylie, then he had to find Samantha Rose and convince her to come back. It was really that simple. When she'd left last night, it was late, too late to get a flight to Salt Lake City. So, she must have spent last night in a St. George hotel.

There was only one airline carrier, SkyWest, with flights to SLC, so in lieu of sleep Coop phoned them last night. As he assumed, Samantha indeed left the house too late last night to get a flight. Their first morning flight took off early at 7:10 a.m. and the next was at 9:55 a.m. Surely, Samantha would be on one of them.

Though Coop rose early, at 5:00 a.m., he could hear Kylie already bustling around. He showered, made coffee, toasted a bagel, then sat down at the table to wait. A few minutes later Kylie came in carrying two Samsonite suitcases. Sighing loudly, she sat down at the table, but still said nothing. Coop poured her cup of coffee and offered half of his burnt bagel. She accepted the coffee, but declined the bagel. Coop refilled his cup, then sat down at the table across from her.

"Coops, you know, I guess I need some more time to think and pray about this," she suddenly blurted, toying with her cup. Her eyes were red and swollen. Apparently, she spent a good part of the night crying. "Maybe, I misunderstood what God wanted."

Coop couldn't help but feel sorry for her. It was obvious her life too was in turmoil.

"I understand," he said, no trace of bitterness or reproach in his voice. "Where will you go?"

"I don't know." Kylie shook her head.

"Can you go back to Roger?"

"Maybe...yes."

"I think that's what you should do," Coop said firmly. "It sounds like Roger is a good man and he's been good to you."

"Have you got any money?"

Coop checked his wallet...fifty-seven dollars. He took all of it and handed it to Kylie.

"I don't suppose you'll be sending any more checks?" She looked up hopefully.

"No, Kylie," Coop shook his head, "I'm completely tapped out." After another moment of silence, he continued, "but I will be sending you divorce papers."

She nodded and finished her coffee. "I'll want half of the value of the house and property, you know."

"That's fair," Coop agreed, "I'll pay you when I can."

Using a tissue, she dabbed the tears from her eyes, quickly hugged Coop, grabbed her suitcases and walked out of the door. Coop knew he should be sad to see her go, but he wasn't. It did, however, make him sad to see her so unhappy. He hoped that would change. But this time it felt more final, maybe because this time he'd at last achieved some sense of closure.

Coop gave Kylie a five-minute head start, then grabbed the keys to the Dodge and headed straight for the airport. Fortunately at this hour traffic was usually light and if he hurried, he should make it before SkyWest boarded the 7:10 flight.

St. George Municipal Airport had recently moved to its new home in the south end of the valley, no more than a stone's throw from the state of Arizona. The old airport sat on an island mesa right in the heart of downtown. For convenience it was unbeatable, but unfortunately its runways were too short to accommodate commercial jets and by its very nature, being a mesa, they could not be lengthened. In the last couple of decades, St. George's population had literally mushroomed, necessitating the construction of the new airport with longer runways and passenger jets.

Now some ten miles out of town, the new airport was built on an elevated, but gently sloping piedmont plain. From there, the view was simply magnificent. To the immediate north across the valley was the uneven panorama of alternating slot canyons and massive red sandstone bluffs, typical of the Navajo formation. Directly behind the Navajo sandstone, rose the craggy blue spires of the ten thousand-foot Pine Valley Mountains. To the northeast, the sculpted crimson/white mesas of Zion Canyon National Park were visible on a clear day. And, to the south and west the vast Mohave Desert spread out forbiddingly, like an endless gray and desolate carpet.

After leaving St. George, Coop sped east on the newly constructed Southern Parkway, then parked in the airport's ten-minute passenger loading zone. Jumping out of the Dodge, he sprinted for the terminal. Fortunately, the metal barrier screen was still in place, blocking passengers from entering the secured area. The TSA officers, however, were milling around and looked as if they were about ready to begin screening. Even at this early hour, the terminal was busy, filled with last minute holiday travelers trying to get home for Thanksgiving dinner.

A minute later a female TSA officer lifted the screen and Coop positioned himself strategically to the left of the metal detectors where he could see the passengers as the filed by. He waited patiently until the plane was fully boarded. There was no Samantha Rose. He was pretty sure he hadn't missed her. After the flight had taken off, he checked at the SkyWest counter to see if she was on manifest for the next flight, but of course that information was confidential.

Coop checked his watch; it was almost 7:30 a.m. Passengers would probably start showing up for the 9:55 flight in an hour or so. This really was not enough time for him to leave the airport. Wandering over to a vending machine, he purchased a cup of coffee, then suddenly remembered he parked in a ten-minute zone.

The second he stepped through the doors he could see it. There fluttering in the early morning breeze was a yellow parking ticket, securely wedged between the wiper and the windshield glass. He couldn't help but laugh at the absurdity of it all. Snatching the parking ticket, he wadded it up and threw it to the ground. That was like charging a man on death row with attempted escape. What difference did a superficial knife wound make when you already had a bullet hole in the heart? After re-parking the Dodge, he went back, picked up the ticket, straightened it out and placed it in his wallet. Sometimes life got so bizarre, so strange, all you could do was laugh.

The passengers for the 9:55 flight came and boarded, but still no sign of Samantha Rose. Coop was beginning to feel a little panicky. Though it was pretty late, maybe she drove her rental car to SLC last night. Once again he went to the SkyWest counter and though they would give no names, they did disclose the first two flights of the day were completely full, even overbooked, due to the holiday rush. The next flight wasn't until 1:37 and it wasn't full. Apparently, the afternoon flight was too late for most travelers to get home for turkey dinner. It was conceivable that was the first available flight for which Samantha could purchase a ticket.

With time to kill, Coop drove back to town and to his office at Urology Associates. Being a holiday, there were no cars in the parking lot, the place looked deserted. Coop unlocked the back door and headed straight for his private office. Piled on his desk was the usual backlog of paperwork. Mechanically, he sorted through it, mostly lab and X-ray slips from the hospital that needed to be signed off. Also there was a memorandum of surgical staff meetings and other hospital functions. He thumbed through several patient referral forms, he'd have to give those to Stan, and a handful of product and seminar flyers.

Mixed in the pile, however, there was one curious-looking, hand-addressed envelope with no return address. Coop picked it up and held it to his nose. It had a slightly familiar odor, one that he couldn't quite put his finger on. Maybe, a bit like his late tack shed or more specifically shoe or saddle leather. He couldn't be sure. Ripping open the envelope, he pulled out a single sheet and fished in his pocket for his reading glasses.

> *Dr. Cooper,*
> *Take care.*
> *As they say, the third time is a charm.*

And that was it! What the hell was that supposed to mean? Was it a joke or a threat? Coop wondered as he wadded up the paper. It was probably from Nickolas Tsongas. His hunger for revenge knew no bounds. Picking up the paper again, Coop tried to smooth it out. Maybe, a professional forensic scientist or a handwriting expert could glean some information from it, but exactly what he had no idea. He'd already contaminated it with his own fingerprints, but maybe others could be lifted. Trying to not contaminate it any further, he carefully stuffed it back in the envelope. He'd show it to Samantha and get her ideas, that is if he ever saw her again.

Finally he finished the tedious paperwork and checked his watch. It was a still a little early, but with nothing else to do he headed back to the airport. As before, he positioned himself in front of the metal detectors.

The 1:37 passengers began to arrive, at first just a trickle, then a flood. They all seemed to show up at once. Frantically, Coop scanned the crowd, trying not miss anyone. No Samantha Rose! His mood plummeted like a skydiver with a tangled parachute.

Maybe, he should try to get on this plane, go to Salt Lake City and search till he found her. But it was too late. The passengers were already mostly boarded and they were getting ready to close the plane's doors. No way would he have time to purchase a ticket and make it through security. Depressed, he turned around and started down the terminal. What should he do now?

Suddenly there she was, striding briskly toward him, towing her suitcase. With each jaunty step, her auburn hair bounced off her back and shoulders.

Abruptly she stopped. There was no question she'd seen him now. Scowling deeply, she dropped her suitcase handle and simply stood there, waiting. Taking in a deep breath, Coop walked toward her.

"Where's Kylie?" she immediately asked.

"She's gone, probably back to Arizona."

Samantha paused and seemed to perceptibly thaw.

"How do you feel about that?"

"Not at all like I thought I would," Coop admitted, "but probably the word that comes to mind would be...uh...relieved."

"So, are you still obsessed with her?"

"So, are you still my lawyer?"

"Well, of course."

"Now, I know you do occasionally practice other kinds of law, other than malpractice?"

"Not if I can help it," Samantha snapped.

"How about divorce law?"

Suddenly she smiled. "I might make an exception."

Coop bent over, picked up the handle to Samantha Rose's suitcase, put his other arm around her shoulders, then steered her toward the Dodge.

"How about some Thanksgiving dinner?" he asked as they left the terminal.

They ate Thanksgiving dinner at the Two Palms restaurant. It was traditional Thanksgiving fare: turkey, dressing, yams, potatoes and gravy, and cranberry sauce. Coop couldn't remember when he'd enjoyed a Thanksgiving dinner more. The food was nothing special, but the company was. This was the way one was supposed to spend the holidays...with loved ones.

Samantha was not a big eater. She mostly picked, then like a food shell game she shuffled everything, rearranging the various piles. At the moment, she was moving the potatoes to where the turkey had been. She took a tiny bite of dressing, then looked up at Coop.

"Your birthday's tomorrow, you know."

Coop shook his head in surprise. In fact, he had totally forgotten. "So, it is," he replied without enthusiasm.

"I got you a present," she grinned.

"I hope not."

Samantha rummaged in her purse, then shoved a pale yellow piece of paper at Coop. It was tissue thin and looked like an invoice. Coop slowly unfolded the paper. Indeed, it was a receipt from **TUC-CIANO'S ITALIAN LEATHER WORKS – MAKERS OF FINE SADDLES SINCE 1910.**

"What is this?" Coop arched an eyebrow.

"It's really quite simple," Samantha was still grinning. "You need a saddle. It's your birthday. This guy makes custom saddles."

"I...I don't know what to say," Coop stammered. No one had ever bought him a present like this.

Samantha leaned over the table and kissed him. "Only thing is, you need to go into his shop tomorrow and tell him all the bells and whistles you want and to be fitted."

Coop wanted to protest they couldn't afford it, but when he saw the smile on her face, he couldn't. In her mind, she had just bought him the perfect present—and she had. So instead, he shook his head in amazement and returned her smile. "Wow, a custom saddle!"

Just as the waiter brought the pumpkin pie, his beeper went off.

"Are you still wearing that thing?" Samantha frowned and nodded toward the pager on his belt.

"Yeah, I guess it's force of habit." As Coop jerked the beeper from the plastic belt holster and checked the message, he added, "I didn't even realize I had it."

"Who is it?"

"The E.R."

"I guess they don't know you're not licensed to practice medicine in this state anymore."

"I guess not," Coop agreed as he silently debated whether to call them back or not.

"Go ahead, call them," Samantha finally said. "If you don't, you're just going to stew about it. Just tell them right up front you can't legally take care of patients in the E.R. right now."

"Yeah, I guess maybe I better, so in the future they won't waste a lot of time trying to track me down." From his shirt pocket, Coop retrieved his cell phone and punched in the number.

"E.R." the voice barked, all business.

"This is Doctor Cooper and I just wanted to tell you...,"

"...Oh, Doctor Cooper!" the receptionist interrupted. "Hold on...let me get the nurse."

Coop shrugged his shoulders at Samantha. "I'm on hold."

A few moments later the nurse breathlessly picked up the phone and immediately began talking. "Doctor Cooper, I'm so glad you called back. We've got a bit of a situation here. We've got Nathan Reed here and he won't let anyone touch him but you."

Coop had already forgotten what he was going to tell them, instead he blurted, "what's wrong?"

"He...he's bleeding to death!"

"From where"

"The bowels."

"I'll be there." Coop flipped his phone off and stood up.

"You've got to be crazy," Samantha blurted. "Stop a minute and let's think this through."

"There's no time."

"If you're caught, and surely you will be," Samantha said, "you'll be charged with practicing medicine without a license."

"If they want that piece of me, they'll have to get in line," Coop quipped, "and I mean way behind everyone else."

"Don't think they won't."

"What would you have me do?"

Samantha paused for only a moment. "Go!" she finally said, "go. I'll take a cab back to the ranch."

It was at least fifteen minutes from the restaurant to the hospital parking lot, but Coop covered it in ten. Jumping out of the Dodge, he dashed for the E.R entrance. The volunteer at the desk instantly recognized him and pushed the release button on the electronic lock. Jerking the door open, Coop sprinted to the central nursing station and was immediately directed to room eleven.

Room eleven was a mess and the smell was overpowering and nauseating. It was a revolting mixture of fresh blood mixed with stool. The odor was greatly augmented by anaerobic bacteria already at work. It reminded Coop of when he was an intern. The sickening stench accompanying colonic bleeders was something one could never forget.

Stepping back, Coop drew in a lungful of untainted air, then holding his breath, plunged into the room.

Nathan was dressed in a rear-tie hospital gown and was lying prostrate on a padded metal gurney. Unfortunately, he was about as white as the sheet he was lying on. Everything below his waist was smeared with blood. Just below Nathan's bare bottom, a large pool of purple semisolid blood, but no actual clots, had accumulated. Nate was groaning softly in pain as the nurse was busily trying to clean up the mess. She barely looked up as Coop entered.

Coop quickly glanced up at the overhead monitor, then leaned over Nathan. He was barely conscious. His respirations, 30/minute, and were labored and strident; his pulse was 120, weak and thready; his blood pressure was bargain basement low at 60/40, but unbelievably there was still no I.V. hanging.

"Where's the I.V.?" Coop demanded.

"He refused," the nurse hurriedly explained, "till you got here."

"Get me all the O negative blood the bank has," Coop ordered, "and all the fresh frozen plasma too. Go! I'll start the I.V."

"Yes, sir," the nurse said smartly.

"And call the O.R., tell them we need a room right now and find the general surgeon on call to help."

As the nurse rushed from the room, Coop grabbed a 14-gauge angiocath, strapped a tourniquet around Nathan's emaciated arm and frantically searched for a vein. With a blood pressure this low, there was nothing to keep the veins from collapsing. Quickly, changing tactics, he jerked down Nate's gown exposing his right shoulder. Feeling for the clavicle, Coop jabbed the needle upward, just under the bone, angling toward the neck. Instantly, there was good blood return. Coop threaded the long plastic sheath over the needle into the subclavicular vein, attached it to connecting tubing, then that to a collapsible plastic bag of Lactated Ringers. Lastly, he opened up the roller-valve completely so it would run wide open. Grabbing another angiocath, he felt for the clavicle on the other side. Within minutes, Coop had two large bore I.V.'s running as fast as they would go.

Just as he was finishing with the second IV, the nurse burst into the room, her arms full of blood and fresh frozen plasma. Coop jerked off the bag of Lactated Ringers from the first I.V., attached a unit of packed red cells, also running it full bore. Then just as he was about to change out the bag of Ringers on the second I.V., an alarm from the overhead bank of monitors began to wail.

Glancing up, he noted with great dismay the EKG had changed. Now, it showed huge V-waves, heralding the onset of a sustained run of V-tach. Not only would a V-tach rhythm pump very little blood, but Coop knew flatline often followed.

Like the downswing of a carpenter's hammer, Coop brought his fist crashing down on Nathan's sternum, attempting to jar his heart out of the life-threatening rhythm, then began rhythmic chest compressions. The nurse grabbed an ambu bag with attached oxygen, placed it on Nate's face and ventilated. Unfortunately, the V-tach continued unabated.

"Charge up the defibrillator," Coop barked to the wide-eyed nurse, "also find me a laryngoscope and endotracheal tube." Then as the nurse turned to leave, he quickly added, "and call a code blue. Get me some help."

But even as she scurried from the room the EKG had already started to level out and by the time she returned with the laryngoscope, it was flatline. Now the only curvilinear lines on the EKG strip were the mechanical waves generated by Coop's chest compressions.

Overhead, the alarms continued to shriek, but eventually they went silent too.

21

The next day was Coop's birthday and in spite of his repeated objections Samantha insisted he go to the saddle shop. Her most persuasive argument, the saddle was already paid for and was non-refundable. Certainly, he did need a saddle and the horses did need to be exercised. When he was a kid, he rode bareback, but no more. Nowadays, he didn't bounce as well when he hit the ground and there was no point in keeping horses if you didn't ride them. It did, however, seem to Coop a bit extravagant, even bordering on irresponsible, considering everything else going on.

After breakfast, Coop, along with Malachi, headed into St. George, to look for Tucciano's Saddle Shop. They invited Samantha Rose, but she declined, stating she wanted to stay at the ranch. Being somewhat vague, she told Coop she had things to do, things she could not do with him hanging around. When pressed, she explained she wanted to go over some items for the trial, i.e. completely familiarize herself with the Westover document and work out a list of potential questions for their upcoming witnesses.

Actually, Tucciano's Italian Leather Works was not located in St. George at all, but southeast of town in the agrarian Little Valley area and fairly close to the new airport. Coop was somewhat familiar with the area as he occasionally bought hay from Bentley's Farm located in the same valley.

Tucciano's shop was part of a new equine complex. In addition to Tucciano's, there also were stables and horses for rent, an enclosed riding arena, miles of outdoor trails, a feed and tack shop, a chuck wagon restaurant, a melodrama live theater featuring an old west gun fight, curio and bakery shops and lastly a riding school. All buildings and shops were located on Cheyenne Street and constructed in the old west style complete with rustic facades, boardwalks and hitching posts. Cheyenne Street, of course, was closed to automobile, allowing only foot, and of course, horse traffic.

Today the parking lot was mostly full. Apparently the long holiday weekend, plus the prolonged Indian summer, was good for business. After finally finding a spot near the back, Coop got out of the Dodge, put Malachi on a leash and headed for the single-street western town. According to a professionally painted directory map strategically place at the town's entrance, Tucciano's was located on the east side of the street and right in the middle of town. With Malachi straining at his leash, he was not good on a leash because almost never had to use one, they stepped onto the boardwalk and headed for Tucciano's.

As Coop opened the door, an overhead bell tinkled and immediately he smelled the distinctive odor of a saddle shop. The air was heavy with a complex mixture of odors: fresh cut leather, tanning and softening chemicals, and saddle soaps and oils. Malachi loved the place. He tugged mightily at his leash, wanting to explore a compelling scent in a different direction. Coop struggled to hold him back.

A quick survey revealed the shop to be essentially an open single room, studio-like establishment. Though open, it nevertheless was divided into distinctive areas: a workshop, a business center and counter, and an exhibition area for displaying new saddles. Scattered around the room were several saddles in various stages of construction, everything from a basic fiberglass tree to several finished ones on wedge-shaped wooden stands. Housed under glass in the business counter was an assortment of leather crafts including a rifle scabbard, holsters, chaps, vests, reins, breast straps and gun belts. The work area, located in the back of the room, was littered with scraps of leather, chemical canisters and bottles, and an array of tools. In a way, it reminded Coop of Nathan Reed's cluttered apartment. Presently, no one was in the room. Coop assumed the owner stepped out for a break.

Coop's grandfather dabbled in leather as a hobby. From hanging around his shop, he was familiar with a lot of the tools scattered around on the shelves and workbenches. Quickly, he picked out an Al Stohlman swivel knife barrel as well as a complete assortment of blades and on a windowsill he spotted a round knife. Strewn about on the benches and cabinets were an assortment of Stohlman mallets and hundreds of leather stamps, a whole array of punches, a concho cutter and a leather shredder. Upon wall shelves and in the open drawers were rivet setters, Osborne cantle pliers, nippers, a scratch compass and a revolving punch with an edger. Walking to the far end of the room, Coop noted on a shelf behind the business counter were various leather dyes and softening oils for sale. Curious, he shuffled over and picked up a bottle of clear oil. Rotating it, he looked at the label. It was nothing more than extra virgin olive oil imported from Italy.

While holding the bottle of oil, Coop paused and surveyed the room a little more closely. Extra virgin olive oil—so what? That must be as common as dun horses or blonde hair in Utah. On a workbench, squeezed in the left hand corner, another item caught his eye. Walking over, he took a closer look. Immediately, he recognized it, an Osborne #145 sewing awl haft, but that's not what gave him pause. He'd forgotten how much a sewing awl haft looked like an ice pick! Transferring the olive oil into the same hand he was holding Malachi's leash, Coop reached over and picked up the tool. It had a varnished maple handle and a two-and-one-fourth inch long steel shaft with a terminal eye for stringing leather cord. Rotating the sewing awl haft, he balanced it in his hand, then slashed the air like a knife. Changing his grip, he hacked downward. Yes, it was possible. This tool could make a wound just like the one that killed Stepper. A bit unsettled, he again sliced the air with it.

At that moment, he heard a toilet flush somewhere in an unseen backroom, then he heard the door creak as it was opened. Hastily, Coop looked around for a place to deposit the oil and sewing awl haft. At that second, Malachi decided to lunge toward a compelling scent across the room. Briefly, Coop juggled the bottle of olive oil, the sewing awl haft and Malachi's leash in his two hands, then lost control of everything. The bottle was airborne for less than a second, then it crashed to the slate floor, shattering into a dozen shards. Clear virgin oil initially puddled, then slowly oozed across the slate floor.

Flushed with embarrassment, Coop turned to face the man now silhouetted in the doorframe.

He was middle-aged with lava black hair, dark brown eyes, an olive complexion and a Roman nose. Obviously, he was of Italian descent.

"Hi, I'm Vincent Tucciano." He stepped forward thrusting a hand toward Coop. "Don't worry about that," he nodded at the broken bottle and laughed. "It's just olive oil. Shouldn't cost you more than a couple hundred dollars."

"Lawrence Cooper," Coop shook his hand. "Let me pay for that." As he reached for his wallet, he considered the name, Tucciano. Where had he heard that name before? Obviously it was Italian, probably from Tuscany, but other than that his nearly perfect memory failed him.

"Nah," Vincent waved his hand in a sign of dismissal, "it's cheap and we've got gallons of the stuff."

"So, Vincent," Coop tried to sound casual, "why olive oil?"

"Call me Vinny," Tucciano ginned. "We just like olive oil. We think it's best for softening and protecting leather. Especially with the extra virgin, there's less oleic aid."

"My grandpa used Neatsfoot Oil," Coop said after finally getting Malachi to sit.

"Nothing wrong with that," Vinny shrugged. "Really any oil is okay as long as it's plant and not petroleum based. You know, no motor oil."

"Why the imported stuff?"

"What can I say?" Vinny shrugged again. "We're Italian."

"Makes sense," Coop agreed, but still wondered.

"I'll take that," Vinny laughed and nodded at the sewing awl haft still in Coop's left hand, "unless you're here to do some work."

Once again Coop blushed and handed over the tool. "I almost forgot I had it. My grandfather liked to work with leather. I recognize a lot of these tools from my childhood."

"That's how I learned the business." Vinny accepted the sewing awl haft from Coop. "My grandfather worked leather in Italy before immigrating to the States. My father, Franco, followed in his footsteps and now I guess it's me."

"So, your father's retired?" *Franco Tucciano*, Coop definitely recognized the name. He knew it was only a matter of time until his photographic memory produced the details.

"Mostly. He still comes in once in a while and gives me a hand. Particularly if I'm swamped." Vincent took a moment to re-shelve the sewing awl haft.

"It's a dying art," Coop added ruefully, "saddle making."

"Well, anyway, it is for this family," Vincent agreed. "My son wants nothing to do with it or the shop."

"Maybe he'll change his mind."

"Maybe, but I wouldn't bet on it. So, what can I do for you today?"

"Uh...my girlfriend, Samantha Rose Jardine, paid to have a custom saddle made for me." Coop walked over to look at the display saddles and added, "beautiful work."

"Ah, yes, the birthday saddle. What a pretty lady. You're a very lucky man."

"Yes, I believe I am," Coop replied with conviction. "She said I needed to come in to be fitted and pick out the style I liked."

"Yeah, that's right," Vinny extracted a photocopied worksheet from a drawer, "there's a whole list of things we need to go over."

For the next half hour Coop and Vincent went through the items on the sheet. Coop chose the style of rigging, skirt, fenders, horn and stirrups. He also selected the size of seat, how high of a cantle and whether the seat was padded or not. Lastly, he had to decide if he wanted a design stamped in the leather and there were literally hundreds of patterns to choose from. After some debate, he settled on a prickly pear cactus design.

Just as they were finishing, the overhead bell tinkled again. Simultaneously, both Vinny and Coop looked up from the work desk to see a bandy-built, white-haired man enter.

"Oh, hi, pops," Vinny greeted, then turned back to Coop. "This is Lawrence Cooper. Dad, he's ordering a new saddle. Mister Cooper, this is my father, Franco Tucciano."

As Coop turned to shake his hand, their eyes momentarily locked. A flash of recognition passed between them. In that instant, Coop remembered who Franco was. Abruptly Tucciano withdrew his hand as though he'd accidently grabbed the hot end of a fireplace poker.

"So, Mister Cooper," Franco hissed through yellow teeth, "*siete voi spendin prezzo del sangue* ?

"Are you spending your blood money?" Vinny translated.

* * *

Back at the ranch, Coop was seated at the kitchen table. Right in front of him was a layered yellow cake and across from the cake sat the pastry chef, a beaming Samantha Rose Jardine. She was obviously having a good time and he was trying to keep a begging Malachi from the cake. Now Coop knew the real reason why she did not want to come with him to Tucciano's Italian Leather Works. It was sitting right in front of him.

"Count them," she laughed. "There's forty-two. Man, that's a lot of candles. Almost a fire hazard."

"Just wait till your birthday," Coop threatened.

"Not nearly as many," she laughed again,

"Only by two."

He had not yet decided whether to tell Samantha about the incident at the saddle shop. He hated to destroy all her planning, her good intentions and her obvious satisfaction of having given him the perfect present. On the other hand, she was bound to find out. Eventually, she would realize there was no saddle.

"Come on, Coop," she encouraged, "make a wish and blow 'em out."

"I don't know if my forty-two year old lungs can muster enough air."

Right after Franco came into the shop, things immediately went downhill. Coop instantly recognized him and was surprised he had not connected name sooner. He must be getting old.

"Coop, blow 'em out," Samantha flashing her irresistible smile. "The wax is melting all over the frosting."

"Okay," Coop relented, took in a big lungful and blew. All candles flickered, then snuffed out. Wow! Finally a good sign. Maybe the gods were tired of toying with him and were moving on to the next poor mortal.

"What did you wish for?"

Of course, Franco Tucciano, the old saddlemaker, was also Gordon Flowers' father-in-law and Jenny Tucciano Flowers' father. Franco was in the family waiting room the day of Gordon's ill-fated surgery and as Coop now remembered, he had not taken the news well. In fact was quite irate.

"How big of a piece do you want?" Samantha held a carving knife, poised above the cake. "And I bought ice cream."

"Not too big, and just one scoop of ice cream."

Right after he'd made the connection, almost like getting close to the end of a crossword puzzle, everything else fell into place. There were just too many coincidences: the Italian virgin oil soaked sponge he found in the field after the fire; the granddaughter Alexis was a nurse and would have easy access to surgical sponges; the sewing awl haft could clearly have been the instrument of Stepper's death; the Yucassote could have been purloined from some leftover after Gordon Flowers death; and lastly the threatening letter he'd opened yesterday that faintly smelled of leather. It all added up to Franco Tucciano!

Samantha handed Coop a large piece of cake and two scoops of ice cream. "It's your birthday," she said, then mistaking his frown added, "live a little."

Then Franco when hissed, "spending your blood money, huh," Coop had not been able to contain himself. Without thinking, he snapped, "'have you killed any horses lately?" With a shocked Vinny looking on, they glared at each other, nose to nose, for several moments, then Franco snarled, "Vincent, this is the man who killed your bother-in-law. He is not welcome in this shop."

"You don't look like you're enjoying your birthday," Samantha Rose observed, sitting down with her own small helping of cake and ice cream. "Something wrong, Coop?"

"No, it's great." Coop tried to smile. "I've just got a lot on my mind."

Vinny tried to reason with him, but the old man stood firm. He flatly informed Vinny since he had not yet paid him all he owed on the shop it was still his. He would make the decisions. Throwing up his hands in frustration, Vincent pulled out his checkbook and refunded Samantha's money.

"Do you want to talk about it?"

"No...," Coop hesitated, remembering the old man's last words.

As Coop stuffed the check in his wallet and made for the door, Franco uttered, "don't think this makes us even, Mister Cooper, not by a long shot." Then he fired one last salvo in Italian, "*occhio per occhio*, an eye for an eye...*una vita per una vita*, a life for a life."

"Yeah," Coop sighed out loud, "Maybe we'd better talk."

Samantha quickly cleared away the dishes, poured two cups of coffee, then sat back down at the table. "Now tell me everything."

Where to start? Coop couldn't think of a good place, so he pulled out the refund check, handed it to her, then blurted, "I'm so sorry about the birthday present."

"Maybe," Samantha looked at the check, then turned it over, "you better fill in the details."

For the next ten minutes Coop told her everything, then simply shook his head and sipped his coffee.

"So, you really think the old man killed Stepper and burned down the tack shed?" Samantha Rose frowned as she refilled their cups.

"I know it's a little hard to believe," Coop agreed, "but you didn't see him, the look in his eyes."

"Maybe, he's got senile dementia."

"Maybe, or senior psychosis might be a better diagnosis," Coop added. "But he is definitely consumed with rage. I honestly think he's capable of murder."

Momentarily the conversation lagged and they drank their coffee and considered all the possibilities, most of them daunting.

"Are you still going to MITH tonight?" Samantha finally asked.

"I don't see any other way, but I must admit I'm more than a little nervous about leaving you."

"I'll be all right." She reached down and petted the dog snuggled at her feet. "Besides, I'll have Malachi to protect me."

"Malachi's a lover not a fighter. He might try to lick someone to death."

"You might be surprised what he'd do if I was threatened."

"You could be right," Coop nodded, remembering how Malachi defended him against Sergeant Kim Gaye. "But how about I call Steve Spaulding or Jacob Heinz to come over and spend the night?"

"Come on, Coop, I'll be okay. It's not even for one whole night. You'll be back before sunup."

"I just plain don't like it." Coop stood his ground. "Either I call one of them or I don't go. I promise, they won't mind."

Grudgingly, Samantha agreed, but when Coop called Steve, he already had plans to go to Mesquite for the evening and Jacob Heinz did not answer his phone.

For a few minutes they again talked about going to the police, but in reality they had nothing, only circumstantial evidence and a gut feeling. And considering Coop's current standing with the department, the suspect's advanced age and their lack of concrete proof, it was unlikely the cops would do anything, except maybe have a good laugh. So in the end, Samantha promised to be vigilant and try to call Jacob again later and Coop promised to be careful and hurry back as fast as he could.

Though Coop tried to keep things light, an uneasy tension filled the house. He fed the horses early, then kissed Samantha goodbye. With the sun well along on its downward arc, Coop hopped into the Dodge and headed for Littlefield.

It was almost sundown when he once again found himself on the same desolate tract of Mojave Desert, driving down the same gravel road toward MITH. With an eye on the dying sun, he tried to gauge his time, then slowed down a bit. He wanted to arrive precisely at dusk for a couple of reasons. One, his telltale dust plume would be less visible. And two, there should still be just enough natural light he wouldn't have to use his equally conspicuous headlights. Since it was a long holiday weekend, Coop was hopeful there would only be a skeletal crew left at MITH, but there was no point in taking chances, he should try to arrive unannounced.

Realizing this time there was probably no way he was going to sneak through the portcullis behind a car, he brought an expandable aluminum ladder, a flashlight, as well as a short 2x6 inch board. Now, he could hear them rattling around in the back as the Dodge jolted over the washboard.

It was almost pitch black when Coop arrived at MITH and without headlights he could barely see the curves and hit most of potholes. Once again just before he rounded the peculiar stone pillar, he parked in the same thicket of mesquite trees. Turning off the ignition, he grabbed the flashlight, ladder and board, then weaved through the creosote bushes toward the compound.

Stumbling through the fast fading light, Coop made his way to the barbwire-capped stucco fence, arriving at a point well south of the iron portcullis. Leaning the ladder against the wall, he carefully climbed to the top, then paused to peek over the crest. For a full five minutes, he waited, systematically surveying the compound. He saw no one, not a single patrolling guard. At last satisfied, he scrambled up to the fence's almost flat crest. He positioned the flat board on top of the barbwire and carefully climbed on top, balancing like a surfer. The wire beneath compressed and flattened with his weight as he inched forward, crossing the wire. After safely making his way across, he reached back, momentarily snagging his shirt as he lifted up the aluminum ladder up and repositioned it on the other side. Carefully, Coop backed down the ladder and hid it in a fern and desert palm thicket. For better or worse, he was back inside MITH.

This time he knew the way. Instead of methodically checking all doors and windows, Coop headed straight for that same tall mesquite tree. Squelching his fear of heights, he climbed it and eased over the parapet onto the flat roof. Still without using the flashlight, he cautiously made his way back to the loose skylight cover. Removing the cap, once again he lowered down through the roof, hanging briefly onto the frame so he could replace the cover. Then like a cat, he dropped straight down on top of the reception desk, landing on his feet this time. There was very little noise and almost no scatter.

Once inside the main pod, Coop silently surveyed the room. Finally deciding it was safe, he turned on his flashlight and sequentially checked out each of the hallways exiting from the main pod. After brief deliberation, he selected the same one he'd taken on his second visit, the one leading to Rob Belton's office, the one labeled, *Business and Administration.* More than likely somewhere in this wing they kept patient records, including a file on Betty Tsongas. With hopes riding high and flashlight bobbing, he started down the hallway.

Coop opened each door as he went. About halfway down the hall he opened a rough-hewn door and shined his flashlight into the darkened room. At first he saw nothing, but as he leaned in he sensed it was a large expansive room. Unlike all the others, however, this one was sparsely decorated, containing almost no southwest paintings or Indian artifacts. It did, however, contain a dozen or so work cubicles with computer bays outfitted with new computers, at least two fax and copy machines, numerous telephones and printers and several rows of custom file cabinets.

Before entering, Coop paused and took a couple of minutes to check the ceiling rafters for any surveillance cameras. Fortunately, there appeared to be none. Smiling self-consciously, he headed straight for the file drawers. One thing for sure, he was getting better at these covert operations.

It took him a few minutes to figure out how the files were organized. Once he mastered their system, it only took him seconds to find the "T" drawer. Quickly, Coop thumbed through the files. There was a Taylor and Thompson and Tripp, and so on, but no Tsongas. He went through them once again, this time more slowly. It didn't matter what speed he used, there still was no folder for Betty Tsongas.

Closing the drawer, Coop found a chair, sat down and turned off his flashlight. He needed a minute to think. There were really only three possibilities. One, MITH was telling the truth and Betty never was a patient here; two, they destroyed the file; or three, the folder was removed and transferred to a more secure location. The first two possibilities were completely out of his hands; he could do absolutely nothing about them. So having no choice, he decided to proceed, operating on the third premise.

Quietly, Coop exited the business office, then continued down the hallway. After a bit more exploring, he found Dr. Rob Belton's office and noticed the same two fur chairs placed before the window. He gave Belton's office a thorough searching, but he still found in it nothing to connect Betty to MITH.

Discouraged, Coop once again stepped back out into the hall. There was nothing else he could do. He might just as well go back to the ranch, back to Samantha Rose and Malachi, then face the music come Monday morning. But just as he turned to go, he saw a small door down the hallway, mostly hidden by a large log pillar. It was probably just another storage closet. He turned and walked away, then stopped. But why not check it out? It would only take a minute. He turned back and rattled the knob. As was common within the hacienda, it was also unlocked. Opening the door, he let himself in.

To his surprise, it was not a closet, but a private office and lavishly furnished. Instead of the prevailing southwest theme, this room was decorated with antique medical paraphernalia. There was a whole array of apothecary medicinal herbs in their original nineteenth-century boxes, a dozen large ceramic herb jars with Chinese lettering, a metal suppository mold, angled glass tubing which Coop recognized as the first urinary catheters, white porcelain urinals and bedpans, a half-dozen glass or porcelain mortars with their pestles and a ceramic inhaler that looked a lot like a present day bong. All these artifacts were housed in several old vintage medicine cabinets, still painted their original white. The center of the room was dominated by a grandly carved ornate desk It looked to be seventeenth-century French. Behind the desk was a priceless matching antique file cabinet.

Hanging on the walls was an array of wood-framed plaques and certificates. Most of them were awards from the health food and herbal medicine industry, but there also was a business license and a large plaque, maybe a personal motto, engraved in gold with foreign words: *Poscis opem nervis corpusque fidele*. From studying Latin in school, Coop could easily decipher it. Loosely translated, it meant, pray for good health and a strong body in old age. Nothing too sinister about that. Coop hoped the same for himself.

After casing the room, Coop returned his attention to the file cabinet. It was a stacked five-drawer unit and was locked. Using all his strength, he tried to jerk a drawer open, but all he accomplished was to nearly topple the cabinet over on himself. Coop hadn't the faintest idea how to pick a lock. Unfortunately, that skill was not taught in medical school. Glancing around, he searched for some way to break and enter. After a few moments, his eyes came to rest on a gold-plated letter opener resting on the desk. Next to it was a polished marble paperweight about the size of a Rubik Cube. Collecting the cube in his right hand and the letter opener in his left, he turned back to the file cabinet. With some difficulty, he wedged the letter opener between the drawer and its frame, directly above the lock, then using the paperweight hammered the letter opener downward. Periodically, he would stop and pry, trying to pop the drawer open. When that failed, he hammered some more, forcing the letter opener deeper into the interface. Finally, using all his body weight for leverage, he pulled down, then jerked. The drawer popped open with a loud crack; simultaneously the letter opener lost its purchase and he lost his balance, tumbling to the floor.

Picking himself up, he positioned the penlight in his mouth, focused the beam and rifled through the folders. Once again it appeared they were organized alphabetically. Rapidly, he shuffled back to the T's, then thumbed more slowly.

Suddenly there it was...the long-missing file of Betty Tsongas! Holding his breath, he skimmed through the half-inch thick file. It was indeed the mother lode. There were dates, times and doses of when the Yuccasote was administered. Coop smiled with satisfaction. At long last the tide had turned; his luck was changing. This was the beginning of the end to his long nightmare.

Grasping the file with his left hand and the flashlight in the right, Coop closed the file drawer and turned to leave the room.

Wait a minute. Hold your horses! He had two other malpractice cases pending, Gordon Flowers and Hector Perdenales Gonzalez. He would eventually need their files too. As long as he was here, it would be foolish, bordering on stupid, not to take their files.

In mid-stride, Coop did a three-sixty and headed back to the file cabinet. Just as he hoped, Gordon Flowers file was in the F's and Hector Gonzalez's was right there in the G's. Confiscating a thick rubber band from the antique desk, Coop rolled together and banded the three files, then once again hurried for the door.

He rapidly made his way back to the central pod and made sure the desk was positioned directly under the skylight. On top of the desk, he stacked a chair, then added several thick telephone directories. Climbing on top of his makeshift scaffold, he pushed the plastic skylight cover up and off to one side, then carefully placed the files on the roof. Then with maximum effort, Coop climbed up through the hole and replaced the skylight cap. He collected the files, then headed for mesquite tree. After wedging the folders under the waistband of his pants, he shimmied down the tree. Once back on solid ground, he again surveyed the grounds, saw no one, then hurried across the compound. Staying low and mostly to the shadows, Coop zigzagged for the aluminum ladder.

Suddenly, an alarm split the night! Coop froze. A second later the floodlights flashed on and swept the compound. A few seconds after that, the grounds came alive, swarming with uniformed security guards.

Staying to the thick foliage and dark shadows, Coop stealthily continued his way toward the ladder.

It wasn't there! He beat down a rush of panic. Had they found it? Is that why the alarms sounded? Frantically, he searched the undergrowth. Wait a minute. Slow down. This palm tree was all wrong. It was leaning in the wrong direction and there were two of them. In the chaos of the moment, he'd gone to the wrong thicket. Taking a couple of deep breaths, he used the portcullis to reestablish his bearings, then veered off to his left. After less than a minute of careful searching, he located the ladder. Pulling it from the thicket, he leaned it up against the stucco fence, then hurriedly started climbing.

"There he is!" A loud voice bellowed.

"Yeah, I see him," another shouted.

A spotlight quickly arched across the night sky, suddenly bathing him in a harsh white light. Behind him a rifle barked and a bullet whined past his left ear, thudding in the stucco and blasting his face with gritty chips. Doggedly, he continued upward, three more steps to reach the top. Another bullet screamed and slammed in the wall just above his head, dusting his hair with white bits of stucco.

"The next one's in your head!" The voice roared from directly behind.

Visibly shaken, Coop hesitated, then stopped. Damn, he was so close. The flat surface of the crest was now within arm's reach. It would only take a couple of seconds to place the board and then... Should he try it? He knew he would never make it. Obviously, the guy with the rifle was a good shot.

Momentarily, the spotlight dipped and the beam slipped off of him. Hastily, Coop grabbed the three-banded files from under his shirt and tossed them over the fence. Quickly, the light refocused on him.

"Down off the ladder, buddy--now!" The voice behind him commanded.

Coop carefully backed down the ladder and raised his hands above his head.

22

Coop was immediately surrounded by an angry swarm of security guards. They searched him, removed his watch and wallet, then handcuffed him and dragged him toward the hacienda. Once again, the tall guard, the one from the night he'd trashed the lab, was there. He immediately recognized Coop.

"Jesus, you again!" he exclaimed, shaking his head in disbelief. He shoved Coop through the main door of the hacienda, then added, "some people never learn."

"I missed you too, Sasquatch," Coop quipped.

Satch cuffed Coop hard on the back of the head. "Shut up, Doc," he snarled, then cuffed him again.

Shoving Coop ahead of them, the guards headed down the south corridor, one of the two Coop had not yet explored. Halfway down, they passed a door identifying it as the security office. They bypassed it and continued on down the hall another forty feet before stopping in front another door. This one had no label. Satch unlocked the door and stepped inside. A moment later, he reappeared, seemed satisfied and nodded to the other guards. Using more force than required, they shoved Coop through the door. As he stumbled forward across the threshold, he got a quick glance at the room, it appeared to be a utility closet, then he tripped and crashed to the floor. As he picked himself up, the guards relocked the door, then his world went black.

Immediately, he sneezed, and sneezed again. The closet reeked of powdered detergents, cleaning solvents and furniture polish. Pinching his nose, Coop tried to stifle his next sneeze, but failed, then failed again. After a few minutes, his eyes accommodated to the darkness and his nose, though still sensitive and stuffy, had calmed enough to allow him to think. Cautiously, he began to explore.

Indeed, he appeared to be in a storage closet. The room was small and rectangular, approximately four-by-eight feet and with no windows. Bracketed to the long walls, floor to ceiling, were wooden shelves stocked with various sizes of cans, boxes and bottles. He found a light switch by the door, but when flipped nothing happened. Reaching up to the ceiling, Coop groped around until he found the round porcelain light fixture. Taking care not to get shocked, he carefully explored it—no light bulb. Involuntarily, he shuddered. This place had all the ambience of the interior of pharaoh's tomb and smelled like a Dow Chemical plant.

Coop felt the insidious, but insistent, creep of claustrophobia. Soon its shipmate panic followed. Fumbling in the dark, he located the door, then backed up as much as he could, which was only a single step. He lunged forward, slamming his shoulder into the solid planks. Nothing gave except his shoulder. With his shoulder now throbbing, he tried it again with the same results. Raising his foot high, he kicked at the door, but unlike in the movies the door held fast. Now raw panic surged, but Coop forced himself to continue with his exploration. Systematically, he searched every square inch of the room. There was nothing, nothing he could use as a tool or weapon and absolutely no way out.

For the next half hour, like a caged zoo animal, he paced around his little cubicle. Finally, exhausted and breathing heavily, he slowed, then stopped. In the dark, he groped until he located a large cardboard box, probably full of toilet paper, and placed it right in the center of the room. He took a minute to consciously slow his breathing, then sat down. The cardboard groaned under his weight, but held.

Coop hated closed dark spaces, even CT scans and MRI's were a nightmare. And being locked in this closet was pretty much the realization of his worst fear, being buried alive. To him, this dark cubicle didn't seem a whole lot different than being crammed in a casket and interred six feet under.

Over the next half-hour, Coop's heart rate and respirations gradually slowed and he finally was capable of rational thought. In his mind, he worked and reworked every possible scenario, then finally resigned himself to what he already knew, there was not way out. There was absolutely nothing for him to do, but wait. Undoubtedly, his captors would eventually return and in the interim he had nothing else to do but work on an escape plan. Realizing he needed a plan was the easy part; the hard part was actually coming up with one.

In the darkness of the closet, time and space melded into one. As single unit, it expanded, warped, then ultimately disappeared into irrelevance. Einstein was at least partially wrong, Coop decided. It wasn't only traveling the speed of light that slowed time, dark crowded spaces, like this closet, did as well. At first, he tried to keep his mind busy trying come up with an escape plan, but as the hours went by all he could focus on was his growing hunger, his mounting thirst and his extreme exhaustion. He forced his mind back to the problem and clenched his jaw muscles with resolve. They would not beat him. He would ignore these physical and psychological sufferings. He would find a way.

Finally, and thankfully, it was morning. Coop could tell by the narrow ribbon of natural light shining in from under the closet door. Other than lacking the basic comforts, he was fine, at least for the time being. With this narrow strip of light, though it really didn't illuminate much, his sense of doom, like early morning dew, evaporated before the rising sun.

Suddenly, the door flew open. The small horizontal band of light in an instant morphed to a blinding shaft of intense white light. Shielding his eyes with a raised arm, Coop saw the vague image of a man emerge from the light. Without comment, a security guard shoved a tray containing orange juice, water and two slices of toast toward him, then immediately dissolved back into the bright corona. The bright light immediately extinguished as the guard slammed the door shut again.

Coop went for the water first, downed it in two gulps, then did the same with the orange juice. With the toast, however, he took his time, slowly chewing and deliberately swallowing. By the time he was half done with the second piece, he wished he'd saved some of the water.

Again he waited in the dark, wondering what was coming next. Obviously, they weren't planning on starving him to death, but what they were planning he could only imagine. There was a good possibility they didn't know what to do. It was apparent from his accommodations they didn't often take prisoners and were ill equipped to handle them.

Certainly by now, they'd discovered the Tsongas, Flowers and Gonzales files were missing. That was some pretty damning evidence, so Coop doubted they would simply turn him loose or as before hand him over to the Washington County Sheriff's Department. So, what would they do? They couldn't hold him like this forever. Or could they? Were they capable of murder? Then disposing of the body? No way for him to know for sure. Like having uninvited relatives drop in and overstay their welcome, they probably weren't quite sure how to handle him. So, in the dark, Coop waited and worried and waited.

Abruptly, the door opened again. Like the sudden release of water from a failed dam, blinding light once again flooded the tiny room. As before, Coop recoiled from the extreme brightness, instinctively raising his arms to protect his eyes. Immersed in the dazzling light, almost like a vision from God, was the shimmering silhouette of a tall man. He had long flowing hazel hair and was dressed in a white peasant smock festooned with fancy red embroidery. His blue jeans were clean, but faded, and his bare feet were clad with leather Roman sandals.

"Doctor Cooper," the man said warmly, "it's good to see you again."

In the intense sunlight, Coop still could not see him clearly, but after a moment the man stepped forward out of the blinding light to the more indirect light of the closet's interior. He motioned to the three security guards to remain outside.

Slowly, Coop's pupils accommodated and re-focused. Now he could clearly see the man standing before him. Not only did he recognize his trademark clothes and facial features, but also his long brown hair and gentle hazel eyes. Yes indeed, he knew this man, but why? Why was he here?

Coop was both puzzled and surprised. None of this made any sense. For there standing before him, like an angelic apparition, was none other than the celebrated healer Doctor Jonathan Clifton Ford!

"Doctor Cooper," Jonathan Clifton Ford reached for Coop's hand. "Doctor Cooper...my...my...what are we going to do with you?"

"Doctor Ford!" Coop accepting his hand while struggling to remain composed. "What are you doing here?"

"Why, I work here. This is my place," Ford beamed. "I'm the Director of MITH. I think you've already met my assistant Doctor Belton."

Ford smiled and grabbed a cardboard case of detergent off the top shelf, then placed it in front of Coop's box of toilet paper. "Let's sit down," he suggested, "and have a some conversation."

Nodding numbly, Coop sat down facing Dr. Ford. "So, what do you want to talk about?"

"You," Ford replied, still smiling. "Whatever are we going to do with you?"

"I'm in favor of letting me go," Coop quipped with a tight smile.

"How about giving me back my files," Ford replied smoothly, "and we might just do that."

"I don't have them." Coop locked eyes with Ford.

"Now, I do tend to believe you," Cliff Ford nodded, "since we did search you last night, but I also think you know where they are."

"No." Coop shook his head slowly. "I have no idea."

"They were in my file cabinet yesterday," Ford continued, "but today I see the lock's been jimmied, the files are gone and just by happenstance we also have an intruder—you. All random and unrelated events? I don't think so. Surely, you can understand my reservation and why I say I don't believe you."

"Maybe, one of your staff took them," Coop suggested. "Anyway, what's the big deal? Betty's dead. They're all dead. So, why do you want their files back?"

"It's important to our research."

"Yeah, I'll bet," Coop said sarcastically. "I'll tell you what, you let me go and I'll show you where they are."

Ford was silent for a few seconds, then abruptly changed the subject. "You know, we could use a good man like you here at MITH."

"What?"

"I said we could use someone like you here at the institute."

"Are you offering me a job?" Coop raised an eyebrow.

"Well, yes," Ford nodded, "but only under certain circumstances."

"That I keep my mouth shut?"

"Well, yes. Of course, we do demand a certain amount of loyalty."

"Uh, well, I'm flattered, but..."

"...But what else have you got going for you?" Ford interrupted.

"With no medical license and no hospital privileges, you're not exactly the most marketable guy in southern Utah."

"You've got a point there."

"And we pay well."

"How well?"

"Six figures to start with the potential for at least that much more in bonuses."

"Nah, I just don't think I'm cut out for this line of work."

"This line of work?" Ford's voice got louder and his demeanor changed. This line of work! This line of work is God's work. Everyone is cut out for this work or at least they'd better be."

"Yeah, well," Coop shrugged. "How did you get in this line of work anyway?

Ford perceptibly relaxed and got a faraway look in his eyes. He sat quietly for a long moment, then cleared his throat. "Well, sir, let me tell you a story." Now his voice was soft, almost reverent. "Many years ago there was a little boy who with his mother lived humbly and on modest means. One day the boy got sick. It was a terrifying disease, which caused severe pain and progressive paralysis. Starting with the big toe, it inched up his body, then jumped from one leg to the other, invading both legs. But still not satisfied, it crept on up to his groin, onto his abdomen and finally to his chest. Once the chest muscles became paralyzed, as you might suspect, being a doctor, the boy had trouble breathing and death came riding a fast horse."

Pausing for a breath, Ford looked at Coop. Coop nodded that he was following.

Ford looked away again, stared at nothing, then continued. "Even though they couldn't afford it, the boy's mother took him to all the best doctors and hospitals. The specialists could do nothing it seems, except generate exorbitant medical bills. The mother grew desperate and sought the services of a healer, a holy man. Arriving with a bagful herbs and heart filled with prayers, he miraculously cured the boy. He was a great and gentle man and like Jesus, a healer. He was a man of God.

"After that, the boy's mission in life was permanently sealed. He immediately dedicated the rest of his life to God and to the natural healing arts."

After a few seconds of silence, Coop asked, "does the disease have a name?"

"The doctors called it Guillian-Barre Syndrome."

"Ah, French polio."

"What?" Ford again returned to the present and focused on Coop.

"That's its nickname, French polio. Both Guillian and Barre were French."

"Oh," Dr. Ford said indifferently, "you are familiar with it."

Again they lapsed into silence, each man lost in his own thoughts.

"It's a self-limiting disease, you know," Coop finally said.

"What?"

"It's self-limiting. Over ninety percent of the time, especially in kids, Guillian-Barre resolves on its own even with no treatment."

What?"

Almost immediately Coop wished he'd kept his mouth shut.

"What!" Ford roared again, his perpetual smile suddenly vanished and his soft doe eyes hardened to fire brown agate. "What are you saying?"

"Forget it," Coop said quickly.

Abruptly Ford rose up from the box, looming over Coop.

"Woe unto them who make light of the work of God!"

"I...I didn't mean anything by it."

Dr. Clifton Ford pivoted on his heel and instantly re-dissolved back into the blinding seam of light. Immediately, the guards slammed and re-locked the door.

Once more, Coop was in the tomb of darkness. Again time slowed and dragged, like a bad college lecture. Coop's mouth became alkali dry and his empty stomach cried out for food, but none arrived. Apparently his punishment for his snubbing the work of God was to withhold food and water. Once again, Coop wished he could take back his crack about Guillian-Barre Syndrome, even though it was true.

From his primitive, but fairly reliable sundial, Coop could tell evening was approaching. The slit of white light beneath the door was fading, slowly replaced by yellow incandescent light. With some effort, he again fought back the rising sense of panic, which seemed to be inversely proportional to the amount of light. Damn, he didn't know if he could make it through another night in this mausoleum.

In the cocoon-like darkness, Coop mulled over this most recent turn of events. Dr. Ford exhibited all the classical symptoms of overt psychosis: fanatical religious obsessions, bursts of paranoia, rapid mood swings and blatant delusions of grandeur. Though Coop knew any psychiatrist worth his salt would never make a definitive diagnosis without further tests, he nevertheless suspected Ford's psychosis was probably the paranoid schizophrenic type. It was possible he was simply a religious nut or even worse, a paranoid schizophrenic religious nut. Right now, however, establishing the correct diagnosis was of little consequence because Dr. Ford was clearly a dangerous man and more than likely was planning to do him harm.

Though he knew it was useless, Coop once again methodically searched the floor, the walls, shelves and rechecked the door. Everything was as solid as a bank vault. Discouraged, he sat back down on the cardboard box and lowered his head down into his hands. Racking his brain, he tried to figure a way out of this mess and failing that, tried to guess what Ford's next move might be. It was like trying to predict the weather without a satellite or the stock market without a computer.

He didn't have long to worry about it, maybe an hour at most, then once again he heard the lock grate as the tumblers turned, then the door slowly swung open. This time there was no blinding shaft of sunlight, but instead the mellow glow from the overhead incandescent light in the hall.

Brusquely, Ford entered, but without his perpetual smile. Instead, his countenance was more of a smirk or the leer of a fox that just discovered a way into the chicken coop. For a few seconds he glowered over Coop.

"Like Goliath of the Old Testament," Ford proclaimed, "you are fast becoming a threat, an obstacle to the establishment of the kingdom of God."

"Huh?" As usual, Coop was having trouble following Ford.

"But when troubles arise," Ford continued, "God always gives us a David, a slingshot and a handful of perfectly-sized pebbles."

Coop didn't like the look in Ford's eyes.

Without further comment, Ford shoved a manila folder toward Coop.

Having no other choice, Coop accepted the file, then turned it over in his hands. It appeared to be a typical MITH patient file. Out of habit, his eyes searched for the name label on the tab. Perhaps by now they'd recovered the files he'd tossed over the fence. His pulse quickened. If they had found the files, he was now expendable. He turned the file over and found the name of the file.

It was not those pilfered files, but nevertheless the name on the folder gave him a start.

With his hands trembling, he let the file slipped through his numb fingers. It ricocheted off the cardboard box, then fell to the floor. As Coop bent over to pick up the file, he glanced up at Ford. The director grinned back at him. With hand still shaking, Coop opened the folder.

It was no mistake. The name on the file was none other than his own: ***Lawrence Addison Cooper***.

Forcing himself to remain calm, Coop quickly thumbed through the folder, speed-reading each page. It appeared to be a complete medical file with dated and signed office visits, various and appropriate lab tests and a spreadsheet showing times, days and doses for every Yuccasote treatment. Coop counted at least twenty entries on this page. Lastly there was an official looking pathology report declaring Lawrence Addison Cooper had been diagnosed with acute myelogenous leukemia. With his mind reeling, Coop shakily handed the folder back to Ford.

"So what do you think?" Cliff Ford asked, still smirking.

"Looks real," Coop admitted.

"Do you want to hear the official backstory that goes along with it?"

"Might just as well," Coop replied without enthusiasm.

"Well it goes something like this," Ford was obviously proud of himself, "you were diagnosed some months ago with a particularly virulent strain of leukemia, but for a number of reasons decided to keep it secret. And as you just saw, we have the pathology report to prove it. Of course, you tried traditional medicine first, seeking treatment out of town to preserve your anonymity, but when that didn't help in desperation you turned to me. After you signed a release form, which as you also see we have, I in good faith treated you with our new food supplement Yuccasote, which has been producing some outstanding results. But unfortunately you had one of those rare idiosyncratic reactions and died. Too bad."

"Let me guess," Coop quipped. "I bled to death."

"Why, sir, that is correct," Ford laughed and slapped a knee. "How did you ever figure that out?"

"Nice plan, but it will never work."

"And why is that, Doctor Cooper?"

"It's really quite elementary, Doctor Watson, there's not enough time. If I'm not back for my court date on Monday, they're going to come looking for me. My girl friend knows where I am. That just gives you a little over thirty-six hours and there's no way Yuccasote can thin my blood that fast."

"God never gives us obstacles," Ford's eyes shinned with missionary zeal, "without giving us a way to overcome."

"I doubt God wants anything to do with his."

Suddenly, Ford stared at Coop, but looked right through him. His eyes glazed over, his face softened a bit and he smiled more benignly. Then as strange as it seemed, he cleared his throat and started to sing.

My eyes have seen the Glory of the coming of the Lord;
He is trampling out the vintage where the grapes of wrath are stored;
He hath loosed the fateful lightening of his terrible swift sword;
His truth is marching on, Halleluiah."

When he finished with the hymn, Dr. Ford nodded to the security guards. Four of them immediately entered the closet and restrained Coop. Though he continued to resist as much as he could, they managed to apply a tourniquet to his right arm, then extend it to expose a prominent antecubital vein. Like a man possessed, Dr. Ford took an angiocath from a black leather medical bag, then eschewing the usual dab of alcohol, plunged it deep into Coop's vein. Once he was sure he had good blood return, Ford retrieved a sixty cc syringe filled with amaretto brown fluid and attached it to a length of plastic connector tubing. He then secured the free end to the angiocath still anchored in Coop's vein. Slowly, and with his right thumb, Ford depressed the syringe's rubber plunger.

Totally exhausted from struggling, Coop lay still and hypnotically watched the brown fluid course through the clear tubing, then disappeared into his anticubital vein.

"Intravenous," Ford grinned maniacally, "works much faster."

23

Show him death,
and he'll be content with fever.
—Old Persian saying

Samantha Rose was sick with worry.

Coop had now been gone for almost twenty-four hours. She'd expected him to return last night. Now the second nightfall was fast approaching and still no sign of him. Even though it was next to impossible, she tried to not dwell on the possibilities, none of them good.

Earlier this morning, she thought about striking out on her own to look for him, but a couple of things prevented her. One, even though she knew vaguely MITH was somewhere south of town in the Mojave Desert, she had no idea exactly where. And furthermore, being from Salt Lake City, she was not familiar with most of the secondary roads in Washington County.

Also, she suspicioned, no she was convinced, they were attacked last night. Though Coop was her primary concern, he was not her only one. He had charged her with guarding the house and ranch and if left unprotected, she was afraid she would return to find the horses slaughtered and the house burned to the ground. It was difficult to know what to do.

Then, there was Malachi to worry about.

Right now, Samantha Rose was on her way down the sloping volcanic hill to pick up Malachi in St. George. As she negotiated the ten miles, her mind replayed the events of last night. Was she being objective? Or was she making way too much of it? She couldn't decide.

It was just after dark and on the eastern horizon there was a promise of a full moon, but just like Coop it hadn't yet made an appearance. Malachi was outside chewing his bone. Coop would let him have bones in the house, but not Samantha. The dog was welcome inside, but bones stayed outside. Suddenly, she'd heard him yelp as if he were in pain. Yes, she was pretty sure it was a yelp and not a bark. Then he yelped again. She flipped on the courtyard lights, grabbed a mop handle for a weapon and with heart pounding stepped outside to look for Malachi.

Suddenly, she heard a commotion over by the horse corrals! Turning toward he sound, she thought she saw movement in the shadows. She edged in closer. Even though she was not certain, she imagined she saw a blurry figure, a vague shape slinking off into the darkness. As she started back to the house, Malachi, whimpering and with tail dragging between his legs, limped toward her.

Back in the light of the kitchen, Samantha Rose examined the dog. He seemed fine except there was a tiny spot of matted blood on the fur over his right hindquarter. On closer inspection, it appeared to be coming from a small puncture site, maybe from barbwire; though it was possible, she supposed, it could have been from a dog or catfight. At first, Malachi acted okay and her anxiety eased a bit, then without warning he started projectile vomiting. A half hour later, he was hit with explosive and bloody diarrhea.

She was frantic. Having never had a dog before, she didn't know what to do. At first she tried to get hold of Jacob Heinz, but he still wasn't home. Then she found the number Coop gave her for Dr. Stephen Spaulding. No luck there either.

The vomiting eventually subsided, but the diarrhea continued for another hour. Surely, Malachi must be getting dehydrated. No question, she had to find a vet. After going through almost every listing in the yellow pages, she finally got a veterinarian on the line. Dr. K. Mortenson (Swedish for Mårtensson--probably evolved from Martin) mumbled something unintelligible under his breath, but nevertheless agreed to see Malachi. He instructed her to bring him to his clinic located on the outskirts of St. George, down River Road. Quickly agreeing, Samantha Rose bundled up the dog and headed for town.

In spite of his gruff demeanor, Dr. Mortenson was, thankfully, one of those caring compassionate veterinarians. Though he was a big man, he had a light step, a soft touch and a gentle voice. With blonde hair thinning and graying and hands the size of a baseball mitt, he had the look of an old football player, probably close to fifty. Without much conversation or the usual pleasantries, Dr. Mortenson thoroughly examined Malachi, drew blood for tests, injected him with a drug cocktail containing Compazine, Fentanyl and Valium, then started an I.V. of normal saline. After taking one more look at his patient, Mortenson washed and dried his hands, then motioned for Samantha to follow. He showed her to a small employee break room featuring a chipped Formica table, two cheap chairs and a half fridge.

"You want a soft drink?" Mortenson nodded for her to sit.

"You have anything diet?"

"Coke or Sprite?"

"Sprite," Samantha replied, "too late in the day for me to have caffeine."

"Not for me." Mortenson laughed as he opened the fridge and selected the drinks.

"You're a better man than me," Samantha joked.

"I'm not certain," Mortenson's blue eyes twinkled, "if I should take that as a subtle dig at my masculinity or consider it faint praise."

"Not meant to be either," Samantha replied, turning red.

"You're not from around here," Dr. Mortenson handed her a diet Sprite, opening a Coke for himself.

"No, Salt Lake City."

"You have family down here?"

"No, I'm a friend of Doctor Cooper."

"Larry Cooper...Coop?" Mortenson asked, then not waiting for an answer he added, "a good man. He took care of my mother's kidney cancer. She's doing great."

"Yes, he is a good man."

"So where is Coop?"

"He...he's out of town." Samantha took a sip of diet Sprite, "I'm watching his place."

"Yeah, he's got that ranch north of town as I recall," Mortenson said. "Nice place. I've been there before. Colicky horse."

"So what do you think?" Samantha nodded toward Malachi.

"The dog's pretty dehydrated, that's why I started the I.V."

"What do you think caused it?" Samantha was sure she wanted to hear the answer.

"I don't know for sure," Mortenson frowned, forehead ridges deepening. "More than likely a virus or he got into something toxic."

"Such as?"

"Well, I've seen dogs do this sort of thing when they get into chocolate or antifreeze or onions. If they get enough, it will kill them. I'm not necessarily saying this was chocolate, but some kind of toxic chemical."

"Could it have been delivered by shot?"

"I don't see why not." Dr. Mortenson raised an eyebrow. "It would work faster that way and be more potent, but why would anyone want to do that?"

"Revenge."

"What?"

"It's kind of a long story. Is there any way to prove this was a poisoning rather than a virus?"

"Sure. One of the blood tests I drew was a toxicology screen, but it won't be back till late tomorrow."

"So, will...do think he will be okay?" Samantha's asked, her perfect face now pinched and drawn with the strain.

"Yeah, I think so," Dr. Mortenson replied. "He already seems a little better, but I'd better keep him here tonight, watch him and continue with the I.V. fluids."

"Do you think I can pick him up tomorrow?"

"Probably," Mortenson nodded, finishing his Coke. "Maybe by late afternoon, but call first to be sure."

"I'll want to check on him anyway," Samantha also finished her Sprite, "so, I'll probably just come in."

"Suit yourself." Dr. Mortenson stood up and yawned.

"How much do I owe you, Doc?" She also stood and fished in her purse.

"*Nein, nada,*" Dr. Mortenson waved his hands as a sign of dismissal, "nothing. Call it professional courtesy."

"But you did a lot here," Samantha protested, "and dragging you out in the middle of the night."

"You did say this was Doctor Larry Cooper's dog?"

"Yes."

"Well, I'd do anything for him. He did the same for my mother. She didn't have any insurance and he wrote off most of her bill."

"You have no idea how much I appreciate this." Samantha Rose shouldered her purse and headed for the door. "You're one of a kind."

"Again faint praise," Mortenson laughed.

"Anything but." Samantha waved goodbye.

When she arrived back at the ranch, there was a message waiting from Jacob Heinz instructing her to call him immediately, regardless of the time. Picking up the phone, Samantha called and explained everything. Of course, Jacob volunteered to come right over, but Samantha told him to wait until tomorrow. It was so late, after 2:00 a.m., and she sincerely doubted anything more would happen tonight.

That was yesterday and now she was almost back into town to pick up Malachi—she hoped. She hadn't called first, but he must be doing better, she reasoned, otherwise they would have called her.

With a start, Samantha realized she was already there, at Mortenson's Animal Hospital and Clinic. It was one of those disconcerting experiences of having arrived at your destination and having absolutely no idea how you got there. Silently she prayed she hadn't run too many red lights.

Samantha checked in the rearview mirror half-expecting to see a cop behind her. Fortunately, there was none. Grabbing her purse, she then walked into the building and inquired of the young receptionist, Jill, as to the status of Malachi. Jill excused herself and said she would go check. Returning a couple minutes later, she reported Malachi was fine and ready to go home. With Jill leading the way, Samantha followed her to one of the back rooms. Malachi was standing in a small chain link enclosure with his tail wagging so vigorously it thumped loudly against the cage wall. When Jill opened the door, Malachi rushed to Samantha and with his tail still beating furiously jumped up on his hind feet to lick her face. Samantha was getting used to Malachi's kisses and breathed a silent sigh of relief he looked so good.

As they walked back to the clinic entrance, Samantha asked if Dr. Mortenson was in. He was not. He was on an emergency call to a horse stable east of town, Jill explained, caring for a foundered mare. Again Samantha tried to pay for the services, but Jill simply waved her off.

"Doctor Mortenson gave me specific instructions that your money is no good here." Mortenson had, however, instructed Jill to tell Samantha all the blood tests were okay except for the coagulation studies. Malachi's blood was a little thin.

Malachi seemed happy to be going back to the ranch and Samantha had to admit, she was too. In spite of the disconcerting episode last night, the ranch was beginning to grow on her. The slower pace and solitude was so different from Salt Lake City, but it was a difference she was beginning to appreciate.

The second she made the last turn onto Coop's private road she spied a red Jeep Grand Cherokee parked in the driveway. She caught her breath and she hurriedly applied the brakes. Was last night's prowler now brazenly waiting for her in her own driveway? Briefly, she considered turning around and heading back into St. George to find the police. But even if she managed to convince them to come back to the ranch, by then surely the Jeep would be gone. Mustering all her courage, she forced herself to go on down the road. She couldn't just turn around and leave, giving him a free run to destroy the place.

As soon as she pulled up, a short energetic man in his early seventies with unruly reddish gray hair jumped out of the Jeep and came straight toward her. Frantically, she grabbed her purse, fumbled in it until she found her pepper spray. With finger on button, she slowly rolled down the window.

"*Guten Abend, ich bin*...uh...I'm Jacob Heinz."

Slowly Samantha exhaled. Discretely, she replaced the Mace back in her purse, then got out to greet Jacob.

After completing the self-introductions and giving Jacob a chance to say hello to Malachi, they went inside. Malachi chose to stay outside, enjoying the residual warmth of the setting sun along with the remainder of his bone.

"Do you want anything to drink?" Samantha offered once inside. "We have cold water, Coke, one or two beers and coffee."

"*Ja, Ja, kaffee*," Jacob nodded enthusiastically. "I gave up *bier* a long time ago. Too much heartburn."

"How about decaf?"

"*Sehr gut*...uh...fine by me."

After making the coffee, Samantha poured two cups, set out a platter of oatmeal cookies, then sat down at the kitchen table opposite Jacob.

"So you're the *fraulein* that's been driving Coop crazy," Jacob said merrily, a twinkle in his eye.

"Right now, he's driving me crazy," Samantha sighed out loud. "Jacob, I...I'm very worried."

"Vhy?" Jacob took a sip of coffee. "Tell me about it."

"He went to MITH last night to see if he could find concrete proof Betty Tsongas was a patient there. If we can't prove that, we're certainly going to lose this trial..."

"*Ja, Ja*, so when was he supposed to return?"

"Late last night or early this morning."

"Umm," Jacob said, holding his cup between his hands. "Are these people dangerous?"

"I don't know," Samantha frowned, "but I think they could be."

"Do you know vhere is this MITH?"

"No, not for sure, but I know it's in the southwest desert, some-where down by Littlefield."

"I know that area a little; I belong to a senior ATV club, you know the four-wheelers. Ve have ridden down some of the roads before and I think I may have seen MITH once from a distance." He stopped to take a sip of coffee. "One day vhen ve vere riding we topped a hill and there was a huge white structure off in the distance with a bunch of palm trees. We didn't know vhat it was, but maybe it was that MITH, I don't know for sure. But there can't be too many of those big places out in the desert."

Samantha was silent for a moment. "I think we should go after him."

"Vhat about the police?"

"We've tried that a couple of times, once after the tack shed fire and then again with Stepper's death...oh...and also when we got Profes-sor Westover's report in the mail. To be honest, Jacob, they know Coop from being arrested and jailed there a couple of times and they don't take him seriously. I suspect they think he's a nut case. Anyway, all we've got for the police to go on is speculation and I sincerely doubt they'll act without something more."

"*Ja, Ja*, then ve should go look for him."

"There's one slight problem." Samantha told Jacob about the attack last night and the poisoning of Malachi.

Heinz considered this new information for a moment, then glanced out the kitchen window. "It's almost dark now," he observed. "Ve'll surely get lost if we go looking in the dark. Let's stay here tonight and protect the ranch. In the morning, I'll call my friend Sophie and have her come over and vatch the place, then ve go find Coop."

Reluctantly, Samantha Rose agreed. Of course, she didn't like the idea of Coop being out there another night and not having the slightest idea of what was going on or where he was. Was he hurt? Was he a prisoner? Or even dead? She immediately drove that thought from her mind. But being strictly pragmatic, Jacob was right. It didn't make much sense for them to go out wandering in the desert in the dead of night and leave the ranch unprotected. Her mind said stay, but her heart was telling her to go.

When they finished their coffee and cookies, she showed Jacob to the guest bedroom, thanked him and said goodnight.

Samantha was fatigued and totally frazzled from the lack of sleep. Needless to say she didn't sleep at all last night and even though she was spent both mentally and physically she still had trouble falling asleep. Obviously, she was too keyed up with worry, worry about Coop and Malachi, though Malachi did seem much better. Finally she managed to slip into a light fitful sleep. On top of the covers next to her, Malachi didn't do much better.

About midnight, Malachi abruptly vaulted off the bed and began pacing and sniffing. A low growl rumbled from his throat and he headed straight for the kitchen door. Instantly awake, Samantha also jumped up, grabbed a flashlight, then keeping a firm hold on Malachi's collar went outside to investigate. She did turn on the flashlight; she didn't need to. The moon was almost full, hovering directly overhead and providing sufficient light. There was nothing amiss in the immediate vicinity of the house, but over by the corrals the horses seemed restless. They kicked up a cloud of dust as they stamped and nervously circled. Still sniffing the air, Malachi lunged for the corrals, but Samantha restrained him.

Samantha was brave, but she was not a fool. After last night, she was not about to go check this out by herself. Returning to the house, she woke up Jacob. As he dressed, Jacob suggested they leave Malachi behind. He didn't think they could keep him quiet and they certainly didn't want him hurt again. Jacob grabbed a large carving knife and Samantha picked up Coop's cast iron fry pan as they left the house. They slowly worked toward the corral. The problem was not seeing, but finding enough shadow for cover in the bright moonlight.

Whinnying nervously, the horses danced and circled the corral. Through the swirling dust and horseflesh, Samantha thought she saw of a shadowy figure right in the center of the melee, then it was gone. She looked at Jacob; he nodded grimly. He'd also seen it. Using hand gestures, Jacob motioned for Samantha to circle around to the back, then he indicated he would go straight in.

Keeping one eye on Jacob and the other on where she was going, Samantha stealthily made her way around the horses. Suddenly, there he was again. Thankfully, he didn't see her; he seemed focused on catching a horse. After a few more minutes, she worked into position directly behind him. With a wave of her hand, she signaled Jacob. Nodding he'd seen her, Jacob still held his position. Samantha could help but wonder if he was as afraid; she sure was. All she knew about Jacob's past was as a youth he'd escaped Nazi Germany with his parents or was it Austria. That must have taken a fair amount of guts.

Abruptly Jacob walked out of the shadows into the bright moonlight and yelled, "Hey, *schweinkopf! Was machen sie heir?*" In the heat of the moment, he reverted to his native language.

Suddenly everything stopped, like someone had hit the pause button on the DVD. Not being chased, it took only seconds for the horses to shy to the far end of the corral and for the dust to settle. This left the intruder standing alone, spotlighted by the full moon. In his right hand he held a length of coiled rope and in his left hand, some kind of a tool that looked a lot like an ice pick. At first, he did not speak or move, but did not seem particularly frightened either. His silver hair glowed softly in the moonlight, though his face remained dark and contorted and his brown eyes blazed with fury.

"Vhat the hell you doing here?" Jacob shouted again, this time more loudly and in English.

The intruder remained silent, but looked around, trying to locate the source of the sound. Finally his fiery brown eyes came to rest on

Jacob, standing less than sixty feet away. Slowly, almost menacingly, he marched toward Jacob. He stopped briefly to open the gate, then passed through it not bothering to re-latch. Unflinching, Jacob stood his ground. Gripping the ice pick-like tool like a dagger, the intruder continued forward, his stride slow and deliberate. When he was within ten feet, he stopped, but still did not speak. He silently glared at Jacob.

Samantha thought Jacob looked visibly relieved when he saw the intruder was an older man, about his same age, but on the other hand he did appear fit and very determined.

The man moved a couple of threatening steps closer, but Heinz still held his ground, the carving knife dangled casually at his side. On the other hand, the intruder held his ice pick up in the ready position.

"*Uomo vecchio*, old man, you best stay out of this," the intruder finally hissed.

"*Greis*, you best get out of here vhile you can." Jacob's butcher knife glinted in the bright moonlight.

So far it was a war of words, a skirmish of name-calling. Samantha silently hoped it stayed that way.

"*Nazista*, I'm warning you," the intruder hacked the air with the ice pick. "This is no concern of yours."

Fascista, you are the one trespassing." Jacob's bearded chin was stubbornly thrust forward. "You leave now and I von't hurt you."

Almost as if cued by music, they slowly stated circling, each looking for an opening. Holding the rope in his left hand, the intruder used it to slap at Jacob, apparently trying to get him to react, then when the opportunity presented he would use the deadly ice pick

"Oh, my God!" Samantha mumbled under her breath. "They're really going to do this!"

Using his left forearm to parry the blows from the rope, Jacob now raised the knife to the ready position, holding it like a sword.

Suddenly, the intruder lunged forward, leading with the ice pick. As quickly as his old arthritic knees would allow, Jacob dodged to the right, but nevertheless Samantha saw the intruder's pick rip through Jacob's shirt and plunge into his left flank. Instantly, Jacob retaliated, slashing wildly with the knife, but his blade carved only the warm moonlit air.

Once again they circled. Samantha could now see the blood

soaking through Jacob's shirt. A seed of doubt flashed in her already anxious mind. This was a fight Jacob may not win! The intruder was quicker and more agile than Jacob. She had to help. Determined, she inched forward.

The intruder lunged again. Jacob barely had time to react. He darted to his left, but once again the ice pick tore trough his clothes. Now he looked frightened.

Samantha continued her silent approach, trying to remain directly behind the intruder. Briefly she caught Jacob's eye. Ever so slightly, he nodded his head, all the while maintaining his focus on the deadly ice pick.

Now, Samantha was in striking distance. She raised the heavy skillet high above her head, then just as the intruder lunged forward she swung down...hard. She missed!

Ouch! The downward momentum of the heavy skillet propelled it into her right kneecap. She almost cried out in pain. Fortunately the intruder missed too. Just in time, Jacob jumped sideways, once again avoiding the deadly ice pick.

Again they started to move in a circle, thrusting and parrying as they went. Limping now, Samantha scurried to stay directly behind the intruder. Like a scene from Shakespeare, silently, almost surreally, the deadly dance continued in the bright moonlight.

Suddenly, the intruder slapped at Jacob with the rope. When he reacted, the intruder lunged forward, again leading with his pick. Jacob skipped sideways, then immediately answered with a vicious swipe of his knife. To avoid the blade, the intruder quickly jumped backwards, bumping into Samantha Rose. Startled, he whirled, but then it was too late.

That's when the fry pan came crashing down.

24

Coop suddenly was seized with a paroxysm abdominal cramps followed by projectile vomiting.

Doubling over, he searched for the plastic mop bucket. Fortunately, he'd not had anything to eat since early morning, but nevertheless he could still taste bile and hydrochloric acid as it regurgitated though in his mouth. Other than those two gastric fluids, it was essentially dry heaves. But dry heaves or not, it was still brutal. With the violent and prolonged retching, his abdominal muscles knotted with spasm. Beads of perspiration, like fog condensing on a warm window, popped out on his forehead and dripped into recesses of his ears and eyes. He already felt weak and dizzy, even before the walls started to spin. They rotated counter clockwise, at first slowly, then faster and faster. Collapsing on the cold concrete floor, he groaned out loud and with each new spasm, he silently wished for death.

After about thirty minutes, the vomiting subsided, but the nausea persisted, as did the occasional need to expectorate large amounts of accumulated mucus. He sensed if he could vomit one last time, he would feel better, but nothing came up except viscous phlegm and green bile. The nausea and churning continued for another hour or so, after which he was totally spent. The injectable Yuccasote was so caustic, so mordant, he honestly didn't know if he could make it through another session. When given p.o. (orally), it must be less harsh, otherwise Coop doubted MITH could convince anyone to take it.

Cold chills and uncontrollable shaking followed the nausea. From the profuse perspiration, his clothes became totally saturated. This coupled with the cold and damp closet air more than likely triggered the intense shivering. Coop longed for the light; he longed to bask in the heat of summer sunshine. In the dark, he searched for a way to warm up, but found only a small stack of dusting rags. At least they were clean. First he used them to towel off, then pieced them across his body, making kind of a mosaic, a patchwork quilt without the needlework.

Slowly, he warmed up enough he could think about things other than basic survival. First, his thoughts turned to the almost impossible riddle, how to get out of here. Or failing that, how to end his own life? Undoubtedly, this was what the gentle healer Dr. Clifton Ford was planning for him anyway. He might just as well beat him to the punch. By doing so, he would save himself a whole lot of pain and deny Ford the satisfaction. That is if you can call killing another human satisfying.

One more time, he fumbled around in the dark, making one a last desperate search. There was absolutely nothing he could use as a tool or a weapon—well, unless he could swing this plastic bucket as a club or throw a deadly roll of toilet paper as a missile. Upon seeing those daunting weapons, he thought derisively, anyone who opened the door would surely turn and run.

Sitting back down on the case of toilet paper, Coop sighed deeply and tried without much success to fight back another surge of claustrophobia. Tight dark spaces invariably make him panic. They always had, since he was a kid, since his cousin locked him in a coal bin, but that was another story.

To take his mind off his tomb-like surroundings, Coop picked up the mop handle, idly rotating it in his hands. It was a good mop, not plastic, but the old fashioned wood kind. He couldn't help but smile. He mopped many a floor with a mop just like this. To earn tuition money for college, he'd once been a night janitor for...

...Wait a minute! Maybe, just maybe, he could use mop handle for a weapon if he had more room. The closet was so cramped he couldn't take a full swing, therefore couldn't generate much force or in the golfing vernacular, he couldn't get much club-head speed. He could, of course, poke with the end of it and maybe if he jabbed hard enough and in just the right place, the solar plexus, he might momentarily stun a security officer. But he'd have to surprise him and overpower him, then what would he do about the others? They always traveled in packs of three or four, and they carried guns. But what if the handle was shorter? Certainly, he could swing it better and maybe...yes, if it was shorter he could even use it as a...but then still there were the other guards. But what if there were fewer of them? Ever so slowly, Coop kicked around those ideas and bit-by-bit a rudimentary plan started to germinate.

Suddenly, the door opened again, allowing a rectangular shaft of yellow light to enter. Following the incandescent light, four burly guards entered, this time without Dr. Ford. Once again the three of them restrained Coop while the fourth, the tall mean one called Satch, applied the tourniquet. Forcibly extending his arm, Satch slapped at his anitcubital fossa, looking for a vein. This time, however, Coop did not struggle, but lay limp and unresisting, like fresh laundry.

With Coop not resisting Satch easily found a vein and inserted the angiocath. When the other guards realized he was not going to resist, they released his arm, stood back and watched. Satch fumbled in his leather bag, found the sixty cc syringe filled with Yuccasote and injected it into Coop's vein. The ease of which he accomplished this made Coop suspect he had some medical training, maybe a nurse or an EMT.

When finished, the Satch stood up, walked behind Coop and de-livered a sharp blow, cuffing him hard on the back of the head, sending him sprawling to the floor and scattering rolls of toilet paper. Grinning maliciously, Satch then kicked him in the ribs as he tried to get up. Winching in pain, Coop doubled over, but did not cry out. He refused to give him the satisfaction. After one final boot, the Satch signaled to the others and they retreated, relocking the door.

Gingerly, Coop got up and checked ribs and the back of his head for injuries. Not too surprising, there appeared to be a slowly expanding hematoma at the base of the skull and another over his ribs. Locating the cardboard box, he righted it, replaced the scattered rolls, then sat down. His ribs were sore, but his head throbbed from the vicious blows. Groaning, he lowered his head onto his lap and massaged his temples. After roughly five minutes, he reached back again and rechecked the hematoma. Though about the size of a fifty-cent piece, it didn't appear to be expanding any further. Nevertheless, it was a sure sign his blood must already be starting to thin.

However, he didn't have long to worry about this. As before, he was soon wracked with a fit of gagging and vomiting. This time, along with the bile and acid, he could taste blood. Again, he perspired profusely and the continual retching produced severe muscle spasms. The paroxysm lasted for approximately thirty minutes and when it finally abated Coop was so weak he could not rise up from the floor. He lay curled in a fetal ball, shivering and without the strength to piece together another patchwork quilt.

As much with self-pity as with pain, Coop cried out loud in the darkness. There was no way he could endure much more of this. His resolve was melting like mountain snow in June. It was not just his determination, but his strength and stamina were also failing. Physically and mentally, he was drained. If he got much weaker, he wouldn't be able to execute his plan.

With maximum effort, Coop forced his mind back to the scheme he was working on. There was no way to know for sure, but it seemed like there was approximately six hours between the first and second doses of Yuccasote. Apparently, Dr. Ford had him on a q.i.d. schedule, every six hours. By using his crude sundial, the light shining under the door, Coop figured when Ford administered the first dose it was early evening, maybe around eight or nine o'clock. That means the second dose was given around two or three a.m. and the next one would be due around eight or nine tomorrow morning. More than likely they would continue giving him a dose every six hours until he spontaneously hemorrhaged. Judging by how fast the hematoma on the back of his head expanded that could happen at any time. Even though he had serious doubts he could make it, he would have to endure two or three more doses for his plan to work.

When the guards arrived next, a shaft of glorious sunlight burst through the opened door. Considering the angle of the light beams, Coop figured it had to be somewhere around eight to nine in the morning. Right on schedule. This time there were only three guards and again he did not resist. It was not a difficult role to play. In fact, he wasn't even sure he was acting. Either way, he did manage to convince the guards he didn't have the strength to struggle. With nothing to do, two of the guards watched while the third, again it was Satch, inserted the needle. When done, once again he cuffed and kicked Coop, then laughed cruelly. He was one mean son-of-a-bitch.

Within minutes, the nausea, vomiting, muscle spasms, chills and fever all returned. If possible, each time was more severe than the last. Once again Coop tasted blood in his vomit. In the dark he couldn't tell for sure, but he suspected it was more than before. Was that how he was going to die, from a massive G.I. hemorrhage? It was certainly possible.

With a growing sense of desperation, Coop wondered it he could actually make it till nightfall and if he did, he had increasing doubts his plan would work. Obviously, he had no choice but to try. He'd already decided suicide was not an option, though his plan was pretty close to suicidal. But he may not have to worry about executing his plan; there was a good chance he would die at any moment just from a spontaneous bleed. If he did survive till nightfall, there was even a better chance he would die executing his most dicey plan. But anything was better than this.

When the door opened for the next dose, Coop was greeted by sunlight again, but this time there were no brilliant slanting rays spotlighting the closet floor, but rather indirect reflected sunlight. According to his calculations, it was early afternoon, probably around 2:00 p.m. With this visit, there were only two guards. Again, he did not resist but lay limp like a jellyfish. Once again, the one guard did nothing but watch as Satch, smilingly cruelly, inserted the angiocath, then injected the thick amaretto liquid. As was becoming his habit, following the injection he delivered another vicious blow to the back of Coop's head.

If all went as planned, by the next dose there would only be one guard, Satch, and if his calculations proved correct it would occur around 8:00 p.m. The dose after that would be the 2:00 a.m. dose and that's when he would make his move—providing he was still alive.

The next time the door opened, Coop was greeted by incandescent light so he knew it was early evening and by his way of reckoning, Sunday night. As he'd hoped, there was only one guard, Satch. Apparently, other than the doctors, Satch was the only one who knew how to start an I.V. Once again Coop did not resist. As Satch fished in his medical bag, he again grinned at Coop. Obviously, he was enjoying this. As soon as he'd released the tourniquet, he delivered another sharp blow to Coop's head.

Maybe the blows to the head were more than just an expression of Satch's sadism, Coop thought bitterly as he rubbed his sore head and examined the alarming hematoma. It could be some kind of a crude coagulation test. Perhaps, the guard was checking to see when Coop's blood was thin enough the blow would result in coma, the result of a subdural bleed. What a guy!

Probably, it was from his weakened condition, but this time the reaction, if possible, was more violent and lasted longer. What kept Coop going, however, was he knew one way or another this was the last one. And it was a damn good thing. With no water or electrolytes, he was now severely dehydrated, constantly dizzy and his muscles felt like denatured protein. Again he tasted blood, but this time there was something different, he vomited up a few chunks. Since he hadn't eaten, he assumed those were blood clots. This was both good and bad. The good, he was still able to clot. The bad, his blood was thin enough to spontaneously seep through the gastric lining and in larger and larger quantities.

For his next injection, he would not have to fake his debilitation. It every way it was real. It required a supreme effort just to keep his wits about him. And he would need his faculties if he were going to pull this off. Would he even have the strength? His plan was very risky and to succeed he would need the precise timing of a military operation and the luck of the Irish. Coop sighed and shook his painful woozy head. Like a man freezing to death, wouldn't it be easier for him to simply close his eyes and drift off? To simply forget this cockamamie plan. He honestly thought he was close enough to death right now he could do just that. He was tempted to close his eyes.

The reason Coop's plan was perilous and had more than a fair chance of becoming a suicide mission was without blood tests he had no way of knowing how thin his blood was becoming. He could only take a wild guess. But there was no doubt about it, by giving the Yuccasote I.V., as Ford said, his blood was become thinner much faster. That's where the blind luck part came in. If his blood was too thin, he surely would die. On the other hand, he dare not set his plan into motion too soon or his plan would certainly fail and he would die from the Yuccasote. That's where the precise timing came in. And of course, this was all made much more difficult without the aid of a timepiece. By now, however, Coop had developed kind of a diurnal rhythm and could pretty much sense, he hoped, when the next dose was due.

When, by his crude calculations, it was approximately fifteen minutes before the 2:00 a.m. dose, Coop firmly set his jaw and staggered to his feet. It was time—time to set his most dubious plan in motion. Propping the mop handle up against the closet wall, he raised his foot and stomped down. His foot simply bounced off. He really must be getting weak. Repositioning the mop handle, he tried again.

C-R-A-C-K!

The wooden handle fractured.

Bending slowly so as not to pass out, he retrieved the shorter piece, about twelve inches long. As he hoped, it had not cleaved straight across, but splintered along the wood grain, leaving a long jagged point that looked like a primitive Stone Age spear.

Next, he raised his shirt, exposing his soft belly. Holding the ragged piece of wood like a dagger, he placed the sharp tip on his tender skin, then hesitated. Mentally, he went through the arguments once again. He could very well die from this foolhardy plan. Was it worth it? Obviously, he was going to die anyway, so what did he have to lose? At least this way he had a slim chance. Taking a deep breath, he prepared for the pain. A muffled cry escaped from his mouth as he raked the razor sharp point of the mop stick across his abdomen.

Like a cracked water pipe, blood instantly gushed from the jagged wound. Coop was both surprised and alarmed at the volume and velocity. Pulling his shirt back over his wound, he collapsed on the floor. He curled up on his right side, still clutching the bloody spear in his right or lower hand. Then he struggled to scoot it and the spear underneath his body. Desperately hoped it was concealed from sight.

Now there was nothing to do, but wait. Coop could feel his shirt becoming wet and sticky as it soaked up the blood like a surgical sponge. A few seconds later, with the shirt was saturated, he could feel it oozing down his belly and onto his flank. Glancing down, he noted with some chagrin a puddle was already forming on the concrete floor. The self-induced hemorrhage showed no sign of slowing or clotting. He quickly looked away.

Briefly, Coop was reminded of what he told patients when asked how he could stand to do surgery. "I don't mind the sight of blood as long as it's not mine." Well, this was *his* blood! For the first time since the ordeal began, Coop silently prayed to the God he wasn't sure he believed in.

As if an ancient alchemist had somehow messed with the Periodic Table of Elements, time instead of gold became the most precious element. To Coop, it was now the most prized possession of all. He wanted to slow it down, to hoard it, to hold it, but he could not. It was slippery; it was intangible. As with grains of sand in an hourglass, with each drop of blood he could feel his precious time tick away.

Maybe he should have waited another ten minutes. Had his timing been off? Had he launched his plan too soon? It was certainly beginning to look like it. Like the dying of a golden sunset, Coop felt his consciousness slowly begin to fade. Desperately, he fought to maintain it, but now there was no question about it, his timing, which needed to be so precise, was off. Way off! He was going to die...

...Suddenly the door jerked open and a rectangle of incandescent light flooded in. Out of the corner of his eye, Coop noted with some satisfaction that once again only one guard entered...Satch. Maybe there was a God after all.

Silhouetted in the doorway, he fiddled with his medical bag, finally extracting a tourniquet, an angiocath and a sixty cc syringe of Yuccasote. With tools in hand, he then approached Coop, still lying on his right side.

Abruptly, he stopped, emitted a muffled gasp, then hesitated. Apparently he'd seen Coop's bloody shirt and the expanding pool of blood on the floor. At first, he appeared unsure, then he stooped over and groped Coop's neck, feeling for a carotid pulse. Going down on his knees, he placed a hand the back of Coop's chest, feeling for the movement of respiration. Apparently satisfied he was still alive Satch grabbed Coop's shoulder and attempted to roll him over onto his back. This movement freed up Coop's right arm, the one clutching the spear.

Mustering all his remaining strength, Coop thrust upward.

25

We chat together: he gives me his prescriptions;
I never follow them, and so I get well.
—Moliere (1622–1673)

The fractured mop handle found its mark, plunging six inches into the exposed soft underbelly of Satch. First shock, then pain registered in his once cruel brown eyes. Clutching his abdomen, he collapsed right on top of Coop. As he fell, the blunt end of the mop stick, still protruding from his abdomen, narrowly missed ramming Coop in the chest.

Almost by reflex, Satch's huge hands clamped around Coop's neck, like a vice, and cutting off his air. Was he going to die of asphyxiation? He hadn't even factored that possibility into his plan. Of all the ways he might die, he'd never even considered strangulation. But even as his consciousness was waning, the guard's grip relaxed.

Calling on reserves he didn't think he had, Coop pushed and rolled Satch off him and over onto his back. As he lay there gasping, Coop struggled to his knees. Satch didn't look so mean now. In fact, he looked more like a patient than a murderer. Sighing in resignation, after all he was still a doctor, Coop reached down and carefully worked the splintered mop handle from his abdomen, then hurriedly examined him. Though in some ways, many ways, he deserved it Coop nevertheless prayed he was not injured too badly.

It was a lower abdominal wound, well away from the liver or spleen. The worst possible scenario, Satch may have punctured the colon or small bowel. Or, maybe even the bladder, if it was full. But none of these potential injuries was immediately life threatening. It would take a couple of hours before he became septic and need critical care. Coop was fairly certain he did not go deep enough to lacerate any of the major vessels and of course he was not on Yuccasote, so Coop sincerely doubted he would bleed to death.

Tying clean dusting rags together, Coop used them to bind both his and the guard's abdominal wounds. His bandage soaked through immediately, but the guard's remained relatively dry. Coop assured Satch he would be okay and he would send help as soon as he could. After checking the guard's abdomen one last time, Coop stood up to go. Swooning, he immediately sank back down to the floor again. His blood pressure must be low. After lowering his head between his knees for a few seconds, his mind began to clear. Once again he stood up, but more slowly this time, and carefully made for the door.

For the first time in two days, Coop walked, or more precisely staggered, out of his closet prison a free man. He should have been overjoyed, but he wasn't. He was much too weak and light headed to rejoice in small victories. He still had a long way to go. Hugging the white plastered wall, he weaved down the corridor toward the central pod. Glancing up at a digital wall clock, he noted the time, 2:15 a.m. His mental clock was pretty accurate after all. As he stumbled past the open door of the security office, he noted there was still no one was manning the desk. So far, other than Satch, the entire compound appeared to be deserted.

It took approximately five minutes for Coop to make his way into the dimly lit central pod. Clutching his blood-soaked belly, he hobbled over to the reception desk and gazed up at the skylight. In his weakened condition there was no way he would be able to scale up through that elevated 4x4 foot opening and onto the roof. Obviously, he was going to have to find another way. Shuffling over to the main entrance, he tried the big door. It was locked from the inside as well. Next, he tried a side door and window with the same result. Exhausted, Coop sank down into the receptionist's chair, dripping blood onto the polished black leather. He needed a moment to think.

If all the doors and windows were locked, there was only one choice left. He was going to have to break out. Surely that would trip some kind of an alarm, so he would have to move fast, at least as fast as his deteriorating condition would allow. The big problem was getting out of the compound. By now they had undoubtedly found and confiscated his ladder—but—but wait a second. Somehow they must be able to open and close the huge portcullis from inside the hacienda. There had be some kind of remote control. He'd personally seen it happen a couple of times. Also, the metal gate was undoubtedly monitored by video camera with two-way audio capabilities as well. Logically, the place for all these controls would be the security office, the very same office he'd just passed.

Summoning as much strength as he could, Coop staggered back down the hallway. Pausing at the security office door, he peeked in. It still looked deserted. Perhaps the guard assigned to the security office was the very same one that he just stabbed, Satch. It was also conceivable that MITH routinely reduced the number of their staff at night and perhaps for holidays even more. But even taking that into consideration, there surely must be more than one guard for the entire compound. Perhaps, the others were assigned to outside patrol duties. But there was no time to worry about that. Looking over his shoulder, he slipped into the security office.

The foyer housed a desk and a couple of chairs, and not much else. There was, however, a second door directly behind the desk. Still dripping blood, Coop limped around the small desk and fumbled with the door. Opening it, he peeked in. It was a much larger room containing several banks of live-feed video monitors, but fortunately still no guards. He shuffled inside and quickly located the two monitors trained on the portcullis. They appeared to receive their feed from two cameras positioned on either side of the roadway, thereby providing opposing views. Though Coop knew it must be live, it looked like a still shot. Nothing moved in the picture.

The immediate problem, however, was how to open the portcullis? There must be some kind of a release mechanism located close to the video monitors, which allowed the operator to see who was at the gate before opening and closing it. Carefully Coop searched the wall, then the small desk and workstation located just below the monitors. Nothing. Then he found it! It was nothing more than a simple red button recessed in the wall and within easy reach of anyone seated at the desk. That had to be it. There was absolutely nothing else.

With hand shaking, Coop pushed the button, then held his breath as he watched the video monitors. Slowly, and with no sound, like a silent movie, the heavy metal portcullis slid open. Coop forced himself to watch the monitors for another full minute to see if opening the gates would attract security. Everything remained quiet.

Turning around, Coop surveyed the room again. Other than the doorway from the foyer, this room was completely devoid of other doors or windows.

Unsteadily, Coop made his way back to the foyer. On his left was a small window he'd not noticed when he first entered. It overlooked a poorly lit desert garden. Coop tried to open it, but it was locked or jammed. He jerked again. The window didn't budge. Turning around, he spied a high-backed wooden chair behind reception desk. He grabbed it and staggered back to the window. Raising the chair high, he slammed it through the window. The glass shattered with a loud crack, but surprisingly triggered no security alarms. Why? Maybe at the time of construction, Coop decided, the architect assumed a window located in the security office did not need to be wired since it was heavily guarded anyway. But whatever the reason, Coop was thankful to hear no wailing of security sirens or the tramp of the guard's military boots. Jerking down the drape, he wrapped his hand and carefully swept away the remaining jagged shards, then tumbled through the window.

Half-stumbling, half-crawling, he worked his way toward the open portcullis. His path was erratic and slow as he tried to stay as much as possible to the shadows. Purposefully, he skirted well around the well-lit central parking lot. It was mostly empty anyway and provided almost no cover. Suddenly, he stopped. There was still a single vehicle parked in the last row, a maroon pickup.

Coop paused for a second look. What the…?

Unbelievably, it was a Dodge pickup—his Dodge pickup!

At first he was bewildered. Why had they brought his truck inside the compound and parked it right in plain sight? Then he remembered. MITH and Dr. Ford were not trying to hide the fact he'd been here. In fact their whole alibi, their forged medical record, was predicated on the premise was a patient there and receiving treatment from Dr. Ford. Under those circumstances, to hide his truck would have been much more suspicious.

But, it really didn't matter. To Coop it was just a damn fortunate stroke of luck. He limped as fast as he could across the asphalt to the Dodge. Groaning, he bent down and felt under the left fender, finally locating his magnetic spare key box. Just that amount of bending, however, made him woozy. Leaning back against the fender, he took a moment to steady himself. Once his head cleared, he used the key to unlock the door, then with great effort, struggled up into the driver's seat.

The Dodge roared to life on the first try. Fortunately, there were some things you could always count on, Dodges and dogs. Shifting to drive, Coop rolled out of the parking lot and headed straight for the open portcullis. Just as he turned down the final straightway, he noted another set of headlights approaching, also heading straight for the portcullis. There was some one coming, another car! Their oncoming headlights bobbed briefly as the wheels bounced over a rock, then leveled out again. From the looks of it, they were coming fast.

Coop punched down on the accelerator. He had to beat them to the portcullis. The other car also sped up and arrived at the gate a fraction of a second sooner. Suddenly braking, they skidded to an angled stop precisely inside the gate and completely blocking the exit.

Also slamming on the brakes, Coop slid to a stop no more than a couple of inches from the bumper of a dark Mercedes Benz. Coop immediately leaned on his horn. The Mercedes didn't budge. Instead, the driver, a man, slowly opened the door and staggered out. A couple of seconds later, the passenger door opened and two females wearing party dresses and high heels stumbled after the man. Holding each other up, they weaved toward the Dodge. Not knowing what else to do, Coop rolled down the window and waited.

The driver tripped as he tried to climb onto the Dodge's running board. Cussing, he finally managed the high step, then poked his head through the window. Instantly, the distinctive aroma malted barley wafted throughout the cab, but that's not what surprised Coop. He started to say something, but the words stuck in his throat. Five minutes ago, he would've bet the ranch, even his life, there was nothing else about this case that could surprise him. If had, he would have lost.

"Where-in-thee-hell did yah learn to drive this friggin' hay wagon, pally?" the driver yelled through the window, then hiccupped loudly.

"Hey, Stevel" Coop said, weakly, "It's me."

At that moment, the two accompanying females arrived. Coop noted they were Spaulding's fairly steady girlfriend, Shannon, and the ever tag along Marty.

"So, it is...." Spaulding slipped from the running board, caught his foot and stumbled to the ground. Cussing, he regained his footing, then stuck his head through the window again.

"Ka-choo!" Coop sneezed from the accumulating fumes of ethanol.

"Well, I'll be god dammed," Spaulding chortled, "if it ain't me old cuttin' buddy, Coops."

Marty leaned in the window, only adding to the collecting fumes and beamed a lopsided grin. "Hi, ya, handsome."

"Oh, me good God, Coops!" Spaulding pushed Marty aside. "You're all bleedy. "What in thee hell happened?"

"It's not important. I need...."

"...Not important!" Spaulding interrupted as peered down at the floorboards. "That's a hell of a whole lot of blood. I should know, for I am thee sandman. And by my calculator...no my calculus, Coops me-man, you've got maybe three or four units right heer on the floor of this friggin' hay wagon."

"You've got to help me get out of here," Coop pleaded. "Move your car, then you can pull right back in and block any pursuit."

"What per'suit, pally? Don't see nobody comin'."

"The guards," Coop nodded over his shoulder. "They're after me."

Spaulding paused a moment to consider. "That's just plain crazy, me ole surgery buddy. The best thing, you to should wait heer and I'll go git thee some help. People can bleed to death," he guffawed, "as you should know."

Coop's was getting light-headed from blood loss or ethanol fumes or both, but he desperately wanted to think this through. "What...uh.. what are you doing here anyway?"

"Well, this heer castle healin'...uh...health or whatever the frig it is, is only thirty minutes from casinos of Mesquite, if ye must know, all on back roads," Spaulding said, stumbling over his thickened tongue. "And ye probably couldn't tell, but we've been a wee drinkin'."

"Really?" Coop mumbled sarcastically. "I hadn't noticed."

"Really? Yeah, well I can hold me booze. Anyways, we sometimes we stop heer and sleep it off. Better than another friggin D.U.I."

"They let you sleep it off!"

"Sir saint Cliffy, you know Doctor chiropractor Ford, the Magnificent, is me brother-in-law. He's a friggin' straight arrow, you know, but he has an apartment heer that he never uses."

"Your brother-in-law?"

"Sure, me first wife was his sister, but prettier."

"You were married before Brenda?" All this came as a revelation. There was a lot, it seems, he didn't know about his best friend.

"Yeah, Brenda, the night slapper, were number two. Alicia, sweet Alicia, Cliffy's sister," he sobbed, "died some few years ago. You know, the friggin' breast cancer."

"No, I didn't know."

"After that Sir Cliffy and I, mainly Cliffy, devoted our lives to finding a cure for this friggin' crab, the cancer, but it ain't been easy."

"So, you work for Doctor Ford?" Coop couldn't believe what he was hearing.

"Yeah, sometimes. After all, he is me brother-in-law."

"What do you do?"

Grinning lopsidedly, Steve shook a finger in Coop's face. "Don't try ye even to trick me, pally."

"Let me guess." Coop took a stab at it. "You supply him with cancer patients for his clinical trials."

"You always were thee fast one, Coops." Spaulding continued to wag his finger in Coop's face. "Nothin' gets you by.

"My patients?"

"Well, yeah, sometimes, me ole cuttin' buddy," Spaulding grinned. "When I see them before surgery, like any good doctor, I give just 'em their options. You know, some alternatives. Not surgery is the only answer."

"But why?" Coop sneezed again. The fumes were getting bad.

"Well, if you must know, mainly to further Saint Cliffy's work at the castle, but also it helps some me pay the friggin' table debts," Spaulding shrugged. It appeared for him alcohol was like the truth serum Sodium Pentothal, "But re-spiteless of what ye may think, Coops me-man, I don't win always thee tables and them bloody shark loans can b...b...bite."

Spaulding lost his balance and grabbed the window frame for support.

"Well," Coop said as firmly as he could. "Well, Steve, I've got to go. Please move your car—now!"

"Okay, buddy, if that's what ye in thee hell want."

Climbing down from the truck, he briefly huddled with the girls, then they separated. The girls faded into the dark shadows of the compound and Spaulding weaved back to the Mercedes Benz. Climbing in, he turned off the ignition, pulled out the keys, then leaned out the window and waved the keys. "Sorry, ole buddy, this Kraut piece-o-shit won't start."

Suddenly it dawned on Coop, the girls had gone for help and Spaulding was stalling! He tried to think, but his head began to spin and his vision blurred. Lowering his head down to the steering wheel, he struggled to remain conscious. He had to do something and damn quick. But really, there was nothing to think about; there was only one way out of here.

Shoving the Dodge in reverse, Coop backed up thirty yards, then loudly revved his mighty Cummings engine as a warning. Still Spaulding didn't move. Without taking his foot off the gas feed, Coop slammed the pickup in drive. Like a Derby thoroughbred bolting from the starting gate, the pickup shot forward. He was going at least thirty miles per hour and still accelerating when he slammed into the car.

The Mercedes's left bumper took the brunt of the collision. As Coop's head snapped backward banging against the rear window, he heard the sickening sound of metal crunching and the explosion of shattering reinforced glass. But the impact also shot-putted the Mercedes out from under the portcullis, creating just enough room for him to clear the gate.

Also staggered by the blow, the Dodge momentarily sputtered and coughed, then roared back to life. Coop backed up once more, disengaging from the Mercedes, then punched the accelerator down to the floor. The Dodge hurled forward through the open portcullis and out to the open desert...to freedom.

Once clear of the gate, Coop slammed on the brakes again. He shook the fog from his head. Apparently, the loss of blood was affecting his photographic memory too. He'd nearly overlooked why he came to MITH in the first place.

Stumbling out of the Dodge, he staggered over to the stucco fence, searching through the thick sagebrush and creosote bushes. Suddenly he found it, right where he tossed it, mostly obscured under a thicket of spiny hopsage. He picked it up and quickly examined it. All three charts were there. At long last, he had the evidence he needed for the Betty Tsongas trial. He lurched back to the pickup and managed to crawl up into the cab. Jamming the truck in gear, he accelerated down the road, rear tires spitting rooster tails of gravel. He swerved at the last second, he barely missing the jutting sandstone pillar.

Coop only had managed to go a couple of hundred yards before he saw double. Suddenly, there were two roads—which one to take? It was difficult to know. Or maybe he was simply seeing them in stereovision and both roads were actually the same road. It was all very confusing, but he'd better slow down if he was going to make it to Littlefield. What was the point of going through all this just to die in a car accident?

Weaving like a drunk and hugging the steering wheel like he was visually impaired, Coop guided the Dodge up the steep canyon wall. Somehow he negotiated the hairpin curves and crested the rimrock, then headed down the three-mile sloping piedmont plain. Finally with relatively flat ground and a fairly straight road, he once again stepped on the gas feed. The truck responded, flying down that lengthy stretch of desert road.

How long could he last? Fighting through his mental fog, Coop tried to figure the possibilities. If a person lost ten or twelve units of blood, he would certainly lose consciousness, then two or three more after that and he'd be dead. Say, fifteen units total of unreplaced blood. If Spaulding was correct at the gate and he had three or four units in the truck, by now he must be up to six or seven units right here in the cab. Then add to that the four or five units he lost before ever getting to the truck and that put him up to around twelve or so. Sure, those were rough estimates, but they were probably in the ballpark? If true, he didn't have much time or blood left.

Even more disconcerting, the bleeding showed no signs of stopping, abating or even clotting. He could feel it trickling down his thighs, soaking his pant legs, collecting around his ankles, then onto the floor. It was warm and tacky and his shoes stuck to the floorboard. Anxiously, he glanced down; the puddle at his feet was still growing!

Abruptly, his vision changed. It was no longer double, but was fading in and out like a car radio with poor reception. Not only his vision, but his consciousness began to waver as well. Somewhere in the back of his mind, he realized he was approaching the end of the piedmont and would soon have to slow down. Wasn't there a sharp curve just outside of Littlefield?

Glancing in his rear view mirror, Coop thought he saw headlights. Was it two or two sets? Was he still seeing double? He didn't know for sure, but without question someone was coming. They were still a ways behind, but from the looks of it they were coming fast. Momentarily, Coop's consciousness waned again and the Dodge drifted onto the apron, bouncing over baseball-sized rocks. Banging his head hard on the ceiling of the cab brought him back. He jerked the steering wheel hard to the left and the pickup tilted back toward the center of the road.

Suddenly, directly ahead, another set of headlights. They rounded a curve and came straight for him. These lights were much closer, brighter and blinding. Why the hell didn't they click off their high beam? Briefly, he glanced at his rear view mirror. Those headlights were still there too—much closer now! He looked forward again. Those lights were right on top of him!

Throwing up his forearm, Coop shielded his eyes as the mental fog blew in. He knew he was losing it, but there was absolutely nothing he could do about it.

Instinctively, he whipped the steering wheel hard to the right. His faithful Dodge responded, immediately careening from the road and bouncing off into the great Mojave Desert.

Then everything went black.

26

Men who are occupied in the restoration
of health to others...they partake of divinity.
For to preserve and renew is almost as noble
as to create.
—*Voltaire (1694–1778)*

Somewhere in the fuzzy recesses of his personal Never Never Land, Coop realized he didn't want to wake up and fought against it. It was really no contest. His preference was to stay right where he was, lying in bed with the beautiful Samantha Rose Jardine.

Everything about this Never Land was white: the paint on the walls and the linoleum covering the floor, even the furniture, the sheets and the comforter. Furthermore, they were both dressed in white night-clothes; she a lacey semi-transparent nightgown and he loose cotton pajama bottoms. More than likely it was mid-morning. This he could tell by the angle of the white sunlight as it streamed through the window, spotlighting the bed. A window adorned with polar white voile curtains, which drawn and tied with a white velvet cord.

Coop was propped up on one elbow and Samantha Rose was curled on her left side facing him. The rust in her hair appeared to combust in the bright sunlight, creating a striking contrast to the ivory sheets. They made love earlier, but now they were simply talking, enjoying each other's company. He made a muffled comment; she threw back her head and laughed. Her voice was musical and her smile, like the sunlight, was bedazzling.

However, this picture was fading fast, bleeding away like life itself, like the lives of Betty Tsongas, Gordon Flowers, Hector Gonzalez and Nathan Reed. The harder Coop tried to cling to it, the faster it whirled and swirled, the white blending into red, like mixing paint at Home Depot.

Then abruptly, it was gone, replaced by a black colorless void, which reminded Coop a lot of the utility closet at MITH. Then suddenly he was transported back to the closet, his blackened tomb, his light-less sarcophagus. He groaned out loud. Desperately, he wanted out of here. Now, unfortunately, the only way out seemed to be a return to consciousness, to wake up. Like a scuba diver carrying too much weight, he struggled toward the surface. As he got closer, he grudgingly opened a single eye, his left eye. To his surprise, he saw nothing but white. Warily, he opened his right eye. It also saw nothing but shades of white.

Indeed, Coop was in a mostly colorless room, everything was clean, bright and white. Initially, he was disoriented. He couldn't decide if this was really consciousness or a variation of his previous dream. He very much wanted to return to the white dream. He looked around for Samantha Rose. Except for him, the bed was empty. Maybe, she got up for a drink or go to the bathroom and would soon return. Glancing down, he saw a white bandage circling his abdomen. That was odd. That particular white wasn't in his earlier dream, but somehow he knew it should be there even though he couldn't remember exactly why.

Then like the breaking of an earthen damn, it all flooded back. But where was the red? The bandage should be red, blood red! It was not. Glancing over at his left arm, he saw an I.V., then followed the plastic tubing all the way up to the collapsible bag of red blood dangling from a stainless steel metal standard. He felt something squeezing his right upper arm. Pulling up the sleeve of his white gown, he saw the black band of a blood pressure cuff, tightly constricting his white biceps. It was connected via black rubber tubing to an automated vital signs monitor, as was the pulse oximeter clipped to the tip of his right index finger. He recognized all this stuff; it was all hospital equipment. He must be in a hospital. But why? And where?

Abruptly, the door opened and a white-frocked nurse entered. She took one look at him and excitedly clapped her hands. "Wonderful!" she exclaimed. "Just wonderful! You're awake."

"Yes, I suppose I am," Coop agreed, but without the same enthu-siasm.

"Well, then, how do you feel, Doctor Cooper?" While waiting for the digital readout of his vital signs, she shoved a thermometer (also connected to same the automated vital signs machine) in his mouth and under his tongue, then retightened his blood pressure cuff,

"U'm-m f-i-ne," Coop croaked. It was not easy talking with his tongue immobilized by the thermometer.

"Vital signs are fine too," the nurse announced brightly as the automated machine flashed a new series of digital numbers. "Blood pressure is up to one-ten-over-sixty, heart rate is eighty-two, temp ninety-nine-point-one and oxygen sat is a whopping ninety-three percent. That makes you my star patient for the day!" Thankfully, she also removed the temperature probe from under his tongue.

"What's my hematocrit?"

The nurse flipped through the chart. "It's actually coming up. As of the six a.m. draw, it was thirty-two."

"How much blood?"

"A lot," the nurse laughed. "You've kept us hopping."

"Then it looks like I'll live," Coop deadpanned.

"From what I hear, nobody was betting that horse yesterday." The nurse checked his abdominal bandage.

"What happened?"

"All I know," the nurse charted his vital signs, then turned to leave, "is that you were in a bad automobile accident and lost a lot of blood."

"How did I get here?"

"I really don't know," the nurse smiled broadly and waved good-bye, "probably by ambulance, like everyone else."

Wearily, Coop sank back onto the bed. He was exhausted and almost immediately dozed again. At first, he slept deeply, like an over-worked intern, then gradually his sleep lightened. How long had he slept? He had no idea. One time he started to waken, but fought against it. This time he was successful. It felt good to be warm, secure and without pain. He liked this present world and decided to stay as long as he could.

In the predawn of his consciousness, he felt something brush against his lips, moist—probably Malachi. He smiled. Malachi was always trying to wake him like that. Smiling, he reached over and stroked his head. It felt more like hair than fur. He stroked again. Puzzled, he cracked his right eye a slit. Indeed, it was hair, rust-colored hair. It was Samantha Rose Jardine!

She leaned over and kissed him again, then pulled up a chair and sat down beside him.

"How are you feeling?" she worry lines etched deeply on her perfect face.

"Never better." Coop grinned.

"*Ja, Ja, du bist ein harter wienerschnitzel.*" Jacob leaned in from the other side of the bed.

Coop grasped his leathery old paw with his left hand and Samantha Rose's smaller softer hand in his right. He started to speak, but no sound came. Tears blurred his vision and choked off his speech.

After a moment, Samantha asked softly, "as Paul Harvey says, would you like to hear the rest of the story?"

Wiping his eyes, Coop nodded.

For the next fifteen minutes, Samantha Rose, with Jacob periodically interrupting to supply salient details, told Coop about their adventures of Friday and Saturday nights. First, she told of Malachi's strange illness, then quickly assured Coop Malachi was fine and she'd gotten special permission from hospital administration to bring him in later. Next she described the melee of Saturday night with the armed intruder at the horse corrals. It was none other than the old saddlemaker, Franco Tucciano. With pride in her voice, she recounted how brave Jacob was during the dramatic standoff. Jacob, however, stubbornly insisted that she was the real hero, then he vividly described the scene with the flying frying pan.

"Wow!" Coop exclaimed. "You both deserve purple hearts."

"Maybe, Jacob," Samantha insisted, "he was wounded in battle."

Coop's grin faded to frown and he turned to Jacob.

"*Nein, nein*, it vas nothing." Heinz lifted up his shirt to show Coop his neatly sutured wound. "It vas just a scratch."

"He sutured it up himself," Samantha laughed, then proudly added, "but I helped."

"*Ja, Ja*, she could assist you vith your next surgery."

"I'm sure she'd be better than Stan Kingsley or that old geezer who helped me the last time." Coop grinned. "What was his name? Heath, Haines, Henry...something like that."

"Nah, I'd better stick to law," Samantha objected, but did seem proud of herself.

"So like I thought," Coop continued, "it was old Tucciano who started the tack shed fire and killed Stepper."

"Yes, apparently he kind of lost it after his son-in-law, Gordon Flowers, died," Samantha replied. "He became obsessed with revenge. I guess he and Gordon were quite close. Closer than with his own son."

"What's going to happen to him?"

"A lot of that depends on you," Samantha Rose replied. "Since you are the only victim, the County Attorney wants to wait and see how you wish to proceed. "Due to his advanced age and because he has no priors, they would prefer he pay restitution, do community service, then forget it...unless...unless, of course, you want to pursue it and have him to go to jail."

"No, not really," Coop shook his head. "If I can get a promise from him it's over, and if he'll pay the expenses to build a new tack shed and replace the saddles and for Stepper, that's good enough for me."

"I think he's already agreed to that," Samantha added.

"So how did I get here?" Coop asked after a moment of pensive silence. "The last thing I remember is leaving MITH, seeing two headlights coming right for me, then swerving. After that, nothing."

"As Paul Harvey said," Samantha smiled, "that is the rest of the rest of the story."

"*Ja, Ja,*" Jacob added enthusiastically. "It vas me and Samantha Rose in the other car."

Samantha nodded, then finished the story. "When you didn't come home on Friday night, I was very worried, but as I mentioned Malachi was sick. I couldn't leave him and also I was concerned about leaving the horses and ranch unprotected. Late Saturday afternoon I got Malachi out of the vet hospital and just as I got home Jacob came over. By then it was almost dark, too late to go search for you and, as you know, that was the night we had to deal with Franco Tucciano. By then so much time had passed, I was literally sick with worry," she paused, a catch in her voice.

After taking a moment to compose herself, she resumed the story. "The next day we had Sophie come over to watch the ranch and take care of the horses and Malachi, then we started searching."

"But ve had no idea of vhere to look," Jacob interjected.

"Jacob thought he had an idea where MITH was," Samantha continued, "but it turned out to be a native desert plant nursery. We looked until we were about to run out of gas, then we turned around and went back into the town of Mesquite. There we filled up with gas, inhaled a burger and headed right back out into the desert. By then it was almost dark, but we still wandered around for hours.

"At about two a.m. we stopped for a bathroom break. Needless to say, we were tired, discouraged and more than a little desperate. After discussing our options for a few minutes, we decided to head down this one last road we'd found just south of the town of Littlefield, then call it quits for the night.

"I was driving and had just rounded a particularly sharp bend and suddenly there were two headlights bearing down, or should I say weaving toward us. I slammed on the brakes. At the same time the other driver swerved and ended up bouncing off into the desert, his truck slamming into a giant Joshua tree.

"Of course, we immediately went over to investigate. That's when I recognized your Dodge pickup. You were unconscious and there was blood everywhere. When we pulled you from the pickup, I thought you were dead."

"*Ich dachte Du wärst tot*," Jacob punctuated his speech with animated hand gestures hands.

"English, Jacob," Coop grinned, "English."

"I thought you vere dead too."

"That's when we noticed the other headlights coming towards us and fast," Samantha continued. "We struggled to get you into the back seat with Jacob, then got out of there as fast as my car would go. In the meantime Jacob worked on you, applied pressure to your wounds and slowed the bleeding.

"Fortunately, as you know, I'm a pretty good driver, but I barely out ran those other two vehicles. Once we reached civilization, Littlefield, Jacob used his cell phone to call the police. Within five minutes an Arizona Highway Patrol cruiser appeared on the horizon with red lights flashing. Seeing the patrol car, our pursuers quickly turned around. Then with the highway patrol escorting us, we then brought you here to Dixie Medical Center. That was two days ago."

"You mean I've been unconscious for two days?" Coop shook his head in disbelief.

"*Ja, Ja*, and damn near died too," Jacob added. "They gave you twenty-two units of blood and several units of clotting factor and plate-lets."

"The doctors said you were fortunate, very fortunate," Samantha Rose sought and found Coop's hand again. "If the wound had penetrated the abdomen you would have died. But it was superficial and did not require major surgery, only a couple dozen skin sutures."

"All...all I can say is...is thank...," Coop choked again as his eyes began to fill.

"Yeah, you owe us big time all right," Samantha teased, her eyes danced with mischief, "and don't think for a minute we don't intend to collect."

"And I intend to pay." Coop used his free hand to wipe the moisture from his eyes.

"*Ja, Ja*, you two *Liebvögel*," Jacob interrupted, "but that's not all."

"I assume you're going to tell me." A twinkle reappeared in Coop's eyes.

"In case you don't remember, you vere in the middle of a malprac-tice trial."

"Oh, yeah, that," Coop said. In fact, he'd forgotten.

"Actually, this is my last case for Cannon, Jeffs and Hanks," Samantha added.

"Huh?"

"Yeah, I resigned."

"What are you going to do?"

"Well, that depends."

"On what?" Coop did his best to remain stoic.

"On things."

"What things?" He enjoyed seeing her squirm.

"On us!" Samantha blurted.

"Oh," Coop scowled. "Uh...uh...I've been thinking...uh...I don't know...uh...but...uh...maybe Saint George does need another good attorney. Someone with a lot of experience. Someone who can do mal-practice, criminal law and even divorce law."

Samantha fired a withering glance. "Or prosecute obnoxious doc-tors. Do you want to hear about the case or not?"

Coop grinned and nodded.

"When we found you, we also found the three files in your truck. So yesterday, with you *in absentia,* I finished our part of the trial And, I must admit with Betty Tsongas's file, plus Doctor Westover's report, we had a pretty strong case. Judge Pleasants gave the case to the jury just this morning."

"And?" Coop asked, holding his breath.

"Here's the verdict." Samantha Rose dangled a folded piece of white computer paper in front of Coop's face, like a carrot.

When he reached for it, she quickly jerked it out of his reach.

"Are you going to make me beg?"

"Maybe a little." Again mischief danced in her eyes. She again let the paper drop a little.

"I can see what kind of a relationship this is going to be."

"Relationship?" she quipped, holding the paper tantalizingly close. "What relationship?"

Like a purse-snatcher, Coop grabbed the paper, then turned his back to read it.

Not guilty!

What a relief. Now more than likely everything else would fall into place and there was a good chance his life could soon return to some semblance of normalcy.

"And," Samantha Rose added, "now that we have both the Flower's and Gonzalez files, we should have no problems with those suits either."

"What about Ford?" Coop rolled back to face Samantha Rose.

"We've given all that information to the county attorney," Samantha said. "First, he wants to speak to you, but he says he fully intends to file charges against Doctor Ford and shut MITH down."

"They may be a vee bit late," Jacob growled. "I've heard that *schleimig* S.O.B. has already disappeared."

"They'll catch him," Samantha insisted. "It's only a matter of time."

Coop frowned at the thought of Ford running free, possibly setting up business somewhere else and again preying on unsuspecting cancer patients. But Samantha was right; surely they would catch him.

"What about Doctor Westover?" Coop asked, his voice husky. "Do we know who killed him?"

"*Jawhol*, it was the tall security guard," Jacob replied. "You know, the one you stabbed at MITH."

"Yeah," Coop frowned and shook his head. "Satch was capable of doing something like that."

"Vell, he's here in the hospital too," Jacob added. "Apparently he confessed to the murder, but he claims it vas an accident. His version is they vere scuffling over some papers, knocked over some chemicals and then the Bunson burner. When the fire erupted, the guard shoved Vestover hard to get away. In the fall, allegedly Vestover hit his head on the lab counter and never made it out."

"Nevertheless," Samantha insisted, "the guard will face charges of murder in the second degree."

"Damn," Coop said, choking up again, "I do feel bad about that."

"So do I," Heinz agreed. "It's a damn shame."

"We all do." Samantha leaned over and gently kissed Coop.

His head bowed in grief, Coop took a moment for his private thoughts. Damn, he'd miss the old guy. He'd been a true friend. When he got better he would go pay his respects to his wife.

"What about my buddy Steve Spaulding?" Coop asked after a few moments. "He was in this up to his chin."

"It's a little tougher with him," Samantha explained. "Unless they catch Doctor Ford and get him to testify, you're the only one who can implicate him. So far, they've found no records to indicate he was an employee or he benefited financially from MITH. Apparently, all transactions were done under the table. So, it will probably boil down to your word against his."

"What could they charge him with?"

"It could be any number of things," Samantha replied. "Fraud, conspiracy to commit fraud, and possibly even an accessory to murder—just for starters."

Coop looked out the window for a few seconds. "Steve was my best friend, but I will testify against him. He did some very bad things and undoubtedly contributed to the deaths of several patients. He should pay for it."

"*Jawhol*, I agree," Jacob nodding his head vigorously. "First, do no harm."

"He was a nice enough fellow," Coop continued, "and a good anesthesiologist. It was the gambling that got him into trouble."

"Yes," Samantha agreed, "but nevertheless he, like everyone else, needs to be held accountable for what he did."

"Anything else?" Coop asked after a moment.

"That's it," Samantha said. "Oh...oh, yeah, except Doctor Kingsley came by yesterday and asked to be released from his contract."

"Yeah, I agree, Stan should be on his own."

"I'll take care of the necessary paperwork," Samantha volunteered, "to dissolve the limited liability partnership.

Coop sighed deeply and gazed out the window. Finally his long nightmare was over.

Leaning over, Samantha brushed a sandy lock of hair and kissed him. "We should probably go and let you get some rest. I'll bring Malachi in this evening."

"*Ja, Ja*, best not to overdue it," Heinz quickly agreed. "But Coop, I've got a big favor to ask before ve go."

"Anything, Jacob, anything."

"Vould you be my best man? You know, me and Sophie..."

"...Jacob!" Coop blurted out with mock indignation. "*Ein alte Geiss, wie du!*"

"Ha, ha, an old goat, huh?" Heinz laughed. "That's pretty good *Deutsch*. You must be practicing. Vell, vill you?"

"Vill I what?" Coop cocked an ear, pretending he didn't hear.

"Vill you be my best man?"

Coop cupped his hands behind his head, then ever so slowly a big grin spread across his face.

"*Jawhol*," he said enthusiastically, "and I know just what I'll get you for a wedding present—the perfect gift."

"Vhat?" Heinz's voice was gravelly and his leathery face skeptical. "*Nein, nein*, no gifts. I don't need nothing."

"Yes, you do," Coop laughed out loud. "Something round, something blue, something pharmaceutical."

Reader's Guide

1. Why did the author include an opening teaser? What did he hope to accomplish?
2. What is the point of the prologue? How does it tie into the rest of the story?
3. Why did the author begin the book with a prank? Other than being amusing, what insight does it provide?
4. In the first chapter, Coop is faced with a common ethical/moral dilemma, one we all have faced. Disregarding the outcome of his surgery, should he have gone into work sick? What were his reasons for doing so?
5. Early on the author uses a literary device known as foreshadowing. When and where?
6. In the second chapter, the author takes us step by step through an operation. Why did he do this? Does this add, or detract from the story?
7. What is Coop's relationship with his wife, Kylie? Why doesn't he go ahead and get a divorce?
8. The author spent a good deal of time explaining how operating rooms and hospitals work. Does this add to the authenticity of the story, or bog it down?
9. Renae, the operating room circulating nurse, is stickler for protocol, but there is more to it than that. Why does she particularly despise Coop, his behavior in the O.R. and why is she so tenacious in seeing him punished?
10. The author uses an acronym as a subtle, maybe not quite so subtle, pun. What was it and where?
11. Coop has three patients die on the operating table from massive hemorrhage. The author thought it important the reader understands the clotting mechanism in order to understand the plot. Did the author succeed in explaining the technical aspects of medicine? Was this educational detour essential to the book? Or, did it detract from it?
12. Is Yuccasote an actual herbal drug? If not, what mechanisms did the author use to make it seem real?
13. What are the issues that complicate Coop and Samantha Rose's relationship? Are there moral/ethical concerns as well?
14. Jacob Heinz plays the role of a classical mentor. Specifically, in what ways does he help Coop?

15. Why do you think Coop has so much trouble with female relationships?

16. Coop and Samantha Rose have definite concerns with holistic medicines compared to FDA (Food and Drug Administration) approved drugs. Specifically, what are their concerns?

17. What was Dr. Jonathan Ford's motive in establishing MITH (Mojave Institute of Therapeutics and Health)?

18. What initially attracted Dr. Stephen Spalding to MITH and what keeps him there?

19. Nathan Reed, like Coop's other patients, initially does well on Yuccasote. Why?

20. After a lengthy delay, Betty Tsongas, Gordon Flowers and Hector Perdenales all eventually return for surgery? Why?

21. Who killed Coop's friend, chemistry professor Dr. Marcus Westover? Why?

22. Dr. Stephen Spaulding has some serious flaws including drinking, practical joking and womanizing, but what is his fatal flaw?

23. Dr. Jonathan Ford feels he has built an impressive health clinic, nevertheless Coop diagnoses him as paranoid schizophrenic. Why?

24. As Coop's troubles begin to mount, he considers suicide. His burgeoning list of problems can be cataloged as personal, professional and legal. What are his personal problems? His professional? His legal? What makes him change his mind?

25. Samantha Rose tries to explain to an angry Coop she can defend him with his three malpractice lawsuits, but not the county's charge of negligent homicide. Why? Why are they different?

26. Yuccasote has some devastating side effects. What are they? It also has some therapeutic benefits. What are they?

27. Why are the families of the deceased patients reluctant to talk about Yuccasote?

28. Frank Tucciano, the old saddlemaker, has an ongoing vendetta. He sets fire to Coop's tack shed, kills his horse and tries to kill his dog as well as his friend, Jacob Heinz. Why?

29. It took Coop's patients months of taking Yuccasote for their blood to become thin enough to spontaneously bleed. Why did it only take Coop a couple of days?

30. What is Coop's relationship with God? Is he really an atheist?